Praise for *New York Times* and *USA TODAY* bestselling author RaeAnne Thayne

"Romance, vivid characters and a wonderful story... really, who could ask for more?"
—Debbie Macomber, #1 *New York Times* bestselling author, on *Blackberry Summer*

"This quirky, funny, warmhearted romance will draw readers in and keep them enthralled to the last romantic page."
—*Library Journal* on *Christmas in Snowflake Canyon*

"A sometimes heartbreaking tale of love and relationships in a small Colorado town... Poignant and sweet."
—*Publishers Weekly* on *Christmas in Snowflake Canyon*

"Plenty of tenderness and Colorado sunshine flavor this pleasant escape."
—*Publishers Weekly* on *Woodrose Mountain*

"Thayne, once again, delivers a heartfelt story of a caring community and a caring romance between adults who have triumphed over tragedies."
—*Booklist* on *Woodrose Mountain*

"Thayne pens another winner... Her main characters are strong and three-dimensional, with enough heat between them to burn the pages."
—*RT Book Reviews* on *Currant Creek Valley*

"RaeAnne has a knack for capturing those emotions that come from the heart."
—*RT Book Reviews*

RaeAnne Thayne

BRAMBLEBERRY HOUSE

HQN™

HQN™

ISBN-13: 978-0-373-80299-9

Recycling programs for this product may not exist in your area.

Brambleberry House

Copyright © 2017 by Harlequin Books S.A.

The publisher acknowledges the copyright holder of the individual works as follows:

His Second-Chance Family
Copyright © 2008 by RaeAnne Thayne

A Soldier's Secret
Copyright © 2008 by RaeAnne Thayne

www.HQNBooks.com

Printed in U.S.A.

CONTENTS

HIS SECOND-CHANCE FAMILY

CHAPTER ONE

As SIGNS FROM heaven went, this one seemed fairly prosaic.

No choir of angels, no booming voice from above or anything like that. It was simply a hand-lettered placard shoved into the seagrass in front of the massive, ornate Victorian that had drifted through her memory for most of her life.

Apartment For Rent.

Julia stared at the sign with growing excitement. It seemed impossible, a miracle. That *this* house, of all places, would be available for rent just as she was looking for a temporary home seemed just the encouragement her doubting heart needed to reaffirm her decision to pack up her twins and take a new teaching job in Cannon Beach.

Not even to herself had she truly admitted how worried she was that she'd made a terrible mistake moving here, leaving everything familiar and heading into the unknown.

Seeing that sign in front of Brambleberry House seemed an answer to prayer, a confirmation that this was where she and her little family were supposed to be.

"Cool house!" Maddie exclaimed softly, gazing up in awe at the three stories of Queen Anne Victorian, with its elaborate trim, cupolas and weathered shake roof. "It looks like a gingerbread house!"

Julia squeezed her daughter's hand, certain Maddie

looked a little healthier today in the bracing sea air of the Oregon Coast.

"Cool dog!" her twin, Simon, yelled. The words were barely out of his mouth when a giant red blur leaped over the low wrought-iron fence surrounding the house and wriggled around them with glee, as if he'd been waiting years just for them to walk down the beach.

The dog licked Simon's face and headbutted his stomach like an old friend. Julia braced herself to push him away if he got too rough with Maddie, but she needn't have worried. As if guided by some sixth sense, the dog stopped his wild gyrations and waited docilely for Maddie to reach out a tentative hand and pet him. Maddie giggled, a sound that was priceless as all the sea glass in the world to Julia.

"I think he likes me," she whispered.

"I think so, too, sweetheart." Julia smiled and tucked a strand of Maddie's fine short hair behind her ear.

"Do you really know the lady who lives here?" Maddie asked, while Simon was busy wrestling the dog in the sand.

"I used to, a long, long time ago," Julia answered. "She was my very best friend."

Her heart warmed as she remembered Abigail Dandridge and her unfailing kindness to a lonely little girl. Her mind filled with memories of admiring her vast doll collection, of pruning the rose hedge along the fence with her, of shared confidences and tea parties and sand dollar hunts along the beach.

"Like Jenna back home is my best friend?" Maddie asked.

"That's right."

Every summer of her childhood, Brambleberry House

became a haven of serenity and peace for her. Her family rented the same cottage just down the beach each July. It should have been a time of rest and enjoyment, but her parents couldn't stop fighting even on vacation.

Whenever she managed to escape to Abigail and Brambleberry House, though, Julia didn't have to listen to their arguments, didn't have to see her mother's tears or her father's obvious impatience at the enforced holiday, his wandering eye.

Her fifteenth summer was the last time she'd been here. Her parents finally divorced, much to her and her older brother Charlie's relief, and they never returned to Cannon Beach. But over the years, she had used the image of this house, with its soaring gables and turrets, and the peace she had known here to help center her during difficult times.

Through her parents' bitter divorce, through her own separation from Kevin and worse. Much worse.

"Is she still your best friend?" Maddie asked.

"I haven't seen Miss Abigail for many, many years," she said. "But you know, I don't think I realized until just this moment how very much I've missed her."

She should never have let so much time pass before coming back to Cannon Beach. She had let their friendship slip away, too busy being a confused and rebellious teenager caught in the middle of the endless drama between her parents. And then had come college and marriage and family.

Perhaps now that she was back, they could find that friendship once more. She couldn't wait to find out.

She opened the wrought-iron gate and headed up the walkway feeling as if she were on the verge of something oddly portentous.

She rang the doorbell and heard it echo through the house. Anticipation zinged through her as she waited, wondering what she would possibly say to Abigail after all these years. Would her lovely, wrinkled features match Julia's memory?

No one answered after several moments, even after she rang the doorbell a second time. She stood on the porch, wondering if she ought to leave a note with their hotel and her cell phone number, but it seemed impersonal, somehow, after all these years.

They would just have to check back, she decided. She headed back down the stairs and started for the gate again just as she heard the whine of a power tool from behind the house.

The dog, who looked like a mix between an Irish setter and a golden retriever, barked and headed toward the sound, pausing at the corner of the house, head cocked, as if waiting for them to come along with him.

After a wary moment, she followed, Maddie and Simon close on her heels.

The dog led them to the backyard, where Julia found a couple of sawhorses set up and a man with brown hair and broad shoulders running a circular saw through a board.

She watched for a moment, waiting for their presence to attract his attention, but he didn't look up from his work.

"Hello," she called out. When he still didn't respond, she moved closer so she would be in his field of vision and waved.

"Excuse me!"

Finally, he shut off the saw and pulled his safety goggles off, setting them atop his head.

"Yeah?" he said.

She squinted and looked closer at him. He looked familiar. A hint of a memory danced across her subconscious and she was so busy trying to place him that it took her a moment to respond.

"I'm sorry to disturb you. I rang the doorbell but I guess you couldn't hear me back here with the power tools."

"Guess not."

He spoke tersely, as if impatient to return to work, and Julia could feel herself growing flustered. She had braced herself to see Abigail, not some solemn-eyed construction worker in a sexy tool belt.

"I…right. Um, I'm looking for Abigail Dandridge."

There was an awkward pause and she thought she saw something flicker in his blue eyes.

"Are you a friend of hers?" he asked, his voice not quite as abrupt as it had been before.

"I used to be, a long time ago. Can you tell me when she'll be back? I don't mind waiting."

The dog barked, only with none of the exuberance he had shown a few moments ago, almost more of a whine than a bark. He plopped onto the grass and dipped his chin to his front paws, his eyes suddenly morose.

The man gazed at the dog's curious behavior for a moment. A muscle tightened in his jaw then he looked back at Julia. "Abigail died in April. Heart attack in her sleep. I'm sorry to be the one to tell you."

Julia couldn't help her instinctive cry of distress. Even through her sudden surge of grief, she sensed when Maddie stepped closer and slipped a small, frail hand in hers.

Julia drew a breath, then another. "I…see," she mumbled. Just one more loss in a long, unrelenting string, she thought. But this one seemed to pierce her heart like jagged driftwood.

It was silly, really, when she thought about it. Abigail hadn't been a presence in her life for sixteen years, but suddenly the loss of her seemed overwhelming.

She swallowed hard, struggling for composure. Her friend was gone, but her house was still here, solid and reassuring, weathering this storm as it had others for generations.

Somehow it seemed more important than ever that she bring her children here.

"I see," she repeated, more briskly now, though she thought she saw a surprising understanding in the deep blue of the man's eyes, so disconcertingly familiar. She knew him. She knew she did.

"I suppose I should talk to you, then. The sign out front says there's an apartment for rent. How many bedrooms does it have?"

He gave her a long look before turning away to pick up another board and carry it to the saw. "Three bedrooms, two of them on the small side. Kitchen's been redone in the last few months and the electricity's been upgraded but the bathroom plumbing's still in pretty rough shape."

"I don't care about that, as long as everything works okay. Three bedrooms is exactly the size my children and I need. Is it still available?"

"Can't say."

She pursed her lips. "Why not?"

He shrugged. "I don't own the place. I live a few houses down the beach. I'm just doing some repairs for the owners."

Something about what he said jarred loose a flood of memories and she stared at him more closely. Suddenly everything clicked in and she gasped, stunned she hadn't realized his identity the instant she had clapped eyes on him.

"Will? Will Garrett?"

He peered at her. "Do I know you?"

She managed a smile. "Probably not. It's been years."

She held out a hand, her pulse suddenly wild and erratic, as it had always been around him.

"Julia Blair. You knew me when I was Julia Hudson. My parents rented a cottage between your house and Brambleberry House every summer of my childhood until I was fifteen. I used to follow you and my older brother, Charlie, around everywhere."

Will Garrett. She'd forgotten so much about those summers, but never him. She had wondered whether she would see him, had wondered about his life and where he might end up. She never expected to find him standing in front of her on her first full day in town.

"It's been years!" she repeated. "I can't believe you're still here."

At her words, it took Will all of about two seconds to remember her. When he did, he couldn't understand why he hadn't seen it before. He had yearned for Julia Hudson that summer as only a relatively innocent sixteen-year-old boy can ache. He had dreamed of her green eyes and her dimples and her soft, burgeoning curves.

She had been his first real love and had haunted his dreams.

She had promised to keep in touch but she hadn't called or answered any of his letters and he remembered how his teenage heart had been shattered. But by the time school started a month later, he'd been so busy with football practice and school and working for his dad's carpentry business on Saturdays that he hadn't really had much time to wallow in his heartbreak.

Julia looked the same—the same smile, the same auburn hair, the same appealing dimples—while he felt as if he had aged a hundred years.

He could barely remember those innocent, carefree days when he had been certain the world was his for the taking, that he could achieve anything if only he worked hard enough for it.

She was waiting for a response, he realized, still holding her hand outstretched in pleased welcome. He held up his hands in their leather work gloves as an excuse not to touch her. After an awkward moment, she dropped her arms to her side, though the smile remained fixed on her lovely features.

"I can't believe you're still here in Cannon Beach," she repeated. "How wonderful that you've stayed all these years! I remember how you loved it here."

He wouldn't call it wonderful. There were days he felt like some kind of prehistoric iceman, frozen forever in place. He had wondered for some time if he ought to pick up and leave, go *anywhere,* just as long as it wasn't here.

Someone with his carpentry skills and experience could find work just about any place. He had thought about it long and hard, especially at night when the memories overwhelmed him and the emptiness seemed to ring through his house but he couldn't seem to work past the inertia to make himself leave.

"So how have you been?" Julia asked. "What about family? Are you married? Any kids?"

Okay, he wasn't a prehistoric iceman. He was pretty certain they couldn't bleed and bleed and bleed.

He set his jaw and picked up the oak board he was shaping for a new window frame in one of the third-floor bedrooms of Brambleberry House.

"You'll have to talk to Sage Benedetto or Anna Galvez about the apartment," he said tersely. "They're the new owners. They should be back this evening."

He didn't quite go so far as to fire up the circular saw but it was a clear dismissal, rude as hell. He had to hope she got the message that he wasn't interested in any merry little trips down memory lane.

She gave him a long, measuring look while the girl beside her edged closer.

After a moment, she offered a smile that was cool and polite but still managed to scorch his conscience. "I'll do that. Thank you. It's good to see you again, Will."

He nodded tersely. This time, he did turn on the circular saw, though he was aware of every move she and her children made in the next few moments. He knew just when they walked around the house with Abigail's clever Irish Setter mix Conan following on their heels.

He gave up any pretense of working when he saw them head across the lane out front, then head down the beach. She still walked with grace and poise, her chin up as if ready to take on the world, just as she had when she was fifteen years old.

And her kids. That curious boy and the fragile-looking girl with the huge, luminescent blue eyes. Remembering those eyes, he had to set down the board and press a hand to the dull ache in his chest, though he knew from two years' experience nothing would ease it.

Booze could dull it for a moment but not nearly long enough. When the alcohol wore off, everything rushed back, worse than before.

He was still watching their slow, playful progress down the beach when Conan returned to the backyard. The dog barked once and gave him a look Will could only describe as peeved. He planted his haunches in front of the worktable and glared at him.

Abigail would have given him exactly the same look for treating an old friend with such rudeness.

"Yeah, I was a jerk," he muttered. "She caught me off guard, that's all. I wasn't exactly prepared for a ghost from the past to show up out of the blue this afternoon."

The dog barked again and Will wondered, not for the first time, what went on inside his furry head. Conan had a weird way of looking at everybody as if he knew exactly what they might be thinking and he managed to communicate whole diatribes with only a bark and a certain expression in his doleful eyes.

Abigail had loved the dog. For that reason alone, Will would have tolerated him since his neighbor had been one of his favorite people on earth. But Conan had also showed an uncanny knack over the last two years for knowing just when Will was at low ebb.

More than once, there had been times when he had been out on the beach wondering if it would be easier just to walk out into the icy embrace of the tide than to survive another second of this unrelenting grief.

No matter the time of day or night, Conan would somehow always show up, lean against Will's legs until the despair eased, and then would follow him home before returning to Brambleberry House and Abigail.

He sighed now as the dog continued to wordlessly reprimand him. "What do you want me to do? Go after her?"

Conan barked and Will shook his head. "No way. Forget it."

He *should* go after her, at least to apologize. He had been unforgivably rude. The hell of it was, he didn't really know why. He wasn't cold by nature. Through the last two years, he had tried to hold to the hard-fought philosophy that just because his insides had been ripped apart and because sometimes the grief and pain seemed to crush the life out of him, he hadn't automatically been handed a free pass to hurt others.

Lashing out at others around him did nothing to ease his own pain so he made it a point to be polite to just about everybody.

Sure, there were random moments when his bleakness slipped through. At times, Sage and Anna and other friends had been upset at him when he pushed away their efforts to comfort him. More than a few times, truth be told. But he figured it was better to be by himself during those dark moments than to do as he'd just done, lash out simply because he didn't know how else to cope.

He had no excuse for treating her poorly. He had just seen her there looking so lovely and bright with her energetic son and her pretty little daughter and every muscle inside him had cramped in pain.

The children set it off. He could see that now. The girl had even looked a little like Cara—same coloring, anyway, though Cara had been chubby and round where Julia's daughter looked as if she might blow away in anything more than a two-knot wind.

It hadn't only been the children, though. He had seen Julia standing there in a shaft of sunlight and for a moment, long-dormant feelings had stirred inside him that he wanted to stay dead and buried like the rest of his life.

No matter how screwed up he was, he had no business being rude to her and her children. Like it or not, he would have to apologize to her, especially if Anna and Sage rented her the apartment.

He lived three houses away and spent a considerable amount of time at Brambleberry House, both because he was busy with various remodeling projects and because he considered the new owners—Abigail's heirs—his friends.

He didn't want Julia Hudson Blair or her children here at Brambleberry House. If he were honest with himself, he could admit that he would have preferred if she had stayed a long-buried memory.

But she hadn't. She was back in Cannon Beach with her children, looking to rent an apartment at Brambleberry House, so apparently she planned to stay at least awhile.

Chances were good he would bump into her again, so he was going to have to figure out a way to apologize.

He watched their shapes grow smaller and smaller as they walked down the beach toward town and he rubbed the ache in his chest, wondering what it would take to convince Sage and Anna to find a different tenant.

CHAPTER TWO

"WILL WE GET to see inside the pretty house this time, Mommy?"

Julia lifted her gaze from the road for only an instant to glance in the rearview mirror of her little Toyota SUV. Even from here, she could see the excitement in Maddie's eyes and she couldn't help but smile in return at her daughter.

"That's the plan," she answered, turning her attention back to the road as she drove past a spectacular hotel set away from the road. Someday when she was independently wealthy with unlimited leisure time, she wanted to stay at The Sea Urchin, one of the most exclusive boutique hotels on the coast.

"I talked to one of the owners of the house an hour ago," Julia continued, "and she invited us to walk through and see if the apartment will work for us."

"I hope it does," Simon said. "I really liked that cool dog."

"I'm not sure the dog lives there," she answered. "He might belong to the man we talked to this morning. Will Garrett. He doesn't live there, he was just doing some work on the house."

"I'm glad he doesn't live there," Maddie said in her whisper-soft voice. "He was kind of cranky."

Julia agreed, though she didn't say as much to her

children. Will had been terse, bordering on rude, and for the life of her she couldn't figure out why. What had she done? She hadn't seen him in sixteen years. It seemed ridiculous to assume he might be angry, after all these years, simply because she hadn't written to him as she had promised.

They had been friends of a sort—and more than friends for a few glorious weeks one summer. She remembered moonlight bonfires and holding hands in the movies and stealing kisses on the beach.

She would have assumed their shared past warranted at least a little politeness but apparently he didn't agree. The Will Garrett she remembered had been far different from the surly stranger they met that afternoon. She couldn't help wondering if he treated everyone that way or if she received special treatment.

"He was simply busy," she said now to her children. "We interrupted his work and I think he was eager to get back to it. We grown-ups can sometimes be impatient."

"I remember," Simon said. "Dad was like that sometimes."

The mention of Kevin took her by surprise. Neither twin referred to their father very often anymore. He had died more than two years ago and had been a distant presence for some time before that, and they had all walked what felt like a million miles since then.

Brambleberry House suddenly came into view, rising above the fringy pines and spruce trees. She slowed, savoring the sight of the spectacular Victorian mansion silhouetted against the salmon-colored sky, with the murky blue sea below.

That familiar sense of homecoming washed over her again as she pulled into the pebbled driveway. She wanted to live here with her children. To wake up in the morning with that view of the sea out her window and the smell of roses drifting up from the gardens and the solid comfort of those walls around her.

As she pulled into the driveway and turned off the engine, she gave a silent prayer that she and the twins would click with the new owners. The one she'd spoken with earlier—Sage Benedetto—had seemed cordial when she invited Julia and her children to take a look at the apartment, but Julia was almost afraid to hope.

"Mom, look!" Simon exclaimed. "There's the dog! Does that mean he lives here?"

As she opened her door to climb out, she saw the big shaggy red dog waiting by the wrought-iron gates, almost as if he somehow knew they were on their way.

"I don't know. We'll have to see."

"Oh, I hope so." Maddie pushed a wisp of hair out of her eyes. She looked fragile and pale. Though Julia would have liked to walk from their hotel downtown to enjoy the spectacular views of Cannon Beach at sunset, she had been afraid Maddie wouldn't have the strength for another long hike down the beach and back.

Now she was grateful she had heeded her motherly instincts that seemed to have become superacute since Maddie's illness.

More than anything—more than she wanted to live in this house, more than she wanted this move to work out, more than she wanted to *breathe*—she wanted her daughter to be healthy and strong.

"I hope we can live here," Maddie said. "I really like that dog."

Julia hugged her daughter and helped her out of her seat belt. Maddie slipped a hand in hers while Simon took his sister's other hand. Together, the three of them walked through the gate, where the one-dog welcoming committee awaited them.

The dog greeted Simon with the same enthusiasm he had shown that morning, wagging his tail fiercely and nudging Simon's hand with his head. After a moment of attention from her son, the dog turned to Maddie. Julia went on full mother-bear alert, again ready to step in if necessary, but the dog showed the same uncanny gentleness to Maddie.

He simply planted his haunches on the sidewalk in front of her, waiting as still as one of those cheap plaster dog statues for Maddie to reach out with a giggle and pet his head.

Weird, she thought, but she didn't have time to figure it out before the front door opened. A woman wearing shorts and a brightly colored tank top stepped out onto the porch. She looked to be in her late twenties and was extraordinarily lovely in an exotic kind of way, with blonde wavy hair pulled back in a ponytail and an olive complexion that spoke of a Mediterranean heritage.

She walked toward them with a loose-hipped gait and a warm smile.

"Hi!" Her voice held an open friendliness and Julia instinctively responded to it. She could feel the tension in her shoulders relax a little as the other woman held out a hand.

"I'm Sage Benedetto. You must be the Blairs."

She shook it. "Yes. I'm Julia and these are my children, Simon and Maddie."

Sage dropped her hand and turned to the twins. "Hey kids. Great to meet you! How old are you? Let me guess. Sixteen?"

They both giggled. "No!" Simon exclaimed. "We're seven."

"Seven? Both of you?"

"We're twins." Maddie said in her soft voice.

"Twins? No kidding? Cool! I've always wanted to have a twin. You ever dress up in each others' clothes and try to trick your mom?"

"No!" Maddie said with another giggle.

"We're not *identical* twins," Simon said with a roll of his eyes. "We're *fraternal*."

"Of course you are. Silly me. 'Cause one of you is a boy and one is a girl, right?"

Sage obviously knew her way around children, Julia thought as she listened to their exchange. That was definitely a good sign. She had observed during her career as an elementary school teacher that many adults didn't really know how to talk to kids. They either tried too hard to be buddies or treated them with obvious condescension. Sage managed to find the perfect middle ground.

"I see you've met Conan," Sage said, scratching the big dog under the chin.

"Is he your dog?" Simon asked.

She smiled at the animal with obvious affection. "I guess you could say that. Or I'm his human. Either way, we kind of look out for each other, don't we, bud?"

Oddly, Julia could swear the dog grinned.

"Thank you again for agreeing to show the apartment to us tonight," she said.

Sage turned her smile to Julia. "No problem. I'm sorry we weren't here when you came by the first time. You said on the telephone that you knew Abigail."

That pang of loss pinched at her again as she imagined Abigail out here in the garden, her big floppy straw hat and her gardening gloves and the tray of lemonade always waiting on the porch.

"Years ago," she answered, then was compelled to elaborate.

"Every summer my family rented a house near here. The year I was ten, my brother and I were running around on the beach and I cut my foot on a broken shell. Abigail heard me crying and came down to help. She brought me back up to the house, fixed me a cookie and doctored me up. We were fast friends after that. Every year, I would run up here the minute we pulled into the driveway of our cottage. Abigail always seemed so happy to see me and we would get along as if I had never left."

The other woman smiled, though there was an edge of sorrow to it. Julia wondered again how Sage had ended up as one of the two new owners of Brambleberry House after Abigail's death.

"Sounds just like Abigail," Sage said. "She made friends with everyone she met."

"I've been terrible about keeping in contact with her," Julia admitted with chagrin as they walked into the entryway of the house, with its sweeping staircase and polished honey oak trim. "I was so sorry to hear about her death—more sorry than I can say that I let so much time go by without calling her. I suppose some foolish part of me just assumed she would always be here. Like the ocean and the seastacks."

The dog—Conan—whined a little, almost as if he understood their conversation, though Julia knew that was impossible.

"I think we all felt that way," Sage said. "It's been four months and it still doesn't seem real."

"Will said she died of a heart attack in her sleep."

"That's right. I find some comfort in knowing that if she could have chosen her exit scene, that's exactly how she would have wanted to go. The doctors said she probably slept right through it."

Sage paused and gave her a considering kind of look. "Do you know Will, then?"

Julia could feel color climb her cheekbones. How foolish could she be to blush over a teenage crush on Will Garrett, when the man he had become obviously wanted nothing to do with her?

"Knew him," she corrected. "It all seems so long ago. The cottage we rented every year was next door to his. We socialized a little with his family and he and my older brother, Charlie, were friends. I usually tried to find a way to tag along, to their great annoyance."

She had a sudden memory of mountain biking through the mists and primordial green of Ecola National Park, then cooling off in the frigid surf of Indian Beach, the gulls wheeling overhead and the ocean song a sweet accompaniment.

Will had kissed her for the first time there, while her brother was busy body surfing through the baby breakers and not paying them any attention. It had just been a quick, furtive brush of his lips, but she could suddenly remember with vivid clarity how it had warmed her until she forgot all about the icy swells.

"He was my first love," she confessed.

Oh no. Had she really said that out loud? She wanted to snatch the words back but they hung between them. Sage turned around, sudden speculation sparking in her exotic, tilted eyes, and Julia could feel herself blushing harder.

"Is that right?"

"A long time ago," she answered, though she was certain she had said those words about a million times already. So much for making a good impression. She was stuttering and blushing and acting like an idiot over a man who barely remembered her.

To her relief, Sage didn't pursue it as they reached the second floor of the big house.

"This is the apartment we're renting. It's been vacant most of the time in the five years I've lived here. Once in a while Abigail opened it up on a short-term basis to various people in need of a comfortable place to crash for a while. Since Anna and I inherited Brambleberry House, we've kept Will busy fixing it up so we could rent out the space."

Will again. Couldn't she escape him for three seconds? "Convenient that he lives close," she said.

"It's more convenient because he's the best carpenter around. With all the work that needs to be done to Brambleberry House, we could hire him as our resident carpenter. Good thing for us he likes to stay busy."

She remembered again the pain in his eyes. She wanted to ask Sage the reason for it, but she knew that would be far too presumptuous.

Anyway, she wasn't here to talk about Will Garrett. She was trying to find a clean, comfortable place for her children.

When Sage opened the door to the apartment, Julia felt a little thrill of anticipation.

"Ready to take a look?" Sage asked.

"Absolutely." She walked through the door with the oddest sense of homecoming.

The apartment met all her expectations and more. Much, much more. She walked from room to room with a growing excitement. The kitchen was small but had new appliances and what looked like new cabinets stained a lovely cherry color. Each of the three bedrooms had fresh coats of paint. Though two of them were quite small, nearly every room had a breathtaking view of the ocean.

"It's beautiful," she exclaimed as she stood in the large living room, with its wide windows on two sides that overlooked the sea.

"Will did a good job, didn't he?" Sage said.

Before Julia could answer, the children came into the room, followed by the dog.

"Wow. This place is so cool!" Simon exclaimed.

"I like it, too," Maddie said. "It feels friendly."

"How can a house feel friendly?" her brother scoffed. "It's just walls and a roof and stuff."

Sage didn't seem to mind Maddie's whimsy. Her features softened and she laid a hand on Maddie's hair with a gentleness that warmed Julia's heart.

"I think you're absolutely right, Miss Maddie," she answered. "I've always thought Brambleberry House was just about the friendliest house I've ever been lucky enough to live in."

Maddie smiled back and Julia could see a bond forming between the two of them, just as the children already seemed to have a connection with Conan.

"When can we move in?" Simon asked.

Julia winced at her son's bluntness. "We've still got some details to work out," she said quickly, stepping in to avoid Sage feeling any sense of obligation to answer before she was completely comfortable with the idea of them as tenants. "Nothing's settled yet. Why don't the two of you play with Conan for a few moments while I talk with Ms. Benedetto?"

He seemed satisfied with that and headed to the window seat, followed closely by his sister and Sage's friendly dog.

Her children were remarkably adept at entertaining themselves. Little wonder, she thought with that echo of sadness. They had spent three years developing patience during Maddie's endless string of appointments and procedures.

When they seemed happily settled petting the dog, she turned back to Sage. "I'm sorry about that. I understand that you need to check references and everything and talk to the co-owner before you make a decision. I'm definitely interested, at least through the school year."

Sage opened her mouth to answer but before she could speak, the dog gave a sudden sharp bark, his ears on alert. He rushed for the open door to the landing and she could hear his claws scrabbling on the steps just an instant before the front door opened downstairs.

Sage didn't even blink at the dog's eager behavior. "Oh, good. That's Anna Galvez. I was hoping she'd be home before you left so she could have a chance to meet you. Anna took over By-the-Wind, Abigail's old book and giftshop in town."

"I remember the place. I spent many wonderful rainy afternoons curled up in one of the easy chairs with a book."

"Haven't we all?" Sage said with a smile, then walked out to the stairs to call down to the other woman.

A moment later, a woman with dark hair and petite, lovely features walked up the stairs, her hand on Conan's fur.

She greeted Julia with a smile slightly more reserved than Sage's warm friendliness. "Hello."

Her smile warmed when she greeted the curious twins. "Hey, there," she said.

Sage performed a quick introduction. "Julia and her twins are moving to Cannon Beach from Boise. Julia's going to be teaching fifth grade at the elementary school and she's looking for an apartment."

"Lovely to meet you. Welcome to Oregon!"

"Thank you," Julia said. "I used to spend summers near here when I was a child."

"She's one of Abigail's lost sheep finally come home," Sage said with a smile that quickly turned mischievous. "Oh, you'll be interested to know that Will was her first love."

To Julia's immense relief, Sage added the latter in an undertone too low for the children to hear, even if they'd been paying attention. Still, she could feel herself blush again. She really *had* to stop doing that every time Will Garrett's name was mentioned.

"I was fifteen. Another lifetime ago. We barely recognized each other when I bumped into him earlier today outside. He seems…very different than he was at sixteen."

Sage's teasing smile turned sober. "He has his reasons," she said softly.

She and Anna gave each other a quick look loaded with layers of subtext that completely escaped Julia.

"Thank you for showing me the apartment. I have to tell you, from what I see, it would be perfect for us. It's exactly what I'm looking for, with room for the children to play, incredible views and within walking distance to the school. But I certainly understand that you need to check references and credit history before renting it to me. Feel free to talk to the principal of the elementary school who hired me, and any of the other references I gave you in our phone conversation. If you need anything else, you have my cell number and the number of the hotel where we're staying."

"Or we could always talk to Will and see what he remembers from when you were fifteen."

Julia flashed a quick look to Sage and was relieved to find the other woman smiling again. She had no idea what Will Garrett remembered about her. Nothing pleasant, obviously, or he probably would have shown a little more warmth when she encountered him earlier.

"Will may not be the best character reference. If I remember correctly, I still owe him an ice-cream cone. He bet me I couldn't split a geoduck without using my hands. I tried for days but the summer ended before I could pay him back."

"Good thing you're sticking around," Anna said. "You can pay back your debt now. We've still got ice cream."

"And geoducks," Sage said. "Maybe you're more agile than you used to be."

She laughed, liking both women immensely. As she gathered the children and headed down the stairs to her car, Julia could only wish for a little more agility. Then she would cross her toes and her fingers that Sage Benedetto and Anna Galvez would let her and her twins rent their vacant apartment.

She couldn't remember when she had wanted anything so much.

"SO WHAT DO you think?" Sage asked as she and Anna stood at the window watching the schoolteacher strap her children into the backseat of her little SUV.

She looked like she had the process down to a science,

Sage thought, something she still struggled with when she drove Chloe anywhere. She could never figure out how to tighten the darn seat belt over the booster chair with her stepdaughter-to-be. She ought to have Julia give her lessons.

"No idea," Anna replied. "I barely talked to her for five minutes. But she seems nice enough."

"She belongs here."

Anna snorted. "And you figured that out in one quick fifteen-minute meeting?"

"Not at all." Sage grinned. She couldn't help herself. "I figured it out in the first thirty seconds."

"We still have to check her references. I'm sorry if this offends you, but I can't go on karma alone on this one."

"I know. But I'm sure they'll check out." Sage couldn't have said how she knew, she just did. Somehow she was certain Abigail would have wanted Julia and her twins to live at Brambleberry House.

"Did you see her blush when Will's name came up?"

Anna shook her head. "Leave it alone, Sage. You engaged women think you have to match up the entire universe."

"Not the entire universe. Just the people I love, like Will."

And you, she added silently. She thought of the loneliness in Anna's eyes, the tiny shadow of sadness she was certain Anna never guessed showed on her expression.

Their neighbor wasn't the only one who deserved to be happy, but she decided she—and Abigail—could only focus on one thing at a time. "Will has had so much pain in his life. Wouldn't you love to see him smile again?"

"Of course. But Julia herself said she hadn't seen him

in years and they barely recognized each other. And we don't even know the woman. She could be married."

"Widowed. She told me that on the phone. Two years, the same as Will."

Compassion flickered in Anna's brown eyes. "Those poor children, to lose their father at such a young age." She paused. "That doesn't mean whatever scheme you're hatching has any chance of working."

"I know. But it's worth a shot. Anyway, Conan likes them and that's the important thing, isn't it, bud?"

The dog barked, giving his uncanny grin. As far as Sage was concerned, references or not, that settled the matter.

CHAPTER THREE

SAGE AND ANNA apparently had a new tenant.

Will slowed his pickup down as he passed Bramble-berry House coming from the south. He couldn't miss the U-Haul trailer hulking in the driveway and he could see Sage heading into the house, her arms stacked high with boxes. Anna was loading her arms with a few more while Julia's children played on the grass not far away with Conan. Even from here he could see the dog's glee at having new playmates.

Damn. This is the price he paid for his inaction. He should have stopped by a day or two earlier and at least tried to dissuade Anna and Sage from taking her on as a tenant.

It probably wouldn't have done any good, he acknowledged. Both of Abigail's heirs could be as stubborn as crooked nails when they had their minds made up about something. Still, he should have at least made the attempt.

But what could he have said, really, that wouldn't have made him sound like a raving lunatic?

Yeah, she seems nice enough and I sure was crazy about her when I was sixteen. But I don't want her around anymore because I don't like being reminded I'm still alive.

He sighed and turned off his truck. He wanted nothing more than to drive past the house and hide out at his place down the beach until she moved on but there was no way on earth his blasted conscience would let him leave three women and two kids to do all that heavy lifting on their own.

He climbed out of his pickup and headed to the trailer. He reached it just as the top box on Anna's stack started to slide.

He lunged for it and plucked the wobbly top box just before it would have hit the ground, earning a surprised look from Anna over the next-highest box.

"Wow! Good catch," she said, a smile lifting her studious features. "Lucky you were here."

"Rule of thumb—your stack of boxes probably shouldn't exceed your own height."

She smiled. "Good advice. I'm afraid I can get a little impatient sometimes."

"Is that it? I thought you just like to bite off more than you can chew."

She made a wry face at him. "That, too. How did you know we needed help?"

He shrugged. "I was driving past and saw your leaning tower and thought you might be able to use another set of arms."

"We've got plenty of arms. We just need some arms with muscle. Thanks for stopping."

"Glad to help." It was a blatant lie but he decided she didn't need to know that.

She turned and headed up the stairs and he grabbed several boxes from inside the truck and followed her, trying to ignore the curious mingle of dread and anticipation in his gut.

He didn't want to see Julia again. He had already

dreamed about her the last two nights in a row. More contact would only wedge her more firmly into his head.

At the same time, part of him—maybe the part that was still sixteen years old somewhere deep inside—couldn't help wondering how the years might have changed her.

Anna was breathing hard by the time they reached the middle floor of the house, where the door to the apartment had been propped open with a small stack of books.

"I could have taken another one of your boxes," he said to Anna.

She made a face. "Show-off. Are you even working up a sweat?"

"I'm sweating on the inside," he answered, which was nothing less than the truth.

The source of his trepidation spoke to Anna an instant later.

"Thanks so much," Julia Blair said in her low, sexy voice. "Those go in Simon's bedroom."

Will lowered his boxes so he could see over them and found her standing in the middle of the living room directing traffic. She wore capris and a stretchy yellow T-shirt. With her hair pulled back into a ponytail, she looked fresh and beautiful and not much older than she'd been that last summer together.

He didn't miss the shock in her eyes when she spied him behind the boxes. "Will! What are you doing here?"

He shrugged, uncomfortable at her obvious shock. Why *shouldn't* he be here helping? It was the neighborly thing to do. Had he really been such a complete jerk the other day that she find his small gesture of assistance now so stunning?

"Do these go into the same room?"

She looked flustered, her cheeks slightly pink. "Um, no. Those are my things. They go in my bedroom, the big one overlooking the ocean."

He headed in the direction she pointed, noting again no sign of a Mr. Blair. On some instinctive level, he had subconsciously picked up the fact that she wore no wedding ring when he had seen her the other day and she had spoken only of herself and her children needing an apartment. Was she widowed, divorced, or never married?

He only wondered out of mild curiosity about the road she might have traveled in the years since he had seen her. Or at least that's what he told himself.

In her bedroom, he found stacks of boxes, some of them open and overflowing with books. The queen-size bed was already made up with a cozy-looking comforter in soft blue tones, with piles of pillows against the headboard.

An image flashed in his head of her tousled and welcoming, her auburn hair spread out on those pillows and a soft, aroused smile teasing the edges of those lovely features.

He dropped the boxes so abruptly he barely missed his toe.

Whoa. Where the hell did that come from?

He had no business thinking about her at all, forget about in some kind of sultry, welcoming pose.

When he returned to the living room, her cheeks were still flushed and she didn't meet his gaze, as if she were embarrassed about something. It was a damn good thing she couldn't know the inappropriate direction of his thoughts.

"I'm sorry." She fidgeted with a stack of books in her hand. "I probably sounded terribly ungracious when you first came in. I just didn't expect you to show up and start hauling my boxes inside."

"No problem."

He started to head toward the door, but she apparently wasn't content with his short response. "Why, again, are you helping me move in?"

He shrugged. What did it matter? He was here, wasn't he? Did they really have to analyze the reasons why? "I was heading home after a job south of here and saw your U-Haul out front. I figured you could use a hand."

"How…neighborly of you."

"Around here we look out for each other." It was nothing less than the truth.

"I remember." She smiled a little. "That's one of the reasons I wanted to come back to Cannon Beach. I remembered that sense of community with great affection."

She set the stack of books down on the coffee table, then turned a searching gaze toward him. "Forgive me, Will, but…for some reason I had the impression you weren't exactly overjoyed to see me the other day."

And he thought he'd been so careful at hiding his reaction. He shifted his weight, not sure how to answer. Any apology would only lead to explanations he was eager to avoid at all costs.

"You took me by surprise, that's all," he finally said.

"A mysterious stranger emerging from your distant past?"

"Something like that. Sixteen seems like a long, long time ago."

She nodded solemnly but said nothing. After an awkward moment, he headed for the door again.

"Anyway, I'm sorry if I seemed less than welcoming." It needed to be said, he decided. Apparently, she was going to be his neighbor and he disliked the idea of this uneasiness around her continuing. That didn't make the words any easier to get out. "You caught me at a bad moment, that's all. But I'm sorry if I gave you the impression I didn't want you here. It was nothing personal."

"I must say, that's a relief to hear."

She smiled, warm and sincere, and for just an instant he was blinded by it, remembering the surge of his blood every time he had been anywhere close to her that last summer.

Before he could make his brain work again, Sage walked up carrying one bulky box.

"What do you have in these, for Pete's sake? Did you pack along every brick from your old place?"

Julia laughed, a light, happy sound that stirred the hair on the back of his neck.

"Not bricks, but close, I'm afraid. Books. I left a lot in storage back in Boise but I couldn't bear to leave them all behind."

So that hadn't changed about her. When she was a kid, she always seemed to have her nose in a book. He and her brother used to tease her unmercifully about being a bookworm.

That last summer, he had been relentless in his efforts to drag her attention away from whatever book she was reading so she would finally notice him....

He dragged his mind away from the past and the dumb, self-absorbed jerk he'd been. He didn't want to remember those times. What was the damn point? That stupid, eager, infatuated kid was gone, buried under the weight of the years and pain that had piled up since then.

Instead, he left Sage and Julia to talk about books and headed back down the sweeping Brambleberry House stairs. On the way, he passed Anna heading back up, carrying a suitcase in each hand. He tried to take them from her but she shook him off.

"I've got these. There are some bulkier things in the U-Haul you could bring up, though."

"Sure," he answered.

In the entryway on the ground floor, he heard music coming from inside Anna's apartment. Through the open doorway, he caught a glimpse of her television set where a Disney DVD was just starting up.

Julia's twins must have finished playing and come inside. He spotted Julia's boy on the floor in front of the TV, his arm slung across Conan's back. Both of them sensed Will's presence and looked up. He started to greet them but the boy put a finger to his mouth and pointed to Abigail's favorite armchair.

Will followed his gaze and found the girl—Maddie—curled up there, fast asleep.

She looked small and fragile, with her too-pale skin and thin wrists. There was something going on with her, but he was pretty sure he was better off not knowing.

He waved to the boy, then headed down the porch steps to the waiting U-Haul.

It was nearly empty now except for perhaps a half-dozen more boxes, a finely crafted Mission-style rocking chair and something way in the back, a bulky-looking item wrapped in an old blanket that had been secured with twine.

He went for the rocking chair first. Might as well get the tough stuff out of the way. It was harder to carry than he expected—wide and solid, made of solid oak—but more awkward than really heavy.

He made it without any trouble up the porch steps and

was trying to squeeze it through the narrow front door without bunging up the doorframe moldings when Sage came down the stairs.

"Okay, Superman. Let me help you with that."

"I can handle it."

"Only because of your freakish strength, maybe."

He felt his mouth quirk. Sage always managed to remind him he still had the ability to smile.

"I had my can of spinach just an hour ago so I think I've got this covered. There are a few more boxes in the U-Haul. Those ought to keep you busy and out of trouble."

She stuck her tongue out at him and he smiled at the childish gesture, with a sudden, profound gratitude for the friendship of those few people around him who had sustained him through the wrenching pain of the last two years.

"Which is it? Are you Popeye or Superman?"

"Take your pick."

"Or just a stubborn male, like the rest of your gender?" She lifted the front end of the chair. "Even Popeye and Superman need help once in awhile. Besides, we wouldn't want you to throw your back out. Then how would all our work get done around here?"

He knew when he was defeated. With a sigh, he picked up the other end. They had another minor tussle about who should walk backward up the stairs but he won that one simply by turning around and starting up.

She didn't let him gloat for long. "I understand you know our new tenant."

His gaze flashed to hers. *Uh-oh. Here comes the inquisition,* he thought. "Knew. Past tense. A long time ago."

The words were becoming like a mantra since she showed up again in Cannon Beach. *A long time ago.* But not nearly long enough. Like a riptide, the memories just seemed to keep grabbing him out of nowhere and sucking him under.

"She's lovely, isn't she?" Sage pressed as they hit the halfway mark on the stairs. "And those kids of hers are adorable. I can't wait until Eben and Chloe finish up their trip to Europe in a few weeks. Chloe's going to be over the moon at having two new friends."

"How are the wedding plans?" he asked at her mention of her fiancé and his eight-year-old daughter. The question was aimed more at diverting her attention than out of much genuine interest to hear about her upcoming nuptials, but it seemed to work.

Sage made a face. "You know I'm not good at that kind of thing. If I had my way, I would happy with something simple on the beach, just Eben and me and Chloe and the preacher."

"I guess when you marry a gazillionaire hotel magnate, sometimes you have to make sacrifices."

"It's still going to be small, just a few friends at the ceremony then a reception later at the Sea Urchin. I'm leaving all the details to Jade and Stanley Wu."

"Smart woman."

She went on about wedding plans and he listened with half an ear.

In a million years, he never would have expected a hippie-chick like Sage to fall for a California businessman like Eben Spencer but somehow they seemed to fit together.

Sage was more at peace than he'd ever known her, settled in a way he couldn't explain.

She was one of his closest friends and had been since she moved to town five years ago and found herself immediately drawn into Abigail's orbit. He loved her as a little sister and he knew she deserved whatever joy she could find.

He wanted to be happy for her—and most of the time he was—but every once in a while, seeing the love and happiness that seemed to surround her and Eben when they were together was like a slow, relentless trickle of acid on an open wound.

Despite knowing Julia was inside, he was relieved as hell when they reached the top of the stairs and turned into the apartment.

"Oh, my Stickley! We bought that when I was pregnant with the twins. I know the apartment is furnished but I couldn't bear to leave it behind. Thank you so much for carrying that heavy thing all that way! That goes right here by the window so I can sit in it at night and watch the moonlight shining on the ocean."

He set it down, his mind on the rocking chair he had made Robin when she was pregnant with Cara. It was still sitting in the nursery along with the toddler bed he had made, gathering dust.

He really ought to do something with the furniture. Sage would probably know somebody who could use it....

Not today, he thought abruptly. He wasn't ready for that yet.

He turned on his heel and headed back down the stairs to retrieve that mysterious blanket-wrapped item. When he reached the U-Haul, he stood for a moment studying it, trying to figure out what it might be—and how best to carry it up the Brambleberry House stairs—when the enticing scent of cherry blossoms swirled around him.

"It's a dollhouse." Julia spoke beside him in a low

voice and he automatically squared his shoulders, though what he was bracing for, he wasn't quite sure.

"My father made it for me years ago. My…late husband tried to fix it up a little for Maddie but I'm afraid it's still falling apart. I really hope it survived the trip."

So she was a widow. They had that in common, then. He cleared his throat. "Should we take the blanket off?"

She shrugged, which he took for assent. He unwrapped the cord and heard a crunching kind of thud inside. Uh-oh. Not a good sign. With a careful look at her and a growing sense of trepidation, he pulled the blanket away and winced as Julia gasped.

Despite her obvious efforts to protect the dollhouse, the piece hadn't traveled well. The construction looked flimsy to begin with and the roof had collapsed.

One entire support wall had come loose as well and the whole thing looked like it was ready to implode.

"I'm sorry," he said, though the words seemed grossly inadequate.

"It's not your fault. I was afraid it wouldn't survive the trip. Oh, this is going to break Maddie's heart. She loved that little house."

"So did you," he guessed.

She nodded. "For a lot of reasons." She tilted her head, studying the wreckage. "You're the carpentry expert. I don't suppose there's any way I can fix this, is there?"

He gazed down at her, at the fading rays of the sun that caught gold strands in her hair, at the sorrow marring those lovely features for a lost treasure.

He gave an inward groan. Dammit, he didn't want to do this. But he was such a sucker for a woman in distress. How could he just walk away?

He cleared his throat. "If you want, I could take a look at it. See what I can do."

"Oh, I couldn't ask that of you."

"You didn't ask," he said gruffly.

She sent him a swift look. "No. I didn't."

"I'm kind of slammed with projects right now. It might take me a while to get to it. And even then, I can't make any guarantees. That's some major damage there. You might be better just starting over."

She forced a smile, though he could see the sadness lingering in her eyes. Her father had made it for her, she had said. He didn't remember much about her father from their summers in Cannon Beach, mostly that the man always seemed impatient and abrupt.

"I can't make any promises," he repeated. "But I'll see what I can do."

"Oh, that would be wonderful. Thank you so much, Will."

Together, they gathered up the shattered pieces of the dollhouse and carried them to his truck, where he set them carefully in the back between his toolbox and ladder.

"I'm happy to pay you for your time and trouble."

As if he would ever accept her money. "Don't worry about it. Let's see if I can fix it first."

She nodded and looked as if she wanted to say something more. To his vast relief, after a moment, she closed her mouth, then returned to the U-Haul for the last few boxes.

CHAPTER FOUR

BETWEEN THE TWO of them, they were able to carry all but a few of the remaining boxes from the U-Haul up the stairs, where they found Sage and Julia pulling books out of boxes and placing them on shelves.

"You're all so wonderful to help me," Julia said, gratitude coursing through her as she smiled at all three of them. "I have to tell you, I never expected such a warm welcome. I thought it would be weeks before I would even know a soul in Cannon Beach besides Abigail. I haven't even started teaching yet but I feel as if I have instant friends."

Sage smiled. "We're thrilled to have you and the twins here. And I think Abigail would be, too. Don't you think, Will?"

He set down the boxes. "Sure. She always loved kids."

"She was nothing but a big kid herself. Remember how she used to sit out on the porch swing for hours with Cara, swinging and telling stories and singing."

"I remember," he said, his voice rough.

Color flooded Sage's features suddenly. "Oh, Will. I'm sorry."

He shook his head. "Don't, Sage. It's okay. I'd better get the last load of boxes."

He turned and headed down the stairs, leaving behind only the echo of his workboots hitting the wooden steps. Julia turned her confused gaze to Anna and Sage and found them both watching after Will with identical expressions of sadness in their eyes.

"I missed something, obviously," she said softly.

Sage gave Anna a helpless look and the other woman shrugged.

"She'll find out sooner or later," Anna said. "She might as well hear it from us."

"You're right," Sage said. "It just still hurts so much to talk about the whole thing."

"You don't have to tell me anything," Julia said quickly. "I'm sorry if I've wandered into things that are none of my business."

Sage glanced down the stairs as if checking to see if Will was returning. When she was certain he was still outside, she turned back, her voice pitched low. "Will had a daughter. She would have been a couple years younger than your twins. Cara. That's who I was talking about. Abigail adored her. We all did. She was the cutest little thing you've ever seen, just full of energy, with big blue eyes, brown curls and dimples. She was full of sugar, our Cara."

Had a daughter. Not has. An ache blossomed in her chest and she knew she didn't want to hear any more.

But she had learned many lessons over the last few years—one of the earliest was that information was empowering, even if the gaining of it was a process often drenched in pain.

"What happened?" she forced herself to ask.

Sage shook her head, her face inexpressibly sad. Anna squeezed her arm and picked up the rest of the story.

"Cara was killed along with Will's wife, Robin, two

years ago." Though Anna spoke in her usual no-nonsense tone, Julia could hear the pain threading through her words.

"They were crossing the street downtown in the middle of the afternoon when they were hit by a drunk tourist in a motorhome," she went on. "Robin died instantly but Cara hung on for two weeks. We all thought—hoped—she was going to pull through but she caught an infection in the hospital in Portland and her little body was too weak and battered to fight it."

She wanted to cry, just sit right there in the middle of the floor and weep for him. More than that, she wanted to race down the stairs and hug her own precious darlings to her.

"Oh, poor Will. He must have been shattered."

"We all were," Sage said. "It was like a light went out of all of us. Will used to be so lighthearted. Like a big tease of an older brother. It's been more than two years since Robin and Cara died and I can count on one hand the number of times I've seen him genuinely smile at something since then."

The ache inside her stretched and tugged and her eyes burned with tears for the teenage boy with the mischievous eyes.

Sage touched her arm. "I'm so glad you're here now."

"Me? Why?"

"Well, you've lost someone, too. You understand, in a way the rest of us can't. I'm sure it would help Will to talk to someone who's experienced some of those same emotions."

Julia barely contained her wince, feeling like the world's biggest fraud.

"Grief is such a solitary, individual thing," she said after an awkward moment. "No one walks the same journey."

Sage smiled and pressed a cheek to Julia's. "I know. But I'm still glad you're here, and I'm sure Will is, too."

Julia was saved from having to come up with an answer to that when she again heard his footsteps on the stairs. A moment later, he came in, muscles bulging beneath the cotton of his shirt as he carried in a trio of boxes.

He had erased any trace of emotion from his features, any sign at all that he contained any emotions at all. Finding out about his wife and daughter explained so much about him. The hardness, the cynicism. The pain in his eyes when he looked at Maddie.

She had a wild urge to take the boxes from him, slip her arms around his waist and hold him until everything was all right again.

"This is the last of it. Where do these go?"

Her words tangled in her throat and she had to clear her throat before she could speak. "The top one belongs in my bedroom. The others are Simon's."

With an abrupt nod, he headed first to her room and then to the one down the hall where Simon slept.

He returned to the living room just as the doorbell downstairs rang through the house.

"Hey, Mom!" Simon yelled up the stairs an instant later. "The pizza guy's here!"

Conan started barking in accompaniment and Julia rolled her eyes at the sudden cacophony of sound. "Are you sure about this? The house was so quiet before we showed up. If you want that quiet again, you'd better speak now while I've still got the U-Haul."

Sage shook her head with a laugh. "No way. I'm not lugging those books back down the stairs. You're stuck here for a while."

Right now, she couldn't think of anywhere she would

rather be. Julia flashed a quick smile to the other two women and Will, grabbed her purse, and headed down the stairs to pay for the pizza.

Simon stood at the door holding on to Conan's collar as the dog wriggled with excitement, his tail wagging a mile a minute.

Her son giggled. "I think he really likes pizza, Mom."

"I guess. Maybe you had better take him into Anna's apartment so he doesn't attack the pizza driver."

With effort, he wrangled the dog through the door and closed the door behind him. Finally, Julia opened the door and found a skinny young man with his cap on backward and his arms full of pizza boxes.

She quickly paid him for the pizza—adding in a hefty tip. She closed the door behind him and backed into the entry, her arms full, and nearly collided with a solid male.

Strong arms came around her to keep her upright.

"Oh," she exclaimed to Will. "I didn't hear you come down the stairs."

"You were talking to the driver," he answered. He quickly released her—much to her regret. She knew she shouldn't have enjoyed that brief moment of contact, but it had been so very long...

She couldn't help noticing the boy she had known now had hard strength in his very grown-up muscles.

"I thought you said the trailer was empty," she said with some confusion as he headed for the door.

"It is. You're done here so I'm heading home."

"You can't leave!" she exclaimed.

He raised an eyebrow. "I can't?"

She held out the boxes in her arms. "You've got to stay for pizza. I ordered way too much for three women and two children."

"Don't forget Conan," he pointed out. "He's crazy about pizza, even though all that cheese is lousy for him."

"Knowing my kids, I'm sure he'll be able to sneak far more than is good for him."

The scent of him reached her, spicy and male and far more enticing than any pizza smells. "I still have too much. Please stay."

He gazed at the door with a look almost of desperation in his eyes. But when he turned back, she thought he might be weakening.

"Please, Will," she pressed.

He opened his mouth to answer but before he could, the door to Abigail's apartment opened and Maddie peeked her head out, looking tousled and sleepy.

"Can we come out now?" she asked.

"As long as the dog's not going to knock me down to get to the Canadian bacon."

At Maddie's giggle, Julia saw a spasm of pain flicker across Will's features and knew the battle was lost.

"I really can't stay." He reached for the doorknob. "Thanks anyway for the invitation, but I've got a lot of work to do at home."

She couldn't push him more, not with that shadow of pain clouding his blue eyes. Surrendering to the inevitable, she simply nodded. "You still need to eat. Take some home with you."

She could see the objections forming on his expression and decided not to take no for an answer. Will Garrett didn't know stubborn until he came up against her.

"What's your pleasure? Pepperoni or Hawaiian? I'd offer you the vegetarian but I think Sage has dibs on that one."

"It's not necessary, really."

"It is to me," she said firmly. "You just spent forty-five minutes helping me haul boxes up. You have to let me repay you somehow. Here, I hope you still like pepperoni and olive."

His eyes widened that she would remember such a detail. She couldn't have explained why—it was just one of those arcane details that stuck in her head. Several times that last summer, they'd gone to Mountain Mike's Pizza in town with her brother and Will always had picked the same thing.

"Maddie, can you hold this for a second?"

She gave the box marked pepperoni to her daughter, then with one hand she opened it and pulled out half the pizza, which she stuck on top of the Hawaiian.

He looked as if he wanted to object, but he said nothing when she handed him the box with the remaining half a pizza in it.

"Here you go. You should have enough for dinner tonight and breakfast in the morning as well. Consider it a tiny way to say thank you for all your hard work."

He shook his head but to her vast relief, he didn't hand the pizza back to her.

"Mom, I can't hold him anymore!" Simon said from behind the door. "He's starving and so am I!"

"You'd better get everyone upstairs for pizza," Will said.

"Right. Good night, then."

She wanted to say more—much more—but with a rambunctious dog and two hungry children clamoring for her attention, she had to be content with that.

BLASTED STUBBORN WOMAN.

Will sat on his deck watching the lights of Cannon Beach flicker on the water as he ate his third piece of pizza.

He had to admit, even lukewarm, it tasted delicious—probably a fair sight better than the peanut butter sandwich he would have scrounged for his meal.

He didn't order pizza very often since half of it usually went to waste before he could get to the leftovers so this was a nice change from TV dinners and fast-food hamburgers.

He really needed to shoot for a healthier diet. Sage was always after him to get more vegetables and fewer preservatives into his diet. He tried but he'd never been a big one for cooking in the first place. He could grill steaks and burgers and the occasional chicken breast but he usually fell short at coming up with something to go alongside the entree.

He fell short in a lot of areas. He sighed, listening to the low rumble of the sea. He spent a lot of his free time puttering around in his dad's shop or sitting out here watching the waves, no matter what the weather. He just hated the emptiness inside the house.

He ought to move, he thought, as he did just about every night at this same time when the silence settled over him with like a scratchy, smothering wool blanket.

He ought to just pick up and make a new start somewhere. Especially now that Julia Hudson Blair had climbed out of the depths of his memories and taken up residence just a few hundred yards away.

She knew.

Sometime during the course of the evening, Sage or Anna must have told her about the accident. He wasn't quite sure how he was so certain, but he had seen a deep compassion in the green of her eyes, a sorrow that hadn't been there earlier.

He washed the pizza down with a swallow of Sam Adams—the one bottle he allowed himself each night.

He knew it shouldn't bother him so much that she knew. Wasn't like it was some big secret. She would find out sooner or later, he supposed.

He just hated that first shock of pity when people first found out—though he supposed when it came down to it, the familiar sadness from friends like Sage and Anna wasn't much easier.

Somehow seeing that first spurt of pity in Julia's eyes made it all seem more real, more raw.

Her life hadn't been so easy. She was a widow, so she must know a thing or two about loss and loneliness. That didn't make him any more eager to have her around— or her kids.

He shouldn't have made a big deal out of the whole thing. He should have just sucked it up and stayed for pizza with her and Sage and Anna. Instead, his kneejerk reaction had been to flee and he had given into it, something very unlike him.

He sighed and took another swallow of beer. From here, he could see her bedroom light. A dark shape moved across the window and he eased back into the shadows of his empty house.

Why was he making such a big deal about this? Julia meant nothing to him. Less than nothing. He hadn't thought about her in years. Yeah, years ago he had been crazy about her when he was just a stupid, starry-eyed kid. He had dreamed about her all that last summer, when she came back to Cannon Beach without her braces and with curves in all the right places.

First love could be an intensely powerful thing for a sixteen-year-old boy. When she left Cannon Beach, his dreams of a long-distance relationship were quickly dashed when she didn't write to him as she had promised. He had tried to call the phone number she'd given him and left several messages that were never returned.

He was heartbroken for a while but he'd gotten over it. By spring, when he'd taken Robin Cramer to the prom, he had completely forgotten about Julia Hudson and her big green eyes.

Life had taught him that a tiny little nick in his heart left by a heedless fifteen-year-old girl was nothing at all to the pain of having huge, jagged chunks of his soul ripped away.

Now, sixteen years later, Julia was nothing to him. He just needed to shake this weird feeling that the careful order of the life he had painstakingly managed to piece together in the last two years had just been tossed out to sea.

He could think of no earthly reason he shouldn't be able to treat her and her children with politeness, at least.

He couldn't avoid interacting with Julia, for a dozen reasons. Beyond the minor little fact that she lived three houses down, he was still working on renovating several of the Brambleberry House rooms. He couldn't avoid her and he sure as hell couldn't run away like a coward every time he saw her kids.

He looked up at Brambleberry House again and his gaze automatically went to the second-floor window. A shape moved across again and a moment later the light went out and somehow Will felt more alone than ever.

"THANK YOU BOTH again for your help today." Julia smiled at Sage and Anna across the table in her new apartment as they finished off the pizza. "I don't know what I would have done without you."

Anna shook her head. "We only helped you with the

easy part. Now you have to figure out where to put everything."

"We have dishes in the kitchen and sheets on the beds. Beyond that, everything else can wait until the morning."

"Looks like some of us need to find that path there sooner than others," Sage murmured, gesturing toward Maddie.

"Not me," Maddie instantly protested, but Julia could clearly see she was drooping tonight, with her elbow propped on the table and her head resting on her fist.

Even with her short nap, Maddie still looked tired. Julia sighed. Some days dragged harder than others on Maddie's stamina. They had spent a busy day making all the arrangements to move into Brambleberry House. Maddie had helped carry some of her own things to her bedroom and had delighted in putting her toys and clothes away herself.

With all the craziness of moving in, Julia hadn't been as diligent as usual about making sure Maddie didn't overextend herself and now it looked as if she had reached the limit of her endurance.

"Time for bed, sweetie. Let's get your meds."

"I'm not ready for bed," she protested, sending a pleading look to Anna and Sage, as if they could offer a reprieve. "I want to stay up and help move in."

"I'm tuckered myself," Julia said. "I'll leave all the fun stuff for tomorrow when we're all rested, okay?"

Maddie sighed with a quiet resignation that never failed to break her heart. She caught herself giving in to the sorrow and quickly shunted it away. Her daughter was still here. She was a miracle and Julia could never allow herself to forget that.

Before she brought in any other boxes, she had made

sure to put Maddie's pill regimen away in a cabinet by the kitchen sink. She poured a glass of water and handed them to her. With the ease of long, grim practice, Maddie downed the half-dozen pills in two swallows, then finished the water to flush down the pills.

Because her daughter seemed particularly tired, Julia helped her into her pajamas then did a quick set of vitals. Everything was within normal ranges for Maddie so Julia pushed away her lingering worry.

"Good night, sweetie," she said after a quick story and kiss. "Your first sleep in the new house!"

"I like this place," Maddie said sleepily as Julia pulled the nightgown over her thin shoulders.

"I like it, too. It feels like home, doesn't it?"

Maddie nodded. "And the lady is nice."

Julia smiled. "Which one? Sage or Anna? I think they're both pretty nice."

Maddie shook her head but her eyes drooped closed before she could answer.

Julia watched her sleep for a moment, marveling again at the lessons in courage and strength and grace her daughter had taught her these last few years.

A miracle, she thought again. As she stood watching over her, she felt the oddest sensation, almost like featherlight fingers touching her cheek.

Weird, she thought. Sage and Anna had warned her Brambleberry House was a typical drafty old house. She would have to do her best to seal up any cracks in Maddie's room.

When she returned to the other room, she found only Simon, curled up in the one corner of the couch not covered in boxes. He had a book in one hand and was petting Conan absently with the other.

What a blessing her son loved to read. Books and his Game Boy had sustained him through many long, boring doctor appointments.

"Did Sage and Anna go downstairs?" she asked.

"I think they're still in the kitchen," Simon answered without looking up from his book.

She heard low, musical laughter before she reached the kitchen. For a moment, she stood in the doorway watching them as they unloaded her grandmother's china into the built-in cabinet.

Here was another blessing. She was overflowing with them. She had come back to Cannon Beach with only a teaching position and her hope that everything would work out. Now she had this great apartment overlooking the sea and, more importantly, two unexpected new friends who were already becoming dear to her.

She didn't think she made a sound but Sage suddenly sensed her presence. She glanced toward her, her exotic tilted eyes lighting in welcome.

"Our girl is all settled for the night?"

Julia nodded. "It was a hectic day. She wore herself out."

"Is she all right?" Anna asked, her features tight with concern.

"Yes. She's fine. She just doesn't have the stamina she used to have." She paused, deciding it was time to reveal everything. "It's one of the long-term side effects of her bone marrow transplant."

"Bone marrow transplant?" Anna exclaimed, her eyes wide with a shock mirrored on Sage's features.

Julia sighed. "Yes. And a round of radiation and two rounds of chemotherapy. I probably should have told you this earlier but Maddie is in remission from acute lymphocytic leukemia."

CHAPTER FIVE

SAYING THE WORDS aloud always left her feeling vaguely queasy, as if she were the one who had endured months of painful treatments, shots, blood draws, the works.

She found it quite a lowering realization that Maddie had faced her cancer ordeal with far more courage than Julia had been able to muster as her mother.

"Oh, Julia." Sage stepped forward and wrapped her into a spontaneous hug. "I'm so sorry you've all had to go through this."

"It's been a pretty bumpy road," she admitted. "But as I said, she's in remission and she's doing well. Much better since the bone marrow transplant. Simon was the donor. We were blessed that they were a perfect match."

"You've had to go through this all on your own?" Anna's dark eyes looked huge and sad.

She knew Anna was referring to Kevin's death and the timing of it. She decided she wasn't quite ready to delve into those explanations just yet so she chose to evade the question.

"I had a strong support network in Boise," she said instead. "Good friends, my brother and his wife, my co-workers at the elementary school there. They all think I'm crazy to move away."

"Why did you?" Anna asked.

"We were all ready for a change. A new start. Three

months ago, Maddie's oncologist took a new job at the children's hospital in Portland. Dr. Lee had been such a support and comfort to us and when she moved, it seemed like the perfect time for us to venture back out in the world."

She sometimes felt as if their lives had been on hold for three years. Between Maddie's diagnosis, then Kevin's death, she and her children had endured far too much.

They needed laughter and joy and the peace she had always found by the ocean.

She smiled at the two other women. "I have to tell you both, I was still wondering if I had made a terrible mistake leaving behind our friends and the safe cushion of support we had in Boise, until we saw the for-rent sign out front of Brambleberry House. It seemed like a miracle that we might have the chance to live in the very house I had always loved so much when I was a little girl, the house where I had always found peace. I took that sign as an omen that everything would be okay."

"We're so glad you found us," Anna said.

"You belong here," Sage added. She squeezed Julia's fingers with one hand and reached for Anna's hand with the other, linking them all together and Julia had to fight back tears, overwhelmed by their easy acceptance of her.

She realized she felt happier standing in this warm kitchen with these women than she could remember being in a long, long time.

"Thank you," she said softly. "Thank you both."

"You smell that?" Sage demanded after a moment.

Anna rolled her eyes. "Cut it out, Sage."

"Smell what?" Julia asked.

"Freesia," Sage answered. "You smelled it, too, didn't you?"

"I thought it was coming from the open window."

Sage shook her head. "Nope. As much as she loved it, Abigail could never get any freesia bulbs to survive in her garden. Our microclimate is just not conducive to them."

"I hope you're not squeamish about ghosts," Anna said after a long sigh. "Sage insists Abigail is still here at Brambleberry House, that she flits through the house leaving behind the freesia perfume she always wore."

Julia blinked, astonished. It seemed preposterous—until she remembered Maddie's words that the lady was nice, and that soft brush against her skin when she had been standing in Maddie's room looking over her daughter almost as if someone had touched her tenderly.

She fought back a shiver.

"You don't buy it?" she said to Anna.

Anna laughed. "I don't know. I usually tend to fall on the side of logic and reason. My intellect tells me it's a complete impossibility. But then, I can't put anything past Abigail. It wouldn't surprise me at all if she decided to defy the rules of metaphysics and stick around in this house she loved. If it's at all within the realm of possibility, Abigail would find a way."

"And Conan is her familiar," Sage added. "You probably ought to know that up front, too. I think the two of them are a team. If Abigail is the brains of the outfit, he's the muscle."

"Okay, now you're obviously putting me on."

Sage shook her head.

"Conan. The dog."

Sage grinned. "Don't look at me like I'm crazy. Just watch and see. The dog is spooky."

"On that, at least, we can agree," Anna said, setting the last majolica teacup in the cupboard. "He's far smarter than your average dog."

"I've seen that much already," Julia admitted. "I'm sorry, but it's a bit of a stretch for me to go from thinking he's an uncommonly smart dog to buying the theory that he's some kind of conduit from the netherworld."

Sage laughed. "Put like that, it does sound rather ridiculous, doesn't it? Just keep your eyes open. You can judge for yourself after you've been here awhile. I wanted to put a disclosure in the rental agreement about Abigail but Anna wouldn't let me."

Anna made a face. "It's a little tough to find an attorney who will add a clause that we might have a ghost in the house."

"There's no *might* about it. You wait and see, Julia."

A ghost and a dog/medium. She supposed there were worst things she could be dealing with in an apartment. "I hope she is still here. I can't imagine Abigail would be anything but a benevolent spirit."

Sage grinned at her. Anna shook her head, but she was smiling as well. "I see I'm outnumbered in the sanity department."

"You're just better at being a grown-up," Sage answered. Her teasing slid away quickly, though, replaced with concern. "And on that note, is there anything special we need to worry about with Maddie? Environmental things she shouldn't be exposed to or anything?"

Julia sighed. She would much rather ponder lighthearted theories of the supernatural than bump up against the harsh reality of her daughter's illness and recovery.

"It's a tough line I walk between wrapping her up in cotton wool to protect her and encouraging as normal a life as possible. Most of the time she's fine, if a little more subdued than she once was. You probably wouldn't know it but she used to be the spitfire of the twins. When they were toddlers, she was always the one leading Simon into trouble."

She gave a wobbly smile and was warmed when Anna reached out and squeezed her hand.

A moment passed before she could trust her voice to continue. "Right now we need to work on trying to regain the strength she lost through the month she spent in the hospital with the bone marrow transplant. I hope by Christmas things will be better."

Sage smiled. "Well, now you've got two more of us—four, counting Abigail and Conan—on your side."

"Thank you," she whispered, immeasurably touched at their effortless acceptance of her and her children.

AFTER SIMON WAS finally settled in bed, Julia stood in her darkened bedroom gazing out at the ripples of the sea gleaming in the moonlight. Though she had a million things to do—finding bowls they could use for cereal in the morning hovered near the top of her list—she decided she needed this moment to herself to think, without rushing to take care of detail after detail.

Offshore some distance, she could see the moving lights of a sea vessel cutting through the night. She watched it for a moment, then her gaze inexorably shifted to the houses along the shore.

There was the cottage where her family had always stayed, sitting silent and dark. Beyond that was Will Garrett's house. A light burned inside a square cedar building set away from the house. His father's workshop, she remembered. Now it would be Will's.

She glanced at her watch and saw it was nearly midnight. What was he working on so late? And did he spend his time out in his workshop to avoid the emptiness inside his house?

She pressed a hand to her chest at the ache there. How did he bear the pain of losing his wife and his child? She remembered the vast sorrow in his gaze when he had looked at Maddie and she wanted so much to be able to offer some kind of comfort to him.

She sensed he wouldn't want her to try. Despite his friendship with Sage and Anna, Will seemed to hold himself apart, as if he had used his carpentry skills to carefully hammer out a wall between himself and the rest of the world.

She ached for him, but she knew there was likely very little she could do to breach those walls.

She could try.

The thought whispered through her head with soft subtlety. She shook her head at her own subconscious. No. She had enough on her plate right now, moving to a new place, taking on a new job, dealing with twins on her own, one of whom still struggled with illness.

She didn't have the emotional reserves to take on anyone else's pain. She knew it, but as the peace of the house settled around her, she had the quiet conviction that she could at least offer him her friendship.

As if in confirmation, the sweet, summery scent of freesia drifted through the room. She smiled.

"Abigail, if you are still here," she whispered, "thank you. For this place, for Anna and Sage. For everything."

For just an instant, she thought she felt again the gentle brush of fingers against her cheek.

WILL MANAGED TO avoid his new neighbors for several days, mostly because he was swamped with work. He was contracted to do the carpentry work on a rehab project in Manzanita. The job was behind schedule because of other subcontractors' delays and the developer wanted the carpentry work done yesterday.

Will was pouring every waking moment into it, leaving his house before the sun was up and returning close to midnight every night.

He didn't mind working hard. Having too much work to do was a damn sight better than having too little. Building something with his hands helped fill the yawning chasm of his life.

But his luck where his neighbors were concerned ran out a week after he had helped carry boxes up to the second-floor apartment of Brambleberry House.

By Friday, most of the basic work on the construction job was done and the only thing left was for him to install the custom floor and ceiling moldings the developer had ordered from a mill in Washington State. They hadn't been delivered yet and until they arrived, he had nothing to do.

Finally he returned to Cannon Beach, to his empty house and his empty life.

After showering off the sawdust and sweat from a hard day's work, he was grilling a steak on the deck—his nightly beer in hand—watching tourists fly kites and play in the sand in the pleasant early evening breeze when he suddenly heard excited barking.

A moment later, a big red mutt bounded into view, trailing the handle of his retractable leash.

As soon as he spied Will, he switched directions and bounded up the deck steps, his tongue lolling as he panted heavily.

"You look like a dog on the lam."

Conan did that weird grin thing of his and Will glanced down the beach to see who might have been on the other end of the leash. He couldn't see anyone—not really surprising. Though he seemed pondeorus most of the time, Conan could pour on the juice when he wanted to escape his dreaded leash and be several hundred yards down the beach before you could blink.

When he turned back to the dog, he found him sniffing with enthusiasm around the barbecue.

"No way," Will muttered. "Get your own steak. I'm not sharing."

Conan whined and plopped down at his feet with such an obviously feigned morose expression that Will had to smile. "You're quite the actor, aren't you? No steak for you tonight but I will get you a drink. You look like you could use it."

He found the bowl he usually used for Conan and filled it from the sink. When he walked back through the sliding doors, he heard a chorus of voices calling the dog's name.

Somehow, he supposed he wasn't really surprised a moment later when Julia Blair and her twins came into view from the direction of Brambleberry House.

Conan barked a greeting, his head hanging over the deck railing. Three heads swiveled in their direction and even from here, he could see the relief in Julia's green eyes when she spotted the dog.

"There you are, you rascal," she exclaimed.

With her hair held back from her face in a ponytail, she looked young and lovely in the slanted early evening light. Though he knew it was unwise, part of him wanted to just sit and savor the sight of her, a little guilty reward for putting in a hard day's work.

Shocked at the impulse, he set down Conan's bowl so hard some water slopped over the side.

"I'm so sorry," Julia called up. Though he wanted to keep them off the steps like he was some kind of medieval knight defending his castle from assault, he stood mutely by as she and her twins walked up the stairs to the deck.

"We were taking him for a walk on the beach," Julia went on, "but we apparently weren't moving quickly enough for him."

"It's my fault," the boy—Simon—said, his voice morose. "Mom said I had to hold his leash tight and I tried, I really did, but I guess I wasn't strong enough."

"I'm sure it's not your fault," Will said through a throat that suddenly felt tight. "Conan can be pretty determined when he sets his mind to something."

Simon grinned at him with a new warmth. "I guess he had his mind set on running away."

"We were going to get an ice cream," the girl said in her whispery voice. He had no choice but to look at her, with her dark curls and blue eyes. A sense of frailty clung to her, as if the slightest breeze would pick her up and carry her out to sea.

He didn't know how to talk to her—didn't know if he could. But he had made a pledge not to hurt others simply because he was in pain. He supposed that included little dark-haired sea sprites.

"That sounds like fun. A great thing to do on a pretty summer night like tonight."

"My favorite ice cream is strawberry cheesecake," she announced. "I really hope they have some."

"Not me," Simon announced. "I like bubblegum. Especially when it's blue bubblegum."

To his dismay, Julia's daughter crossed the deck until she was only a few feet away. She looked up at him out of serious eyes. "What about you, Mr. Garrett?" Maddie asked. "Do you like ice cream?"

Surface similarities aside, she was not at all like his roly-poly little Cara, he reminded himself. "Sure. Who doesn't?"

"What kind is your favorite?"

"Hmmm. Good question. I hate to be boring but I really like plain old vanilla."

Simon hooted. "That's what my mom's favorite flavor is, too. With all the good flavors out there—licorice or coconut or chocolate chunk—why would you ever want plain vanilla? That's just weird."

"Simon!" Julia's cheeks flushed and he thought again how extraordinarily lovely she was—not much different from the girl he'd been so crazy about nearly two decades ago.

"Well, it is," Simon insisted.

"You don't tell someone they're weird," Julia said.

"I didn't say *he* was weird. Just that eating only vanilla ice cream is weird."

Will found himself fighting a smile, which startled him all over again. "Okay, I'll admit I also like praline ice cream and sometimes even chocolate chip on occasion. Is that better?"

Simon snickered. "I guess so."

He felt the slightest brush of air and realized it was Maddie touching his arm with her small, pale hand. Suddenly he couldn't seem to catch his breath, aching inside.

"Would you like to come with us to get an ice-cream cone, Mr. Garrett?" she asked in her breathy voice. "I bet if you were holding Conan's leash, he couldn't get away."

He glanced at her sweet little features then at Julia. The color had climbed even higher on her cheekbones and she gave him an apologetic look before turning back to her daughter.

"Honey, I'm sure Mr. Garrett is busy. It smells like he's cooking a steak for his dinner."

"Which I'd better check on. Hang on."

He lifted the grill and found his porterhouse a little on the well-done side, but still edible. He shut off the flame, using the time to consider how to answer the girl.

He shouldn't be so tempted to go with them. It was an impulse that shocked the hell out of him.

He had spent two years avoiding social situations except with his close friends. But suddenly the idea of sitting here alone eating his dinner and watching others enjoy life seemed unbearable.

How could he possibly go with them, though? He wasn't sure he trusted himself to be decent for an hour or so, the time it would take to walk to the ice-cream place, enjoy their cones, then walk home.

What if something set him off and brought back that bleak darkness that always seemed to hover around the edges of his psyche? The last thing he wanted to do was hurt these innocent kids.

"Thanks for the invitation," he said, "but I'd better stay here and finish my dinner."

Conan whined and butted his head against Will's leg, almost as if urging Will to reconsider.

"We can wait for you to eat," Simon said promptly. "We don't mind, do we, Mom?"

"Simon, Mr. Garrett is busy. We don't want to badger him." She met his gaze, her green eyes soft with an expression he couldn't identify. "Though we would love to have you come along. All of us."

"I don't want you to have to wait for me to eat when you've got strawberry cheesecake and bubblegum ice-cream cones calling your name."

Julia nodded rather sadly, as if she had expected his answer. "Come on, kids. We'd better be on our way."

Conan whined again. Will gazed from the dog to Julia and her family, then he shook his head. "Then again, I guess there's no reason I can't warm my steak up again when we get back from the ice-cream parlor. I'm not that hungry right now anyway."

His statement was met with a variety of reactions. Conan barked sharply, Julia's eyes opened wide with surprise, Simon gave a happy shout and Maddie clapped her hands with delight.

It had been a long time since anyone had seemed so thrilled about his company, he thought as he carried his steak inside to cover it with foil and slide it in the re-frigerator.

He didn't know what impulse had prompted him to agree to go along with them. He only knew it had been a long while since he had allowed himself to enjoy the quiet peace of an August evening on the shore.

Maybe it was time.

CHAPTER SIX

THIS WAS A mistake of epic proportions.

Will walked alongside Julia while her twins moved ahead with Conan. Simon raced along with the dog, holding tightly to his leash as the two of them scared up a shorebird here and there and danced just out of reach of the waves. Maddie seemed content to walk sedately toward the ice-cream stand in town, stopping only now and again to pick something up from the sand, study it with a serious look, then plop it in her pocket.

Will was painfully conscious of the woman beside him. Her hair shimmered in the dying sunlight, her cheeks were pinkened from the wind, and the soft, alluring scent of cherry blossoms clung to her, feminine and sweet.

He couldn't come up with a damn thing to say and he felt like he was an awkward sixteen-year-old again.

Accompanying her little family to town was just about the craziest idea he had come up with in a long, long time.

She didn't seem to mind the silence but he finally decided good manners compelled him to at least make a stab at conversation.

"How are you settling in?" he asked.

She smiled softly. "It's been lovely. Perfect. You know, I wasn't sure I was making the right choice to move here but everything has turned out far better than I ever dreamed."

"The apartment working out for you, then?"

"It's wonderful. We love it at Brambleberry House. Anna and Sage have become good friends and the children love being so close to the ocean. It's been a wonderful adventure for us all so far."

He envied her that, he realized. The sense of adventure, the willingness to charge headlong into the unknown. He had always been content to stay in the house where he had been raised. He loved living on the coast—waking up to the sound of scoters and grebes, sleeping to the murmuring song of the sea—but lately he sometimes felt as if he were suffocating here. It was impossible to miss the way everyone in town guarded their words around him and worse, watched him out of sad, careful eyes.

Maybe it was time to move on. It wasn't a new thought but as he walked beside Julia toward the lights of town, he thought perhaps he ought to do just as she had—start over somewhere new.

She was looking at him in expectation, as if she had said something and was waiting for him to respond. He couldn't think what he might have missed and he hesitated to ask her to repeat herself. Instead, he decided to pick a relatively safe topic.

"School starts in a few weeks, right?" he asked.

"A week from Tuesday," she said after a small pause. "I plan to go in and start setting up my classroom tomorrow."

"Does it take you a whole week to set up?"

"Oh, at least a week!" Animation brightened her features even more. "I'm way behind. I've got bulletin boards to decorate, class curriculum to plan, students' pictures and names to memorize. Everything."

Her voice vibrated with excitement and despite his discomfort, he almost smiled. "You can't wait, can you?"

She flashed him a quick look. "Is it that obvious?"

"I'm glad you've found something you enjoy. I'll admit, back in the day, I wouldn't have pegged you for a schoolteacher."

She laughed. "I guess my plans to be a rich and famous diva someday kind of fell by the wayside. Teaching thirty active fifth-graders isn't quite as exciting as going on tour and recording a platinum-selling record."

"I bet you're good at it, though."

She blinked in surprise, then gave him a smile of such pure, genuine pleasure that he felt his chest tighten.

"Thank you, Will. That means a lot to me."

Their gazes met and though it had been a long, long time, he knew he didn't mistake the currents zinging between them.

A gargantuan mistake.

He was almost relieved when they caught up with Maddie, who had slowed her steps considerably.

"You doing okay, cupcake?" Julia asked.

"I'm fine, Mommy," she assured her, though her features were pale and her mouth hung down a little at the edges.

He wondered again what the story was here—why Julia watched her so carefully, why Maddie seemed so frail—but now didn't seem the appropriate time to ask.

"Do you need a piggyback ride the rest of the way to the ice-cream stand?" Julia asked.

Maddie shook her head with more firmness than before, as if that brief rest had been enough for her. "I can make it, I promise. We're almost there, aren't we?"

"Yep. See, there's the sign with the ice-cream cone on it."

Somehow Maddie slipped between them and folded her hand in her mother's. She smiled up at Will and his chest ached all over again.

"I love this place," Maddie announced when they drew closer to Murphy's Ice Cream.

"I do, too," Will told her. "I've been coming here for ice cream my whole life."

She looked intrigued. "Really? My mom said she used to come here, too, when she was little." She paused to take a breath before continuing. "Did you ever see her here?"

He glanced at Julia and saw her cheeks had turned pink and he wondered if she was remembering holding hands under one of the picnic tables that overlooked the beach and stealing kisses whenever her brother wasn't looking.

"I did," he said gruffly, wishing those particular memories had stayed buried.

Maddie looked as if she wanted to pursue the matter but by now they had reached Murphy's.

He hadn't thought this whole thing through, he realized as they approached the walk-up window. Rats. Inside, he could see Lacy Murphy Walker, who went to high school with him and whose family had owned and operated the ice-cream parlor forever.

She had been one of Robin's best friends—and as much as he loved her, he was grimly aware that Lacy also happened to be one of the biggest gossips in town.

"Hi, Will." She beamed with some surprise. "Haven't seen you in here in an age."

He had no idea how to answer that so he opted to stick with a polite smile.

"We're sure loving the new cabinets in the back," she went on. "You did a heck of a job on them. I was saying the other day how much more storage space we have now."

"Thanks, Lace."

Inside, he could see the usual assortment of tourists but more than a few local faces he recognized. The scene was much the same on the picnic tables outside.

His neck suddenly itched from the speculative glances he was getting from those within sight—and especially from Lacy.

She hadn't stopped staring at him and at Julia and her twins since he walked up to the counter.

"You folks ready to order?"

He hadn't been lumped into a *folks* in a long time and it took him a moment to adjust.

Sometimes he thought that was one of the things he had missed the most the last two years, being part of a unit, something bigger and better than himself.

"Hang on," he said, turning back to Julia and her twins. "Have you decided?" he asked, in a voice more terse than he intended.

"Bubblegum!" Simon exclaimed. "In a sugar cone."

Lacy wrote it down with a smile. "And for the young lady?"

Maddie gifted Lacy with a particularly sweet smile. "Strawberry cheesecake, please," she whispered. "I would like a sugar cone, too."

"Got it." Again Lacy turned her speculative gaze at him and Julia, standing together at the counter. "And for the two of you?"

The two of you. He wanted to tell her there was no *two of you*. They absolutely were *not* a couple, just two completely separate individuals who happened to walk down the beach together for ice cream.

"Two scoops of vanilla in a sugar cone," he said.

"Make that two of those." Julia smiled at Lacy and he felt a little light-headed. It was only because he hadn't eaten, he told himself. Surely his reaction had nothing to do with the cherry blossom scent of her that smelled sweeter than anything coming out of the ice cream shop.

Lacy gave them the total and Will pulled out his wallet.

"My treat," he said, sliding a bill to Lacy.

She reached for it at the same time Julia did.

"It is not!" Julia exclaimed. "You weren't even planning to come along until we hounded you into it. Forget it, I'm paying."

Even more speculative glances were shooting their way. He could see a couple of his mother's friends inside and was afraid they would be on the phone to her at her retirement village in San Diego before Lacy even scooped their cones.

Above all, he wanted to avoid attention and just win this battle so they could find a place to sit, preferably one out of view of everyone inside.

"Nobody hounded anybody. I wanted to come." *For one brief second of insanity,* he thought, but didn't add. "I'm paying this time. You can pick it up next time."

The minute the words escaped his mouth, he saw Lacy's eyes widen. *Next time,* he had said. Rats. He could just picture the conversation that would be buzzing around town within minutes.

You hear about Will Garrett? He's finally dating again, the new teacher living in Abigail's house. The pretty widow with those twins. Remember, her family used to rent the old Turner place every summer.

He grimaced to himself, knowing there wasn't a darn thing he could do about it. When a person lived in the same town his whole life, everybody seemed to think they had a stake in his business.

"Are you sure?" Julia still looked obstinate.

He nodded. "Take it, Lace," he said.

To his vast relief, she ended the matter by stuffing the bill into the cash register and handing him his change.

"It should just be a minute," she said in a chirpy kind of voice. She disappeared from the counter, probably to go looking for her cell phone so she could start spreading the word.

"Thank you," Julia said, though she still looked uncomfortable about letting him treat.

"No problem."

"It really doesn't seem fair. You didn't even want to come with us."

"I'm here, aren't I? It's fine."

She looked as if she had something more to say but after a moment she closed her mouth and let the matter rest when Lacy returned with the twins' cones.

"Here you go. The other two are coming right up."

"Great service as always, Lacy," he said when she handed him and Julia their cones. "Thanks."

"Oh, no problem, Will." She smiled brightly. "And let me just say for the record that it's so great to see you out enjoying…ice cream again."

Heat soaked his face and he could only hope he wasn't blushing. He hadn't blushed in about two decades and he sure as hell didn't want to start now.

"Right," he mumbled, and was relieved when Simon spoke up.

"Hey, Mom, our favorite table is empty. Can we sit out there and watch for whales?"

Julia smiled and shook her head ruefully. "We've been here twice and sat at the same picnic table both times. I guess that makes it our favorite."

She studied Will. "Are you in a hurry to get back or do you mind eating our cones here?"

He would rather just take a dip in the cold waters of the Pacific right about now, if only to avoid the watching eyes of everyone in town. Instead, he forced a smile.

"No big rush. Let's sit down."

He made the mistake of glancing inside the ice-cream parlor one time as he was sliding into the picnic table across from her—just long enough to see several heads swivel quickly away from him.

With a sigh, he resigned himself to the rumors. Nothing he could do about them now anyway.

SHE WAS QUITE certain Conan was a canine but just now he was looking remarkably like the proverbial cat with its mouth stuffed full of canary feathers.

Julia frowned at the dog, who settled beside the picnic table with what looked suspiciously like a grin. Sage and Anna said he had an uncanny intelligence and some hidden agenda but she still wasn't sure she completely bought it.

More likely, he was simply anticipating a furtive taste of one of the twins' cones.

If Conan practically hummed with satisfaction, Will resembled the plucked canary. He ate his cone with a sto-

icism that made it obvious he wasn't enjoying the treat—
or the company—in the slightest.

She might have been hurt if she didn't find it so terribly sad.

She grieved for him, for the boy she had known with
the teasing smile and the big, generous heart. His loss
was staggering, as huge as the Pacific, and she wanted
so desperately to ease it for him.

What power did she have, though? Precious little, especially when he would only talk in surface generali-
ties about mundane topics like the tide schedule and the
weather.

She tried to probe about the project he was working
on, an intriguing rehabilitation effort down the coast,
but he seemed to turn every question back to her and
she was tired of talking about herself.

She was also tired of the curious eyes inside. Good
heavens, couldn't the poor man go out for ice cream without inciting a tsunami of attention? If he wasn't being
so unapproachable, she would have loved to give their
tongues something to wag about.

How would Will react if she just grabbed the cone out
of his hand, tossed it over her shoulder into the sand, and
planted a big smacking kiss on his mouth, just for the
sheer wicked thrill of watching how aghast their audi-
ence might turn?

It was an impulse from her youth, when she had
been full of silly dreams and impetuous behavior. She
wouldn't do it now, of course. Not only would a kiss
horrify Will but her children were sitting at the table
and they wouldn't understand the subtleties of social tit-
for-tat.

The idea was tempting, though. And not just to give the gossips something to talk about.

She sighed. It would be best all the way around if she just put those kind of thoughts right out of her head. She had been alone for two years and though she might have longed for a man's touch, she wasn't about to jump into anything with someone still deep in the grieving process.

"What project are you working on next at Brambleberry House?" she asked him.

"New ceiling and floor moldings in Abigail's old apartment, where Anna lives now," he answered. "On the project I'm working on in Manzanita, the developer ordered some custom patterns. I liked them and showed them to Anna and she thought they would be perfect for Brambleberry House so we ordered extra."

"What was wrong with the old ones?"

"They were cracking and warped in places from water damage a long time ago. We tried to repair them but it was becoming an endless process. And then when she decided to take down a few walls, the moldings in the different rooms didn't match so we decided to replace them all with something historically accurate."

He started to add more, but Maddie slid over to him and held out her cone.

"Mr. Garrett, would you like to try some of my strawberry cheesecake ice cream? It's really good."

A slight edge of panic appeared around the edges of his gaze. "Uh, no thanks. Think I'll stick with my vanilla."

She accepted his answer with equanimity. "You might change your mind, though," she said, with her innate generosity. "How about if I eat it super slow? That way if decide you want some after all, I'll still have some left for you to try later, okay?"

He blinked and she saw the nerves give way to astonishment. "Uh, thanks," he said, looking so touched at the small gesture that her heart broke for him all over again.

Maddie smiled her most endearing smile, the particularly charming one she had perfected on doctors over the years. "You're welcome. Just let me know if you want a taste. I don't mind sharing, I promise."

He looked like a man who had just been stabbed in the heart and Julia suddenly couldn't bear his pain. In desperation, she sought a way to distract him.

"What will you do on Brambleberry House after you finish the moldings?" she finally asked.

He looked grateful for the diversion. "Uh, your apartment is mostly done but the third-floor rooms still need some work. Little stuff, mostly, but inconvenient to try to live around. I figured I would wait to start until after Sage is married and living part-time in the Bay Area with Eben and Chloe."

"I understand they're coming back soon from an extended trip overseas. We've heard a great deal about them from Sage and Anna. The twins can't wait to meet Chloe."

"She's a good kid. And Eben is good for Sage. That's the important thing."

He was a man who loved his friends, she realized. That, at least, hadn't changed over the years.

He seemed embarrassed by his statement and quickly returned to talking about the repairs planned for Brambleberry House. She listened to his deep voice as she savored the last of her cone, thinking it was a perfect summer evening.

The children finished their treats—Maddie's promise to Will notwithstanding—and were romping with Conan in the sand. Their laugher drifted on the breeze above the sound of the ocean.

For just an instant, she was transported back in time, sitting with Will atop a splintery picnic table, eating ice-cream cones and laughing at nothing and talking about their dreams.

By unspoken agreement, they stood, cones finished, and started walking back down the beach while Conan herded the twins along ahead of them.

"I'm boring you to tears," Will said after some time. "I'm sorry. I, uh, don't usually go on and on like that about my work."

She shook her head. "You're not boring me. On the contrary. I enjoy hearing about what you do. You love it, don't you?"

"It's just a job. Not something vitally important to the future of the world like educating young minds."

She made a face. "My, you have a rosy view of educators, don't you?"

"I always had good teachers when I was going to school."

"Good teachers wouldn't have anywhere to teach those young minds if not for great carpenters like you," she pointed out. "The work you've done on Brambleberry House is lovely. The kitchen cupboards are as smooth as a satin dress. Anna told me you made them all by hand."

"It's a great old house. I'm trying my best to do it justice."

They walked in silence for a time and Julia couldn't escape the grim realization that she was every bit as attracted to him now as she had been all those years ago.

Not true, she admitted ruefully. Technically, anyway. She was far *more* aware of him now, as a full-grown woman—with a woman's knowledge and a woman's needs—than she ever would have been as a naive, idealistic fifteen-year-old girl.

He was bigger than he had been then, several inches taller and much more muscled. His hair was cut slightly shorter than it had been when he was a teenager and he had a few laugh lines around his mouth and his eyes, though she had a feeling those had been etched some time ago.

She was particularly aware of his hands, square-tipped and strong, with the inevitable battle scars of a man who used them in creative and constructive ways.

She didn't want to notice anything about him and she certainly wasn't at all thrilled to find herself attracted to him again. She couldn't afford it. Not when she and her children were just finding their way again.

Hadn't she suffered enough from emotionally unavailable men?

"Look what I found, Mom!" Maddie uncurled her fingers to reveal a small gnarled object. "What is it?"

As she studied the object, Julia held her daughter's hand, trying not to notice how thin her fingers seemed. It appeared to be an agate but was an odd color, greenish gray with red streaks in it.

"We forgot to bring our rocky coast field book, didn't we? We'll have to look it up when we get back to the house."

"Do you know, Mr. Garrett?" Maddie presented the object for Will's inspection.

"I'm afraid I'm not much of a naturalist," he said, rather curtly. "Sage is your expert in that department. She can tell you in a second."

"Oh. Okay." Maddie's shoulders slumped, more from fatigue than disappointment, Julia thought, but Will didn't pick up on it. Guilt flickered in his expression.

"I can look at it," he said after a moment. "Let's see."

Will reached for her hand and he examined the contents carefully. "Wow. This is quite a find. It's a bloodstone agate."

"I want to see," Simon said.

"It's pretty rare," Will said. He talked to them about some of the other treasures they could find beachcombing on the coast until they reached his house.

"I guess this is your stop," Julia said as they stood at the steps of his deck.

He glanced up the steps, as if eager to escape, then looked back at them. "I'll walk you the rest of the way to Brambleberry House. It's nearly dark. I wouldn't want you walking on your own."

It was only three houses, she almost said, but he looked so determined to stick it out that she couldn't bring herself to argue.

"Thank you," she said, then gave Maddie a careful look. Her daughter hadn't said much for some time, since finding the bloodstone.

"Is it piggyback time?" Julia asked quietly.

Maddie shrugged, her features dispirited. "I guess so. I really wanted to make it the whole way on my own this time."

"You made it farther this time than last time. And farther still than the time before. Come on, pumpkin. Your chariot awaits." Julia crouched down and her daughter climbed aboard.

"I can carry her," Will said, though he looked as if

he would rather stick a nail gun to his hand and pull the switch.

"I've got her," she answered, aching for him all over again. "But you can make sure Simon and Conan stay away from the surf."

They crossed the last hundred yards to Brambleberry House in silence. When they reached the back gate, Will held it open for them and they walked inside where the smells of Abigail's lush late-summer flowers surrounded them in warm welcome.

She eased Maddie off her back. "You two take Conan inside to get a drink from Anna while I talk to Mr. Garrett, okay?"

"Okay," Simon said, and headed up the steps. Maddie followed more slowly but a moment later Julia and Will were alone with only the sound of the wind sighing in the tops of the pine trees.

"What's wrong with Maddie?"

His quiet voice cut through the peace of the night and she instinctively bristled, wanting to protest that nothing was wrong with her child. Absolutely nothing. Maddie was perfect in every way.

The words tangled in her throat. "She's recovering from a bone marrow transplant," she answered in a low voice to match his. It wasn't any grand secret and he certainly deserved to know, though she didn't want to go through more explanations.

"It's been four months but she hasn't quite regained her strength. She's been a fighter through everything life has thrown at her the last two and a half years, though— two rounds of chemo and a round of radiation—so I know it's only a matter of time before she'll be back to her old self."

CHAPTER SEVEN

HE HEARD HER words as if she whispered them on the wind from a long distance away.

Bone marrow transplant. Chemotherapy. Radiation. Cancer.

He had suspected Maddie was ill, but *cancer*. Damn it. The thought of that sweet-faced little girl enduring that kind of nightmare plowed into him like a semitruck and completely knocked him off his pins.

"I'm sorry, Julia."

The words seemed horrifyingly inadequate but he didn't have the first idea what else to say in this kind of situation. Besides, hadn't he learned after the dark abyss of the last two years that sometimes the simplest of sentiments meant the most?

The sun had finally slipped beyond the horizon and in the dusky twilight, she looked young and lovely and as fragile as her daughter.

"It's been a long, tough journey," she answered. "But I have great hope that we're finally starting to climb through to the other side."

He envied her that hope, he realized. That's what had been missing in his world for two years—for too long there had seemed no escape to the unrelenting pain. He missed Robin, he missed Cara, he missed the man he used to be.

But this wasn't about him, he reminded himself. One other lesson he had learned since the accident that stole his family was that very few people made it through life unscathed, without suffering or pain, and Julia had obviously seen more than her share.

"A year and a half, you said. So you must have had to cope with losing your husband in the midst of dealing with Maddie's cancer?"

In the twilight, he saw her mouth open then close, as if she wanted to say something but changed her mind.

"Yes," she finally answered, though he had a feeling that wasn't what she intended to tell him. "I guess you can see why I felt like we needed a fresh start."

"She's okay now, you said?"

"She's been in remission for a year. The bone marrow transplant was more a precaution because the second round of chemo destroyed her immune system. We were blessed that Simon could be the donor. But as you can imagine, we're all pretty sick of hospitals and doctors by now."

He released a breath, his mind tangled in the vicious thorns of remembering those last terrible two weeks when Cara had clung to life, when he had cried and prayed and begged for another chance for his broken and battered little girl.

For nothing.

His prayers hadn't done a damn bit of good.

"It's kind of surreal, isn't it?" Julia said after a moment. "Who would have thought all those summers ago when we were young that one day we'd be standing here in Abigail's garden together talking about my daughter's cancer treatment?"

He had a sudden, savage need to pummel something—

to yank the autumn roses up by the roots, to shatter the porch swing into a million pieces, to hack the limbs off Abigail's dogwood bushes.

"Life is the cruelest bitch around," he said, and the bitter words seemed to scrape his throat bloody and raw. "Makes you wonder what the hell the point is."

She lifted shocked eyes to his. "Oh, Will. I'm so sorry," she whispered, and before he realized her intentions, she reached out and touched his arm in sympathy.

For just a moment the hair on his arm lifted and he forgot his bitterness, held captive by the gentle brush of skin against skin. He ached for the tenderness of a woman's touch—no, of *Julia's* touch— at the same time it terrified him.

He forced himself to take a step back. Cool night air swirled between them and he wondered how it was possible for the temperature to dip twenty degrees in a millisecond.

"I'd better go." His voice still sounded hoarse. "Your kids probably need you inside."

Her color seemed higher than it had been earlier and he thought she looked slightly disconcerted. "I'm sure you're right. Good night, then. And…thank you for the ice cream and the company. I enjoyed both."

She paused for the barest of moments, as if waiting for him to respond. When the silence dragged on, an instant's disappointment flickered in her eyes and she began to climb the porch steps.

"You're welcome," he said when she reached the top step. She turned with surprise.

"And for the record," he went on, "I haven't enjoyed much of anything for a long time but tonight was…nice."

Her brilliant smile followed him as he let himself out

the front gate and headed down the dark street toward his home, a journey he had made a thousand times.

He didn't need to think about where he was going, which left his mind free to wander through dark alleys.

Cancer. That cute little girl. Hell.

Poor thing. Julia said it was in remission, that things were better except lingering fatigue. Still, he knew this was just one more reason he needed to maintain his careful distance.

His heart was a solid block of ice but if it ever started to melt, he knew he couldn't let himself care about Julia Blair and her children. He couldn't afford it.

He had been through enough pain and loss for a hundred lifetimes. He would have to be crazy to sign up for a situation with the potential to promise plenty more.

When he was ready to let people into his life again—if he was ever ready—it couldn't be a medically fragile little girl, a boy with curious eyes and energy to burn, and a lovely auburn-haired widow who made him long to taste life again.

SHE DIDN'T SEE Will again for several days. With the lead-up to the start of school and then the actual chaos of adjusting to a new classroom and coming to know thirty new students, she barely had time to give him more than a passing thought.

But twice in the early hours of the morning as she graded math refresher assignments and the obligatory essays about how her students had spent the summer, she had glimpsed the telltale glimmer of lights in his workshop through the pines.

Only the walls of Abigail's old house knew that both times she had stopped what she was doing to stand at the window for a few moments watching that light and wondering what he was working on, what he was thinking about, if he'd had a good day.

It wasn't obsession, she told herself firmly. Only curiosity about an old friend.

Other than those few silent moments, she hadn't allowed herself to think about him much. What would be the point?

She had seen his reaction to the news of Maddie's cancer, a completely normal response under the circumstances. He had been shocked and saddened and she certainly couldn't blame him for the quick way he distanced himself from her.

She understood, but it still saddened her.

Now, the Friday after school started, she pulled into the Brambleberry House driveway to find his pickup truck parked just ahead of her SUV. Before she could contain the instinctive reaction, her stomach skittered with anticipation.

"Hey, I think that's Mr. Garrett's truck," Simon exclaimed. "See, it says Garrett Construction on the side."

"I think you must be right." She was quite proud of herself for the calm reply.

"I wonder what's he doing here." Simon's voice quivered with excitement and she sighed. Her son was so desperately eager for a man in his life. She couldn't really blame him—except for Conan, who didn't really count, Simon was surrounded by women in every direction.

"Do you think he's working on something for Sage and Anna? Can I help him, do you think? I could hand him tools or something. I'm really good at that. Do you think he'll let me?"

"I don't know the answer to any of your questions,

kiddo. You'll have to ask him. Why don't we go check it out?"

Both children jumped out of the vehicle the moment she put it in Park. She called to them to wait for her but either they didn't hear her or they chose to ignore her as they rushed to the backyard, where the sound of some kind of power tool hummed through the afternoon.

She caught up with them before they made it all the way.

"I don't want you bothering Will—Mr. Garrett—if he's too busy to answer all your many questions. He has a job to do here and we need to let him."

The rest of what she might have said died in her throat when they turned the corner and she spotted him.

Oh mercy. He wore a pair of disreputable-looking jeans, a forest green T-shirt that bulged with muscle in all the right places, and a leather carpenter's belt slung low like a gunfighter's holster. The afternoon sun picked up golden streaks in his brown hair and he had just a hint of afternoon stubble that made him look dangerous and delectable at the same time.

Oh mercy.

Conan was curled under the shade nearby and his bark of greeting alerted Will's to their presence.

The dog lunged for Simon and Maddie as if he hadn't seen them in months instead of only a few hours and Will even gifted them with a rare smile, there only for an instant before it flickered away.

He drew off his leather gloves and shoved them in the back pocket of his jeans. "School over already? Is it that late?"

"We have early dismissal on Fridays. It's only three o'clock," Julia answered.

"We've been out for a few hours already," Maddie informed him. "Usually we get to stay at the after-school club until Mama finishes her work in her classroom."

"Is that right?"

"It's really fun," Simon answered. "Sometimes we have to stay in Mom's room with her and do our homework if we have a lot, but most of the time we go to extracurriculars. Today we played tetherball and made up a skit and played on the playground for a long time."

"Sounds tiring."

"Not for me," Simon boasted. "Maybe for Maddie."

"I'm not tired," Maddie protested.

His gaze met Julia's in shared acknowledgment that Maddie's claim was obviously a lie.

"What's the project today?" she asked.

"Last time I was here I noticed the back steps were splintering in a few places. I had a couple of hours this afternoon so I decided to get started on replacing them before somebody gets hurt."

Simon looked enthralled. "Can we help you fix them? I could hand you tools and stuff."

That subtle panic sparked in his eyes, the same uneasiness she saw the day they went for ice cream, whenever she or the children had pushed him for more than he was willing to offer.

She could see him trying to figure a way out of the situation without hurting Simon and she quickly stepped in.

"We promised Sage we would pick a bushel of apples and make our famous caramel apple pie, remember? You finally get to meet Chloe in a few hours when she and her father arrive."

Simon scowled. "But you said in the car that if Mr. Garrett said it was okay, we could help him."

She sent a quick look of apology to Will before turning back to her son. "I know, but I could really use your help with the pies."

"Making pies is for girls. I'd rather work with tools and stuff," Simon muttered.

Will raised an eyebrow at this blatantly chauvinistic attitude. "Not true, kid. I know lots of girls who are great at using tools and one of my good friends is a pastry chef at a restaurant down the coast. He makes the best brambleberry pie you'll ever eat in your life."

"Brambleberry, like our house?" Maddic asked.

"Just like."

"Cool!" Simon said. "I want some."

"No brambleberries today," Julia answered. "We're making apple, remember? Let's go change our clothes and get started."

Simon's features drooped with disappointment. "So I don't get to help Mr. Garrett?"

"Simon—"

"I don't mind if he stays and helps," Will said.

"Are you sure?"

He nodded, though she could still see a shadow of reluctance in his eyes. "Positive. I'll enjoy the company. Conan's a good listener but not much of a conversationalist."

She smiled at the unexpected whimsy. "Conversing is one thing Simon does exceptionally well, don't you, kiddo?"

Simon giggled. "Yep. My dad used to say I could talk for a day and a half without needing anybody to answer back."

"I guess that means you probably talk in your sleep, right?"

Simon giggled. "I don't, but Maddie does sometimes. It's really funny. One time she sang the whole alphabet song in her sleep."

"I was only five," Maddie exclaimed to defend herself.

"And you're going to be fifteen before we finish this pie if we don't hurry. We all need to change out of school clothes and into apple-picking and porch-fixing clothes."

Simon looked resigned, then his features brightened. "Race you!" he called to Maddie and took off for the house. She followed several paces behind with Conan barking at their heels, leaving Julia alone with Will.

"I hope he doesn't get in your way or talk your ear off."

"Don't worry. We'll be fine."

"Feel free to send him out to play if you need to."

They lapsed into silence. She should go upstairs, she knew, but she had suddenly discovered she had missed him this last week, silly as that seemed after years when she hadn't given the man a thought.

She couldn't seem to force herself to leave. Finally she sighed, giving into the inevitable.

She took a step closer to him. "Hold still," she murmured.

Wariness leapt into the depths of his blue eyes but he froze as if she had just cast his boots in concrete.

He smelled of leather and wood shavings, and hot, sun-warmed male, a delicious combination, and she wanted to stand there for three or four years and just enjoy it. She brushed her fingers against the blade of his cheekbone, feeling warm male skin.

At her touch, their gazes clashed and the wariness in his eyes shifted instantly to something else, something raw and wild. An answering tremble stirred inside her and for a moment she forgot what she was doing, her fingers frozen on his skin.

His quick intake of breath dragged her back to reality and she quickly dropped her hand, feeling her own face flame.

"You, um, had a little bit of sawdust on your cheek. I didn't want it to find its way into your eye."

"Thanks." She wasn't sure if it was her imagination or not but his voice sounded decidedly hoarse.

She forced a smile and stepped back, though what she really wanted to do was wrap her arms fiercely around his warm, strong neck and hold on for dear life.

"You're welcome," she managed.

With nothing left to be said, she turned and hurried into the house.

SHE TRIED HARD to put Will out of her mind as she and Maddie plucked Granny Smith apples off Abigail's tree. She might have found it a bit easier to forget about him if the ladder didn't offer a perfect view of the porch steps he was fixing.

Now she paused, her arm outstretched but the apple she was reaching to grab forgotten as she watched him smile at something Simon said. She couldn't hear them from here but so far it looked as if Simon wasn't making too big a pest of himself.

"Is this enough, Mama?" Maddie asked from below, where she stood waiting by the bushel basket.

Julia jerked her attention back to her daughter and the task at hand. "Just a moment." She plucked three more and added them to the glistening green pile in the basket.

"That ought to do it."

"Do we really need that many apples?"

"Not for one pie but I thought we could make a couple of extras. What do you think?"

She thought for a moment. "Can we give one to Mr. Garrett?"

Maddie looked over at the steps where Simon was trying his hand with Will's big hammer and Julia saw both longing and a sad kind of resignation in her daughter's blue eyes.

Maddie could be remarkably perceptive about others. Julia thought perhaps her long months of treatment—enough to make any child grow up far too early—had sensitized her to the subtle behaviors of others toward her. The way adults tried not to stare after she lost her hair, the stilted efforts of nurses and doctors to befriend her, even Julia's attempts to pretend their world was normal. Maddie seemed to see through them all.

Could Maddie sense the careful distance Will seemed determined to maintain between them?

Julia hoped not. Her daughter had endured enough. She didn't need more rejection in her life right now when she was just beginning to find her way again.

"That's a good idea," she finally answered Maddie, hoping her smile looked more genuine than it felt. "And perhaps we can think of someone else who might need a pie."

She lifted the bushel and started to carry it around the front of the house. She hadn't made it far before Will stepped forward and took the bushel out of her hands.

"Here, I'll carry that up the stairs for you."

She almost protested that it wasn't necessary but she could tell by the implacable set of his jaw that he wouldn't accept any arguments from her on the matter.

"Thank you," she said instead.

She and Maddie followed him up the stairs.

"Where do you want this?" he asked.

"The kitchen counter by the sink."

"We have to wash every single apple and see if it has a worm," Maddie informed him. "I hope we don't find one. That would be gross."

"That's a lot of work," he said stiffly.

"It is. But my mama's pies are the best. Even better than brambleberry. Just wait until you try one."

Will's gaze flashed to Julia's then away so quickly she wondered if she'd imagined the quick flare of heat there.

"Good luck with your pies."

"Good luck with your stairs," she responded. "Send Simon up if you need to."

He nodded and headed out the door, probably completely oblivious that he was leaving two females to watch wistfully after him.

CHAPTER EIGHT

ABOUT HALFWAY THROUGH helping Julia peel the apples, Maddie asked if she could stop for a few minutes and take a little rest.

"Of course, baby," Julia assured her.

Already Maddie had made it an hour past the time when Julia thought she would give out. School alone was exhausting for her, especially starting at a new school and the effort it took to make new friends. Throw in an hour of after-school activities then picking the apples and it was no wonder Maddie was drooping.

A few moments later, Julia peered through the kitchen doorway to the living room couch and found her curled up, fast asleep.

Julia set down the half-peeled apple, dried her hands off on her apron, and went to double-check on her. Yes, it might be a bit obsessive, but she figured she had earned the right the last few years to a little cautious overreaction.

Maddie's color looked good, though, and she was breathing evenly so Julia simply covered her with her favorite crocheted throw and returned to the kitchen.

Her job was a bit lonely now, without Maddie's quiet observations or Simon's bubbly chatter. With nothing to distract her, she found her gaze slipping with increasing frequency out the window.

She couldn't see much from this angle but every once

in a while Will and Simon would pass into the edge of her view as they moved from Will's power saw to the porch.

She had nearly finished peeling the apples when she suddenly heard a light scratch on the door of her apartment over the steady hammering and the occasional whine of power tools.

Somehow she wasn't surprised to find Conan standing on the other side, his tail wagging and his eyes expectant.

"Let me guess," she murmured. "All that hammering is interfering with your sleep."

She could swear the dog dipped his head up and down as if nodding. He padded through the doorway and into the living room, where he made three circles of his body before easing down to his stomach on the floor beside Maddie's couch.

"Watch over her for me, won't you?"

The dog rested his head on his front paws, his attention trained on Maddie as if the couch where she slept was covered in peanut butter.

"Good boy," Julia murmured, and returned to the kitchen.

She finished her work quickly, slicing enough apples for a half-dozen pies.

She assembled the pies quickly—cheating a little and using store-bought pie shells. She had a good pie crust recipe but she didn't have the time for it today since Eben and Chloe would be returning soon.

Only two pies could cook at a time in her oven and they took nearly forty minutes. After she slid the first pair in, she untied her apron and hung it back on the hook in the kitchen.

Without giving herself time to consider, she grabbed the egg timer off the stovetop, set it for the time the pies needed and stuck it in her pocket, then headed down the stairs to check on Simon.

It was nearly five-thirty but she couldn't see any sign of Anna or Sage yet. Sage, she knew, would be meeting Eben and Chloe at the small airstrip in Seaside, north of Cannon Beach. As for Anna, she sometimes worked late at her store in town or the new one in Lincoln City she had opened earlier in the summer.

She followed the sound of male voices—Will's lower-pitched voice a counterpoint to Simon's mile-a-minute higher tones.

She stepped closer, still out of sight around the corner of the house, until she could hear their words.

"My mom says next year I can play Little League baseball," Simon was saying.

"Hold the board still or we'll have wobbly steps, which won't do anyone any good."

"Sorry."

"Baseball, huh?" Will said a moment later.

"Yep. I couldn't play this year because of Maddie's bone transplant and because we were moving here. But next year, for sure. I can't wait. I played last year, even though I had to miss a lot of games and stuff when Mad was in the hospital."

She closed her eyes, grieving for her son who had suffered right along with his sister. Sometimes it was so easy to focus on Maddie's more immediate needs that she forgot Simon walked each step of the journey right along with her.

"Yeah, I hit six home runs last year. I bet I could do a lot more this year. Did you ever play baseball?"

"Sure did," Will answered. "All through high school and college. Until a few years ago, I was even on a team around here that played in the summertime."

"Probably old guys, huh?"

Julia cringed but Will didn't seem offended, judging by his quick snort of laughter—the most lighthearted sound she had heard from him since she'd been back.

"Yeah. We have a tough time running the bases for all the canes and walkers in the way."

Julia couldn't help herself, she laughed out loud, drawing the attention of both Will and Simon.

"Hi, Mom," Simon chirped, looking pleased to see her. "Guess what? Mr. Garrett played baseball, too."

"I remember," she said. "Your Uncle Charlie dragged me to one of his summer league games the last time I was here and I got to watch him play. He hit a three-run homer."

"Trying to impress you," Will said in a laconic tone.

She laughed again. "It worked very well, as I recall."

That baseball game had been when she first starting thinking of Will as more than just her brother's summer-vacation friend. She hadn't been able to stop thinking about him.

What, exactly, had changed since she came back? she wondered. She still couldn't seem to stop thinking about him.

"My mom likes baseball, too," Simon said. "She said maybe next month sometime we can go to a Mariners game, if they're in the playoffs. It's not very far to Seattle."

His eyes lit up with sudden excitement. "Hey, Mr. Garrett, you could come with us! That would be cool."

Will's gaze met hers and for an instant she imagined sharing hot dogs and listening to the cheers and sitting beside him for three hours, his heat and strength just inches away from her.

"I do enjoy watching the Mariners," Will said, an un-readable look in his eyes. "I'm pretty busy next month but if you let me know when you're going, I can see how it fits my schedule."

"We haven't made any definite plans," Julia said, hoping none of the longing showed in her expression.

She hadn't realized until this moment that Simon wasn't the only one in their family who hungered for a man in their lives.

And not just any man, either. Only a strong, quiet carpenter with callused hands and a rare, beautiful smile.

She decided to quickly change the subject. "The stairs look wonderful. Are you nearly finished?"

Before he could answer, they heard sudden excited barking from the front of the house.

Julia laughed. "I guess Conan needed to go out. It's a good thing he has his own doggy door."

"Hang on a minute," Will said. "That's his *somebody's home* bark."

A moment later they heard a vehicle pull into the driveway.

"Conan!" a high, excited voice shrieked and the dog woofed a greeting.

"That would be Chloe," Will said.

By tacit agreement, the three of them walked together toward the front of the house. When they rounded the corner, Julia saw a dark-haired girl around the twins' age with her arms around the dog's neck.

Beside her, Sage—glowing with joy—stood beside a man with commanding features and brilliant green eyes.

"Hey, guys!" Sage beamed at them. "Julia, this is Chloe Spencer and her dad, Eben."

Julia smiled, though she would have known their identities just from the glow on Sage's features—the same one that flickered there whenever she talked about her fiancé and his daughter.

"Eben, this is Julia Blair."

The man offered a smile and his hand to shake. "The new tenant with the twins. Hello. It's a pleasure to meet you finally. Sage has told me a great deal about you and your children the last few weeks."

Sage had told her plenty about Eben and Chloe as well. Meeting them in person, she could well understand how Sage could find the man compelling.

It seemed an odd mix to her—the buttoned-down hotel executive who wore an elegant silk power tie and the free-thinking naturalist who believed her dog communicated with her dead friend. But Julia could tell in an instant they were both crazy about each other.

Eben Spencer turned to Will next and the two of them exchanged greetings. As they spoke, she couldn't help contrasting the two men. Though Eben was probably more classically handsome in a *GQ* kind of way, with his loosened tie and his rolled up shirt sleeves, she had to admit that Will's toolbelt and worn jeans affected her more.

Being near Eben Spencer didn't make her insides flutter and her bones turn liquid.

"And who's this?" Eben was asking, she realized when she jerked her attention back to the conversation.

Color soaked her cheeks and she hoped no one else noticed. "This is one of my kiddos. Simon, this is Mr. Spencer and his daughter, Chloe."

"I'm eight," Chloe announced. "How old are you?"

Simon immediately went into defensive mode. "Well," he said slowly, "I won't be eight until March. But I'm taller than you are."

Chloe made a face. "*Everyone* is taller than me. I'm a shrimp. Sage says you have a twin sister. How cool! Where is she?"

He looked to Julia for an answer.

"Upstairs," she answered. "I'll go wake her, though. She's been anxious to meet you."

As if on cue, her timer beeped. "Got to run. That would be my pies ready to come out of the oven."

"You're making pie?" Chloe exclaimed. "That's super cool. I just *love* pie."

She smiled, charmed by Sage's stepdaughter-to-be. "I do, too. But not burnt pie so I'd better hurry."

She tried to be quiet as she slid the pies from the oven and carefully set them on a rack to dry, but she must have clattered something because Maddie began to stir in the other room.

She stood in the doorway and watched her daughter rise to a sitting position on the couch. "Hey, baby. How are you feeling?"

Maddie gave an ear-popping yawn and stretched her arms above her head. "Pretty good. I'm sorry, Mama. I said I would help you make pies and then I fell asleep."

"You helped me with the hard part, which was picking the apples and washing them all."

"I guess."

She still looked dejected at her own limitations and Julia walked to her and pulled her into a hug. "You helped me a ton. I never would have been able to finish without you. And while you were sleeping soundly, guess who arrived?"

Her features immediately brightened. "Chloe?"

"Yep. She's outside with Simon right now."

"Can I go meet her?"

She smiled at her enthusiasm. One thing about Maddie, even in the midst of her worst fatigue, she could go from full sleep to complete alertness in a matter of seconds.

"Of course. Go ahead. I'll be down in a minute—I just have to put in these other pies."

A few moments later, she closed her apartment door and headed down the stairs. The elusive scent of freesia seemed to linger in the air and she wondered if that was Abigail's way of greeting the newcomers. The whimsical thought had barely registered when Anna's door— Abigail's old apartment—slowly opened.

She instinctively gasped, then flushed crimson when Will walked out, a measuring tape in hand.

What had she expected? The ghostly specter of Abigail, complete with flashy costume jewelry and a wicked smile?

"Hi," she managed.

He gave her an odd look. "Everything okay?"

"Yes. Just my imagination running away with me."

"I was double-checking the measurements for the new moldings in Anna's apartment. I'm hoping to get to them in a week or so."

"All done with the stairs, then?"

"Not quite. I'm still going to have to stain them but the bulk of the hard work is done."

"You do good work, Will. I'm very impressed."

"My dad taught me well."

The scent of freesia seemed stronger now and finally she had to say something. "Okay, tell me something. Can you smell that?"

Confusion flickered across his rugged features. "I smell sawdust and your apple pie baking. That's it."

"You don't smell freesia?"

"I'm not sure I know what that is."

"It's a flower. Kind of light, delicate. Abigail used to wear freesia perfume, apparently. I don't remember that about her but Anna and Sage say she did and I believe them."

He still looked confused. "And you're smelling it now?"

She sighed, knowing she must sound ridiculous. "Sage thinks Abigail is sticking around Brambleberry House."

To her surprise, he laughed out loud and she stared, arrested by the sound. "I wouldn't put it past her," he said. "She loved this old place."

"I can't say I blame her for that. I'm coming to love it, too. There's a kind of peace here—I can't explain it. Maddie says the house is friendly and I have to tell you, I'm beginning to believe her."

He shook his head, but he was smiling. "Watch out or you'll turn as wacky as Sage. Next thing I know, you'll be balancing your chakras every five minutes and eating only tofu and bean sprouts."

She gazed at his smile for a long moment, arrested by his light-hearted expression. He looked young and much more relaxed than she had seen him in a long time, almost happy, and her heart rejoiced that she had been able to make him smile and, yes, even laugh.

His smile slid away after a moment and she realized she was staring at his mouth. She couldn't seem to look away, suddenly wildly curious to know what it would be like to kiss him again.

Something hot kindled in the blue of his eyes and she caught her breath, wanting his touch, his kiss, more than she had wanted anything in a long time.

He wasn't ready, she reminded herself, and eased

back, sliding her gaze from his. No sooner had she made up her mind to step away and let the intense moment pass when she could swear she felt a determined hand between her shoulderblades, pushing her forward.

She whirled around in astonishment, then thought she must be going crazy. Only the empty stairs were behind her.

"What's wrong?" Will asked. Though his words were concerned, that stony, unapproachable look had returned to his expression and she sighed, already missing that brief instant of laughter.

"Um, nothing. Absolutely nothing. My imagination seems to be in overdrive, that's all."

"That's what you get for talking about ghosts."

She forced a smile and headed for the door. Just before she walked through it, she turned and aimed a glare at the empty room.

Stay out of my love life, Abigail, she thought. *Or any lack thereof.*

She could almost swear wicked laughter followed behind her.

Damn it. He wasn't at all ready for this.

Will followed Julia out the door, still aware of the heat and hunger simmering through him.

He had almost kissed her. The urge had been so strong, he had been only seconds away from reaching for her.

She wouldn't have stopped him. He sensed that much— he had seen the warm welcome in her eyes and had known she would have returned the kiss with enthusiasm.

He still didn't know why he had stopped or why she had leaned away then looked behind her as if fearing her children were skulking on the second-floor landing watching them.

He didn't know why they hadn't kissed but he was enormously grateful they had both come to their senses.

He didn't want to be attracted to another woman. Sure, he was a man and he had normal needs just like any other male. But he had been crazy about his wife. Kissing another woman—even *wanting* to kiss another woman—still seemed like some kind of betrayal, though intellectually he knew that was absurd.

Robin had been gone for more than two years. As much as he had loved her, he sometimes had to work hard to summon the particular arrangement of her features and the sound of her voice.

He was forgetting her and he hated it. Sometimes his grief seemed like a vast lake that had been frozen solid forever. Suddenly, as if overnight, the ice was beginning to crack around the edges. He wouldn't have expected it to hurt like hell but everything suddenly seemed more raw than it had since the accident.

He pressed his fist to the ache in chest for just a moment then headed for the backyard, where he had set up his power tools. His gaze seemed to immediately drift to Julia and he found her on the brick patio, laughing at something Sage had said, the afternoon sunlight finding gold strands in her hair. He could swear he felt more chunks of ice break free.

She must have sensed the weight of his stare—she turned her head slightly and their gazes collided for a brief moment before he broke the connection and picked up his power saw and headed for his truck.

On his next trip to get the sawhorses, he deliberately

forced himself not to look at her. He was so busy *not* looking at her that he nearly mowed down Eben.

"Sorry," he muttered, feeling like an ass.

Eben laughed. "No problem. You look like your mind's a million miles away."

He judged her to be only about twenty-five feet, but he wasn't going to quibble. "Something like that," he murmured.

He hadn't expected to like Eben Spencer. When Sage had first fallen for the man, Will had been quite certain he would break her heart. As he had come to know him these last few months, he had changed his mind. Eben was deeply in love with Sage.

The two of them belonged together in a way Will couldn't have explained to save his life.

"You look like you could use a hand clearing this up."

He raised an eyebrow. "No offense, but you're not really dressed for moving my grimy tools."

"I don't mind getting a little dirty once in a while." The other man hefted two sawhorses over one shoulder, leaving Will only his toolbox to carry.

"Thanks," he said when everything had been slid into the bed of his pickup truck.

"No problem," Eben said again. "You're staying for dinner, aren't you? Sage has decided to throw an impromptu party since Chloe and I are back in town for a few days. I really don't want to be the only thing around here with a Y chromosome. Beautiful as all these Brambleberry women are, they're a little overwhelming for one solitary man."

"Don't forget you've got Simon Blair around now."

Eben laughed. "Well, that does help even the scales a little, but I have a feeling Sage and the others will be lost in wedding plans. I wouldn't mind company while I'm manning the grill."

He was tempted. He knew he shouldn't be but his empty house had become so oppressive sometimes he hated walking inside it.

"Got anything besides veggie burgers?"

"Sage talked to Jade and Stanley and they're sending over some choice prime-cut steaks from The Sea Urchin—the kind you can't buy at your average neighborhood grocery store."

"Sage *must* be in love if she's chasing down steaks for you," Will said, earning a chuckle from Eben.

"She might be a vegetarian but she's very forgiving of those of us who aren't quite as enlightened yet."

"Maybe she's just biding her time until you're married, then she'll start substituting your bacon for veggie strips and your hamburgers for mushroom, bean-curd concoctions."

Eben smiled, his expression rueful. "I'm so crazy about her, I probably wouldn't mind." He paused. "Stay, why don't you? Anna and Sage would love to have you."

What about Julia? He wondered. His attention shifted to her and that longing came out of nowhere again, knocking him out at the knees.

"Sure," he said, before he could give himself a chance to reconsider. "I just need to run home and wash off some of this sweat and sawdust."

"Great. We'll see you in a few minutes then."

He drove away, already regretting the momentary impulse to accept the invitation.

CHAPTER NINE

AN HOUR LATER, after taking a quick shower and changing his clothes, Will stood beside Eben at the grill, beer in hand, asking himself again why he had possibly thought this might be a good idea.

It was a lovely evening, he had to admit that. A breeze blew off the ocean, cool enough to be refreshing but not cold enough to have anybody reaching for a sweater.

The sweet sound of children's laughter rang through the Brambleberry House yard as Chloe and the twins threw a ball for Conan. Sage, Julia and Anna were sitting at a table on the weathered brick patio looking over wedding magazines.

Abigail would have adored seeing those she loved most enjoying themselves together. This casual, informal kind of gathering was exactly the kind of thing she loved best.

He only wished he could enjoy himself as he used to do, that he didn't view the whole scene with his chest aching and this deep sense of loss in his gut.

"My people at The Sea Urchin tell me the work you've done on the new cabinetry in the lobby is spectacular," Eben said as he turned the steaks one last time.

Will forced a smile. "I had great bones to work with. That helps on any project."

"She's a beautiful old place, isn't she?" Eben's smile

was much more genuine. "I'm sorry I haven't had the opportunity yet to see what you've accomplished there. I'm looking forward to tomorrow when I have a chance to check out the progress of the last three weeks while Chloe and I have been overseas. I've been getting daily reports but it's not the same as seeing it firsthand."

"I think you'll be happy with it. You've got some real craftsmen working on The Sea Urchin."

"Including you." He took a sip of his beer, then gave Will an intent look. "In fact, I've got a proposition for you."

Will raised an eyebrow, curiosity replacing the ache, if only temporarily. Another job? he wondered. As far as he knew, The Sea Urchin was the only Spencer Hotels property along the coast.

"Spencer Hotels could always use a master carpenter. We've got rehab projects going in eight different properties right now alone. There's always something popping. What would you say to signing on with us, traveling a little? You could take your pick of the jobs, anywhere from Tokyo to Tuscany. We've got more than enough work to keep you busy, with much more in the pipeline."

He blinked, stunned at the offer. He was just a journeyman carpenter in piddly little Cannon Beach. What the hell did he know about either Tokyo or Tuscany?

"Whoa," he finally managed through his shock. "That's certainly…unexpected."

"I've been thinking about it for a while. When I received the glowing report from my people here, it just seemed a confirmation of what had already been running around my head. I think you'd be perfect for the job. I usually try to hire workers from the various communities where my hotels are located—good business practice, you know—but I also like to have my own man overseeing the work."

"I don't know what good I would be in that capacity. I don't speak any language except good old English and a little bit of Spanish."

"The Spanish might help. But we always have translators on site, so that's not really a concern. I'm looking for a craftsman. An artisan. From what I've seen of your work, you definitely qualify. I also want someone I can trust to do the job right. And again, you qualify."

He had to admit, he was flattered. How could he not be? He loved his work and took great pride in it. When others saw and acknowledged a job well done, he found enormous satisfaction.

For just a moment, he allowed himself to imagine the possibilities. He had lived his entire life in Cannon Beach—in the very same house, even. Though he loved the town and loved living on the coast, maybe it was time to pick up and try something new, see the world a little.

On the other hand. he wasn't sure the ghosts that haunted him were ready for him to move on.

"You don't have to give me any kind of answer tonight," Eben said at his continued silence. "Just think about it. If you decide you're interested, we can sit down while I'm here and talk details."

"I'll think about it," he agreed. "I…it's a little overwhelming. It would be a huge change for me."

"But maybe not an unwelcome one," Eben said, showing more insight than Will was completely comfortable with.

"Maybe not." He paused. "I've got a buddy up in Ketchikan who's been after me to come up and go into business with him. I've been tossing the idea around."

"That might be good for you, too. Look at all your options. Take all the time you need. As far as I'm concerned, you can consider the Spencer Hotels offer an indefinite one with no time limit."

"What offer?"

He hadn't even noticed Sage had joined them until she spoke. Now she slipped her arm through the crook of Will's elbow and gave his arm an affectionate squeeze. Of all his friends, Sage was the most physical, and he always appreciated her hugs and kisses on the cheek and the times, like now, when she squeezed his arm.

He didn't like to admit it, but he sometimes ached for the soft comfort of a woman's touch, even the touch of a woman he considered more in the nature of a little sister than anything else.

"You won't like it," Eben predicted.

She made a face. "Try me. Believe it or not, I can be remarkably open-minded sometimes."

"Good. It might be a good idea for you to keep that in mind," Eben said with a wary expression.

"What are you up to?"

"I'm trying to steal Will away from Cannon Beach to come work for Spencer Hotels."

She dropped her arm and glared with shock at both of them. "You can't leave! We need you here."

"Says the woman who's going to be moving to San Francisco herself in a few months," Will murmured.

She tucked a loose strand of wavy blonde hair behind her ear, flushing a little at the reminder. "Not full-time. We'll be here every summer so I can still run the nature center camps. And we're planning to spend as much time up here as we can—weekends and school holidays."

"But you'll still be in the Bay Area most of the time, right?"

"Yes." She made a face. "I'm selfish, I know. I just don't want things to change."

"Things change, Sage. Most of the time we have no choice but to change, too, whether we want to or not."

She squeezed his arm again, her eyes suddenly moist. He saw memories of Robin and Cara swimming there and he didn't want to ruin her night by bringing up the past.

"I'm not going anywhere right now," he said. "Let's just enjoy the evening while we can."

Eben kissed his fiancée on the tip of her nose, an intimate gesture that for some reason made Will's chest ache. "These steaks are just about ready and I think your bean burger is perfect, though I believe that statement is a blatant oxymoron."

She laughed and headed off to tell the others dinner was ready.

"Give my offer some thought," Eben said when Sage was out of earshot. "Like I said, you don't have to answer right away. Maybe you could try it for six months or so to see how the traveling lifestyle fits you."

"I'll think about it," he agreed, which was an understatement of major proportions.

THEY ATE ON the brick patio, protected from the wind blowing off the sea by the long wall of Sitka spruce on the seaward edge of the yard.

While he and Eben had been grilling, the women had set out candles of varying heights around the patio and turned on the little twinkling fairy lights he had hung in the trees for Abigail a few summers earlier.

It seemed an odd collection of people but somehow

the mix worked. Sage, with her highly developed social conscience. Anna with her quiet ambition and hard work ethic. Eben, dynamic businessman, and Julia, warm and nurturing, making sure plates were full, that the potato salad was seasoned just so, that drinks were replenished.

A group of very different people brought together because of Abigail, really.

Conversation flowed around him like an incoming tide finding small hidden channels in the sand and he was mostly content to sit at the table and listen to it.

"You're not eating your steak."

He looked up to find Julia watching him, her green eyes concerned. Though she sat beside him, he hadn't been ignoring her for the last hour but he hadn't exactly made any effort to seek her out, still disconcerted by that moment in the hallway when he had wanted to kiss her more than he wanted oxygen.

"Sorry," he mumbled and immediately applied himself to the delicious cut in front of him.

"You don't have to eat it just because I said something." She pitched her voice low so others didn't overhear. "I was just wondering if everything is okay. You seem distracted."

He was distracted by *her*. By the cherry blossom scent of her, and her softness so close to him and the inappropriate thoughts he couldn't seem to shake.

"You don't know me anymore, Julia. For all you know, maybe I'm always this way."

As soon as the sharp words left his mouth, a cold wind suddenly forced its way past the line of trees to flutter the edges of the tablecloth and send the lights shivering in the treetops.

He didn't miss the hurt that leapt into her eyes or the way her mouth tightened.

He was immediately contrite. "I'm sorry. I'm not really fit company tonight."

"No, you're not. But it happens to all of us." She turned away to talk to Eben, on her other side, and the prime-cut steak suddenly had all the appeal of overdried beef jerky.

He would have to do a better job of apologizing for his sharp words, he realized. She didn't deserve to bear the brunt of his temper.

His chance didn't come until sometime later when everyone seemed to have finished dinner. Julia stood and started clearing dishes and Will immediately rose to help her, earning a surprised look and even a tentative smile from her.

"Where are we taking all this stuff?" he asked when he had an armload of dishes.

"My apartment. My dishwasher is the newest and the biggest. Most of the dishes came out of my kitchen anyway and I can make sure those that belong to Sage or Anna are returned to their rightful homes."

He followed her up the stairs, then headed down for another load. When he returned, she was rinsing and loading dishes in the dishwasher and he immediately started helping.

She flashed him one quick, questioning look, then smiled and made room for him at the sink.

The sheer domesticity of it stirred that same weird ache in his throat and he could feel himself wanting to shut down, to flee to the safety and empty solitude of his house down the beach.

But he had come this far. He could tough it out a little longer.

"I owe you an apology for my sharpness," he said after a moment. "A better one than the sorry excuse I gave you outside."

Her gaze collided with his for just a moment before she returned her attention to the sink. "You don't owe me anything, Will. I overstepped and I'm sorry. I've been overstepping since I came back to Cannon Beach."

She sighed and turned around, her hip leaning against the sink. "You were absolutely right, we don't have any kind of…anything. We were friends a long time ago, when we were both vastly different people. That was in the past. Somehow I keep forgetting that today we're simply two people who happen to live a few houses apart and have the same circle of friends."

"That's not quite true."

She frowned. "Which part isn't true?"

"That we were friends so long ago."

Hurt flickered in her eyes but she quickly concealed it and turned back to the sink. "My mistake, then. I guess you're right. We didn't know each other well. Just a few weeks every summer."

He should just stop now before he made things worse. What was the point in dragging all this up again?

"That's not what I meant. I only meant that the way we left things was definitely more than just friends."

She stared at him, sudden awareness blossoming in the green of her eyes.

"It took me a long time to get over you," he said, and the admission looked as if it surprised her as much as it did him. "When you didn't answer my letters, I figured everything I thought we had was all in my head. But it still hurt."

"Oh, Will." She dried her hands on a dish towel. "I would have written you but…things were so messed up. I was messed up. The day we returned home from our last summer in Cannon Beach, my parents told us they were divorcing. This was only two weeks before school started. My dad ended up with Charlie and the house in Los Angeles, and my mom took me to Sacramento with her. I had to start a new school my junior year, which was terrible. I didn't even get your letters until almost the end of the school year when my dad finally bothered to forward them from L.A."

She touched his arm, much the way Sage had earlier, but Sage's touch hadn't given him instant goosebumps or make him want to yank her into his arms.

"I should have written to explain to you what was going on," she went on. "I'm sorry I didn't, but I never forgot you, Will. This probably sounds really stupid, but the time I spent with you that summer was the best thing that happened to me in a long time, either before it or after, and I didn't want to spoil the memory of it."

She smiled, her hand still on his arm. He was dying here and he doubted she even realized what effect she was having on him. "You have no idea how long it took me to stop comparing every other boy to you."

"What can I say? I'm a hell of a kisser."

He meant the words as a flippant joke and she gave him a startled laugh, then followed up with a sidelong glance. "I do believe I remember that about you," she murmured.

The intimacy of the room seemed to wrap around

them. For one wild moment, he felt sixteen again, lost in the throes of first love, entranced by Julia Hudson.

He could kiss her.

The impulse to taste her, touch her, poured through him and he was powerless to fight it. He took a step forward, expecting her to back away. Instead, her gaze locked with his and he saw in her eyes an awareness—even a longing—to match his own.

Still he hesitated, the only sound in the kitchen their mingled breathing. He might have stayed in an eternity of indecision if she hadn't leaned toward him slightly, just enough to tumble the last of his defenses.

In an instant, his mouth found hers and captured her quick gasp of surprise.

So long. So damn long.

He had forgotten how soft a woman's mouth could be, how instantly addictive it could be to taste desire.

Part of him wanted to yank back and retreat to his frozen lake where he was safe. But he was helpless to fight the tide of yearning crashing over him, the heat and sensation and pure, delicious pleasure of her softness against him.

IT SEEMED IMPOSSIBLE, but he tasted better than she remembered, of cinnamon and mint and coffee.

She should be shocked that he would kiss her, after being quite blunt that he wasn't interested in starting anything. But it seemed so right to be here in his arms that she couldn't manage to summon anything but grateful amazement.

She slid her arms around his neck, letting him set the pace and tone of the kiss. It was gentle at first, sweet and comfortable. Two old friends renewing something they had once shared.

Just as it had so many years earlier, being in his arms felt right. Completely perfect.

Their bodies had changed over the years—he was much broader and more muscled and she knew giving birth to twins had softened her edges and given her more curves.

But they still seemed to fit together like two halves of the same planed board.

She was aware of odd, random sensations as the kiss lingered—the hard countertop digging into her hip where he pressed her against it, the silk of his hair against her fingers, the smell of him, leathery and masculine.

And freesia.

The smell of flowers drifted through her kitchen so strongly that she opened one eye to make sure Abigail wasn't standing in the doorway watching them.

An instant later, she forgot all about Abigail—or any other ghosts—when Will pulled her closer and deepened the kiss, his tongue playing and teasing in a way that demonstrated quite unequivocally that he had learned more than a few things in the intervening years since their last kiss on the beach.

Heat flared, bright and urgent, and she dived right into the flames, holding him closer and returning the kiss.

She had no idea how long they kissed—or just how long they might have continued. Both of them froze when they heard the squeak of the entry door downstairs.

Will wrenched his mouth away, breathing hard, and stared at her and her heart broke at the expression on his face—shock and dismay and something close to anguish.

He raked a hand through his hair, leaving little tufts looking as if he'd just walked into a wind tunnel.

"That was… I shouldn't have…"

He seemed so genuinely upset, she locked away her hurt and focused on trying to ease his turmoil. "Will, it's okay."

"No. No, it's not. I shouldn't have done that. I've… I've got to go."

Without another word, he hurried out of the kitchen and her apartment and she heard the thud of his boots as he rushed down the wooden stairway and out the door.

She leaned against the counter, her breathing still ragged. She felt emotionally ravaged, wrung out and hung to dry.

She was still trying to figure out what just happened when she heard a knock on her door.

She wasn't sure she was at all ready to face anyone but when the knock sounded again, she knew she wouldn't be able to hide away there in her kitchen forever.

"It's open," she called.

The door swung open and a moment later Anna Galvez walked into the apartment.

"What's up with Will? He passed me on the stairs and didn't even say a word before he headed out the door like the hounds of hell were nipping at his heels."

She gave Julia a careful look. "Are you okay? You look flushed. Did you and Will have a fight or something?"

"That blasted *or something* will get you every time," Julia muttered under her breath.

"You're going to have to give me a break here. I've been working all day on inventory and my brain is mush. Do you want to explain what that means?"

"Not really." She sighed, not at all comfortable talking about this. But right now she desperately needed a friend and Anna definitely qualified. "He kissed me," she blurted out.

Surprise then delight flickered across Anna's features. "Really? That's wonderful!"

"Is it? Will obviously didn't think so."

"Will doesn't do anything he doesn't want to do. If he hadn't wanted to kiss you, he wouldn't have."

"He was horrified afterward."

"A little overdramatic, don't you think?"

"You should have seen his face! I don't think he's ready. He's lost so much."

"So have you. I don't hear you saying you're not ready."

But their situations were vastly different, a point she wasn't prepared to point out to Anna. Will had been happily married when his wife died. She, on the other hand, had let Kevin go long before his fatal car accident.

"He will figure things out in his own time. Don't worry," Anna went on. "He's a wonderful man who's been through a terrible tragedy. But he'll get through it. Have a little faith."

Right now faith was something Julia had in very short supply. She could tumble hard and fast for Will Garrett. It wouldn't take a hard push—she had been in love with him when she was fifteen years old and she could easily see herself falling again.

But what would be the point, if he had his heart so tightly wrapped in protective layers that he wouldn't let anyone in?

CHAPTER TEN

IT WAS JUST a damn kiss.

Three weeks later, Will backed his truck into the Brambleberry House driveway, fighting a mix of dread and unwilling anticipation.

He knew both reactions were completely ridiculous. What the hell was he worrying about? She wouldn't even be here—he had finally managed to work the molding job into his schedule only after squeezing in a time when he could be certain Julia and her children were safely tucked away at the elementary school.

The very fact that he had to resort to such ridiculous manipulations of his own schedule simply to avoid seeing a certain woman bugged the heck out of him.

He ought to be tougher than this. He should have been completely unfazed by their brief encounter, instead of brooding about it for the better part of three weeks.

So he had kissed her. Big deal. The world hadn't stopped spinning, the ocean hadn't suddenly been sucked dry, the Coast Range hadn't suddenly tumbled to dust.

Robin hadn't come back to haunt him.

He knew his reaction to the kiss had been excessive. He had run out of her apartment at Brambleberry House like a kid who had been caught smoking in the boy's room of the schoolhouse.

Yeah, he had overreacted to the shock of discovering not all of him was encased in ice—that he could desire another woman, could long to have her wrapped around him.

He still wanted it. That was what had bothered him for three weeks. Even though he hadn't seen her in all that time, she hadn't been far from his thoughts.

He remembered the taste of her, sweet and welcoming, the softness of her skin under his fingers, the subtle peace he had so briefly savored.

He couldn't seem to shake this achy sense that with that single kiss, everything in his world had changed, in a way he couldn't explain but knew he didn't like.

He didn't want change. Yeah, he hated his life and missed Robin and Cara so much he sometimes couldn't breathe around the pain. But it was *his* pain.

He was used to it now, and somewhere deep inside, he worried that letting go of that grief would mean letting go of his wife and baby girl, something he wasn't ready to face yet.

He knew his reaction was absurd. Plenty of people had lost loved ones and had moved ahead with their lives. His own mother had married again, just a few years after his father died, when Will was in his early twenties. She had moved to San Diego with her new husband, where the two of them seemed to be extremely happy together. They played golf, they went sailing on the bay, they enjoyed an active social life.

Will didn't begrudge his mother her happiness. He liked his stepfather and was grateful his mother had found someone else.

Intellectually, he knew it was possible, even expected, for him to date again sometime. He just wasn't sure he was ready yet—indeed, that he would ever be ready.

It had just been a kiss, he reminded himself. Not a damn marriage proposal.

As he sat in the driveway, gearing himself to go inside, the moist sea breeze drifted through his cracked window and he could suddenly swear he smelled cherry blossoms.

It was nearing the end of September, for heaven's sake, and was a cool, damp morning. He had absolutely no business smelling the spring scent of cherry blossoms on the breeze.

No doubt it was only the power of suggestion at work—he was thinking about Julia and his subconscious somehow managed to conjure the scent that always seemed to cling to her.

He closed his eyes and for just a moment allowed his mind to wander over that kiss again—the way she had responded to him with such warm enthusiasm, the silky softness of her mouth, the comfort of her hands against his skin.

Just a damn kiss!

His sigh filled the cab of the pickup and he stiffened his resolve and reached for the door handle.

Enough. Anna and Sage weren't paying him to sit on his butt and moon over their tenant. He had work to do. He'd been promising Anna for weeks he would get to her moldings and he couldn't keep putting it off.

A Garrett man kept his promises.

He climbed out and strapped on his tool belt with a dogged determination he would have found amusing under other circumstances, then grabbed as many of the moldings out of the back as he could lift.

He carried them to the porch and set them as close to the house as he could, then went back to his pickup for the rest. Judging by the steely clouds overhead, they were in for rain soon and he needed to keep the custom-cut oak dry.

He nearly dropped his second load when the front door suddenly swung open. A second later, Conan bounded through and barked with excitement.

He set the wood down with the other pile and gave the dog the obligatory scratch. "You're opening the door by yourself now? Pretty soon you're going to be driving yourself to the store to pick up dog food. You won't need any of us anymore."

"Until that amazing day arrives, he'll continue to keep us all as willing slaves. Hi, Will."

His entire insides had clenched at the sound of that first word spoken in a low, musical voice, and he slowly lifted his gaze to find Julia standing in the doorway.

She looked beautiful, fresh and lovely, and he could almost feel the churn of his heart.

"What are you doing here?" he said abruptly. "I figured you'd be at school."

Too late, he realized all that his words revealed—that he had given her more than a minute's thought in the last three weeks. She wasn't a stupid woman. No doubt she would quickly read between the lines and figure out he had purposely planned the project for a time when he was unlikely to encounter her.

To his vast relief, she didn't seem to notice. "I should be. At school, I mean. But Maddie's caught some kind of a bug. She was running a fever this morning and I decided I had better stay home and keep an eye on her."

"Is it a problem, missing your class?"

She shook her head. "I hate having to bring in a substitute this early in the school year but it can't be helped. The school district knew when they hired me that my daughter's health was fragile. So far they've been amazingly cooperative."

"She's okay, isn't she?"

All he could think about even as he asked the question was the irony of the whole thing. Above all else, he had tried his best to avoid bumping into her. So how, in heaven's name, had he managed to pick the one day she was home to finish the job?

"I think she's only caught a little cold," Julia answered. "At least that's what I hope it is. She's sniffly and coughing a bit but her fever broke about an hour ago. I hope it's just one of those twenty-four hour bugs."

"That's good."

"Her night was a little unsettled but she's sleeping soundly now. I figured rest was the best thing for her so I'm letting her sleep as long as she needs to beat this thing."

"Sounds like a smart plan."

"I guess you're here to do the moldings in Anna's apartment."

He nodded curtly, not knowing what else to say.

"Do you have more supplies in your truck that need to come in? I can help you carry things."

"This is it." His voice was more brusque than he intended and Conan made a snarly kind of growl at him.

Will just barely managed not to snarl back. He didn't need a dog making him feel guilty. He could do that all on his own.

It wasn't Julia's fault she stirred all kinds of unwelcome feelings in him and it wasn't at all fair of him to take out his bad mood on her.

He forced himself to temper his tone. "Would you mind holding the door open for me, though? It's going to rain soon and I'd hate for all this oak to get wet."

"Oh! Of course." She hurried to open the door. The only tricky part now was that he would have to move past her to get inside, he realized. He should have considered that little detail.

Too late now.

He let out a sigh of defeat and picked up several of the moldings and squeezed past her, doing his best not to bang the wood on the doorway on his way inside.

Going in wasn't so tough. Walking back out for a second load with his arms unencumbered was an entirely different story. He was painfully aware of her—that scent of spring, the heat of her body, the flicker of awareness in her green eyes as he passed.

Oh, he was in trouble.

His only consolation was that she seemed just as disconcerted by his presence.

"I guess you probably have a key to Anna's apartment, don't you?" she asked.

He nodded. "I have keys to the whole house so I can come and go when I'm working on something. All but your apartment. I gave it back to Anna and Sage when I finished up on the second floor."

"Good to know," she murmured.

He cleared his throat, set down the moldings in the entry and fished in his pocket, then pulled out the Brambleberry keyring. Of course, his hands seemed to fumble as he tried to find the right one to fit the lock for Anna's apartment, but he finally located it and opened her door.

"Would you mind holding the apartment door open as well? I need to be careful not to hit the wood on the frame. If you could guide it through, that would be great."

"Sure!" She hurried to prop open the door with an eagerness that made him blink. Even though it was akin to torture, he had to walk past her all over again and he forced himself to put away this sizzle of awareness and focus on the job.

She followed him inside as he carried the eight-foot-long moldings in and set them behind Anna's couch.

"Can I give you a hand with anything else?" Julia asked. "To be honest, I'm a bit at loose ends this morning and was looking for a distraction. I've already finished my lesson plans for the next month and I'm completely caught up with my homework grading. I was just contemplating rearranging my kitchen cabinets in alphabetical order, just to kill the boredom. I'd love the chance to do something constructive."

That was just about the last thing on earth he needed right now, to have to work with Julia looking on. She was the very definition of distraction. With his luck, he'd probably be so busy trying not to smell her that he would glue his sleeve to the wood.

His hesitation dragged on just a moment too long, he realized as he watched heat soak her cheeks.

"You're used to working alone and I would probably only get in the way, wouldn't I? Forget I said anything."

He hated her distress, hated making her think he didn't want her around. Was he a coward or was he a man who could contain his own unwanted desires?

"I *am* used to working alone," he said slowly, already regretting the words. "But I guess I wouldn't mind the company."

It was almost worth his impending discomfort to see her face light up with such delight. She must really be bored if she could get so excited about handing him tools and watching him nail up moldings.

"I'll just run up and grab the walkie-talkie I let the

kids use when they're sick to call out to me when they need drinks and things. That way Maddie will be able to find me when she wakes up."

He nodded, though she didn't seem to expect much of an answer as she hurried out the door and up the stairs.

What the hell had he just done? he wondered. The whole point of scheduling this project during this time had been to avoid bumping into her. He certainly didn't expect to find himself inviting her to spend the next hour or so right next to him, crowding his space, posing far too much of a temptation for his peace of mind.

"What are you grinning at?" he growled to Conan.

The dog just woofed at him and settled onto the rug in front of the empty fireplace. When Abigail was alive, that had always been his favorite place, Will remembered.

He supposed it was nice to see a few things didn't change, even though he felt as if the rest of his life was a deck of cards that had suddenly been thrown into the teeth of the wind.

SHE WAS A fool when it came to Will Garrett.

Up in her apartment, Julia quickly ran a brush through her hair. She thought about touching up the quick makeup job she'd done that morning but she figured Will would probably notice—and wonder—if she put on fresh lipstick.

Would he really notice? The snide voice in her head asked. He had made it plain he wasn't interested in her. Or at least that he didn't want to be interested in her, which amounted to the same thing.

More reason she was a fool for Will Garrett. Some part of her held out some foolish hope that this time might be different, that this time he might be able to see beyond the past.

Her conversation with Anna seemed to play through her head again. *He's a wonderful man who's been through a terrible tragedy. But he'll get through it. Have a little faith.*

She understood grief. Understood and accepted it. Despite their marital problems toward the end, she had mourned Kevin's death for the children's sake and for the sake of all those dreams they had once shared, the dreams that had been lost along the way somewhere.

She understood Will's sorrow. But she also accepted that she had missed him these last few weeks.

He hadn't been far from her thoughts, even as she went about the business of living—settling into the school year, getting to know her new students and co-workers at the elementary school, helping Simon and Maddie with their schoolwork.

She glanced out the window at his workshop, tucked away behind his house beneath the trees. How many nights had she stood at the window, watching the lights flicker there, wondering how he was, what he was thinking, what he might be working on?

She was obsessed with the man. Pure and simple. Perhaps they would both be better off if she just stayed up here with her daughter and pushed thoughts of him out of her head.

She sighed. She wasn't going to, because of that whole being-a-fool thing again. She couldn't resist this chance to talk to him again, to indulge herself with his company and perhaps come to know a little more about the man he had become.

She opened Maddie's door and found her daughter still

sleeping, her skin a healthy color and her breathing even. Julia scribbled a quick note to tell her where she was.

"I have the other walkie-talkie so just let me know when you wake up," she wrote and slipped the note under the other wireless handset on Maddie's bedside table where she couldn't miss it.

She spent one more moment watching the miracle of her daughter sleeping.

It was exactly the reminder she needed to wake her to the harsh reality of just how cautious she needed to be around Will Garrett.

Girlhood crushes were one thing, but she had two children to worry about now. She couldn't risk their feelings, couldn't let them come to care any more about a man who quite plainly wasn't ready to let anyone else into his life.

She would walk downstairs and be friendly in a polite, completely casual way, she told herself as she headed for the door. She wouldn't push him, she wouldn't dig too deeply.

She would simply help him with his project and try to bridge the tension between them so they could remain on friendly terms.

Anything else would be beyond foolish, when she had her children's emotional well-being to consider.

CHAPTER ELEVEN

WHEN SHE RETURNED to Anna's apartment, she found Conan sleeping on his favorite rug but no sign of Will. His tools and the boards he had brought in were still in evidence but Will wasn't anywhere to be found so Julia settled down to wait.

A moment later, she heard the front door open. Conan opened one eye and slapped his tail on the floor but didn't bother rising when Will came in carrying a small tool box and a container of nails.

He faltered a little when he saw her, as if he had forgotten her presence, or, worse, had maybe hoped it was all a bad dream. She was tempted again to abandon the whole idea and return upstairs to Maddie. But some part of her was still intensely curious to know why he seemed so uncomfortable in her presence.

He obviously wasn't completely impervious to her or he wouldn't care whether she hung around or not, any more than it bothered him to have Conan watching him work.

Was that a good sign, or just more evidence that she ought to just leave the poor man alone?

"Are you sure there's not anything else I can bring inside for you?" she asked. "I'm not good for much but I can carry tools or something."

"No. This should be everything I need."

He said nothing more, just started laying out tools,

and she might have thought he had completely forgotten her presence if not for the barest clenching of muscle along his jawline and a hint of red at the tips of his ears.

She knew she shouldn't find that tiny reaction so fascinating but she couldn't seem to stop staring.

She found *everything* about Will Garrett fascinating, she acknowledged somewhat grimly.

From the tool belt riding low on his hips to the broad shoulders he had gained from hard work over the years to the tiny network of lines around his eyes that had probably once been laugh lines.

She wanted to hear him laugh again. The strength of her desire burned through her chest and she would have given anything just then to be able to come up with some kind of hilarious story that would be guaranteed to have him in stitches.

"Since you're here, can you do me a favor?" he spoke suddenly as she was wracking her brain trying to come up with something.

"Of course." She jumped up, pathetically grateful for any task, no matter how humble.

"I need to double-check my measurements. I've checked them several times but I want to be sure before I make the final cuts."

"I guess you can't be too careful in your line of work."

"Not when you're dealing with oak trim that costs an arm and a leg," he answered.

"It's gorgeous, though."

"Worth every penny," he agreed, and for one breathless moment, he looked as if he wanted to smile. Just before the lighthearted expression would have broken free, his features sobered and he held out the end of the tape measure to her.

He was a man who devoted scrupulous attention to detail, she thought as they measured and re-measured the circumference of the room. He had kissed her the same way, thoroughly and completely, as if he couldn't bear the idea of missing a single second.

Her stomach quivered at the memory of his arms around her and the intensity of his mouth searching hers.

Maybe this hadn't been such a grand idea, the two of them alone here in the quiet hush of a rainy day morning with only Conan for company.

"What do you do when you don't have a fumbling and inept—but well-meaning—assistant to help you out with things like this?" she asked, to break the sudden hushed intimacy.

He shrugged. "I usually make do. I have a couple of high school kids who help me sometimes. Most jobs I can handle on my own but sometimes an extra set of hands can definitely make the work a lot easier."

She was grateful again that she had offered help, even if he still seemed uneasy about accepting.

"Well, I can't promise that my hands are good for much, but I'm happy to use them for anything you need."

As soon as the words left her mouth, she realized how they could be misconstrued. She flushed, but to her vast relief he didn't seem to notice either her blush or her unintentionally provocative statement.

"Thanks. I appreciate that."

He paused after writing down one more measurement then retracting the tape measure. "Robin was always after me to hire a full-time assistant," he said after a moment.

This was the first time he had mentioned his wife to her on his own. It seemed an important step, somehow, as if he had allowed himself to lower yet another barrier between them.

Julia held her breath, not wanting to say anything that might make him regret bringing up the subject.

"You didn't do it, though?"

He shrugged. "I like working on my own. I can pick the music I want, can work at my own pace, can talk to myself when I need to. Yeah, I guess that probably makes me a little on the crazy side."

She laughed. "Not crazy. I talk to myself all the time. It helps to have Conan around, then I can at least pretend I'm talking to him."

He smiled. One moment he was wearing that remote, polite expression, then next, a genuine smile stole over his handsome features. She stared at it, her pulse shivering.

She wanted to leap up and down and shriek with glee that she had been able to lighten his features, even if only for a moment, but then he would definitely think *she* was the crazy one.

"Maybe I need a dog to take on jobs with me, just so I don't get a reputation as the wild-eyed carpenter who carries on long conversations with himself."

"I'm sure Sage and Anna would consider renting Conan out by the hour," she offered.

He smiled again—twice in as many minutes!—and turned to the dog. "What do you say, bud? Want to be my permanent assistant?"

Conan snuffled and gave a huge yawn that stretched his jaws, then he flopped over on his other side, turning his back toward both of them.

Julia couldn't help laughing. "Sorry, Will, but I think that's a definite no. You wouldn't want to interfere with his strenuous nap schedule. I guess you'll have to make do with me for now. I just hope I haven't messed up your rhythm too much."

"No. You're actually helping."

"You don't have to sound so surprised!" she exclaimed. "I do occasionally have my uses."

"Sorry. I didn't mean it that way."

She managed a smile. "No problem. Believe it or not, I've got a pretty thick skin."

They worked in silence and Will seemed deep in thought. When he spoke some time later, she realized his mind was still on what he'd said about hiring an assistant.

"Sometimes Robin would come with me on bigger jobs to lend a hand, until Cara came along, anyway," he said. "She started to crawl early—six months or so—and was into everything. She barely gave Robin a second to breathe for chasing her."

Again, she sensed by the stiff set of his shoulders that he wasn't completely comfortable talking about his family. She wasn't sure why he had decided to share these few details but she was beyond touched that he was willing to show her this snapshot of their life together.

"I can imagine it was hard to get any work done while you were chasing a busy toddler," she said.

He nodded. "She wasn't afraid of anything, our Cara. If Robin or I didn't watch her, she'd be out the back door and halfway to the ocean before we figured out where she had gone. We had to put double child-locks on every door."

He smiled a little at the memory but she could still sense the pain around the edges of his smile. She couldn't help herself, she reached out and touched his forearm, driven only by the need to comfort him.

His skin was warm, covered in a layer of crisp dark hair. He looked down at her fingers on his darker skin and she thought she saw his Adam's apple move as he swallowed.

"Maddie was like that, too," she said after a moment, lifting her hand away.

"Maddie?"

"I know. Hard to believe. She was a much busier toddler than Simon. She was always the ringleader of the two of them."

She smiled at the memory. "When they still could barely walk, they used to climb out of their cribs in the night to play with their toys. I couldn't figure out how they were doing it so I set up the video camera with a motion sensor and caught Maddie moving like a little monkey to climb out of hers. She didn't need any help but Simon apparently wasn't as skilled so Maddie would climb out and then push a half-dozen stuffed animals over the top railing of his crib so he could use them to climb out. It was quite a system the little rascals came up with."

He paused in the middle of searching through his toolbox, his features far more interested than she might have expected. "So what did you do? Take out all the stuffed animals from the room?"

She made a face. "No. Gave in to the inevitable. We bought them both toddler beds so they wouldn't break their necks climbing out"

"Did they still get up in the night?"

"Not as much. I think it was the lure of the forbidden that kept them trying to escape."

He laughed—a real, full-fledged laugh. She watched the shadows lift from his eyes for just a moment, saw in that light expression some glimmer of the Will she had known, and she could swear she felt the tumble and thud of her heart.

She was an idiot for Will Garrett, only now she didn't have the excuse of being fifteen, flush with the heady excitement of first love.

After entirely too short a time, his laughter slid away and he turned his attention back to the project. "How do you feel about heights?"

"Moderately okay, within reason."

"It would help if you could hold the trim up while I nail it, as long as you don't mind climbing the ladder."

"Not at all."

For the next twenty minutes, they spoke little as they worked together to hang the trim. They finished two walls quickly but the other two weren't as straightforward. One had a fireplace and chimney flue that Will needed to work the trim around and the other had a jog that she thought must contain ductwork.

As she waited for Will to figure out the angles for the cuts, Julia sat on the couch, enjoying the animation on his features as he calculated. She wondered if he knew how his eyes lit up while he was working, how he seemed to vibrate with an energy she didn't see there at other times.

At last he figured out the math involved to make sure the moldings matched up correctly. He left for a moment and she heard his power saw out on the porch.

"You love this, don't you?" she asked when he returned carrying the cut pieces of trim.

He shrugged. "It's a living."

"It's more than that to you. I can tell. I keep remembering how much you complained about your dad making you go out on jobs with him that summer."

His laugh was rueful, tinged with embarrassment. "I

was a stupid sixteen-year-old punk without a brain in my head. All I wanted to do was hang out with my friends and try to impress pretty girls."

She shook her head. "You were *not* a punk. You were by far the most decent boy I knew."

The tips of his ears turned that dusky red again. "Funny, you always seemed like such a sensible kind of girl."

"I was sensible enough to know when a boy is different from the others I'd met. All they wanted to do was flirt and see how many bases they could steal. They weren't interested in talking about serious things like the political science class they had taken the year before or the ecological condition of the shoreline."

"Did I do that?"

"You don't remember?"

He slanted her a sidelong look. "All I remember is trying to figure out whether I dared try sliding in to second base."

She blushed, though she couldn't help smiling, too. "I guess you were just more subtle about that particular goal than the other boys, then."

"Either that or more chicken."

She laughed. She couldn't help herself. To her delight, he laughed along with her and the unexpected sound of it even had Conan lifting his head to watch the two of them with what looked suspiciously like satisfaction.

She remembered Sage's assertion that the dog was working in cahoots with Abigail.

Just now—with the rain pattering softly against the window and this peculiar intimacy swirling around them—the idea didn't seem completely ludicrous.

"Okay, I think I've finally got this figured out," he said after a moment. "I think I'm ready for my assistant."

She pushed her ladder closer to his since they were working with a much smaller length of trim.

As he was only a few feet away from her, she was intensely aware of him—his scent, leathery and masculine, and the heat that seemed to pulse from him.

He wasn't smiling or laughing now, she noted. In fact, he seemed tense suddenly and in a hurry to finish this section of the job.

"I can probably handle the rest on my own," he said, his voice suddenly sounding strained. "None of the remaining lengths of trim are very long so I shouldn't need your help holding them in place."

"I can stick around, just in case you need me."

His gaze met hers and she thought he would tell her not to bother but he simply nodded. "Sure. Okay."

She was so relieved he wasn't going to send her away that she wasn't paying as close attention to what she was doing as she should have been while she descended the ladder at the same time Will descended his own ladder next to her.

In her distracted state, she misjudged the last rung and stumbled a little at the bottom.

"Whoa! Careful there," he exclaimed, reaching out instinctively to catch her.

For one moment, they froze in that suspended state, with his strong arms around her and her arms trapped between their bodies. Her startled gaze flew to his and she thought she saw awareness and desire and the barest shadow of resignation there.

WILL STARED AT HER, his heart pumping in his chest like an out-of-control nail gun. A desperate kind of hunger prowled through him, wild and urgent. Though he knew she was far from it, she felt small and fragile in his arms.

He could feel the heat of her burning his skin, could smell that soft, mouthwatering scent of cherry blossoms.

He closed his eyes, fighting the inevitable with every ounce of strength he had left. But when he opened his eyes, he found her color high, her lips parted slightly, her eyes a deep and mossy green, shadowed with what he was almost positive was a heady awareness to match his own.

He should stop this right now, should just release her, push her from Anna's apartment and lock the door snugly behind her. The tiny corner of his brain that could still manage to string together a coherent thought told him that was exactly the course of action he ought to follow.

But how could he? She was so soft, so sweetly, irresistibly warm, and he had been cold for so damn long.

He heard a groan and realized it came from his own throat just an instant before he lowered his mouth and kissed her.

She sighed his name, just a whispered breath between their mouths, but the sound seemed to sink through all the layers of careful protection around his heart.

She wrapped her arms around his neck, responding eagerly to his kiss. Tenderness surged through him, raw and terrifying. He wanted to hang on tight and never let go, wanted to stand in Abigail's old living room for the rest of his life with a soft rain clicking against the windows and Julia Hudson Blair in his arms.

They kissed for a long time, until he was breathing hard and light-headed, until her mouth was swollen, until his body cried out for more and more.

He didn't know how long they would have continued—forever if he'd had his way—when suddenly he heard the one thing guaranteed to shatter the moment and the mood like a hard, cold downpour.

"Mama? Are you there? I woke up."

The sweet, high voice cut through the room like a buzz saw. He stiffened, his insides cold suddenly, and frantically looked to the doorway, aghast at what he had done and that her daughter had caught them at it.

He only knew a small measure of relief when he realized the voice was coming from the walkie-talkie she had brought downstairs.

Julia was breathing just as hard as he was, her eyes wide and dazed and her cheeks flushed.

Even through his dismay, he had to clench his fists at his side to keep from reaching for her again.

She drew in a deep, shuddering breath, then walked to the walkie-talkie and picked it up.

"I'm here, baby," she said, her voice slightly ragged. "How are you feeling?"

"My throat still hurts a little but I'm okay," Maddie answered. "Where are you, Mama?"

Julia flashed a quick glance at him, then looked away. "Downstairs with W Mr. Garrett. Didn't you see my note?"

"Yes, when I woke up. But I was just wondering if you were still down there."

"I am."

"Is Conan there with you?"

Will saw her sweep the room with her gaze until she found the dog still curled up by the couch. "He's right here. I'll bring him up with me if you want some company."

"Thanks, Mama."

She clipped the walkie-talkie to her belt, angled slightly away from him so he couldn't see her expression, then she seemed to draw another deep breath before she turned to face him.

"I...have to go up. Maddie needs me."

"Right." He ached to touch her again, just one more time, but he fiercely clamped down on the desire, wanting her gone almost as much as he wanted to sweep her into his arms again.

Without warning, he was suddenly furious. Damn her, *damn her,* for making him want again—for this churn of his blood pouring into the frozen edges inside him. Pain prickled through him, like he had just shoved frostbitten fingers into boiling water.

He didn't want this, didn't want to feel again. Hadn't he made that clear? So why the hell did she have to come in here, with her sweet smile and her warm eyes and her soft curves.

"Will—"

"Don't say anything," he bit out. "This was a mistake. It's been a mistake for me to spend even a minute with you since you came back to town."

At his sudden attack, shock and hurt flared in her green eyes and he hated himself all over again but that didn't change what he knew he had to do.

"You didn't think it was a mistake a moment ago," she murmured.

He couldn't deny the truth of that. "I'm attracted to you. That's obvious, isn't it? I have been since I was sixteen years old. But I don't want to be. You're in my way every single time I turn around."

He lashed out, needing only to make her understand

even as he was appalled at his words, at the way her spine seemed to stiffen with each syllable.

Still, he couldn't seem to hold them back once he started. They gushed between them, ugly and harsh.

"You're always coming around to help me work, showing up at my house dragging your kids along, crowding me every second. Don't you get it? I don't want you around! Why can't you just leave me alone?"

Conan rose and growled and for the first time in Will's memory the dog looked menacing. At the same time, a branch outside Anna's apartment clawed and scratched against the window, whipped by a sudden microburst of wind.

Julia seemed to ignore all the external distractions. She drew in a deep breath, her face paler than he had ever seen it.

"That's not fair," she said, her voice low and tight.

He raked a hand through his hair, hating himself, hating her, hating Robin and Cara for leaving him this empty, harsh, cruel husk of a man. "I know. I know it's not fair. You don't deserve to bear the weight of all that, Julia. I know that, but I can't help it. I'm sorry, but it's the truth. I need you to leave me alone. Please. I can't do this anymore. I can't. Not with you. Not with anyone."

The branch scraped the glass harder and he made a mental note to prune it for Sage and Anna, even as he fought down the urge to pound something, to smash his fists hard into the new drywall he had put in a few months earlier.

She studied him for a long moment, her features taut.

"Okay," she finally murmured and headed for the door to Anna's apartment.

Before she left, she turned around to face him one last

time. "I appreciate your frankness. Since I know you're a fair man, I'm sure you'll allow me the same privilege."

What the hell was he supposed to say to that? He waited, though he wanted nothing more than to shove the door closed behind her and lock it tight.

"I have something I want to say, though I know it's not my place and none of my business. Still, I think you need to hear it from someone."

She paused, and seemed to be gathering her thoughts. When she spoke, her words sliced at him like a band saw.

"Will, do you really think Robin and Cara would want this for you?"

"Don't."

He couldn't bear a lecture or a commentary or whatever she planned. Not now, not about this.

She shook her head. "No. I'm going to say this. And then you can push me away all you want, as you've been doing since I came back to Cannon Beach. I want you to ask yourself if your wife and little girl would want you to spend the rest of your life wallowing in your pain, smothering yourself in it. From all I've heard about Robin, it sounds as if she was generous and loving to everyone. Sage has told me what a good friend she was to everyone, how people were always drawn to her because of her kindness and her cheerful nature. I'm sorry I never had the chance to meet her. But from what I've heard of her, I can't imagine Robin would find it any tribute to her kind and giving nature that you want you to close yourself away from life as some kind of…of penance because she's gone."

She looked as if she had more she wanted to say, but to his relief she only gave him one more long look then turned to gesture to Conan. The dog added his glare to hers, giving Will what could only be described as the snake-eye, then followed her out the door.

Will stood for a long moment, an ache in his chest and her scent still swirling around him. He closed his eyes, remembering again the sweetness of her touch, how fiercely he had wanted to hold on tight, to surrender completely and let her work her healing magic.

He had to leave.

That was all there was to it. He couldn't stay in Cannon Beach with Julia and her kids just a few houses away. There was no way in the small community of year-round residents that he could avoid her, and seeing her, spending any time with her, was obviously a mistake.

He had meant what he said. She crowded him and he couldn't deal with it anymore.

He knew after his outburst just now that she wouldn't make any effort to spend time with him, but they were still bound to bump into each other once in a while and he had just proved to himself that he had no powers of resistance where she was concerned.

He had no other option but to escape.

He pulled out his cell phone. He knew the number was there—he had dialed it only the night before but in the end he had lost his nerve and hung up.

With the wind still whipping the tree branches outside like angry fists, he found it quickly, hit the button to redial and waited for it to ring.

As he might have expected, he was sent immediately to voice-messaging. For a moment he considered hanging up again but the sweet scent of spring flowers drifted to him and he knew this was what he had to do.

He drew in a breath. "Eben, this is Will Garrett," he began. "I'd like to talk about your offer, if it's still open."

CHAPTER TWELVE

"Simon, hands to yourself."

Her son snatched his fingers back an instant before they would have dipped into the frosting on the frill-bedecked sheet cake for Sage's wedding shower.

"I only wanted a little smackeral," he complained.

Julia sighed, even as she fought a smile. This was why she was destined to be a lousy mother, she decided. How on earth was she supposed to have the gumption to properly discipline her son when he knew he could charm her every time by quoting Winnie the Pooh?

"No smackerals, little or otherwise," she said as sternly as she could manage. "After the bridal shower you can have all the leftovers you want but Sage wouldn't want grimy little finger trails dipping through her pretty cake, would she?"

"Sage wouldn't mind," he grumbled.

All right, he was probably correct on that observation. Sage was remarkably even-tempered for a bride and she adored Julia's twins and spoiled them both relentlessly.

But as their mother, it was Julia's responsibility to teach them little things like manners, and she couldn't let him get away with it, smackerals or not.

"I mind," she said firmly. "Tell you what, if you promise to help Anna and me put all the chairs and tables away after the shower, you can appease your sugar buzz with one of the cookies you and Maddie and I made last night."

He grinned and reached for one. "Can I take one to Mad? She's in her room."

"As long as you don't forget where you were taking it and eat that one too along the way."

"I would *never* do that!" he protested, with just a shade too much offended innocence.

Julia shook her head, smiling as she put the finishing touches on the cake.

Simon paused at the doorway. "Can we eat our cookies outside and play with Conan for a while since the rain *finally* stopped?"

"Of course," she answered. After an entire week straight of rain, she knew both of her children were suffering from acute cases of cabin fever.

A moment later, she heard the door slam then the pounding of two little sets of feet hurtling down the stairs, joined shortly after by enthusiastic barking.

Unable to resist, she moved to the window overlooking the backyard just in time to see Maddie pick up an armful of fallen leaves and toss them into the air, her face beaming with joy at being outside to savor the October sunshine. Not far away, Conan and Simon were already wrestling in the grass together.

The two of them loved this place—the old house, with its quirks and its personality, the yard and Abigail's beautiful gardens, the wild and gorgeous ocean just a few footsteps away.

They were thriving here, just as she had hoped. They already had good friends at school, they were doing well in their classes. Maddie's health seemed to have taken a giant leap forward and improved immeasurably in the nearly two months they had been in Cannon Beach.

She should be so happy. Her children were happy, her job was working out well, they had all settled into a routine.

So why couldn't she shake this lingering depression that seemed to have settled on her shoulders as summer slid into autumn? She shifted her gaze from the Brambleberry House yard to another house just a few hundred yards up the beach.

There was the answer to the question of why she couldn't seem to shake her gray mood. Will Garrett. She hadn't seen him since their disastrous encounter nearly two weeks earlier but her insides still churned with dismay when she remembered his blunt words telling her to leave him alone, and then her own presumptuous reply.

She had been way out of line to bring Robin and Cara into the whole thing, to basically accuse him of dishonoring his wife and daughter's memory simply because he continued to push Julia away.

She had had no right to tell him how he ought to grieve or to pretend she knew what his wife might have wanted for him. She had never even met the woman.

Because of her lingering shame at her own temerity, she was almost grateful she hadn't seen him since, even to catch a glimpse of him through the pines as he moved around his house.

That's what she told herself, anyway. If she stood at her window at night watching the lights in his house, hoping for some shadow to move across a window, well, that was her own pathetic little secret.

With one last sigh, she forced herself to move away from the window and return to the kitchen and the cake.

A few moments later, with a final flourish, she judged it ready and carefully picked it up to carry it downstairs to Anna's apartment.

Since her arms were full, she managed to ring the doorbell with her elbow. Anna opened almost immediately. Though she smiled, Julia didn't miss the troubled expression in her eyes.

She was probably just busy setting up for the shower, Julia told herself. She knew Anna had been distracted with problems at her two giftshops as well, though she seemed reluctant to talk about them.

Julia smiled and held out the cake. "Watch out. Masterpiece coming through."

Anna's expression lifted slightly as she looked at the autumn-themed cake, with its richly colored oak and maple leaves and pine boughs, all crafted of frosting.

Sage wasn't one for frilly lace and other traditional wedding decorations. Given her job as a naturalist and her love of the outdoors, Julia and Anna had picked a nature theme for the shower they were throwing and the cake was to be the centerpiece of their decorations.

"Oh! Oh, it's beautiful!"

"Told you it would be," Julia said with undeniable satisfaction as she carried the cake inside Anna's apartment to a table set in a corner.

"You were absolutely right," Sage said from the couch. "I can't believe you did all that in one afternoon!"

Julia shrugged. "I don't have a lot of domestic skills but I can decorate a cake like nobody's business. I told you I put myself through college working in a bakery, so if the teaching thing ever falls through, I've at least got something to fall back on."

She grinned at them both and was surprised when they didn't smile back. Instead, they exchanged grim looks.

"What is it? What's wrong? Is it the cake? I tried to decorate it just as we discussed."

"It's not the cake," Anna assured her. "The cake is gorgeous."

"Did somebody cancel, then?"

"No. Everybody's still coming, as far as I know." Sage sighed. "I just hung up the phone with Eben."

She frowned. "Is everything okay with Chloe?"

"No. Nothing like that. Julia, it's not Eben or Chloe or anything to do with the shower. It's Will."

Her stomach cramped suddenly and for a moment she couldn't seem to breathe. "What…what's wrong with Will?"

"He's leaving," Anna said, her usual matter-of-fact tone sounding strained.

"Leaving?"

Sage nodded, her eyes distressed. "Apparently he's taken a traveling job with Spencer Hotels. A sort of carpentry trouble-shooter, traveling around to their renovation sites and overseeing the work of the local builders. He's starting right after the wedding. He accepted the job a few weeks ago but apparently Eben didn't seem to think it was anything worth mentioning to me until just now on the phone, purely in passing."

She scowled, apparently at her absent fiancé. Julia barely noticed, too lost in her own shock. Two weeks ago. She didn't miss the significance of that, not for a minute.

They had kissed right here in this very living room and she could think of nothing else but how he had all but begged her to leave him alone and then in her hurt, she had said such nervy, terrible things to him.

Ask yourself if your wife and little girl would want you to spend the rest of your life wallowing in your pain, smothering yourself in it.

Oh, what had she done? Now he had taken a traveling job with Eben's company and she could hardly seem to work her brain around it. He was leaving Cannon Beach—the home he loved, his friends, the business he had work so hard to build.

Because of her.

She knew it had to be so. What other reason could he have?

She had made him too uncomfortable, had pushed too hard.

I can't imagine Robin would find it any tribute that you want you to close yourself away from life as some kind of penance because she's gone.

Her face burned and her stomach seemed to twist into a snarled tangle. What had she *done?*

"What do you think, Julia?"

She jerked her mind back to the conversation to realize Sage was speaking to her and as her silence dragged on, both women were giving her curious looks.

It was obvious they expected some response from her but as she hadn't heard the question, she didn't know at all what to say.

"I'm sorry. What?"

"I said that you've known him longer than any of us. What could he be thinking?"

"Oh no. I don't know him," she murmured. "Not really."

Perhaps that was the trouble, she admitted to herself. She had this idealized image of Will from years ago when she had loved him as a girl. Had she truly allowed herself to accept the reality of all the years and the pain between them?

She had pushed him, harder than he was ready to be pushed. She had backed him into a corner and he was looking for some way out.

This was all her fault and she was going to have to figure out a way to make things right. She couldn't let Will leave everything he cared about behind because of her.

The doorbell rang suddenly and Conan jumped up from his spot on the floor where he had been watching them. Now he hurried to Anna's open apartment door, his tail wagging furiously and for one wild moment her heart jumped at the thought that it might be Will.

Foolish, she realized almost instantly. Why would he be here?

More likely it was Becca Wilder, the teenager she had hired to corral the twins for the evening while she was busy with Sage's shower.

Her supposition was confirmed a moment later when Anna went to answer the door and Julia heard the voice of Jewel Wilder, Becca's mother and one of Sage's friends, who had offered to drop Becca off when she came to the shower herself.

She couldn't do anything about Will right now, she realized. Sage's bridal shower was supposed to start any moment now and she couldn't let the celebration be ruined by her guilt.

THREE HOURS LATER, as Sage said goodbye to the last of her guests, Julia began gathering discarded plates and cups, doing her best to ignore her head that throbbed and pulsed with pain.

She knew exactly why her head was pounding—the

same reason her heart ached. Because of Will and his stubborn determination to shut himself off from life and because of her own stubborn, misguided determination to prevent him.

For Sage's sake, she had done her best to put away her anxiety and guilt for the evening. She had laughed and played silly wedding shower games and tried to enjoy watching Sage open the gifts from her eclectic collection of friends.

Beneath it all, the ache simmered and seethed, like a vat of bitter bile waiting to boil over.

Will was leaving his home, his friends, his wife and daughter's resting places. She couldn't let him do it, not if he was leaving because of her.

She carried the plates and dishes into the kitchen, where she found Anna wrapping up the leftover food.

"It was a wonderful party," Julia said.

"I think everyone had a good time," Anna agreed. "But listen, you don't have to help clean up. I can handle it. Why don't you go on upstairs with the twins?"

"I just checked with Becca and they're both down for the night. She's heading home with her mom and is leaving the door open so we can hear them down here."

Anna stuck a plate of little sandwiches into her refrigerator, then gave Julia a placid smile.

"That's great. Since the twins are asleep, this would be the perfect chance for you to go and talk some sense into Will."

Julia stared at her, completely astounded at the suggestion. "Where did that come from?"

Anna smiled. "My brilliantly insightful mind."

"Which I never realized until this moment is a little on the cracked side. Why would he listen to me?"

"Well, somebody needs to knock some sense into him and Sage and I both decided you're the best one for the job."

"Why on earth would you possibly think *that?* You've both been friends with him for a long time. I just moved back. He'll listen to what you have to say long before he'll listen to me."

Not to mention the tiny little detail that she suspected *she* was the reason he was leaving in the first place— and the fact that he had basically ordered her to stay away from him.

She wasn't about to admit that to Anna, though.

"We're like sisters to him," Anna answered. "Naggy, annoying little sisters. You, on the other hand, are the woman he has feelings for."

She bobbled the plate she was loading into the dishwasher but managed to catch it before it shattered on the floor.

"Wrong!" she exclaimed. "Oh, you couldn't be more wrong. Will doesn't have feelings for me. He…he might, if he would let himself, but he's wrapped himself up so tightly in his pain he won't let anyone through. Or not me, at least. No, he absolutely doesn't have feelings for me."

Anna studied her for a long moment, then smiled unexpectedly. "Our mistake, then, I guess. Sage and I were quite convinced there was something between the two of you. Will's been different ever since you came back to Cannon Beach."

"Different, how?" she asked warily.

"I can't quite put my finger on how, exactly. I wouldn't say he's been happier, but he's done things he hasn't in two years. Going for ice cream with you and your kids.

Coming to the barbecue with Eben and Chloe without putting up a fight. Sage and I both thought you were slowly dragging him back to life, whether he wanted you to or not, and we were both thrilled about it. He kissed you, didn't he?"

Julia flushed. "Yes, but he wasn't happy about either time."

Anna's eyebrow rose. "There was more than one time?"

She sighed. "A few weeks ago, when I helped him hang the new moldings in your living room. We had a fight afterward and I said horrible things to him, things I had no right to say. And now I find out he took a job with Eben's company, and accepted it two weeks ago. I just can't believe it's a coincidence."

"All the more reason you should be the one to convince him to stay," Anna said.

"He told me to stay away from him," Julia whispered, hurting all over again at the harshness of his words.

"Are you going to listen to him? Go on," Anna urged. "I'll keep an eye on Simon and Maddie for you. There's nothing stopping you."

Except maybe her guilt and her nerves and the horrible, sinking sensation in her gut that she was pushing a man away from everything that he cared about, just so he could escape from her.

Before she could formulate further arguments, a huge shaggy beast suddenly hurried into the room, a leash in his mouth and Sage right on his heels.

"Conan, what has gotten into you, you crazy dog?" she exclaimed. "I can put you out."

But the dog didn't listen to her. He headed straight to

Julia, plopped down at her feet and held the leash out in his mouth with that familiar expectant look.

She groaned. "Not you, too?"

Sage and Anna exchanged glances and Julia was quite certain she heard Sage snigger.

"Looks like you're the chosen one," Anna said with a smile.

"You can't fight your destiny, Jules," Sage piped in. "Believe me, I've tried. The King of Brambleberry House has declared you're tonight's sacrificial lamb. You can't escape your fate."

She closed her eyes, aware as she did that the pain in her head seemed to have lifted while she was talking to Anna. "I suppose you're telling me Conan wants me to talk to Will, too."

"That's what it looks like to me," Sage said.

"Same here."

Julia stared at Anna—prosaic, no-nonsense Anna, who looked just as convinced as Sage.

"You're both crazy. He's a dog, for heaven's sake!"

Sage grinned. "Watch it. If you offend him, you'll be stuck for life giving him his evening walk."

"Rain or shine," Anna added. "And around here, it's usually rain."

She studied them all looking so expectantly at her and gave a sigh of resignation. "This isn't fair, you know. The three of you ganging up on me like this."

In answer, Sage clipped the leash on Conan's collar and held the end out for Julia. Anna left the room, returning a moment later with Julia's jacket from the closet in the entryway.

"What if Will doesn't want to talk to me?"

It was a purely rhetorical question. She knew perfectly well he wouldn't want to talk to her, just as she was grimly aware she was only trying to delay the inevitable moment when she had to gather her nerve and walk down the beach to his house.

"You're an elementary school teacher," Anna said with a confident grin. "You're good at making your students do things they don't want to do, aren't you?"

Julia snorted. "I have a feeling Will Garrett might be just a tad harder to manage than my fifth-grade boys."

"We all have complete faith in you," Sage said.

Before she was quite aware of how they had managed it, they ushered her and Conan out the front door and closed it behind her. She was quite surprised when she didn't hear the click of the door locking behind her. She wouldn't have put anything past them at this point.

Conan strained on his leash to be gone but she stood on the porch steps of Brambleberry House trying to gather her frayed nerves as she listened to the distant crash of the sea and the cool October breeze moaning in the tops of the pines.

Finally she couldn't ignore Conan's urgency and she followed the walkway around the house to the gate that opened to the beach.

It would probably be a quicker route to just take the road to his house but she wasn't in a huge hurry to face him anyway.

Conan seemed less insistent as they walked along the shoreline, after he had marked just about every single rock and tuft of grass they passed.

It gave her time to remember her last summer on Cannon Beach. She passed the rock where she had been sitting when he kissed her for the *last* time—not counting more recent incidences—the night before she left Cannon Beach when she was fifteen.

She paused and ran her finger along the uneven surface, remembering the thrill of his arms around her and how she had been so very certain she had to be in love with him.

She'd had nothing to compare it to, but she had been quite sure at fifteen that this must be the real thing.

And then the next day her world had shattered and she had been shuttled to Sacramento with her mother, away from everything safe and secure in her life.

Still, even as her parents' marriage had imploded, she had held the memory of a handsome boy close to her heart.

At first she thought the moisture on her cheeks was just sea spray, then she realized it was tears, that she was crying for lost innocence and for the two people they had been, and for all the pain that had come after for both of them.

She wiped at her cheeks as she knelt and hugged Conan to her. The dog licked at her cheeks and she smiled a little at his attempts to comfort her.

"I'm being silly again, aren't I? I'm not fifteen anymore and I'm not that dreamy-eyed girl. I'm thirty-one years old and I need to start acting like it, don't I?"

The dog barked as if he agreed with her.

With renewed resolve, she squared her shoulders and stood again, gathering her courage around her.

She had to do this. Will's life was here in Cannon Beach. It had always been here, and she couldn't ruin that for him.

She swallowed her nerves and headed for the lights she could see flickering in his workshop.

CHAPTER THIRTEEN

HE WOULD MISS THIS.

Will stood in his father's workshop—his workspace now, at least for another few days—and routered the edge of a shingle while a blues station played on the stereo.

He had always found comfort within these walls, with the air sweet with freshly cut wood shavings and sawdust motes drifting in the air, catching the light like gold flakes.

He left the door ajar, both for ventilation and to let the cool, moist sea air inside. In the quiet intervals without the whine and hum of his power tools, he could hear the ocean's low murmur just down the beach.

This was his favorite spot in the world, the place where he had learned his craft, where he had forged a connection with his stern, sometimes austere father, where he had figured out many of his own strengths and his weaknesses.

Before Robin and Cara died, he used to come out here so he could have a quiet place to think. Sage probably would have given it some hippy new age name like a transcendental meditation room or something.

He just always considered it the one place where his thoughts seemed more clear and cohesive.

He didn't so much need a place to think these days as he needed an escape on the nights when the house seemed too full of ghosts to hold anyone still breathing.

In a few days when he started working for Eben Spencer's company, everything would be different. He expected his workspaces for the next few months would be any spare corner he could find in whatever hotel around the globe where Eben sent him to work.

Who would have ever expected him to become an itinerant carpenter? *Have tools, will travel.*

His first job was outside of Boston but Eben wanted to send him to Madrid next and then on to Portofino, Italy before he headed to the Pacific Rim. And that was only the first month.

Will shook his head. Italy and Spain and Singapore. What the hell was he going to do in a foreign country where he didn't know a soul and didn't speak the language?

It all seemed wildly exotic for a guy who rarely left his coastal hometown, who only possessed a current passport because he and Robin had gone on a cruise to Mexico the year before Cara came along.

The work would be the same. That was the important thing. He would still be doing the one thing he was good at, the one thing that filled him with satisfaction, whether he was in Portofino or Madrid or wherever else Eben sent him.

Maybe those ghosts might even have a chance to rest if he wasn't here dredging them up every minute.

He sure hoped he was making the right choice.

He set down the finished shingle and picked up another one from the dwindling pile next to him. Only a few more and then he only had to nail them to the roof to be finished. A few more hours of work ought to do it.

Against his will, he shot another glance out the window at the big house on the hill, solid and graceful against the moonlit sky.

The lights were out on the second floor, he noted immediately, then chided himself for even noticing.

He was almost certain he wasn't really trying to outrun any ghosts by taking the job with Spencer Hotels. But he knew he couldn't say the same for the living woman who haunted him.

He sighed as his thoughts inevitably slid back to Julia, as they had done so often the last two weeks. Tonight was Sage's bridal shower, he knew. He had seen cars coming and going all night.

Julia was probably right in the middle of it all, with her sweet smile and the sunshine she seemed to carry with her into every room.

For a man who wanted to push her away, he sure spent a hell of a lot of time thinking about her. He sighed again, and could almost swear he smelled the cherry blossom scent of her on the wind.

But a moment later, when the router was silent as he picked up another shingle, he thought he heard a snuffling kind of noise outside the door, then a dark red nose poked through.

An instant later, Conan was barking a greeting at him and Julia was walking through the doorway behind him.

Will yanked up his safety glasses and could do nothing but stare at her, wondering how his thoughts had possibly conjured her up.

Her cheeks were flushed, her hair tousled a little by the wind, but she was definitely flesh and blood.

"Hi," she murmured, and he was certain her color climbed a little higher on her cheeks.

She looked fragile and lovely and highly uncomfortable. No wonder, after the things he had said to her the last time they had spoken.

"I'm sorry to bother you… I…we…" Her voice trailed off.

"Wasn't tonight Sage's big bridal shower?"

"It was. But it's over now and everyone's gone. After the shower, Conan needed a walk and he picked me to take him and Sage and Anna made me come down here to talk to you."

She finished in a rush, without meeting his gaze.

"They made you?"

Her gaze finally flashed to his and he saw a combination of chagrin and rueful acceptance. "You know what they're like. I have a tough enough time saying no to them individually. When they combine forces, I'm pretty much helpless to resist."

"Why did they want you to talk to me?" he asked, though he had a pretty strong inkling.

She didn't answer him, though, only moved past him into the workshop, her attention suddenly caught by the project he was working on.

Damn it.

He could feel his own cheeks start to flush and wished, more than anything, that he had had the foresight to grab a tarp to cover the thing the minute she walked in.

"Will," she exclaimed. "It's gorgeous!"

He scratched the back of his neck, doing his best to ignore how the breathy excitement in her voice sent a shiver rippling down his spine. "It's not finished. I'm working on the shingles tonight, then I should be ready to take it back up to Brambleberry House."

She moved forward for a closer look and he couldn't seem to wrench his gaze away from her starry-eyed delight at the repaired dollhouse he had agreed to work on the day she moved in.

"It's absolutely stunning!"

She drew her finger along the curve of one of the cupola's with tender care. Will could only watch, grimly aware that he shouldn't have such an instant reaction just from the sight of her soft, delicate hands on his work.

"You fixed it! No, you didn't just fix it. This is beyond a simple repair. It was such a mess, just a pile of broken sticks, when you started! And from that, you've created a work of art!"

"I don't know that I'd go quite that far."

"I would! Oh, Will, it's beautiful. Better than it ever was, even when it was new from my father."

To his horror, tears started to well up in her eyes.

"It's just a dollhouse. Not worth bawling about," he said tersely, trying to keep the sudden panic out of his voice.

She gave a short laugh as she swiped at her cheeks. "They're happy tears. Oh, believe me. Will, it's wonderful. I can't tell you how much this will mean to Maddie. She tried to be brave about it but she was so heartbroken when I told her the dollhouse hadn't survived the move. It was one of her last few ties to her father and she has always cherished it, I think because he gave it to her right after her diagnosis, a few days before he…"

Her voice trailed off for a moment and he thought she wasn't going to complete the sentence, but then she drew in a breath and straightened her shoulders. "Before he left us."

Will stared at her, trying to make sense of her words. "I didn't realize your husband died so soon after Maddie's cancer was discovered."

She sighed. "He didn't," she said slowly. "His car accident was eighteen months after her diagnosis but…we were separated most of that time. We were a few months shy of finalizing our divorce when he died."

She lifted her chin almost defiantly when she spoke the last part of the sentence.

He wondered at it, even as he tried to figure out how the hell a man with a beautiful wife and two kids—one with cancer—could walk away from his family in the middle of a crisis.

He left us, she had said quite plainly. He didn't miss the meaning of that now. The man had a daughter with cancer and he had been the one to walk away from them.

Will had a sudden fierce wish that he could have met her husband just once before he died, to teach the bastard a lesson about what it meant to be a man.

She was waiting for him to answer, he realized.

"I'm sorry," he finally said, wincing at the inane words. "That must have been hard on you and the kids during such a rough time."

She managed a wobbly smile. "You could say that."

"All this time, you never said anything about your marriage. I had no idea it was rocky."

She sighed and leaned against the work table holding the resurrected dollhouse.

"I don't talk about it much, especially when the kids are around. I don't want them thinking less of their father."

He raised an eyebrow at that, but said nothing. He had his own opinions about it but he didn't think she would be eager to hear them.

"Maddie's diagnosis kicked Kevin in the gut. The stark truth is, he just couldn't handle it. His mother died of cancer when he was young, a particularly vicious form that lingered for a long time, and I think he just couldn't bear the thought that he might lose someone else he loved in the same way."

What kind of strength had it taken her to deal with a crumbling marriage at the same time she was fighting for her daughter's life? He couldn't even imagine it.

He studied her there in his workshop and saw shadows in her eyes. There was more to the story, he sensed.

"Was there someone else?" Some instinct prompted him to ask.

She gave him a swift, shocked look. "How did you know that? I haven't told anyone else. Not even Sage and Anna know that part."

"I don't know. Just a guess." He couldn't very well tell her he was becoming better than he ought to be at reading her thoughts in her lovely green eyes.

She sighed, tracing a finger over one of the arched windows on the dollhouse. "A coworker. He swore he only turned to her after we separated—after Maddy's diagnosis—because he was hurting so much inside and so afraid for the future."

"That doesn't take away much of the sting for you, I imagine."

"No. No, it doesn't. I was angry and bitter for a long time. I mean, I was the one dealing with appointments and sitting through Maddie's chemotherapy with her and holding her when she threw up for hours afterward. I was scared, too. Not scared, I was *terrified*. I used to check on her dozens of times a night, just to make sure she was still breathing. I still do when she's having a rough night. It was a miracle I could function, most days. I was just as scared, but I didn't turn to someone else. I toughed it out by myself because I had no choice."

He couldn't imagine such a betrayal—more than that, he couldn't understand why she could seem to be such a happy person now after what she had been through.

Most women he knew would be bitter and angry at the world after surviving such an ordeal but Julia seemed to bubble over with joy, finding delight in everything.

She had been over the moon that he had repaired a dollhouse her bastard of an almost-ex-husband had worked on. He figured most betrayed women would have smashed the dollhouse to pieces themselves out of spite so they wouldn't have one more reminder of their cheating spouse.

"I don't know why I told you all that," she said after a moment, her cheeks slightly pink. "I didn't come here to relive the past."

Since she seemed eager to change the subject, he decided he wouldn't push her.

"That's right," he answered. "Sage and Anna sent you."

"I would have come anyway," she admitted. "They just gave me a push in this direction."

He found that slightly hard to believe, given his rudeness the last time they met.

"Why?" he asked.

She let out a breath, then confirmed his suspicion. "I… Sage just found out from Eben tonight that you're leaving."

He picked up another shingle, stalling for time. He did *not* want to get into this, especially not with her, though he had been half-expecting something like this for two weeks, since he accepted Eben's offer.

"That's right," he finally said. It would have been rude to turn the router on again—not to mention, Conan wouldn't like it—but he was severely tempted, if only to cut her off.

She seemed to have become inordinately fascinated with one of the finials on the dollhouse.

"I know this is presumptuous and I have no real right to ask…"

Her voice trailed off and he sighed, yanking his safety glasses off his head and setting them aside. He had a feeling he wasn't going to be finishing the dollhouse anytime soon.

"Something tells me you're going to ask anyway."

She twisted her hands together, her color still high. "You love Cannon Beach, Will. I know you do."

"Yeah. I do love it here. I always have."

"Help me understand, then, why you would suddenly decide to leave the town you have lived in for thirty-two years. This is your home. You have friends here, a thriving business. Your whole life is here!"

"What life?"

He hadn't meant to say something that raw, that honest, but his words seemed to hang between them and he couldn't yank them back.

It was the truth, anyway.

He didn't have a life, or at least not much of one. Everything he had known and cared about was gone and he couldn't walk anywhere in Cannon Beach without stumbling over a memory of a time when he thought he had owned the world, when he was certain he had everything he could ever possibly want.

Since Julia came to town, everything seemed so much harder, his world so much emptier—something else he wasn't about to explain to her.

Her eyes were dark with sorrow and something else that looked suspiciously like guilt.

"Maybe I was ready for a change," he finally said. "You just said it yourself, I've lived here my entire life. That's pretty pathetic for a grown man to admit, that he's never been anywhere, never done anything. Eben offered me the job some time ago. I gave it a lot of thought and finally decided the time was right."

She didn't look convinced. After another long, awkward moment, she clenched her hands together and lifted her gaze to his, her mouth trembling slightly.

"Will you tell me the truth? Are you leaving because of me?"

He shifted his gaze away, wishing his hands were busy with the router again. Unfortunately, his gaze collided with Conan's, and the dog gave him an entirely too perceptive look.

"Why would you say that?" he stalled.

She stepped closer, looking again as if she wanted to weep. "I've been sick inside ever since Sage told me you were taking this job with Eben's company."

"You shouldn't be, Julia. This is not on you. Let it go."

She shook her head. "I pushed you too hard the other day. I said terrible things. I had no right, Will. I have a terrible habit of always thinking I know what's best for everyone else."

Her short laugh held no trace of humor. "I don't know why. I mean, I've made a complete mess of my own life, haven't I? So why would I dare think I have any right to tell anyone else what to do with their life? But I was wrong, Will. I shouldn't have said what I did."

"Everything you said was right on the money. I knew it even while I was reacting so strongly. I've thought the same things myself, deep in my subconscious. Robin wouldn't want me to hide away from life, to sit out here in my workshop and brood while the world carries on without me. That wasn't what she was about, what *we* were about. But even though I've thought the same thing, I can't deny that hearing it from you was tough."

"I'm so sorry."

He sighed at the misery in her voice and surrendered to the inevitable. He stepped forward and picked up her knotted fingers, feeling them tremble in his hands.

"I care about you, Julia, more than I thought I could ever care about anyone again. When I'm with you, I feel like I'm sixteen again, sitting on the beach with the prettiest girl I've ever seen. But it scares the hell out of me. I'm not ready. That's the bald, honest truth. I'm not ready and I'm afraid I don't know if I ever will be."

"That's why you're leaving?"

"I'd be lying if I said you had nothing to do with my decision to take the job with Eben. But leaving—trying something new—has been on my mind for some time. I was considering it long before you showed up again, back when you were just a distant memory of a past that sometimes feels like it should belong to someone else."

He paused, struck by the contrast of her soft, delicate hands in his fingers that were hard and roughened by years of work.

"I guess you could say you're part of the reason I'm leaving, but you're not the only reason. I need a change. If I stay here, buried under the weight of the past, I'm afraid I'll slowly petrify like a piece of driftwood."

She took a long time to answer. Just when he was about to release her hands and step away, she clutched at his fingers with hands that still trembled.

"Would it make any difference if I...if I were the one to leave?"

He stared at her, taken aback. "Where would you go? You love your new job, Brambleberry House. Everything."

Sadness twisted across her lovely features. "I do love it here and the twins are thriving. But I have much less invested in Cannon Beach than you do. I've only been here a short time. We started over here, we can start over somewhere else."

That she would even contemplate making such a sacrifice for his sake completely astounded him.

"You can't do that for me, Julia. I would never ask of it you."

"You didn't ask. I'm offering. I hate the idea that I had anything to do with your decision to leave. I blew in to town out of nowhere and ruined everything."

"You ruined nothing, Julia."

Whether he liked it or not, tenderness churned through him and he couldn't bear her distress. He lifted their joined hands and pressed his mouth to the warm skin at the back of her hand.

She shivered at his touch and he couldn't help himself. He pulled her into his arms, where she settled with a soft sigh.

"You ruined nothing," he repeated. "If anything, you made me realize I can't exist in this halflife forever. I have to move forward or I'll suffocate and right now taking this job with Eben feels like the best way to do that."

"I don't want you to leave," she murmured, her arms around his waist and her cheek against his chest.

He closed his eyes, stunned by the soft, contented peace that seemed to swirl through him. Right at this moment, he didn't want to think about leaving. Hell, he didn't want to move a muscle ever again.

They stood together for a long time, in a silence broken only by the sea outside the door and the dog's snuffly breaths as he slept.

When at last she lifted her face to his, he gave a sigh of surrender and lowered his mouth to hers.

CHAPTER FOURTEEN

HIS KISS WAS slow and gentle, like standing in a torpid stream, and it seemed to push every single thought from her head.

After their last kiss and the words they had flung at each other afterward, she had been certain she wouldn't find herself here in his arms again.

The unexpectedness of it added a poignant beauty to the moment and she leaned into him, savoring his hard strength against her.

He kissed her for long, drugging moments, until her knees were weak and her mind a pleasant muddle.

Through the soft haze that seemed to surround her, she had a vague awareness that there a subtle difference this time, something that had been missing the other times they kissed.

It took her several moments to pinpoint the change. Those other times they had kissed, he had always held part of himself back and she had sensed the reluctance underlying each touch, even when she doubted he was fully aware of it himself.

This time, that hesitancy was gone. All she tasted in his kiss was tenderness and the sweet simmer of desire.

She smiled against his mouth, unable to contain the giddy joy exploding through her.

"What's so funny?" he murmured.

"Nothing," she assured him. "Absolutely nothing. It's just… I've just missed you."

He stared at her for a long moment, his face just inches from hers, then he groaned and kissed her again. This time his mouth was wild, urgent, and she responded eagerly, pouring all the emotions in her heart into their embrace.

She was in love with him.

Even as her body stirred to life, as their mouths tangled together, as she seemed to sink into the hard strength of his arms, the truth seemed to washed over her like the storm-churned sea and she reeled under the unrelenting force of it.

He was leaving in three days and had just made it quite plain he wouldn't change his mind. Nothing but heartache awaited her. She knew it, just as she knew she was powerless to change the inevitable.

But that didn't matter. Right here, right now, she was in his arms and she couldn't waste this moment by worrying about how much she would bleed inside when he walked away.

She tightened her arms around him and he made a low sound in the back of his throat and his arms tightened around her.

"Julia," he murmured. Just her name and nothing else.

"I'm here," she whispered. "Right here."

She brushed a kiss against the skin of his jawline, savoring the scent of sawdust and hard-working male. He made a low sound in his throat that sent an answering shiver rippling down her spine.

"You're cold."

"A little," she admitted, though her reaction was more from the desire spinning wildly through her system.

"I'm sorry. I like to keep it cool out here when I'm working, especially at night to keep me awake."

He paused for a moment, his gaze a murky blue. "We could go inside," he said, with a soberness that told her exactly what he meant by the words—and how much it cost him to make the suggestion.

A hundred doubts and insecurities zinged through her head. It would be tough enough for her to handle his departure. How could she possibly let him walk away after sharing such intimacies without her heart shattering into a million pieces?

But how could she walk away *now,* when he was offering her so much more of himself than she ever thought he would?

"Are you sure?" she asked.

He paused, taking his time before answering. "I'm not sure of anything, Julia. I only know I want you and this feels more right than anything else has in a long, long time."

"Oh, Will." She framed his face with her hands and kissed him again, pouring all her heart into the kiss.

When at last he drew back, both of them were trembling, their breathing ragged.

"I don't know if I can promise you anything," he said, his voice a low rasp in the night. "Hell, I'm almost a hundred percent certain I can't. But right now I can't bear the thought of letting you out of my arms."

"I'm not going anywhere," she said.

"Not even inside, where it's warmer and far more comfortable than my dusty workshop?"

She smiled, aware of the cold seeping through her jacket despite the heat of his embrace. "All right."

He returned her smile with one of his own and she

shivered all over again at the unexpectedness of it. "I'm not going to let you freeze to death out here. Come on inside."

Conan was already standing by the door waiting for them, she saw when she managed to wrench her gaze away from Will's, as if the dog had heard and understood their complete conversation.

She shook her head at his spooky omniscience, but didn't have time to ponder it before Will was holding her hand and walking inexorably toward his house.

It had started to rain again while she was inside the workshop, a fine, cold mist that settled in her hair and made her grateful for the warmth that met them inside the house.

She hadn't been inside his home since that last summer so long ago, though she had seem glimpses of it through the window the day they had gone for ice cream, another lifetime ago.

She had the fleeting impression as she followed him inside of a roomy, comfortable place with a vaguely neglected air to it. He slept here but she had the feeling he spent as little time as possible within these walls.

Conan stopped in the kitchen and plopped down on a rug by the door but Will led her to a large family room with two adjoining deep sofas facing a giant plasma television on one wall.

"Are you still cold?" he asked. "I can start a fire. That should take the chill out of the air."

"You don't have to."

"It will only take a moment."

Without waiting for an answer, he moved to the hearth and started laying out kindling. She didn't mind, sensing he needed the time and space, just as she did, to regain a little equilibrium.

She shrugged out of her jacket and settled into one of the plump sofas, nerves careening through her.

It had been a long time for her and she hoped she wasn't unforgivably rusty. She would have been completely terrified if she didn't have the feeling he hadn't been with anyone since his wife's death.

"I imagine you have a spectacular view when it's daylight."

He gave her a rueful smile as he set a match to the kindling. "I guess. I've been looking at it every day of my life. I tend to forget how breathtaking it is. Maybe traveling a little—seeing other sights for a change—will help me appreciate what I've taken for granted all my life."

Somehow she didn't think the reminder of his imminent departure was accidental. She tried to pretend it didn't matter, even as sorrow pinched at her.

"Do you know where Eben's sending you first?"

"Outside of Boston. I'll be there for a few weeks then I guess I'm off to Italy. Quite a change for a guy who's never left the coast."

The tinder was burning brightly now so he added a heavier log. The flames quickly caught hold of it. Already, the room seemed warmer, though she wasn't sure if that was from the fire or from the nerves shimmering through her.

Will stood for a moment, watching the fire. When he seemed confident the log would burn, he turned back to her, his features impassive.

"Is something wrong?" she finally said, when the silence between them dragged on.

His sigh sounded deep, heartfelt. "You scare the hell out of me."

She tensed. "Do you want me to leave?"

"About as much as I want to take a table saw to my right arm," he admitted. "In other words, absolutely not."

Despite her nerves, she couldn't contain the laughter bubbling through her as he moved toward her and sat on the sofa beside her. He reached for her hand, but didn't seem in a rush to kiss her again.

This was lovely, she thought, sitting here gazing into the flickering firelight with a soft rain sliding against the window and his fingers tracing patterns on hers.

"I don't know if this is any consolation," she said after a moment, "but you're not the only one who's nervous. It's, uh, been a long time for me. I'd be surprised if you couldn't hear my knees knocking from there."

He gave her a careful look. "Do *you* want to leave?"

She mustered a shaky smile. "About as much as I want to *watch* you take a table saw to your right arm. In other words, absolutely not."

"Good," he murmured.

Finally he kissed her and at the delicious heat, the familiar taste and scent of him, her nerves disappeared. She was suddenly filled with the sweet assurance that this was right. She loved Will Garrett, had loved him since she was a stupid, naive girl.

She wanted this, wanted him, and even if this was all they would ever share, she wouldn't allow any regrets.

He kissed her until she was trembling, aching for more. She held him close, pouring all the emotions she couldn't verbalize into her kiss.

By the time he worked the buttons of her blouse, her head was whirling. When he pushed aside the lacy cups of her bra to touch her, she almost shattered apart right there as a torrent of sensations poured through her.

Oh, it had been far too long since she had remembered what it was to be touched with such heat and tenderness. She had forgotten this slow churn of her blood, the restless ache that seemed to fill every cell.

She arched against him, reveling in his hard strength against her curves, in his rough hands against her sensitive skin.

He groaned, low in his throat, and lowered his head to take her in his mouth. She clutched him close, her hands buried in his hair, as he teased and tasted.

His breathing was ragged when he lifted his clever, clever lips from her breast and found her mouth again while he shrugged out of his own shirt.

She couldn't help shivering as his hard strength covered her again.

"Are you still cold?" he murmured.

"Not even close," she answered, framing his face in her hands and kissing him fiercely. He responded with a groan and any tentativeness disappeared in a wild rush of heat.

In moments, they were both naked. Silhouetted in the dancing firelight, he was gorgeous, hard and muscled, ruggedly male.

"Okay, now I'm nervous again," she admitted.

"We can stop right now if you want," he said gruffly. "It might just kill me to let you out of my arms, but we don't have to go any further."

"No. I don't want to stop. Just kiss me again."

He willingly obeyed and for several long moments, only their mouths connected, then at last he pulled her close, trailing kisses from her mouth to the sensitive skin of her neck.

"Okay now?" he murmured, his body warm and hard against her.

"Oh, much, much better than okay," she breathed, her mouth tangling with his again as he pressed her back against the soft cushions of the sofa.

It was everything she might have dreamed—tender and passionate, sexy and sweet. When he filled her, she cried out, stunned at the emotions pouring through her, and she had to choke back the words of love she knew he wasn't ready to hear.

His mouth was hard and urgent on hers as he began to slowly move inside her and she lifted her hips to meet him.

Oh, she had missed this. She hadn't fully appreciated how much until right this moment.

How was she ever going to be able to go back to her solitary life?

She pushed the grim thought away, unwilling to let anything destroy the beauty of this moment.

He moved more deeply inside her and she gasped his name, feeling as breathless and shaky as the time she and Will had sneaked out to go cliff diving.

He withdrew then pushed inside her again and the contrast between the tenderness of his kiss and the wild urgency of his body sent her spinning and soaring over the edge.

With a groan, he joined her, his hands gripping hers tightly.

As they floated together back to earth, he shifted and pulled her on top of him, tugging a knit throw from the back of the sofa to cover them.

She nestled into his heat and his strength, a delicious lassitude soaking into her muscles, more content than she could ever remember being in her life.

SHE MUST HAVE slept for a few moments, tucked into the safe shelter of his arms. When she blinked her eyes open, the grandfather clock in the hallway was tolling midnight.

Like Cinderella, she knew the spell was ending and she would have to slip away home.

She shifted her gaze to Will and found him watching her. Was he regretting what they had shared? To her frustration, she could read nothing in his veiled expression.

She sat up, reaching for her blouse as she went. "I need to go back to Brambleberry House. Sage and Anna are going to be sending a search party out after me."

He sat up and she had to force herself to look away from that broad, enticing expanse of muscles.

"Oh, somehow I doubt that. I have a feeling they know exactly where you are."

"You're probably right," she answered ruefully. "A little on the spooky side, those two."

He raised an eyebrow as he slid into his jeans. "A little?"

She smiled. "Okay. A lot. I should still go, much as I don't want to."

He was quiet for a long moment, watching out of those veiled features as she worked the buttons of her shirt.

"Julia, I can't promise you anything," he finally said.

She met his gaze, doing her best to keep the devastation at bay. "You said that earlier, and I understand, Will. I do. I don't expect anything."

He raked a hand through his hair. "I'm just so damn

screwed up right now. I wish things could be otherwise. I'm just…"

She returned to him and cut his words off with a kiss, hoping he didn't taste the desperation in her kiss. This would be the one and only time for them, she knew.

He didn't have to say the words for her to accept the reality that nothing had changed. He was still leaving in a few days, and she would be left here alone with her pain.

"Will, it's okay," she lied. "My eyes were wide open when I walked into your house. No illusions here, I promise."

"I'm so sorry." His voice was tight with genuine regret and she shook her head.

"I'm not. Not for an instant."

She drew in a breath, gathering the last vestiges of courage left inside her for what somehow she suddenly knew she had to say.

"While we're tossing our cards out on the table, I think I should tell you why I'm here."

His expression turned wary. "Why?"

She sighed. "You haven't figured it out? I'm in love with you, Will."

The words hovered between them, raw and naked, and she had to smile a little at the sudden panic in his eyes.

"I know. It was a big shock for me, too. I'm not telling you that as some kind of underhanded tactic to convince you to stay. I know that nothing I say will change your mind and, believe me, I don't expect my feelings to change your decision in any way. I just felt that you should know. I wouldn't be here with you right now if I didn't love you—it's just not the kind of thing I do."

"I think some part of me guessed as much," he admitted.

"You've been in my heart for sixteen years, Will. Through my parents' divorce, through my own difficult teen years, through the breakup of my marriage, some part of me remembered that summer with you as a wonderful, magical time. Maybe the best summer of my life. You were my first love and I've never forgotten you."

"Julia…"

She shook her head, willing herself not to cry. Not now, not yet. "You don't have to say it. I know, we were different people then. And to be honest, the place you held in my heart was precious but only a tiny, dusty little spot, a corner I peeked into once in awhile with a smile and fond memories but then quickly forgot again."

She forced a smile. "And then I came back to Cannon Beach and here you were. As I came to know you all over again, I revisited those memories and realized that the boy I fell in love with back then had become a good, honorable man. A man who takes great pride in a job well done, who talks to dogs, who cares deeply about his neighbors and is kind to children…even when they make him bleed inside."

She touched his cheek, wishing with all her heart that he was ready to accept the precious, healing gift she so wanted to offer him.

Even as she touched him, though, she didn't miss his slight, barely perceptible flinch.

"Don't. Don't love me, Julia." His voice was ragged, anguished. "I'll only hurt you."

"I know you will." She managed a wobbly smile, even though she could swear she heard the sound of her heart cracking apart. "But I'll survive it."

She kissed him again, a soft, sincere benediction, then stepped away to shrug into her jacket. "I have to go."

He didn't argue, just pulled on his own shirt and boots. "I'll walk you back."

"I have Conan. I'll be fine."

"I'll walk you back," he said firmly.

She nodded, realizing that arguing with him would only be a waste of strength and energy, two commodities she had a feeling she would be needing in the days ahead.

In truth, she didn't mind. These were probably her last few moments with him and she wanted to savor every second.

Conan was again waiting expectantly by the back door. He cocked his head, his expression quizzical. She had no idea what he could read in their expressions but he whined a little.

More than anything, she wanted to bury her face in his fur and sob but she managed to keep her composure as Will handed her an umbrella and picked up a flashlight hanging on a hook by the door.

The slow, steady rain perfectly matched her mood. She shivered a little and zipped up her jacket, then headed toward Brambleberry House.

Will didn't share the umbrella—instead, he simply pulled the hood of his Gore-Tex jacket up, which given the dark and the rain effectively obscured his features.

They walked in silence and even Conan seemed subdued, almost sad. Instead of his usual ebullient energy, he plodded along beside her with his head hanging down.

As for Will, he seemed as distant and unreachable as the Cape Meares lighthouse.

She shouldn't have told him her feelings, she thought. He already carried enough burdens. He didn't need that one, too.

He finally spoke when they approached the gates of

Brambleberry House, but they weren't words she wanted to hear.

"Julia, I'm sorry," he said.

"Please don't be sorry we made love. I'm not."

"I should be. Sorry about that, I mean. But I'm not. It was…right. That's not what I meant. Mostly, I guess I'm sorry things can't be different, that we have all these years and pain between us."

She touched his cheek. "The years and the pain shaped us, Will. They're part of who we are now."

He turned his head and kissed her fingers, then pulled her into his arms once more. His kiss was tender, gentle, with an underlying note of finality to it. When he drew away, her throat ached with unshed tears.

"You're not leaving until after the wedding, are you?"

He nodded. "Sage would kill me if I missed her big day. My flight leaves the next morning."

"Well, I'll see you then, anyway. Goodbye, Will."

She had a million things she wanted to say but this wasn't the time. None of them would make a difference anyway.

Instead, she managed one last shaky smile and tugged Conan up the stairs and into the entry, forcing herself not to look back as she heard his muffled footsteps on the sidewalk.

Anna's apartment door opened the moment Julia closed the front door behind her, and Sage and Anna both peeked their heads out into the entryway. They had changed into pajamas and she could smell the aroma of popcorn from inside the apartment.

Conan hurried inside as soon as she unclipped his leash, probably looking for any stray kernels that might have been dropped. She would have smiled if she thought she could manage it.

"So?" Sage demanded. "What happened? You were gone *forever*. Did you talk Will into staying?"

As much as she had come to love both the other women in just the few short months she had been in Cannon Beach, she couldn't bear their curiosity right now, not when her emotions had been scraped to the bone.

"No," she said, her voice low. "His mind is made up."

Sage made a sound of disgust but Anna gave her a searching, entirely perceptive look. She was suddenly aware that her hair was probably a mess and she no doubt had whisker burns on her skin.

"It's not your fault, Julia," she said after a moment. "I'm sure you tried your best."

She fought an almost hysterical urge to laugh. To hide it, she yanked off her jacket and hung it back in the closet. "He has his reasons. He didn't take the job with Eben on a whim, I can promise you that."

"That still doesn't make it right!" Sage exclaimed.

"As people who…who care about him, we owe it to Will to respect his decision, even if we don't agree with it or think it's necessarily the best one for him."

Sage looked as if she wanted to argue but Anna silenced her with a long, steady look.

"He won't change his mind?" Anna asked.

"I don't think so," Julia said.

To her surprise, though Sage was usually the demonstrative one, this time Anna was the one who pulled her into her arms for a hug. "Thanks for trying. I know it was hard for you."

You have no idea, she thought, even as Sage hugged her as well. For just a moment, Julia thought she smelled freesia and it was almost as if Abigail herself was there offering understanding and comfort.

"Don't badger him about it, okay?" she said. "It was a hard decision for him to make but I think taking the job is something he...he needs to do right now."

"Are you okay?" Anna murmured.

For one terrible moment, the sympathy in her friend's voice almost made her weep but she blinked away the tears. "Fine. Just fine. Why wouldn't I be?"

Anna didn't look convinced but to her immense relief, she didn't push. "You look exhausted. You'd better get some rest."

She nodded with a grateful look. "It's been a long day," she agreed. "Good night."

She quickly turned and hurried up the stairs, praying she could make it inside before breaking down.

After she closed the door behind her, she checked on the twins and found them sleeping peacefully, then returned to the darkened living room. Against her will, she moved to the windows overlooking his house and saw lights on again in his workshop.

The thought of him in his solitary workshop by himself, putting the finishing touches on Maddie's spectacular dollhouse was the last straw. Tears slid down her cheeks to match the rain trickling down the window and she stood for a long time in the dark, aching and alone.

CHAPTER FIFTEEN

THREE DAYS LATER, he stood on the edge of the dance floor in the elegant reception room of The Sea Urchin, doing his level best not to spend the entire evening staring at Julia like the lovesick teenager he had once been.

He hadn't seen her since the night they had shared together but he was quite certain he hadn't spent more than ten minutes without thinking about her—remembering the softness of her skin, her sweet response to him, the shock that had settled in gut when she told him she loved him.

Just now she was dancing with her son, laughing as she tried to show him the steps of the fox-trot. She looked bright and vibrant and beautiful in a lovely, flowing green dress that matched her eyes. Despite her apparent enjoyment in the evening, he was almost certain he had caught a certain sadness in her eyes whenever their gazes happened to collide, and his heart ached, knowing he had put it there.

He couldn't stay much longer. He was leaving in the morning and still had work to do packing and closing up his house for an indefinite time. Beyond that, it hurt more than he ever would have dreamed to keep his distance from Julia, to stand on the sidelines and watch her, knowing he could never have her.

He needed to at least talk to Sage before he escaped, he knew. When the music ended and she returned to the edge of the dance floor on the arm of ancient Mr. Delarosa, one of Abigail's old friends, he hurried to claim her before anyone else.

"Have any dances left for an old friend?"

Surprise flickered in her eyes, then she gave him a brilliant smile. "Of course!"

He wasn't much of a dancer but he did his best, grateful at least that it was another slow song and he wasn't going to have to make an idiot out of himself by trying to shake and groove.

"You make a stunning bride, kiddo," he said when they fell into a rhythm. "Who ever would have believed it?"

He gave an exaggerated wince when she punched him lightly in the shoulder.

"You know I'm teasing," he said, squeezing the fingers he held. "I'm thrilled for you and Eben, Sage. I really am. You're a beautiful bride and it was a beautiful ceremony."

"It was, wasn't it? I only wish Abigail could have been here."

"I don't doubt she was, in her own way."

She smiled, as he intended. "I think you're probably right. I was quite sure I smelled freesia at least once while Eben and I were exchanging our vows."

"I'm glad the weather held for you." It had been a gorgeous, sunny day, warm and lovely, a rarity on the coast for October.

"I thought for sure we were going to have to move everything inside for the ceremony but the weather couldn't have been more perfect."

"That's because Mother Nature knows she owes you big-time for all your do-gooder, save-the-world efforts. She wouldn't dare ruin your big day with rain."

She laughed softly then sobered quickly. "I forgot, I'm not supposed to be speaking to you. I'm still mad at you."

"Don't start, Sage. We've been over this. I'm going. But it's not forever—I'll be back."

"It won't be the same."

"Nothing will. Look at you, Mrs. Spencer. You're moving to San Francisco with Eben and Chloe. Things change, Sage."

"I'm going to miss you, darn it. You're the big, annoying, overprotective brother I've always wanted, Will."

He was more touched than he would dare admit. "And since the day you moved in to Brambleberry House, you've been like a bratty little sister to me, always sure you know what's best for everyone."

She made a harumph kind of sound. "That's because I do. For instance, I am quite certain you're making a huge mistake to leave Cannon Beach and a certain resident of Brambleberry House who shall remain nameless."

"Who? Conan?"

She smacked his shoulder again. "You know who I mean. Julia."

He shook his head. "Leave it alone, Sage."

"I won't." She stuck her chin out with a stubbornness he should have expected, knowing Sage. "If Abigail were here, she would tell you the exact same thing. You can't lie to me, you have feelings for Julia, don't you?"

"None of your business. This is a great band, by the way. Where did you find them?"

"I didn't, Jade Wu did. You know perfectly well she handled all the wedding details. And I won't let you change the subject. What kind of idiot walks away from a woman as fabulous as Julia, who just happens to be crazy about him?"

"I'm going to leave you right here in the middle of the dance floor if you don't back off," he warned her. Though he spoke amicably enough, he put enough steel in his voice that he hoped she got the message.

She gave him a piercing look and then her gaze suddenly softened. "You're as miserable as she is! You know you are."

He shifted his gaze to Julia, who was dancing and smiling with the owner of the bike shop—who just happened to be the biggest player in town.

"She doesn't look miserable to me."

They were several couples away from them on the dance floor, but just at that moment, her partner swung her around so she was facing him. They made eye contact and for one sizzling moment, it was as if they were alone in the room.

He caught his breath, snared by those deep green eyes for a long moment, until her partner turned her again.

"She does a pretty good job of hiding it, but she is," Sage said.

She paused, then met his gaze. "Did I ever tell you how I almost lost Eben and Chloe because I was too afraid of being hurt to let them inside my heart?"

"I don't think you did," he said stiffly.

"It's a long story but look at the happy ending, just because I decided Eben's love was worth far more to me than my pride. You're the most courageous man I know, Will. You've walked through hell these last few years. I know that, know that you've endured more than anyone should have to—a pain that most of us probably couldn't even guess at. Don't you think you've been through enough? You deserve happiness. Do you really think you're going to find it traveling around the world, leaving behind your home and everyone who loves you?"

"I don't know," he said, more struck by her words than he cared to admit. "But I'm going anyway. This is your wedding day. I don't want to fight with you about this. I appreciate your concern for me, but everything will be fine."

She sighed and probably would have said more but Eben came up behind them at that moment.

"What does a guy have to do to get a dance with his bride?"

"Just ask," Will said. "She's all yours."

He kissed Sage on the cheek and released her. "Thanks for the dance and the advice," he said. "Congratulations again to both of you."

Much as he loved her, he was relieved to walk away and leave her to Eben. He didn't need more of her lectures about how he was making a mistake to leave or her not-so-subtle hints about Julia.

What he needed was to get out of here, and soon. He couldn't take much more.

He made it almost to the door when he felt a sharp tug on his jacket. He turned around and found Maddie Blair standing beside him wearing a frilly blue party dress and a blazing smile.

His heart caught just a little but he probed around and realized he no longer had the piercing pain he used to whenever he saw Julia's dark-haired daughter.

"Hi," she said.

He forced himself to smile back. "Hi yourself."

"I had to tell you how much I love, love, *love* my doll-house. It's the best dollhouse in the whole world! Thank you so much!"

"I'm glad you like it."

"Did you know it has a doorbell that really works? And it even has a secret closet in the bedroom that you open a special way."

"I believe I did know that."

He had finally finished the dollhouse late into the night two days before and had dropped it off at Brambleberry House, leaving it covered with a tarp on the porch for Julia to find. He knew it was cowardly to drop it off in the middle of the night. He should have picked a time when he could help carry it up the stairs for her, but he hadn't been able to face her.

"I would like to dance with you," Maddie announced, leaving him no room for arguments.

"Um, sure," he said, not knowing how to wiggle out of it. "I'd like that."

It wasn't even a lie, he realized to his surprise. He held out his arm in a formal kind of gesture and she grinned and slipped her hand into the crook of his elbow. Together they worked their way through the crowd to the dance floor.

While they danced, Maddie kept up an endless stream of conversation during the dance—about her dolls, about how she was going to go visit Chloe in San Francisco some time, about some mischief her brother had been up to.

He listened to her light chatter while the music poured around him, making appropriate comments whenever she stopped to take a breath.

"You're the best dancer I've danced with tonight," she said when the song was almost at an end. "Simon stepped on my toes a million times and I think he even broke one. And Chloe's dad wouldn't stop looking at Sage the whole time we danced. I think that's rude, don't you, even if they did just get married. Grown-ups are weird."

Will couldn't help it, he looked down at Maddie's animated little face and laughed out loud.

"You have a nice laugh," she observed, watching him through her wise little eyes that had endured too much. "I like it."

"Thanks," he answered, a little taken aback.

"You know what?" she whispered, as if confiding state secrets, and he had to bend his head a little lower to hear her, until their faces were almost touching.

"What?" he whispered back.

"I like you, too." She smiled at him, then before he realized what she intended, she stood on her tiptoes and kissed his cheek.

He stared at her as her words seemed to curl through him, squeezing the air from his lungs and sending all the careful barriers he thought he had built around his heart tumbling with one big, hard shove.

"Thanks," he finally said around the golf ball-size lump in his throat. "I, uh, like you, too."

It wasn't quite true, he realized with shock. His feelings for this little girl and her brother ran deeper than simple affection.

He had tried so hard to keep them all at bay but somehow when he wasn't looking, Julia's twins had sneaked into his heart. He cared about them—Simon, with his inquisitive mind and his eagerness to please, and Maddie with her unrelenting courage and the simple joy she seized from life.

How the hell had he let such a thing happen? He thought he had been so careful around them to keep his distance but something had gone terribly wrong.

He remembered Maddie offering to eat her ice cream slowly so he could have a taste if he wanted, Simon talking about baseball and inviting him to watch a Mariners' game, budding hero worship in his eyes.

He loved Julia's children.

Just as he loved their mother.

He stopped stock-still on the dance floor. It *couldn't* be true. It couldn't. His gaze found Julia, standing at the refreshment table talking to Anna. She looked graceful and lovely. When she felt his gaze, she turned and gave him a tentative smile and he suddenly wanted nothing more than he wanted to yank her into his arms and carry her out of here.

"Are you okay, Mr. Garrett?" Maddie asked.

"I…yes. Thank you for the dance," he said, his voice stiff.

"You're welcome. Will you come play Barbies with me sometime?"

He had to get out of there, right now. The noise and the crowd were pressing in on him, suffocating him.

"Maybe. I'll see you later, okay?"

She nodded and smiled, then slipped away. On his way out the door, his gaze caught Julia's one more time and he hoped to hell the shock of his newfound feelings didn't show in his expression.

She gave him another tentative smile, which he acknowledged with a jerky nod, then he slipped out the door.

He climbed into his pickup in a kind of daze and pulled out of The Sea Urchin's parking lot in the pale twilight, not knowing where he was heading, only that he had to get away. He thought he was driving aimlessly, following the curve of the ocean, but before he quite realized it, he found himself at the small cemetery at twilight, just as the sunset turned the waves a soft, pale blue.

He parked outside the gates, knowing he didn't have long since the cemetery was supposed to be closed after dark. Leaves crunched underfoot as he followed the familiar path, listening to the quiet reverence of the place.

He stopped at his father's grave first, under the spreading boughs of a huge, majestic oak tree. It was a fitting resting place for a man who could work such magic with his hands and a piece of wood. He stopped, head bowed, remembering the many lessons he had learned from his father. Work hard, play hard, cherish your family.

Not a bad mantra for a man to follow.

After long moments, he let out a breath and walked over a small hill to Abigail's grave, decorated with many tokens of affection. Sage had left her a wedding invitation, he saw, and a flower from her bouquet, and Will couldn't help smiling.

He saved the toughest for last. With emotion churning through him, he followed the trail around another curve, almost to the edge by the fence, where two simple headstones marked Robin's and Cara's graves.

He hadn't been here in a few months, he realized with some shock. Right after the accident he used to come here every day, sometimes twice a day. He had hated it, but he had come. Those visits had dwindled but he had always tried to come at least once a week to bring his wife whatever flowers were in season.

Like Abigail, Robin had loved flowers.

Guilt coursed through him as he realized how he had neglected his responsibilities.

He rounded the last corner and there they were, silhouetted in the dying sun. Two simple markers—Robin

Cramer Garrett, beloved wife. Cara Robin Garrett, cherished daughter.

Emotions clogged his throat. Oh, he missed them. He walked closer, then he blinked in shock, certain the dusky twilight must be playing tricks with his eyesight.

A few weeks after the accident, Abigail had asked him if she could plant a rosebush between Robin's and Cara's graves. He had been wild with grief, inconsolable, and wouldn't have cared whether she planted a whole damn flower garden, so he had given his consent.

He hadn't paid it much attention, other than to note a few times in the summer that if she had still been alive, Abigail would have been devastated to know she must have planted a sterile bush. He hadn't seen a single bloom on it in two years.

Now, though, as he stood in the cool October air, he stared in shock at the rosebush. It was covered in flowers—hundreds of them, in a rich, vibrant yellow.

This couldn't be right. He didn't know a hell of a lot about horticulture but he was fairly certain roses bloomed in summer. It was mid-October now, and had been colder than usual the last few weeks, rainy and dank.

It made absolutely no sense but he couldn't ignore the evidence in front of him. Abigail's roses were sending their lush, sweet fragrance into the air, stirring gently in a soft breeze.

Let go, Will. Life moves on.

He could almost swear he heard Abigail's words on the breeze, her voice as brisk and no-nonsense as always.

He sank down onto the wooden bench he had built and stared at the flower-heavy boughs, softly caressing the marble markers.

Let go.

His breathing ragged, he gazed at the flowers, stunned by the emotion pouring through him like a cleansing, healing rainstorm, something he hadn't known since his family was taken from him with such sudden cruelty.

Hope.

It was hope.

These roses seemed a perfect symbol of it, a precious gift Abigail had left behind just for him, as if she knew that somehow he would need to see those blossoms at exactly this moment in his life to remind him of things he had lost along the way.

Hope, faith. Love.

Life moves on.

Whether he was ready for it or not, he loved Julia Blair and her children. They had showed him that his life was not over, that if he could only find the courage, his future didn't have to be this grim, empty existence.

She had roared back into his life like a hurricane, blowing away all the shadows and darkness, the bone-deep misery that had been his companion for two years.

He couldn't say the idea of loving her and her kids still didn't scare the hell out of him. He had already lost more than he could bear. But the idea of living without them—of going back to his gray and cheerless life—scared him more.

He sat on the bench for a long time while the cemetery darkened and the roses danced and swayed in the breeze, surrounding him with their sweet perfume.

When at last he stood up, his cheeks were wet but his heart felt a million times lighter. He headed for the cemetery gates, with only one destination in mind.

CHAPTER SIXTEEN

"MAMA, I JUST love weddings." Though she was drooping with fatigue, Maddie's eyes were bright as Julia helped her out of her organza dress.

"It was lovely, wasn't it?"

"Sage was so pretty in her dress. She looked like an angel. And Chloe did a good job throwing the flower petals, didn't she? She didn't even look one bit nervous!"

Julia smiled at Maddie's enthusiasm. "She was the best flower girl I've ever seen."

"Do you think when you get married, I could wear a dress like Chloe's and throw flower petals, too?"

She winced, not at all sure how to answer. "Um, honey, I've already been married, to your dad," she finally said.

"But you could get married again, couldn't you? Chloe said you could because her dad was already married before, too, to her mom. Then her mom died just like Daddy and now her dad is married again to Sage."

Julia forced a smile. "Isn't it lucky he found Sage?"

She, on the other hand, had given her heart to Will Garrett, wholly and completely, and somehow she knew she would never be able to love anyone else. Will wasn't ready for it. For all she knew, he would *never* be ready. If Will couldn't bring himself to love her back, she was afraid she would spend the rest of her life alone.

But she wasn't about to confide her heartache to her daughter. "You need to get to sleep, kiddo. It's been a big day and I know you're tired. Simon's already in his bed, sound asleep."

She helped Maddie into her nightgown and was tucking her under the covers when Maddie touched her hand.

"Mama, I think you should marry Mr. Garrett."

Julia nearly tripped over Maddie's slippers in her astonishment. "Wh…why would you say that?"

"Well, lots of reasons. He smells nice and I just love the dollhouse he made me."

Not the worst reasons for a seven-year-old girl to come up with to marry a man, she supposed.

"And maybe if you married him, he wouldn't be so sad all the time. You make him smile, Mama. I know you do."

Tears burned in her eyelids at Maddie's confident statement and she knelt down to fold her daughter into her arms.

"Go to sleep, pumpkin," she said through the emotions clogging her throat. "I'll see you in the morning."

She turned off the light and closed her door, then moved to Simon's room to check on him. He was sleeping soundly, his blankets already a tangle at his waist. She tucked them back over his shoulders then returned to the living room, lit only by a small lamp next to her Stickley rocking chair.

Though she tried to fight the impulse, she finally gave in and moved to the window overlooking Will's house. No lights were on there, she saw. Was he asleep already?

He was leaving in the morning. Maybe he intended to get a solid night's rest for traveling across the country.

The emotions Maddie had stirred in her finally broke free and she felt tears trickling down her cheeks. He hadn't said a word to her all day. She had felt his gaze several times, both during the ceremony and then after at the reception, but he hadn't approached her.

After his dance with Maddie, she had intended to track him down—if only to tell him goodbye before he left for his new job—but he had rushed out of The Sea Urchin so fast she hadn't had the chance.

She didn't need a pile of two-by-fours to fall on her head to figure out he didn't want to talk to her again.

She swiped at her tears with her palm. He hadn't even left town yet and she already missed him like crazy. Despite her determined claims to him that she wouldn't regret making love, she couldn't deny that the tender intimacy they had shared had only ratcheted up her pain to a near-unbearable level.

Sage's joy today had only served to reinforce to Julia that she was unlikely ever to know that kind of happiness with Will. He might have opened up his emotions to her a few nights ago but now they were as tightly locked and shoved away as they had been since she returned to town. If she needed proof, she only had to look at the careful distance he maintained at the wedding.

What a strange journey she had traveled since making the decision to return to Cannon Beach. She never would have guessed when she took that teaching job several months ago that she would find love and heartbreak all in one convenient package.

He was leaving in the morning and she could do nothing to stop him.

She sobbed, just a little, then the sound caught in her throat when she suddenly thought she smelled freesia.

"Oh, Abigail," she murmured. "I wish you were here

to tell me what to do, how I can reach Will. I don't think I can bear this."

Silence met her impassioned plea, but an instant later she jumped a mile when she felt something wet brush her hand.

"Conan! You scared the life out of me! Where were you?"

The dog had followed her and the twins upstairs when they returned to Brambleberry House from the wedding, apparently needing company since Anna was still busy cleaning up at the reception and Sage and Eben were staying at The Sea Urchin for the night until they left for their honeymoon in the Galapagos in the morning.

He must have gone into her room to lie down, since she hadn't seen him when she came out of Simon's room and had forgotten he was even there. Still, she had to admit she was grateful for the company. The dog leaned against her leg, offering his own unique kind of support and sympathy.

"Thanks," she whispered, as they sat together in her dim apartment looking out at the lights of town.

But his steady comfort didn't last long. After a moment, his ears pricked up and he suddenly barked and rushed for the door, his tail wagging.

She sighed. "You want to go out *again?* We let you out when we came home!"

He whined a little and watched her out of those curiously intelligent eyes. With a sigh, she abandoned any fleeting hope she might have briefly entertained about sinking into a hot bubble bath to soak away her misery, for a while anyway.

"All right, you crazy dog. Just let me find some shoes first."

She had changed after the reception into worn jeans and her oldest, most comfortable sweater. Now she grabbed tennis shoes and headed down the stairs.

The moment she opened the outside door, Conan rocketed down the porch steps and toward the front gate, then disappeared from sight.

Oh rats. She forgot to check that the gate was still closed. Conan usually stuck close to home, preferring his own territory, but if he smelled a cat anywhere in the vicinity, all bets were off.

What was she supposed to do now? No one else was home, the twins were sleeping upstairs and the dog was loose. She couldn't let him wander free, though.

"Conan," she called. "Get back here."

He barked from what sounded like just the other side of the ironwork fence, but she couldn't see him in the darkness.

"Here, boy. Come on."

He didn't respond to the command and with a sigh, she headed down the sidewalk, hoping he wasn't in the mood for a playful game of tag. She wasn't at all in the mood to chase him.

"Come on, Conan. It's cold." She walked through the gate, then froze when she saw in the moonlight just why the dog hadn't answered her summons.

He was busy greeting a man who stood silent and watchful on the other side of the fence.

Will.

She stared at him, stunned to find him here, tonight, and wondering if she had left any evidence of the tears she had just shed for him. All those emotions just under the surface threatened to break through again—sorrow and regret, doubt, sadness.

Love.

Especially love.

She wanted to go to him, throw her arms around his waist and beg him not to leave.

"I didn't see you there," she said instead, hoping her emotional tumult didn't show up in her voice.

He said nothing, just continued to pet the dog and watch her. She walked a little closer.

"Is everything okay?"

"No." His voice sounded hoarse, ragged. "I don't think it is."

He stepped closer to her, so near she could smell the scent of his aftershave, sexy and male. Her heart, already pounding hard since the instant she saw him standing in the darkness, picked up a pace.

"What is it?"

He was quiet for a long time—so long she was beginning to worry something was seriously wrong. Finally, to her immense shock he reached out and grasped her fingers and pulled her even closer.

"I had to come. Had to see you."

"Why?"

His slow sigh stirred her hair. "I love you, Julia."

"Wh-what did you say?" She jerked her hand away and scrambled back. Her heartbeat accelerated and she couldn't seem to catch her breath as shock rippled through her.

He raked a hand through his hair. "I didn't mean to just blurt it out like that. I must sound like an idiot."

"I'm… I'm sorry. You don't sound like an idiot. I just… I wasn't expecting that. You're leaving tomorrow. Aren't you leaving?"

A tiny flutter of joy started in her heart but she was

afraid to let it free, afraid he would only crush it and leave her feeling worse than ever.

"Yes. I'm leaving."

She expected his words but they still scored her heart. He said he loved her, but he was leaving anyway?

"I wish I didn't have to go but I gave my word to Eben and I'm committed, at least for a few weeks, until he can find someone else to take my place."

He reached for her hand again and she could feel her fingers trembling in his hard, callused palm. "And then I'd like to come back. To Cannon Beach and to you."

While she was still reeling from his words, he paused, then touched her cheek softly. "You were so right about everything you've said to me. I need to move forward, to give myself the freedom to taste all life has to offer again. It's time. I've known it's time, but I've been so afraid. That's a tough thing for a man to admit, but it's the truth. I was afraid to let myself love you, afraid I was somehow…betraying Robin and Cara by all the feelings I was starting to have for you."

She squeezed his fingers. "Oh, Will. You'll never stop loving them. I would never ask that of you. That's exactly the way it should be. But the heart is a magical thing. Abigail taught me that. When you're ready, when you need it to, it can miraculously expand to make room."

He studied her for a long moment and then suddenly he smiled. Only when she saw his mouth tilt, saw the genuine happiness in his expression, did she realize he truly meant what he said. *He loved her.* She still couldn't quite absorb it, but his eyes in the soft moonlight were free of any lingering grief and sorrow.

He loved her.

He cupped his hands around her face and kissed her

then, soft and gentle in the cool October air. She wrapped her arms around his waist as a sweet, cleansing joy exploded through her.

"My heart has made room for you, Julia. For you and your beautiful children. How could it help but find a place? You already had your own corner there sixteen years ago. I think some part of me was just waiting for you to return and move back in."

His mouth found hers again, and in his kiss she tasted joy and healing and the promise of a sweet, beautiful future.

Not far away, a huge mongrel dog sat on his haunches watching them both with satisfaction in his eyes while the soft, flowery scent of freesia floated in the autumn air.

* * * * *

A SOLDIER'S SECRET

To my brothers, Maj. Brad Robinson, US Air Force, and high school teacher and coach Mike Robinson. Both of you are heroes!

CHAPTER ONE

LIGHTS WERE ON in her attic—lights that definitely hadn't been gleaming when she left that morning.

A cold early March breeze blew off the ocean, sending dead leaves skittering across the road in front of her headlights and twisting and yanking the boughs of the Sitka spruce around Brambleberry House as Anna Galvez pulled into the driveway, behind an unfamiliar vehicle.

The lights and the vehicle could only mean one thing.

Her new tenant had arrived.

She sighed. She *so* didn't need this right now. Exhaustion pressed on her shoulders with heavy, punishing hands and she wanted nothing but to slip into a warm bath with a mind-numbing glass of wine.

The day had been beyond ghastly. She could imagine few activities more miserable than spending an entire humiliating day sitting in a Lincoln City courtroom being confronted with the unavoidable evidence of her own stupidity.

And now, despite her battered ego and fragile psyche, she had to go inside and make nice with a stranger who wouldn't even be renting the top floor of Brambleberry House if not for the tangled financial mess that stupidity had caused.

In the backseat, Conan gave one sharp bark, though

she didn't know if he was anxious at the unfamiliar vehicle parked in front of them or just needed to answer the call of nature.

Since they had been driving for an hour, she opted for the latter and hurried out into the wet cold to open the sliding door of her minivan. The big shaggy beast she inherited nearly a year earlier, along with the rambling Victorian in front of her, leaped out in one powerful lunge.

Tail wagging, he rushed immediately to sniff around the SUV that dared to enter his territory without his permission. He lifted his leg before she could kick-start her brain and Anna winced.

"Conan, get away from there," she called sternly. He sent her a quizzical look, then gave a disgruntled snort before lowering his leg and heading to one of his favorite trees instead.

She really hoped her new tenant didn't mind dogs.

She hated the idea of a stranger in Sage's apartment. If she had her way, she would keep it empty, even though Sage and her husband and stepdaughter had their own beach house now a half mile down the shore for their frequent visits to Cannon Beach from their San Francisco home.

But after Anna vehemently refused to accept financial help from Sage and Eben, Sage had insisted she at least rent out her apartment to help defray costs.

The two of them were co-owners of the house and Sage's opinion certainly had weight. Besides, Anna was nothing if not practical. The apartment was empty, she had a fierce, unavoidable need for income and she knew many people were willing to pay a premium for furnished beachfront living space.

Army Lieutenant Harry Maxwell among them.

She gazed up at the lights cutting through the twilight

from the third-story window. She was going to have to go up there and welcome him to Brambleberry House. No question. It was the right thing to do, even if the long, exhausting day in that courtroom had left her as bedraggled and wrung-out as one of Conan's tennis balls after a good hard game of fetch on the beach.

She might want to do nothing but climb into her bed, yank the covers over her head and weep for her shattered dreams and her own stupidity, but she had to put all that aside for now and do the polite thing.

She grabbed her laptop case from the passenger seat just as her cell phone rang. Anna swallowed a groan when she saw the name and phone number.

She wasn't sure what was worse—making nice with a stranger now living in her home or being forced to carry on a conversation with the bubbly real estate agent who had facilitated the whole deal.

With grim resignation, she opened her phone and connected the call. "Anna Galvez speaking."

"Anna! It's Tracy Harder!"

Even if she hadn't already noted Tracy's information on the caller ID, she would have recognized the other woman's perky enthusiasm in an instant.

"So have you seen him yet?" Tracy asked.

Anna screwed her eyes shut as if she could just make those upstairs lights—and Tracy—disappear. "I just pulled up to the house, Tracy. I've been in Lincoln City all day. I haven't had a chance to even walk into the house yet. So, no, I haven't seen him. I'm planning to go up to say hello in a moment."

"You are the luckiest woman in town right now. I mean it! You have absolutely *no* idea."

"You're right," she said, unable to keep the dry note

out of her voice. "But I'm willing to bet you're about to enlighten me."

Tracy gave a low, sultry laugh. "I know we didn't mention a finder's fee on top of my usual property management commission, but you just might want to kick a bonus over my way after you meet him. The man is gorgeous. Yum, that's all I have to say. *Yum!*"

Just what she needed. A player who would probably be entertaining a long string of model types at all hours of the day and night. "As long as he pays his rent on time and only needs a two-month lease, I don't care what he looks like."

"That's because you haven't met him yet. How much longer will Julia Blair and her kids be renting the second floor? I might be interested when she moves out— I'd love to be beneath that man."

Anna couldn't help her groan, both at Tracy's not so subtle sexual innuendo and at the idea of the real estate agent's wild boys living in the second-floor apartment.

"Julia and Will aren't getting married until June," she answered. With any luck, Lieutenant Maxwell would be long gone by then, leaving behind only his nice fat rental check.

"When she moves out, let me know. That might be a good time for us to talk about a more long-term solution to Brambleberry House. You can't keep taking in temporary renters to pay for the repairs on it. The place is a black hole that will suck away every penny you have."

Didn't she just know it? Anna let herself in the front door, noting that the paint on the porch was starting to crack and peel.

Replacing the furnace the month before had taken just about her last dime of discretionary income—not that she had much of that, as she tried to shore up her faltering business amid scandal and chicanery. The house needed a new roof, which was going to cost more than buying a brand-new car.

"Now listen," Tracy went on in her ear as Anna opened the door to her apartment to set down her laptop, Conan on her heels. "I told you I've got several fabulous potential buyers on the hook with both the cash and the interest in a great old Victorian on the coast. You need to think about it, Anna. I mean it."

"I guess I didn't realize there was such a market for big black holes these day."

Tracy laughed. "When you have enough money, no hole is too big or too black."

And when you had none, even a pothole could feel like an insurmountable obstacle. Anna swallowed another sigh. "I appreciate the offer and your help finding a tenant for the attic apartment."

"But you're not interested in selling." Tracy's voice was resigned.

"Not right now."

"You're as stubborn as Abigail was. I'm telling you, Anna, you're sitting on a gold mine."

"I know." She sat down in Abigail's favorite armchair. "But for now it's my gold mine. Mine and Sage's."

"All right, but when you change your mind, you know where to find me. And I want you to call me after you meet our Lieutenant Maxwell."

As far as Anna was concerned, the man wasn't *our* anything. Tracy was welcome to him. "Thanks again for dealing with the details of the rental agreement," she answered. "I'll let you know how things are going in a week or two. 'Bye, Tracy."

She ended the call and set down her phone, then leaned her head back against the floral upholstery. Conan sat beside her and, like the master manipulator he was, nudged one of her hands off the armrest and onto his head.

She scratched him between the ears for a moment, trying to let the peace she usually found at Brambleberry House seep through her. After a few moments— just when her eyelids were drifting closed—Conan slid away from her and moved to the door. He planted his haunches there and watched her expectantly.

"Yeah, I know, already," she grumbled. "I plan to go upstairs and say hello. I don't need you nagging me about it. I just need a minute to work up to it."

Still, she climbed out of the chair. After a check in the mirror above the hall tree, she did a quick repair of her French twist, grabbed Conan's leash off the hook by the door and put it on him, then headed up the stairs to meet her new neighbor.

As she trailed her fingers on the railing worn smooth by a hundred years of Dandridge hands, she reviewed what she knew about the man. Though Tracy had handled the details, Anna knew Lieutenant Maxwell had impeccable references.

He was an army helicopter pilot who had just served two tours of duty in the Middle East. He was currently on medical leave, recovering from injuries sustained in a hard landing in the midst of enemy fire.

He was single, thirty-five years old and willing to pay a great deal of money to rent her attic for only a few months.

When Tracy told her his background, Anna wanted to reduce the rent. She was squeamish about charging full price to an injured war veteran, but he refused to accept any concession.

Fine, she thought now as she paused on the third-floor landing. But she could still be gracious and welcoming to the man and hope that he would find the healing and peace at Brambleberry House that she usually did.

Outside his door, the scent of freesia curled around her and she closed her eyes for a moment, missing Abigail with a fierce ache. Conan didn't let her wallow in it. He gave a sharp bark and started wagging his tail furiously.

With a sigh, Anna knocked on the door. A moment later, it swung open and she forgot all about being kind and welcoming.

Tracy had told the God's-honest truth.

Yum.

Lieutenant Maxwell was tall—perhaps six-two—with hair the color of aged whiskey and chiseled, lean features. He wore a burgundy cotton shirt and faded jeans with a small, fraying hole below the knee.

He had a small scar on the outside of his right eye that only made him look vaguely piratelike and his right arm was encased in a dark blue sling.

The man was definitely gorgeous, but there was something more to it. If she had passed him on the street, she would have called him compelling, especially his eyes. She gazed into their hazel depths and felt an odd tug of recognition. For a brief, flickering moment, he seemed so familiar she wondered if they had met before.

The question registered for all of maybe two seconds before Conan suddenly began barking an enthusiastic welcome and lunged for Lieutenant Maxwell as if they were lifelong friends.

"Conan, sit," she ordered, disconcerted by her dog's reaction. He wasn't one for jumping all over strangers. Despite his moods and his uncanny intelligence, Conan was usually well-mannered, but just now he strained against the leash as if he wanted to knock her new tenant to the ground and lick his face off.

"Sit!" she ordered, more sternly this time. Conan gave her a disgruntled look, then plopped his butt to the floor.

"Good dog. I'm sorry," she said, feeling flustered. "Hi. You must be Harry Maxwell, right?"

Something flashed in his eyes, too quickly for her to identify it, but she thought he looked uncomfortable.

After a moment, he nodded. "Yeah."

With that single syllable, he sounded as cold and remote as Tillamook Rock. She blinked, not quite sure how to respond. He obviously didn't want to be best friends here, he was only renting her empty apartment, she reminded herself.

Despite Conan's sudden ardor, it was probably better all the way around if they all maintained a careful distance during the duration of Harry Maxwell's rental agreement. He was only here for a short time and then he would probably head back to active duty. No need for unnecessarily messy entanglements.

Taking her cue from his own reaction, she forced her voice to be brisk, professional. "I'm Anna Galvez, one of the owners of Brambleberry House. This is my dog, Conan. I don't know what's come over him. I'm sorry. He's not usually so…ardent…with strangers. Every once in a while he greets somebody like an old friend. I can't explain it but I'm very sorry if his exuberance makes you uncomfortable."

He unbent enough to reach down and scratch the dog's chin, which had the beast's tail thumping against the floor in ecstasy.

"Conan? Like the barbarian?" he asked.

"Actually, like the talk-show host. It's a long story."

One he obviously wasn't interested in hearing about, if the remote expression on his handsome features was any indication.

She tugged Conan's leash when he tried to wrap himself around the soldier's legs and after another disgruntled moment, the dog condescended enough to sit beside her. "I'm sorry I wasn't here when you arrived so I could show you around. I wasn't expecting you for a day or two."

"My plans changed. I was released from the military hospital a few days earlier than I expected. Since I didn't have anywhere else to go right now, I decided to head out here."

How sad, she thought. Didn't he have any family eager to give him a hero's welcome?

"Since I was early, I planned to get a hotel room for a couple days," he added, "but the property management company said the apartment was ready and available."

"It is. Everything's fine. I'm just sorry I wasn't here."

"The real estate agent handled everything."

Not everything Tracy probably *wanted* to handle, Anna mused, then was slightly ashamed of herself for the base thought.

This whole situation felt so awkward, so out of her comfort zone.

"You were able to find everything you needed?" she asked. "Towels, sheets, whatever?"

He shrugged. "So far."

"The kitchen is fully stocked with cookware and so forth but if you can't find something, let me know."

"I'll do that."

Despite his terse responses, Anna was disconcerted by

her awareness of him. He was so big, so overwhelmingly male. She would be glad when the few months were up, though apparently Conan was infatuated with the man.

She had a sudden fierce wish that Tracy had found a nice older lady to rent the attic apartment to, but somehow she doubted too many older ladies were interested in climbing forty steps to get to their apartment.

Thinking of the steps reminded her of his injury and she nodded toward the sling on his shoulder. "I'm really sorry I wasn't here to help you carry up boxes. I guess you managed all right."

"I don't have much. A duffel and a suitcase. I'm only here for a short time."

"I know, but it's still two long flights of stairs."

She thought annoyance flickered in his eyes, as if he didn't like being reminded of his injury, but he quickly hid it.

"I handled things," he said.

"Well, if you ever need help carrying groceries up or anything or if you would just like the name of a good doctor around here, just let me know."

"I'm fine. I don't need anything. Just a quiet place to hang for a while until I'm fit to return to my unit."

She had the impression Lieutenant Harry Maxwell wasn't a man who liked being in any kind of position to need help. She supposed she probably shouldn't be holding her breath waiting for him to ask for it.

"I'm afraid I can't promise you complete quiet. Conan is mostly well-behaved but he does bark once in a while. I should also warn you if Tracy didn't mention it that there are children living in the second-floor apartment. Seven-year-old twins."

"They bark, too?"

She searched his face for any sign of a sense of humor but his expression revealed nothing. Still, she couldn't help smiling. "No, but they can be a little…energetic… at times. Mostly in the afternoons. They're gone most of the day at school and then they're usually pretty quiet in the evenings."

"That's something, then."

"In any case, they won't be here at all for several days. Their mother, Julia, is a teacher. Since they're all out of school right now for spring break, they've gone back to visit her family."

Before Lieutenant Maxwell could respond, Conan broke free of both the *sit* command and her hold on the leash and lunged for him again, dancing around his legs with excitement.

Anna reached for him again. "Conan, stop it right now. That's enough! I'm so sorry," she said to her new tenant, flustered at the negative impression they must be making.

"No worries. I'm not completely helpless. I think I can still manage to handle one high-strung mutt."

"Conan is not like most dogs," she muttered. "Most of the time we forget he even *is* a canine."

"The dog breath doesn't give him away?"

She smiled at his dry tone. So some sense of humor did lurk under that tough shell. That was a good sign. Brambleberry House and all its quirks demanded a strong constitution of its occupants.

"There is that," she answered. "We'll get out of your way and let you settle in. Again, if you need anything, don't hesitate to call. My phone number is right next to the phone or you can just call down the stairs and I'll usually hear you."

"I'll do that," he murmured, his mouth lifting slightly from its austere lines into what almost passed for a smile.

Just that minimal smile sent her pulse racing. With effort, she wrenched her gaze away from the dangerously masculine appeal of his features and tugged a reluctant Conan behind her as she headed back down the stairs.

Nerves zinging through her, Anna cursed to herself as she let herself back in to her apartment. She did *not* need this right now, she reminded herself sternly.

Her life was already a snarl of complications. She certainly didn't need to add into the mix a wounded war hero with gorgeous eyes, lean features and a mouth that looked made for trouble.

HE FORGOT ABOUT the damn dog.

Max shut the door behind the two of them—Anna Galvez and Conan. His last glimpse of the dog was of him quivering with a mix of excitement and friendly welcome and a bit of *why-aren't-you-happier-to-see-me?* confusion as she yanked his leash to tug him behind her down the stairs.

It had been shortsighted of him not to think of Abigail's mutt and his possible reaction to seeing Max again. He hadn't even given Conan a single thought—just more evidence of how completely the news of Abigail's death had knocked him off his pins.

The dog had only been a pup the last time he'd seen him before he shipped to the Middle East for his first tour of duty. During those last few days he had spent at Brambleberry House, Max had played hard with Conan. They'd run for miles on the beach, hiked up and down the coast range and played hours of fetch in the yard.

Had it really been four years? That was the last time

he had had a chance to spend any length of time here, a realization that caused him no small amount of guilt.

Conan should have been one of the first things on his mind after he found out about Abigail's death—several months after the fact. He could only blame his injuries and the long months of recovery for sending any thoughts of the dog scattering. It looked as if he was well-fed and taken care of. He supposed he had to give points to the woman—Anna Galvez—for that, at least.

He wasn't willing to concede victory to her, simply because she seemed affectionate to Abigail's mutt.

Anna Galvez. Now there was a strange woman, at least on first impressions. He couldn't quite get a handle on her. She was starchy and stiff, with her hair scraped back in a knot and the almost-masculine business suit and skirt she wore.

He would have considered her completely unappealing, except when she smiled, her entire face lit up as if somebody had just turned on a thousand-watt spotlight and aimed it right at her.

Only then did he notice her glossy dark hair, the huge, thick-lashed eyes, the high, elegant cheekbones. Underneath the layers of starch, she was a beautiful woman, he had realized with surprise, one that in other circumstances he might be interested in pursuing.

Didn't matter. She could be a supermodel and it wouldn't make a damn bit of difference to him. He had to focus on the two important things in his life right now— healing his shattered arm and digging for information.

He wasn't looking to make friends, he wasn't here to win any popularity contests, and he certainly wasn't interested in a quick fling with one of the women of Brambleberry House.

CHAPTER TWO

SHE COULD NEVER get enough of the coast.

Anna walked along the shore early the next morning while Conan jumped around in the sand, chasing grebes and dancing through the baby breakers.

The cool March wind whipped the waves into a froth and tangled her hair, making her grateful for the gloves and hat Abigail had knitted her last year. Offshore, the seastacks stood sturdy and resolute against the sea and overhead gulls wheeled and dived in the pale, early morning sky.

It all seemed worlds away from growing up in the high desert valleys of Utah but she loved it here. After four years of living in Oregon, she still felt incredibly blessed to be able to wake up to the soft music of the sea every single day.

Abigail had loved beachcombing in the mornings. She knew every inlet, every cliff, every tide table. She could spot a California gray whale's spout from a mile away during the migration season and could identify every bird and most of the sea life nearly as well as Sage, who was a biologist and naturalist by profession.

Oh, Anna missed Abigail. She could hardly believe it had been nearly a year since her friend's death. She still sometimes found herself in By-the-Wind—the book and gift store in town she first managed for Abigail and then purchased from her—looking out the window and expecting Abigail to stop by on one of her regular visits.

I know the store is yours now but you can't blame an old woman for wanting to check on things now and again, Abigail would say with that mischievous smile of hers.

Anna's circumstances had taken a dramatic shift since Abigail's death. She had been living in a small two-room apartment in Seaside and driving down every day to work in the store. Now she lived in the most gorgeous house on the north coast and had made two dear friends in the process.

She smiled, thinking of Sage and Julia and the changes in all their lives the past year. When she first met Sage, right after the two of them inherited Brambleberry House, she had thought she would never have anything in common with the other woman. Sage was a vegetarian, a save-the-planet sort, and Anna was, well, focused on her business.

But they had developed an unlikely friendship. Then when Julia moved into the second-floor apartment the next fall with her darling twins, Anna and Sage had both been immediately drawn to her. Many late-night gabfests later, both women felt like the sisters she had always wanted.

Now Sage was married to Eben Spencer and had a new stepdaughter, and Julia was engaged to Will Garrett and would be marrying him as soon as school was out in June, then moving out to live in his house only a few doors down from Brambleberry House.

Both of them were deliriously happy, and Anna was thrilled for them. They were wonderful women who deserved happiness and had found it with two men she was enormously fond of.

If their happy endings only served to emphasize the

mess she had made of her own life, she supposed she only had herself to blame.

She sighed, thinking of Grayson Fletcher and her own stupidity and the tangled mess he had left behind.

She supposed one bright spot from the latest fiasco in her love life was that Julia and Sage seemed to have put any matchmaking efforts on hiatus. They must have accepted the grim truth that had become painfully obvious to her—she had absolutely no judgment when it came to men.

She trusted the wrong ones. She had been making the same mistake since the time she fell hard for Todd Ashman in second grade, who gave her underdog pushes on the playground as well as her first kiss, a sloppy affair on the cheek. Todd told her he loved her then conned her out of her milk money for a week. She would probably still be paying him if her brothers hadn't found out and made the little weasel leave her alone.

She sighed as Conan sniffed a coiled ball of seaweed and twigs and grasses formed by the rolling action of the sea. That milk money had been the first of several things she had let men take from her.

Her pride. Her self-respect. Her reputation.

If she needed further proof, she only had to think about her schedule for the rest of the day. In a few hours, she was in for the dubious joy of spending another delightful day sitting in that Lincoln City courtroom while Grayson Fletcher provided unavoidable evidence of her overwhelming stupidity in business and in men.

She jerked her mind away from that painful route. She wasn't allowed to think about her mistakes on these morning walks with Conan. They were supposed to be therapy, her way to soothe her soul, to recharge her energy for the day ahead. She would defeat the entire purpose by spending the entire time looking back and cataloguing all her faults.

She forced herself to breathe deeply, inhaling the mingled scents of the sea and sand and early spring. Since Sage had married and moved out and she'd taken over sole responsibility of Conan's morning walks, she had come to truly savor and appreciate the diversity of coastal mornings. From rainy and cold to unseasonably warm to so brilliantly clear she could swear she could see the curve of the earth offshore.

Each reminded her of how blessed she was to live here. Cannon Beach had become her home. She had never intended it to happen, had only escaped here after her first major romantic debacle, looking for a place far away from her rural Utah home to lick her wounds and hide away from all her friends and family.

She had another mess on her hands now, complete with all the public humiliation she could endure. This time she wasn't about to run. Cannon Beach was her home, no matter what, and she couldn't imagine living anywhere else.

They had walked only a mile south from Brambleberry House when Conan suddenly barked with excitement. Anna shifted her gaze from the fascination of the ocean to see a runner approaching them, heading in the direction they had come.

Conan became increasingly animated the closer the runner approached, until it was all Anna could do to hang on to his leash.

She guessed his identity even before he was close enough for her to see clearly. The curious one-handed gait was a clear giveaway but his long, lean strength and brown hair was distinctive enough she was quite certain she would have figured out it was Harry Maxwell long before she could spy the sling on his arm.

To her annoyance, her stomach did an uncomfortable little twirl as he drew closer. The man was just too darn good-looking, with those lean, masculine features and the intense hazel eyes. It didn't help that he somehow looked rakishly gorgeous with his arm in a sling. An injured warrior still soldiering on.

She told herself she would have preferred things if he just kept on running but Conan made that impossible, barking and straining at his leash with such eager enthusiasm that Lieutenant Maxwell couldn't help but stop to greet him.

Maybe he wasn't quite the dour, humorless man he had appeared the day before, she thought as he scratched Conan's favorite spot, just above his shoulders. Nobody could be all bad if they were so intuitive with animals, she decided.

Only after he had sufficiently given the love to Conan did he turn in her direction.

"Morning," he said, a weird flash of what almost looked like unease in his eyes. Why would he possibly seem uncomfortable with her? She wasn't the one who practically oozed sex appeal this early in the morning.

"Hi," she answered. "Should you be doing that?"

He raised one dark eyebrow. "Petting your dog?"

"No. Running. I just wondered if all the jostling bothers your arm."

His mouth tightened a little and she had the impression again that he didn't like discussing his injury. "I hate the sling but it does a good job of keeping it from being shaken around when I'm doing anything remotely strenuous."

"It must still be uncomfortable, though."

"I'm fine."

Back off, in other words. His curtness was a clear signal she had overstepped.

"I'm sorry. Not my business, is it?"

He sighed. "I'm the one who's sorry. I'm a little frustrated at the whole thing. I'm not a very good patient and I'm afraid I don't handle limitations on my activities very well."

She sensed that was information he didn't share easily and though she knew he was only being polite she was still touched that he would confide in her. "I'm not a good patient, either. If I were in your shoes, I would be more than just a little frustrated."

Some of the stiffness seemed to ease from his posture. "Well, it's a whole lot more fun flying a helicopter than riding a hospital bed, I can tell you that much."

They lapsed into silence and she would have expected him to resume his jog but he seemed content to pet Conan and gaze out at the seething, churning waves.

It hardly seemed fair that, even injured as he was and just out of rehab, he didn't seem at all winded from the run. She would have been gasping for breath and ready for a little oxygen infusion.

"It looks like it's shaping up to be a gorgeous day, doesn't it?" she said. "Forecasters are saying we should have clear and sunny weather for the next few days. You picked a great time of year to visit Cannon Beach."

"That's good."

"I don't know if you've had a chance to notice this yet but on one of the bookshelves in the living room, I left you a welcome packet. I forgot to mention it when I stopped to say hello last night."

"I didn't see it. What kind of welcome packet?"

"Not much. Just a loose-leaf notebook, really, with some local sightseeing information. Maps of the area, trail guides, tide tables. I've also included several menus from my favorite restaurants if you want to try some of the local cuisine, as well as a couple of guidebooks from my store."

She had spent an entire evening gathering and collating the information, printing out pages from the Internet and marking some of her favorite spots in the guide books. All right, it was a nerdy, overachiever thing to do, she realized now as she stood next to this man who simmered with such blatant male energy.

She really needed to get a life.

Still, he didn't look displeased by the effort. If she didn't know better, she would suspect him of being perilously close to a surprised smile. "Thank you. That was… nice."

She made a face. "A little over-the-top, I know. Sorry. I tend to be a bit obsessive about those kinds of things."

"No, it sounds perfect. I'll be sure to look through it as soon as I get a chance. Maybe you can tell me the best place for breakfast around here. I haven't had much chance to go shopping."

"The Lazy Susan is always great or any of the B and Bs, really."

Or you could invite him to breakfast.

The thought whispered through her mind and she blinked, wondering where in the world it came from. That just wasn't the sort of thing she did. Now, Abigail would have done it in a heartbeat, and Sage probably would have as well, but Anna wasn't nearly as audacious.

But the thought persisted, growing stronger and stronger. Finally the words seemed to just blurt from her mouth. "Look, I'd be happy to fix something for you. I was in the mood for French toast anyway and it's silly to make it just for me."

He stared at her for a long moment, his eyes wide with surprise. The silence dragged on a painfully long time, until heat soaked her cheeks and she wanted to dive into the cold waves to escape.

"Sorry. Forget it. Stupid suggestion."

"No. No, it wasn't. I was just surprised, that's all. Breakfast would be great, if you're sure it's not too much trouble."

"Not at all. Can you give me about forty-five minutes to finish with Conan's morning walk?"

"No problem. That will give me a chance to finish my run and take a shower."

Now there was a visual she didn't need etched into her brain like acid on glass. She let out a breath. "Great. I'll see you then."

With a wave of his arm, sling and all, he headed back up the beach toward Brambleberry House.

With strict discipline, she forced herself not to watch after him. Instead, she gripped Conan's leash tightly so he wouldn't follow his new best friend and forced him to come with her by walking with firm determination in the other direction.

What just happened there? She had to be completely insane. Temporarily possessed by the spirit of Abigail that Sage and Julia seemed convinced still lingered at Brambleberry House.

She faced what was undoubtedly shaping up to be another miserable day sitting in the courtroom listening to more evidence of her own foolishness. And because she felt compelled to attend every moment of the trial, she had tons of work awaiting her at both the Cannon Beach and Lincoln City stores.

So what was she thinking? She had absolutely no business inviting a sexy injured war veteran to breakfast.

Remember your abysmal judgment when it comes to men, she reminded herself sternly.

It was just breakfast, though. He was her tenant and it was her duty to get to know the man living upstairs in her home. She was just being a responsible landlady.

Still, she couldn't control the excited little bump of anticipation. Nor could she ignore the realization that she was looking forward to the day more than she had anything else since before Christmas, when everything safe and secure she thought she had built for herself crashed apart like a house built on the shifting, unstable sands of Cannon Beach.

THIS MIGHT BE easier than he thought.

Fresh from the shower, Max pulled a shirt out of his duffel, grateful it was at least moderately unwrinkled. It wouldn't hurt to make a good impression on his new landlady. So far she didn't seem suspicious of him—he doubted she would have invited him to breakfast otherwise.

Now *there* was an odd turn of events. He had to admit, he was puzzled as all hell by the invitation. Why had she issued it? And so reluctantly, too. She had looked as shocked by it as he had been.

The woman baffled him. She seemed a contradiction. Yesterday she had been all prim and proper in her business suit, today she had appeared fresh and lovely as a spring morning and far too young to own a seaside mansion and two businesses.

He didn't understand her yet. But he would, he vowed.

Not so difficult to puzzle out had been his own reaction to her. When he had seen her walking and had recognized Conan, he had been stunned and more than a little disconcerted by the instant heat pooling in his gut.

Rather inconvenient, that surge of lust. His unwilling attraction to Anna Galvez. He would no doubt have a much easier time focusing on his goal without that particular complication.

How, exactly, was he supposed to figure out if Ms. Galvez had conned a sweet old lady when he couldn't seem to wrap his feeble male brain around anything but pulling all that thick, glossy hair out of its constraints, burying his fingers in it and devouring her mouth with his?

He yanked off the pain-in-the-ass waterproof covering he had to use to protect his most recent cast from yet another reconstructive surgery and carefully eased his arm through the sleeve of the shirt. He was almost—but not quite—accustomed to the pain that still buzzed across his nerve endings whenever he moved the arm.

It wasn't as bad as it used to be. After more than a dozen surgeries in six months, he could have a little mobility now without scorching agony.

He had to admit, he couldn't say he was completely sorry about his unexpected attraction to Anna Galvez. In some ways it was even a relief. He hadn't been able to summon even a speck of interest in a woman since the crash, not even to flirt with the pretty army nurses at the hospital in Germany and then later at Walter Reed.

He had worried that something internal might have been permanently damaged in the crash, since what he had always considered a relatively healthy libido seemed to have dried up like a wadi in a sandstorm.

He had even swallowed his pride and asked one of the doctors about it just before his discharge and had been told not to worry about it. He'd been assured that his body had only been a little busy trying to heal, just as his mind had been struggling with his guilt over the deaths of two members of his flight crew.

When the time was right, he'd been told, all the plumbing would probably work just as it had before.

It might be inconvenient that he was attracted to Anna Galvez, inconvenient and more than a little odd, since he had never been attracted to the prim, focused sort of woman before, but he couldn't truly say he was sorry about it.

And if he needed a reminder of why he couldn't pursue the attraction, he only needed to look around him at the familiar walls of Brambleberry House.

For all he knew, Anna Galvez was the sneaky, conniving swindler his mother believed her to be, working her wiles to gull his elderly aunt out of this house and its contents, all the valuable antiques and keepsakes that had been in his father's family for generations.

He wouldn't know until he had run a little reconnaissance here to see where things stood.

His father had been the only child of Abigail's solitary sibling, her sister Suzanna, which made Max Abigail's only living relative.

Though he hadn't really given it much thought—

mostly because he didn't like thinking about his beloved great-aunt's inevitable passing—he supposed he had always expected to inherit Brambleberry House someday.

Finding out she had left the house to two strangers had been more than a little bit surprising.

She must not have loved you enough.

The thought slithered through his mind, cold and mean, but he pushed it away. Abigail had loved him. He could never doubt that. For some inexplicable reason, she had decided to give the house to two strangers and he was determined to find out why.

And this morning provided a perfect opportunity to give Anna Galvez a little closer scrutiny, so he'd better get on with things.

Buttoning a shirt with one good hand genuinely sucked, he had discovered over the last six months, but it wasn't nearly as tough as trying to maneuver an arm that didn't want to cooperate through the unwieldy holes in a T-shirt or, heaven forbid, a long-sleeved sweater, so he persevered.

When he finished, he put the blasted sling on again, ran a comb through his hair awkwardly with his left hand, then headed for the stairs, his hand on the banister he remembered Abigail waxing to a lustrous sheen just so he could slide down it when he was a boy.

Delicious smells greeted him the moment he headed downstairs—coffee, bacon, hash browns and something sweet and yeasty. His stomach rumbled but he reminded himself he was a soldier, trained to withstand temptation.

No matter how seemingly irresistible.

He paused outside Abigail's door, a little astounded at the sudden nerves zinging through him.

It was one thing to inhabit the top floor of Brambleberry House. It was quite another, he discovered, to return to Abigail's private sanctuary, the place he had loved so dearly.

The rooms beyond this door had been his haven when he was a kid. The one safe anchor in a tumultuous, unstable childhood—not the house, he supposed, as much as the woman who had been so much a part of it.

No matter what might be happening in his regular life—whether his mother was between husbands or flushed with the glow of new love that made her forget his existence or at the bitter, ugly end of another marriage—Abigail had always represented safety and security to him.

She had been fun and kind and loving and he had craved his visits here like a drunk needed rotgut. He had looked forward to the two weeks his mother allowed him with fierce anticipation the other fifty weeks of the year. Whenever he walked through this door, he had felt instantly wrapped in warm, loving arms.

And now a stranger lived here. A woman who had somehow managed to convince an old woman to leave her this house.

No matter how lovely Anna Galvez might be, he couldn't forget that she had usurped Abigail's place in this house.

It was hers now and he damn well intended to find out why.

He drew in a deep breath, adjusted his sling one more time, then reached out to knock on Abigail's door.

CHAPTER THREE

SHE OPENED THE door wearing one of his aunt's old ruffled bib aprons.

He recognized it instantly, pink flowers and all, and had a sudden image of Abigail in the kitchen, bedecked with jewels as always, grinning and telling jokes as she cooked up a batch of her famous French toast that dripped with caramel and brown sugar and pralines.

He had to admit he found the dichotomy a little disconcerting. Whether Anna was a con artist or simply a modern businesswoman, he wouldn't have expected her to be wearing something so softly worn and old-fashioned.

He doubted Abigail had ever looked quite as appealing in that apron. Anna Galvez's skin had a rosy glow to it and the friendly pink flowers made her look exotically beautiful in contrast.

"Good morning again," she said, her smile polite, perhaps even a little distant.

Maybe he ought to forget this whole thing, he thought. Just head back out the door and up the stairs. He could always grab a granola bar and a cola for breakfast.

He wasn't sure he was ready to face Abigail's apartment just yet, and especially not with this woman looking on.

"Something smells delicious in here, like you've gone to a whole lot of work. I hope this isn't a big inconvenience for you."

Her smile seemed a little warmer. "Not at all. I enjoy cooking, I just don't get the chance very often. Come in."

She held the door open for him and he couldn't figure out a gracious way to back out. Doing his best to hide his sudden reluctance, he stepped through the threshold.

He shouldn't have worried.

Nothing was as he remembered. When Abigail was alive, these rooms had been funky and cluttered, much like his aunt, with shelves piled high with everything from pieces of driftwood to beautifully crafted art pottery to cheap plastic garage-sale trinkets.

Abigail had possessed her own sense of style. If she liked something, she had no compunction about displaying it. And she had liked a wide variety of things.

The fussy wallpaper he remembered was gone and the room had been painted a crisp, clean white. Even more significant, a few of the major walls had been removed to open up the space. The thick, dramatic trim around the windows and ceiling was still there and nothing jarred with the historic tone of the house but he had to admit the space looked much brighter. Cleaner.

Elegant, even.

He had only a moment to absorb the changes before a plaintive whine echoed through the space. He followed the sound and discovered Conan just on the other side of the long sofa that was canted across the living room.

The dog gazed at him with longing in his eyes and though he practically knocked the sofa cushions off with his quivering, he made no move to lunge at him.

Max blinked at the canine. "All right. What's with the dog? Did somebody glue his haunches to the sofa?"

She made a face. "No. We're working on obedience. I gave him a strict *sit-stay* command before I opened the door. I'm afraid it's not going to last, as much as he wants to be good. I'm sorry."

"I don't mind. I like dogs."

He particularly liked this one and had since Conan was a pup Abigail had rescued from the pound, though he certainly couldn't tell her that.

She took pity on the dog and released him from the position with a simple "Okay."

Conan immediately rushed for Max, nudging at him with that big furry red-gold head, just as a timer sounded through the room.

"Perfect. That's everything. Do you mind eating in the kitchen? I have a great view of the ocean from there."

"Not at all."

He didn't add that Abigail's small kitchen, busy and cluttered as it was, had always been his favorite room of the house, the very essence of what made Brambleberry House so very appealing.

He found the small round table set with Abigail's rose-covered china and sunny yellow napkins. A vase of fresh flowers sent sweet smells to mingle with the delicious culinary scents.

"Can I do anything?"

"No, everything's all finished. I just need to pull it from the oven. You can go ahead and sit down."

He sat at one of the place settings where he had a beautiful view of the sand and the sea and the haystacks offshore. He poured coffee for both of them while Conan perched at his feet and he could swear the dog was grinning at him with male camaraderie, as if they shared some secret.

Which, of course, they did.

In a moment, Anna returned to the table with a casserole dish. She set it down then removed covers from the other plates on the table and his mouth watered again at the crispy strips of bacon and mound of scrambled eggs.

"This is enough to feed my entire platoon, ma'am."

She grimaced. "I haven't cooked for anyone else in a while. I'm afraid I got a little carried away. I hope you're hungry."

"Starving, actually."

He was astonished to find it was true. The sea air must be agreeing with him. He'd lost twenty pounds in the hospital and though the doctors had been strictly urging him to do something about putting it back on, he hadn't been able to work up much enthusiasm to eat anything.

Nice to know *all* his appetites seemed to be returning.

He took several slices of bacon and a hefty mound of scrambled eggs then scooped some of the sweet-smelling concoction from the glass casserole dish.

The moment he lifted the fork to his mouth, a hundred memories came flooding back of other mornings spent in this kitchen, eating this very thing for breakfast. It had been his favorite as long as he could remember and he had always asked for it.

"This is—" *Aunt Abigail's famous French toast,* he almost said, but caught himself just in time. "Delicious. Really delicious."

When she smiled, she looked almost as delectable as the thick, caramel-covered toast, and just as edible. "Thank you. It was a specialty of a dear friend of mine. Every time I make it, it reminds me of her."

He slanted her a searching look across the table. She sounded sincere—maybe *too* sincere. He wanted to take her apparent affection for Abigail at face value but he couldn't help wondering if his cover had been blown. For all he knew, she had seen a picture of him in Abigail's things and guessed why he was here.

If she truly were a con artist and knew he was Abigail's nephew come to check things out, wouldn't she lay it on thick about how much she adored his aunt to allay his suspicions?

"That's nice," he finally said. "It sounds like you cared about her a lot."

She didn't answer for several seconds, long enough that he wondered if she were being deliberately evasive. He felt as if he were tap-dancing through a damn minefield.

"I did," she finally answered.

Conan whined a little and settled his chin on his fore-paws, just as if he somehow understood exactly whom they were talking about and still missed Abigail.

Impossible, Max thought. The dog was smart but not *that* smart.

"I've heard horror stories about army food," Anna said, changing the subject. "Is it as awful as they say?"

Even as he applied himself to the delicious breakfast, his mind couldn't seem to stop shifting through the nu-ances and implications of every word she said and he wondered why she suddenly seemed reluctant to discuss Abigail after she had been the one to bring her into the conversation. Still, he decided not to push her. He would let her play things her way for now while he tried to fig-ure out the angles.

"Army food's not bad," he said, focusing on her question. "Army hospital food, that's another story. This is gour-met dining to me after the last few months."

"How long were you in the hospital?"

Just as she didn't want to talk about Abigail, he sure as hell didn't want to discuss his time in the hospital.

"Too damn long," he answered, then because his voice sounded so harsh, he tried to amend his tone. "Six months, on and off, with rehab and surgeries and everything."

Her eyes widened and she set down her own fork. "Oh, my word! Tracy—the real estate agent with the property management company—told me you had been hurt in Iraq but I had no idea your injuries were so severe!"

He fidgeted a little, wishing they hadn't landed on this topic. He hated thinking about the crash or his injuries—or the future that stretched out ahead of him, darkly uncertain.

"I wasn't in the hospital the entire time. A month the first time, mostly in the burn unit, but I needed several surgeries after that to repair my shoulder and arm then skin grafts and so on. All of it took time. And then I picked up a staph infection in the meantime and that meant another few weeks in the hospital. Throw in a month or so of rehab before they'd release me and here we are."

"Oh, I'm so sorry. It sounds truly awful."

He chewed a mouthful of fluffy scrambled eggs that suddenly tasted like foam peanuts. He knew he was lucky to make it out alive after the fiery hard landing. That inescapable fact had been drilled into his head constantly since the crash, by himself and by those around him.

For several tense moments after they had been hit by a rocket-fired grenade as they were picking up an injured soldier that October day to medevac, he had been quite certain this was the end for him and for the four others on his Black Hawk.

He thought he was going to be a grim statistic, another one of those poor bastards who bit it just a week before their tour ended and they were due to head home.

But somehow he had survived. Two of his crew hadn't been so lucky, despite his frantic efforts and those of the other surviving crew member. They had saved the injured Humvee driver, so that was something.

That first month had been a blur, especially the first few days after the crash. The medical transport to Kuwait and then to Germany, the excruciating pain from his shattered arm and shoulder and from the second- and third-degree burns on the right side of his body…and the even more excruciating anguish that still cramped in his gut when he thought about his lost crew members.

He was aware, suddenly, that Conan had risen from the floor to sit beside him, resting his chin on Max's thigh.

He found enormous comfort from the soft, furry weight and from the surprising compassion in the dog's eyes.

"How are you now?" Anna asked. "Have the doctors given you an estimate of what kind of recovery you're looking at?"

"It's all a waiting game right now to see how things heal after the last surgery." He raised his arm with the cast. "I've got to wear this for another month."

"I can't imagine how frustrating that must be for you. I don't know about you, but I'm not the most patient person in the world. I'm afraid I would want results immediately."

They definitely had that much in common. Though his instincts warned him to filter every word through his suspicions about her, he had to admit he found her concern rather sweet and unexpected.

"I do," he admitted. "But I was in the hospital long

enough to see exactly what happened to those who tried to rush the healing process. Several of them pushed too hard and ended up right back where they started, in much worse shape. I won't let that happen. It will take as long as it takes."

"Smart words," she said with an odd look and only then did he realize that it had been one of his aunt's favorite phrases, whether she was talking about the time it took for cookies to bake or for the berries to pop out on her raspberry canes out back.

He quickly tried to turn the conversation back to her. "What about you? For a woman who claims she's impatient for results, you've picked a major project here, renovating this big house on your own."

"Brambleberry House belonged to a dear friend of mine. Actually, the one whose French toast recipe you're eating." She smiled a little. "When she died last year, she left it to me and to another of her lost sheep, Sage Benedetto. Sage Benedetto-Spencer, actually. She's married now and lives in San Francisco with her husband and stepdaughter. In fact, you're living in what used to be her apartment."

He knew all about Sage. He'd been hearing about her for years from Abigail. When his aunt told him she had taken on a new tenant for the empty third floor several years ago, he had instantly been suspicious and had run a full background check on the woman, though he hadn't revealed that information to Abigail.

Nothing untoward had showed up. She worked at the nature center in town and had seemed to be exactly as she appeared, a hardworking biologist in need of a clean place to live.

But five years later, she was now one of the owners

of that clean abode—and she had recently married into money.

That in itself had raised his suspicions. Maybe she and Anna had a whole racket going on. First they conned Abigail, then Sage set her sights on Eben Spencer and tricked him into marrying her. What other explanation could there be? Why would a hotel magnate like Spencer marry a hippie nature girl like Sage Benedetto?

"So you live down here and rent out the top two floors?"

She sipped her coffee. "For now. It's a lot of space for one woman and the upkeep on the place isn't cheap. I had to replace the heating system this year, which took a huge chunk out of the remodeling budget."

There was one element of this whole thing that didn't jibe with his mother's speculation that they were gold-digging scam artists, Max admitted. If they were only in this for the money, wouldn't they have flipped the house, taken their equity and split Cannon Beach?

It didn't make sense and made him more inclined to believe she and Sage Benedetto truly had cared for Abigail, though he wasn't ready to concede anything at this point.

"The real estate agent who arranged the rental agreement with me mentioned you own a couple of shops on the coast but she didn't go into detail."

If he hadn't been watching her so carefully, he might have missed the sudden glumness in her eyes or the subtle tightening of her lovely, exotic features.

He had obviously touched on a sore subject, and from his preliminary Internet search of her and Sage, he was quite certain he knew why.

"Yes," she finally said, stirring her scrambled eggs around on her plate. "My store here in town is near the post office. It's called By-the-Wind Books and Gifts."

"By-the-Wind? Like the jellyfish?" he asked.

"Right. By-the-wind sailors. My friend Abigail loved them. The store was hers and she named it after a cross-wind one year sent hundreds of thousands of them washing up on the shore of Cannon Beach. I started out managing the store for her when I first came to town. A few years ago when she hit seventy-eight she decided she was ready to slow down a little, so I made an offer for the store and she sold it to me."

Abigail had adored her store as much as she loved this house. She wasn't the most savvy of businesswomen but she loved any excuse to engage a stranger in conversation.

"So you've opened a second store now," he asked.

She shifted in her seat, her hands clenching and unclenching around the napkin in her lap. "Yes. Last summer I opened one in Lincoln City. By-the-Wind Two."

She didn't seem nearly as eager to talk about her second store and he found her reaction interesting and filed it away to add to his growing impressions about Anna Galvez.

He had limited information about the situation but his Internet search had turned up several hits from the Lincoln City newspaper about her store manager being arrested some months ago and charged with embezzlement and credit card fraud.

Max knew from his research that the man was currently on trial. He didn't, however, have any idea at all if Anna was the innocent victim the newspapers had portrayed or if she perhaps had deeper involvement in the fraud.

Before coming back to Brambleberry House, he had been all too willing to believe she might have been involved, that she had managed to find a convenient way to turn her manager into the scapegoat.

It was a little harder to believe that when he was sitting across the table from her and could smell the delicate scent of her drifting across the table, when he could feel the warmth of her just a few feet away, when he could reach out and touch the softness of her skin…

He jerked his mind from that dangerous road. "You must be doing well if you've got two stores. Any plans to expand to a third? Maybe up north in Astoria or farther south in Newport?"

"No. Not anytime in the near future. Or even in the not-so-near future." She forced a smile that stopped just short of genuine. "Would you like more French toast?"

He decided to allow her to sidetrack him for now, though he wasn't at all finished with this line of questioning. Instead, he served up another slice of the French pastry.

Being here in this kitchen like this was oddly surreal and he almost expected Abigail to bustle in from another part of the house with her smile gleaming even above the mounds of jewelry she always wore.

She wouldn't be bustling in from anywhere, he reminded himself. Grief clawed at him again, the overwhelming sense of loss that seemed so much more acute here in this house.

Oh, he missed her.

He suddenly felt a weird brush of something against his cheek and he had a sudden hideous fear he might be crying. He did a quick finger-sweep but didn't feel any wetness. But he was quite certain he smelled something flowery and sweet.

Out of nowhere, the dog suddenly wagged his tail and

gave one happy bark. Max thought he saw something out of the corner of his gaze but when he turned around he saw only a curtain fluttering in the other room from one of the house's famous drafts.

He turned back to find Anna Galvez watching him, her eyes wary and concerned at the same time.

"Is everything okay, Lieutenant Maxwell?" she asked.

He shook off the weird sensation, certain he must just be tired and a little overwhelmed about being back here. *Lieutenant Maxwell,* she had called him. Discomfort burned under his skin at the fake name. This whole thing just felt wrong somehow, especially sitting here in Abigail's kitchen. He wanted to just tell her the truth but some instinct held him back. Not yet. He would let the situation play out a little longer, see what she did.

But he couldn't have her calling him another man's name, he decided. "You don't have to call me Lieutenant Maxwell. You can call me Max. That's what most people do."

A puzzled frown played around that luscious mouth. "They call you Max and not Harry?"

"Um, yeah. It's a military thing. Nicknames, you know?"

The explanation sounded lame, even to him, but she appeared to buy it without blinking. In fact, she gifted him with a particular sweet smile. "All right. Max it is. You may, of course, call me Anna."

He absolutely was *not* going to let himself get lost in that smile, no matter his inclination, so he forced himself to continue with his subtle interrogation. "Are you from around here?"

She shook her head. "I grew up in a small town in the mountains of Utah."

He raised an eyebrow, certain he hadn't unearthed that little tidbit of information in his research. "Utah seems like a long way from here. What brought you to the Oregon coast?"

Her eyes took on that evasive film again. "Oh, you know. I was ready for a change. Wanted to stretch my wings a little. That sort of thing."

He had become pretty good over the years at picking up when someone wasn't being completely honest with him and his lie radar was suddenly blinking like crazy.

She was hiding something and he wanted to know what.

"Do you have family back in Utah still?"

The tension in her shoulders eased a little. "Two of my older brothers are still close to Moose Springs. That's where we grew up. One's the sheriff, actually. The other is a contractor, then I have one other brother who's a research scientist in Costa Rica."

"No sisters?"

"Just brothers. I'm the baby."

"You were probably spoiled rotten, right?"

Her laugh was so infectious that even Conan looked up and grinned. "More like endlessly tormented. I was always excluded from their cool boy stuff like campouts and fishing trips. Being the only girl and the youngest Galvez was a double curse, one I'm still trying to figure out how to break."

This, at least, was genuine. She glowed when she talked about her family—her eyes seemed brighter, her features more animated. She looked so delicious, it was all he could do not to reach across the table and kiss her right here over his aunt's French toast.

Her next words quickly quashed the bloom of desire better than a cold Oregon downpour.

"What about you?" she asked. "Do you have family somewhere?"

How could he answer that without giving away his identity? He decided to stick to the bare facts and hope Abigail hadn't talked about his particular twisted branch of the family tree.

"My father died when I was too young to remember him. My mother remarried several times so I've got a few stepbrothers and stepsisters scattered here and there but that's it."

He didn't add that he didn't even know some of their names since none of the marriages had lasted long.

"So where's home?" she asked.

"Right now it's two flights of stairs above you."

She made a face. "What about before you moved up-stairs?"

Brambleberry House was the place he had always considered home, even though he only spent a week or two here each year. Life with his mother had never been exactly stable as she moved from boyfriend to boyfriend, husband to husband. Before he had been sent to military school when he was thirteen, he had attended a dozen different schools.

Abigail had been the rock in his insecure existence. But he certainly couldn't tell that to Anna Galvez. Instead, he shrugged.

"I'm career army, ma'am. I'm based out of Virginia but I've been in the Middle East for two tours of duty. I've been there the last four years. That feels as much home as anywhere else, I guess."

CHAPTER FOUR

OH, THE POOR MAN.

Imagine considering some military base a home. She couldn't quite fathom it and she felt enormously blessed suddenly for her safe, happy childhood.

Her family might have been what most people would consider dirt-poor. Her parents were illegal immigrants who had tried to live below the radar. As a result, her father had never been paid his full worth and when he had been killed in a construction accident, the company he worked for had used his illegal immigrant status as an excuse not to pay any compensation to his widow or children.

Yes, her family might not have had much when she was a kid but she had never lived a single moment of her childhood when she didn't feel her home was a sanctuary where she could always be certain she would find love and acceptance.

Later, maybe, she had come to doubt her worth, but none of that stemmed from her girlhood.

And now she had Brambleberry House to return to at the end of the day. No matter how stressful her life might seem sometimes, this house welcomed her back every night, solid and strong and immovable.

It saddened her to think of Harry Maxwell moving

from place to place with the military, never having anything to anchor him in place.

"I suppose if you had a wife and children, you would probably be recovering with them instead of at some drafty rented house on the Oregon shore."

"No wife, no kids. Never married." He paused, giving her a careful look. "What about you?"

She had always wanted a big, rambunctious family just like the one she'd known as a girl but those childhood dreams spun in the tiny bedroom of that Moose Springs house seemed far away now.

Her life hadn't worked out at all the way she planned. And though there were a few things in her life she wouldn't mind a do-over on—especially more recent events—she couldn't regret all the paths she had followed that had led her to this place.

"Same goes. I was engaged once but…it didn't work out."

Before he could respond, Conan lumbered to his feet and headed for the door.

"That's a signal," she said with a smile. "Time for him to go out and if I don't move on it, we'll all be sorry. Excuse me, won't you?"

Though he had a doggie door to use when she wasn't home, Conan much preferred to be waited on and to go out through the regular door like the rest of the higher beings. She opened her apartment door and then the main door into the house for him and watched him bound eagerly to his favorite corner of the yard.

When she returned to the kitchen, she found Lieutenant Maxwell clearing dishes from the table.

"That was delicious. It was very kind of you to invite me. A little unexpected, but kind nonetheless."

"You're welcome. I'll be honest, it's not the sort of thing I usually do but…well, it *is* the sort of thing Abigail would have done. She was always striking up conversations with people and taking them to lunch or whatever. I had the strangest feeling this morning on the beach that she would want me to invite you to breakfast."

She heard the absurdity of her own words and made a face. "That probably sounds completely insane to you."

"Not completely," he murmured.

"No, it is. But I'm not sorry. I enjoyed making breakfast and I suppose it's only fitting that I know at least a little about the person living upstairs. At least now you don't feel like a stranger."

"Well, I appreciate the effort and the French toast. It's been…a long time since I've had anything as good."

He gave her a hesitant smile and at the sight of it on those solemnly handsome features, her stomach seemed to do a long, slow roll.

Oh, bad idea. She had no business at all being attracted to the man. He was her tenant, and a temporary one at that. Beyond that, the timing was abysmal. She had far too much on her plate right now trying to save By-the-Wind Two and see that Grayson Fletcher received well-deserved justice. She couldn't afford any distractions, especially not one as tempting as Lieutenant Harry Maxwell.

"I'm glad you enjoyed it," she said, forcing her voice to be brisk and businesslike.

Conan came back inside before he could answer. He headed straight for the lieutenant, who reached down to pet him. The absent gesture reminded her of another detail she meant to discuss with him.

"I'm afraid I'm going to be tied up in Lincoln City

most of today. Some days I can take Conan with me since I have arrangements with a kennel in town but they were full today so he has to stay home. I hope he doesn't make a pest of himself."

"I doubt he'll bother me."

"With the dog door, he can come as he likes. I should probably tell you, he thinks he owns the house. He's used to going up the stairs to visit either Sage when she lived here or Julia and the twins. If he whines outside your door, just send him back downstairs."

"He won't bother me. If he whines, I'll invite him inside. He's welcome to hang out upstairs. I don't mind the company."

He petted the dog with an unfeigned affection that warmed her, though she knew it shouldn't. Most people liked Conan, though Grayson Fletcher never had. That in itself should have been all the red flags she needed that the man was trouble.

"Well, don't feel obligated to entertain him. I would just ask that you close the gate behind you if you leave so he can't leave the yard. He tends to take off if there's a stray cat in the neighborhood."

"I'll do that." He paused. "Would you have any objection if I take Conan along if I go anywhere? He kind of reminds me of a…dog I once knew."

At the sound of his name, the dog barked eagerly, his tail wagging a mile a minute.

Conan would adore any outing, she knew, but she couldn't contain a few misgivings.

"Conan can be a little energetic when he wants to be. Are you certain you can restrain him on the leash if he decides to take off after a squirrel or something?"

"Because of this, you mean?" he asked stiffly, gesturing to the sling. "My other arm still works fine."

She nodded, feeling foolish. "Of course. In that case, I'm sure Conan would love to go along with you anywhere. He loves riding in the car and he's crazy about any excuse to get some exercise. I'm afraid my schedule doesn't allow me to give him as much as he would like. Here, let me grab his leash for you just in case."

She headed for the hook by the door but Conan had heard the magic word—*leash*—and he bounded in front of her, nearly dancing out of his fur with excitement.

Caught off balance by seventy-five pounds of dog suddenly in her way, she stumbled a little and would have fallen into an ignominious heap if Lieutenant Maxwell hadn't reached out with his uninjured arm to help steady her.

Instant heat leaped through her, wild and shocking. She was painfully cognizant of the hard male strength of him, of his mouth just inches away, of those hazel eyes watching her with a glittery expression.

She didn't think she had ever, in her entire existence, been so physically aware of a man. Of his scent, fresh-washed and clean, of the muscles that held her so securely, of the strong curve of his jawline.

She might have stayed there half the morning, caught in the odd lassitude seeping through her, except she suddenly was quite certain she smelled freesia as she had earlier during breakfast.

The scent eddied around them, subtle and sweet, but it was enough to break the spell.

She jerked away from him before she could do something abysmally stupid like kiss the man.

"I'm sorry," she exclaimed. "I'm so clumsy sometimes. Are you all right? Did I hurt you?"

A muscle worked in his jaw, though that strange light lingered in his eyes. "I'm not breakable, Anna. Don't worry about it."

Despite his words, she was quite certain she saw lines of pain bracketing his mouth. With three older brothers, though, she had learned enough about the male psyche to sense he wouldn't appreciate her concern.

She let out a long breath. This had to be the strangest morning of her life.

"Here's the leash," she said. "If you decide to take Conan with you, just call his name and rattle this outside my door and he should come running in an instant."

He nodded. For a moment, she thought he might say something about the surge of heat between them just now, but then he seemed to change his mind.

"Thanks again for breakfast," he said. "I would offer to return the favor but I'm afraid you'd end up with cold cereal."

She managed a smile, though she was certain it wasn't much of one. He gazed at her for a long moment, his features unreadable, then he headed for the door.

Conan danced around behind him, his attention glued to the leash, but she managed to close the door before the dog could escape to follow him up the stairs.

He whined and slumped against the door and she leaned against it, absently rubbing the dog's ears as that freesia scent drifted through the apartment again.

"Cut it out, Abigail," she spoke aloud. Lieutenant Maxwell would surely think she was crazy if he heard her talking to a woman who had been dead nearly a year.

Still, there had been that strange moment at breakfast

when she had been almost positive he sensed something in the kitchen. His eyes had widened and he had seemed almost disconcerted.

Ridiculous. There had been nothing there for him to sense. Abigail was gone, as much as she might wish otherwise. She was just too prosaic to believe Sage and Julia's theory that their friend still lingered here at Brambleberry House.

And even if she did buy the theory, why would Abigail possibly make herself known to Harry Maxwell? It made no sense.

Sage believed Abigail had played a hand in her relationship with Eben, that she had carefully orchestrated events so they would both finally be forced to admit they belonged together.

Though Julia didn't take things quite that far, she also seemed to believe Abigail had helped her and Will find their happily-ever-after.

But Abigail had never even met Harry Maxwell. Why on earth would she want to hook him up with Anna?

She heard the ludicrous direction of her thoughts and shook her head. She had far too much to do today to spend any more time speculating on the motives of an imaginary matchmaking ghost.

She wasn't about to let herself fall prey to any beyond-the-grave romantic maneuvering between her and a certain wounded soldier with tired, suspicious eyes.

MAX RETURNED TO his third-floor aerie to be greeted by his cell phone belting out his mother's ringtone.

He winced and made a mental note to change it before she caught wind of the song one of his bunkmates at

Walter Reed had programmed as a joke after Meredith's single visit to see him in the six months after the crash.

His mother wouldn't be thrilled to know he heard Heart singing "Barracuda" every time she called.

When he was on painkillers, he had found it mildly amusing—mostly because it was right on the money. Now he just found it rather sad. For much the same reason.

He thought about ignoring her but he knew Meredith well enough to be sure she would simply keep calling him until he grew tired of putting her off, so he finally picked it up.

With a sigh, he opened his phone. "Hi, Mom," he greeted, feeling slightly childish in the knowledge that he only used the word because he knew it annoyed her.

She had been insisting since several years before he hit adolescence that he must call her Meredith but he still stubbornly refused.

"Where were you, Maxwell? I've been calling you for an hour." Her voice had that prim, tight tone he hated.

"I was at breakfast. I must have left my phone here."

He decided to keep to himself the information that he was downstairs eating Abigail's French toast with Anna Galvez.

"You said you would call me when you arrived."

"You're right. That's what I said."

He left his sentence hanging between them, yet another strategy he had learned early in his dealings with her mother. She wouldn't listen to explanations anyway so he might as well save them both the time and energy of offering.

The silence dragged on but he held his ground. Finally she heaved a long-suffering sigh and surrendered.

"What have you found?" she asked. "Have those women gutted the house and sold everything in it?"

He gazed around at the apartment with its new coat of paint and kitchen cabinets and he thought of the downstairs apartment, with its spacious new floor plan.

"I wouldn't exactly say that."

"Brambleberry House was filled with priceless antiques. Some of them were family heirlooms that should have gone to you. I can't believe Abigail didn't do a better job of preserving them for you. You're her only living relative and those family items should be yours."

Since she had backed down first, he let her ramble on about the injustice of it all—as if Meredith cared about anyone's history beyond her own.

"I was apparently mistaken to let you visit her all those summers. When I think of the expense and time involved in sending you there, I just get furious all over again."

He happened to know Abigail had paid for every plane ticket and Meredith had looked on those two weeks as her vacation from the ordeal of motherhood but he decided to let that one slide, too.

"She must have been crazy at the end," Meredith finally wound down to say. "That's the only explanation that makes sense. Why else would she leave the house to a couple of strangers when she could have left it to her favorite—and only—nephew?"

"We've had this conversation before," he said slowly. "I can't answer that, Mom."

"What do you intend to do, then? Have you spoken with an attorney yet about contesting the will?"

"It's been nearly a year since Abigail died. I can't just show up out of nowhere and start fighting over the house."

He didn't need Brambleberry House. What did he care

about some decaying old house on the coast? He certainly didn't need any inheritance from Abigail. His father had been a wealthy, successful land developer.

Though he died suddenly, he had been conscientious—or perhaps grimly aware of his wife's expensive habits. He had left his young son an inviolable trust fund that Meredith couldn't touch.

Through wise investments over the years, Max had parlayed that inheritance into more money than one man—or ten—could spend in a lifetime.

The money didn't matter to him. Abigail did. She had been his rock through childhood and he owed her at least some token effort to make sure she had been competent in her last wishes.

"You most certainly can fight over it! That house should belong to you, Maxwell. You're entitled to it."

He rolled his eyes. "I'm not entitled to anything."

"That's nonsense," Meredith snapped. "You have far more claim on Brambleberry House than a couple of grubby little gold diggers. Did you contact Abigail's attorney yet?"

He sighed, ready to pull the old bad-connection bit so he could end the call. "I've been in town less than twenty-four hours, Mom. I haven't had a chance yet."

"You have to swear you'll contact me the moment you know anything. The very *moment*."

He had a fleeting, futile wish that his mother had been as concerned when her son was shot down by enemy fire as she apparently was about two strangers inheriting a house she had despised.

The moment the thought registered, he pushed it quickly away. He had made peace a long time ago with the reality that his mother had a toxic, self-absorbed personality.

He couldn't change that at thirty-five any more than he had been able to when he was eight.

For the most part, both of them rubbed together tolerably well as long as they were able to stay out of the other's way.

"I'll do that. Goodbye, Mom."

He hung up a second later and gazed at the phone for a long moment, aware she hadn't once asked about his arm. Just like Meredith. She preferred to pretend anything inconvenient or unpleasant just didn't exist in her perfect little world.

If Brambleberry House had been some worthless shack somewhere, she wouldn't have given a damn about it. She certainly wouldn't have bothered to push him so hard to check into the situation.

And he likely would have ignored her diatribes about the house if not for his own sense of, well, *hurt* that Abigail hadn't bothered to leave him so much as a teacup in her will.

It made no sense to him. She had loved him. Her Jamie, she called him, a nickname he had rolled his eyes at. James had been his father's name and it was his middle name. Abigail seemed to get a kick out of being the only one to ever call him that.

They had carried on a lively e-mail correspondence no matter where he was stationed and he thought she might have mentioned sometime in all that some reason why she was cutting him out of her will.

He had allowed his mother to half convince him Sage Benedetto and Anna Galvez must have somehow finagled their way into Abigail's world and conned her into leaving the house and its contents to them. It now seemed a silly notion. Abigail had been sharp as a tack. She would have seen through obvious gold-digging.

But she was also very softhearted. Perhaps the women had played on her sympathy somehow.

Or maybe she just had come to love two strangers more than she loved her own nephew.

He sighed, disgusted with the pathetic, self-pitying direction of his thoughts.

After spending the last hour with Anna Galvez, he wasn't sure what to think. She seemed a woman of many contradictions. Tough, hard-as-nails businesswoman one moment, softly feminine chef with an edge of vulnerability the next.

It could all be an act, he reminded himself. Still, he couldn't deny his attraction to her. She was a lovely woman and he was instinctively drawn to her.

Under other circumstances, he might have even liked her.

He heard a vehicle start up below and moved to the window overlooking the driveway. He saw her white, rather bland minivan carefully back out of the driveway then head south toward Lincoln City.

The woman was a mystery, one he was suddenly eager to solve.

CHAPTER FIVE

THIS WAS A STUPID IDEA.

Just after noon, Max slipped into the condiment aisle of the small grocery store in town, cursing his bad luck—and whatever idiotic impulse had led him to ever think he could get away with assuming a false identity in this town.

He must have been suffering the lingering effects of the damn painkillers. That was the only explanation that made sense.

It had seemed like such a simple plan. Just slip into town incognito, then back out again without anybody paying him any mind.

The idea should have worked. Cannon Beach was a tourist town, after all, and he figured he would be considered just one more tourist.

He had forgotten his aunt had known every permanent resident in town. Scratch that. Abigail probably had known every single person along the entire northern coast.

He felt ridiculous, hovering among the ketchup and steak sauce and salad dressing bottles. He peeked around the corner again, trying to figure out how he could get out of the store without being caught by the woman with the short, steel-gray hair and trendy tortoiseshell glasses.

Betsy Wardle had been one of Abigail's closest friends. He knew the two of them used to play Bunco on a regular basis. If Betsy recognized him, the entire jig would be up.

He had met her several times before, as recently as four years earlier, the last time he stayed with his aunt.

He couldn't see any way to avoid having her recognize him now. The worst of it was, Betsy was an inveterate gossip. Word would be out all over town that Abigail's nephew was back, and of course that word would be quick to travel in Anna's direction.

He had two choices, as he saw it. He could either leave his half-full grocery cart right here and do his best to hightail it out of the store without being caught or he could just play duck-and-run and try to avoid her until she paid for her groceries and left.

He shoved on his sunglasses and averted his face just in time as she rounded the corner with her cart. He pushed past her, hoping like hell she was too busy picking out gourmet mustard to pay him any attention.

To be on the safe side, he turned in the direction she had just come and would have headed several aisles away but he suddenly heard an even more dreaded sound than Betsy Wardle's soft southern drawl.

Anna Galvez was suddenly greeting the older woman with warm friendliness.

He groaned and closed his eyes. Exactly the last person he needed to see right now when Betsy could expose him at any second. What was she doing here? Wasn't she supposed to be in Lincoln City right now?

He definitely needed to figure out a way out of here fast. He started to head toward the door when Betsy's words stopped him and he paused, pretending to compare the nutritional content of two different kinds of soy chips while he listened to their conversation one aisle over.

"How is your court case going against that awful man?" Betsy was asking.

"Who knows?" Anna answered with a discouraged-sounding sigh.

"The whole thing is terrible. Unconscionable. That's what I say. I just can't believe that man would work so hard to gain your trust and then take advantage of a darling girl like you. It's just not fair."

"Oh, Betsy. Thank you. I appreciate the support of you and Abigail's other friends. It means the world to me."

He wished he could see through the aisle to read her expression. She sounded sincere but he couldn't tell just by hearing her voice.

"I know I've told you this before and you've turned me down but I mean it. If you need me to testify on your behalf or anything, you just say the word. Why, when I think of how much you did for Abigail in her last years, it just breaks my heart that you're suffering so now. You were always at Brambleberry House helping with her taxes or paying bills for her or whatever she needed. You're a darling girl and I wouldn't hesitate a minute to tell that Lincoln City jury that very thing."

"Thank you, Mrs. Wardle," Anna answered. "While, again, I appreciate your offer, I don't think it will come to that. I'm not the one on trial, Grayson Fletcher is."

"I know that, honey, but from what I've read in the papers, it sounds like it's mostly his word against yours. I'm just saying I'm happy to step up if you need it."

"You're a dear, Mrs. Wardle. Thank you. I'll be sure to let the prosecutor know."

They chatted for a moment longer, about books and gardening and the best time to plant rhododendron bushes. Just as he was thinking again about trying to escape the store without being identified, he heard Anna say goodbye to the other woman. Out of the corner of his eye, he saw Betsy heading to the checkout counter that was at the end of his aisle.

He turned blindly to head in the other direction and suddenly ran smack into another cart.

"Oh!" exclaimed Anna Galvez.

"Sorry," he mumbled, keeping his head down and hoping she was too distracted to notice him.

No such luck. She immediately saw through the sunglasses. "Lieutenant Maxwell! Hello!"

"Oh. Hi. I didn't see you there," he lied. "This is a surprise. I thought you were going to be out of town today."

Her warm smile chilled at the edges. "My, uh, obligation was postponed for the rest of the afternoon. So instead I'm buying refreshments for one of the teen book clubs that meets after school at By-the-Wind. They're discussing a vampire romance so I'm serving tomato juice and red velvet cake. A weird combination, I know, but they have teenage stomachs so I figured they could handle it."

"Don't forget the deviled eggs."

She laughed. "What a great idea! I wish I'd thought of it in time to make some last night."

When she smiled, she looked soft and approachable and so desirable he forgot all about keeping a low profile. All he wanted to do was kiss her right there next to the organic soup cans.

He jerked his gaze away. "I guess I'd better let you get back to the shopping then. Your vampirettes await."

"Right."

He paused. "Listen, after I'm done here, I was thinking about taking a quick hike this afternoon. I know you said your dog could hang out with me but since you're here, maybe I'd better check that it's still okay with you."

"Absolutely. He'll be in dog heaven to have somebody else pay attention to him."

"Thanks. I'll bring him home about six or so."

"Take your time. I probably won't be done at the store until then anyway."

She smiled again, and it was much more warm and open than the other smiles she'd given him. He could swear it went straight to his gut.

"In truth," she went on, "this will take a big weight off my shoulders. I worry about Conan when I have to work long hours. Sometimes I take him into By-the-Wind with me since he loves being around people, but that's not always the easiest thing with a big dog like Conan. You're very sweet to think of including him."

Sweet? She thought he was *sweet?* He was a lieutenant with the U.S. Army who had been shot down by enemy fire. The last thing he felt was sweet.

"I just wanted a little company. That's all."

He didn't realize his words came out a growl until he saw that soft, terrifying smile of hers fade.

"Of course. And I'm sure he'll enjoy it very much. Have fun, then. I believe there were several area trail guides among the travel information I left in your apartment. If you don't find what you're looking for, we have several others in the store."

"I just figured I would take the Neah-Kah-Nie Mountain trail."

She stared at him in surprise. "You sound like you're familiar with the area. I don't know why, but for some reason, I assumed you hadn't been to Cannon Beach before."

He cursed the slip of his tongue. He was going to

have to watch himself or he would be blurting out some of the other hikes he'd gone on with Aunt Abigail over the years.

"It's been a while," he answered truthfully enough. "I'm sure everything has changed since I was here last. A good trail guide will still come in handy, I'm sure. I'll be sure to grab it back at the house before I leave."

"If you get lost, just let Conan lead the way out for you. He'll head for food every time."

"I'll keep that in mind."

He smiled, hoping she wouldn't focus too much on his past experience in Cannon Beach. "Have fun with your reading group."

"I'll do that. Enjoy your hike."

With a last little finger wave, she pushed her cart toward the checkout. He watched her go, wondering how she could manage to look so very delicious in a conservative gray skirt and plain white blouse.

This was a stupid idea, he echoed his thought of earlier, for a multitude of reasons. Not the least of which was the disturbing realization that each time he was with her, he found himself more drawn to her.

How was he supposed to accomplish his mission here to check out the situation at Brambleberry House when all his self-protective instincts were shouting at him to keep as much distance as possible between him and Anna Galvez?

THEY WERE LATE.

Anna sat at her home office computer, pretending to work with her spreadsheet program while she kept one eye out the window that overlooked the still-empty driveway.

Worry was a hard, tangled knot in her gut. It was nearly seven-thirty and she had watched the sun set over the Pacific an hour earlier. They should have been home long before now.

Without Conan, the house seemed to echo with silence. She had always thought that an odd turn of phrase but she could swear even the sound of her breathing sounded oddly magnified as she sat alone in her office gazing out the window and fretting.

She worried for her dog, yes. But she also worried about a certain wounded soldier with sad, distant eyes.

They were fine, she told herself. He had assured her he could handle Conan even at his most rambunctious. He was a helicopter pilot, used to situations where he had to be calm under pressure and he was no doubt more than capable of coping with any difficulty.

Still, a hundred different scenarios raced through her brain, each one more grim than the last.

Anything could have happened out there. Neah-Kah-Nie Mountain had stunning views of the coastline but the steep switchbacks on the trail could be treacherous, especially this time of year when the ground was soaked.

She pushed the worry away and focused on her computer again. After only a few moments, though, her thoughts drifted back to Harry Maxwell.

How odd that it had never occurred to her that he might have visited Cannon Beach before. Is that why he seemed so familiar? Had he come into By-the-Wind at some point?

But if he had, wouldn't he have mentioned it at breakfast when she had talked about buying the store from Abigail?

It bothered her that she couldn't quite place how he

seemed so familiar. She usually had a great memory for faces. But thousands of customers walked through By-the-Wind in a given year. There was no logical reason she would remember one man, no matter how compelling.

And he was compelling. She couldn't deny her attraction for him, though she knew it was completely ridiculous.

He was her tenant. That's all she could allow him to be at this complicated time in her life—not that he had offered any kind of indication he was interested in anything else.

Breakfast had been a crazy impulse and she could see now how foolish. It created this false sense of intimacy, as if an hour or so together made them friends somehow, when in reality he had only been at Brambleberry House a day.

No more breakfasts. No more chance encounters on the beach, no more bumping into him at the supermarket. When he and Conan returned safely from their hike—as she assured herself they would—she would politely thank him for taking her dog along with him, then for the rest of his time at Brambleberry House, she intended to do her absolute best to pretend the upstairs apartment was still empty.

It was a worthy goal and sometime later, when her pulse ratcheted up a notch at the sight of headlights pulling into the driveway, she told herself her reaction was only one of relief and maybe a little annoyance that he had left her to worry so long.

She forgot all about keeping her distance, though, when she saw him in the pale moonlight as he gingerly climbed out of his SUV then leaned on Conan as he limped his way toward the house.

CHAPTER SIX

SHE BURST THROUGH her apartment into the foyer just as he opened the front door, Conan plodding just ahead of him.

Max looked up with surprise at her urgent entrance, then she saw something that looked very much like resignation flash in his expression before her attention was caught by his bedraggled condition. Mud covered his Levi's and he had a long, ugly scrape on his cheek.

"Oh, my word! Are you all right? What happened?"

He let out a long breath and she thought for a moment he would choose not to answer her.

"I'm fine. Nothing to worry about."

"Nothing to worry about?" she exclaimed. "Are you crazy? You look like you fell off a cliff."

He raised an eyebrow but said nothing and she could swear her heart stuttered to a stop.

"That's not really what happened. Surely you didn't fall off a cliff, did you?"

"Not much of one."

"Not much of one! What kind of answer is that? Either you fell off a cliff or you didn't."

"I slid on a some loose rocks and fell. It was only about twenty feet, though."

Only twenty feet. She tried to imagine falling twenty feet and then calmly talking about it as if she had merely stumbled over a curb. It was too big a stretch for her and her mind couldn't quite get past it.

"I'm so sorry! Did you hurt your arm when you fell?"

He shrugged. "I might have jostled it a little when I was trying to catch a handhold but I managed to stay off it for the most part and land on my left side."

"Please, just tell me Conan didn't trip you or something to make you fall."

He gave a rough laugh and she realized with some shock this was the first time she had heard him laugh. Smile, yes. Laugh, not until just this moment, when he was battered and bleeding and looking like something one of Conan's feline nemeses would drag in.

He reached down to scratch the dog's ears. "Not at all. He was off the leash about five meters ahead of me at the time I slipped. You should be very proud of him, actually. He's a real hero."

"Conan? My Conan?"

"If not for him, I probably would have slipped farther down the scree and gone off the cliff," he answered. "I don't know how he did it, as steep as that thing was, but he made it down the hill where I had fallen and practically dragged me back up, through the mud and the rocks and everything. With my stupid arm and shoulder, I'm not sure I could have climbed back up on my own."

She shuddered at the picture he painted, which sounded far worse than anything she had been conjuring up in her imagination before they arrived home. Twenty feet! It was a wonder he didn't have a couple dozen broken bones!

"I'm so glad you're both okay!"

"I shouldn't be," he admitted. "It was luck, pure and simple. I should never have gone across that rock field. I could tell it wasn't stable but I went anyway. I don't blame you if you don't trust me to take your dog again. But I have to tell you, if not for Conan, I'm not sure I would be here right now. The dog is amazing."

Conan grinned at both of them with no trace of humility. She shook her head, fighting the urge to wrap her arms around her brave, wonderful dog and hold on tight.

"It was lucky you took him, then. And of course you can take him again. Anytime. Maybe he's your guardian angel."

Conan barked as if he agreed completely with that sentiment.

"Or at least helping him out," Max said with a rueful smile.

"You're so certain your guardian angel is a man?"

He made a face. "I haven't really given it much thought. Most women I know would have knocked me to the ground before I could take a step across dangerous terrain in the first place. A preemptive strike, you know?"

"Sounds like you know some interesting women, Lieutenant Maxwell."

"I had an…older relative who taught me most women are interesting if a man is wise enough to allow them room to be."

She blinked. Now there was something Abigail might have said. She wouldn't have expected the philosophy to be echoed by a completely, thoroughly masculine man like Harry Maxwell but she was beginning to think there was more to the helicopter pilot than she'd begun to guess at.

"We could stand out here in the hall having this interesting discussion but why don't you come inside instead and let me help you clean up and put some medicine and bandages on those cuts on your face?"

As she might have predicted, he looked less than thrilled at the prospect. He even limped for the stairs and she felt terrible she had kept him standing even for these few moments.

"Thanks, but that's not necessary. I can handle it."

She raised an eyebrow. "One-handed?"

He paused on the bottom stair with a frustrated sigh. "There is that."

"Come on, Max. I'm happy to do it."

"I don't want to put you to any trouble."

"I had three rough-and-tumble older brothers and always seemed the permanently designated medic. I think I spent half my childhood bandaging some scrape or other. I'm not squeamish at the sight of blood and I have a fairly steady hand with a bottle of antiseptic. You could do worse, Lieutenant Maxwell."

He studied her for a moment, then sighed again and she knew she had won when he stepped gingerly down from the bottom stairs.

"I'm sorry you have to do this. First your dog and now you. The inhabitants of Brambleberry House are determined to look out for me, aren't you?"

Somebody has to do it, she almost said, but wisely held her tongue while Conan barked his own answer as Max followed her into her living room.

ANNA GALVEZ INTRIGUED him more every time he saw her.

Earlier in the grocery store she had worn that slim gray skirt and white blouse with her hair tucked away and had looked as neat and tidy as a row of newly sharpened pencils.

Tonight, as she led the way into her apartment he was entranced by her unrestrained hair as it shivered and gleamed under the overhead lights in a luscious cloud that reached past her shoulders.

She had on the same white blouse from earlier—or at least he thought it was the same one. But she had traded the skirt for a pair of jeans and she was barefoot except for a flirty pair of turquoise flip-flop slippers.

As she led him inside Abigail's apartment, he caught sight of just a hint of pale coral toenail polish peeking through and he found the contrast of that with her slim brown feet enormously sexy.

If he were wise, he would turn right around and race up the stairs as fast as he could go with his now gimpy foot from the ankle he was certain he twisted in the fall.

The hard reality was he wouldn't be going anywhere fast. He hesitated to take off his hiking boot for fear the whole ankle would balloon to the size of a basketball the moment he did. It had ached like crazy the whole way down the mountain and he had a feeling he'd only made it home because his SUV was an automatic and his right leg was fine to work the gas pedal and the brake.

Like it or not, he was stuck in this apartment with Anna for the time being. He could probably do a credible job of washing the worst of the dirt and tiny pieces of mountain from his face but he had a couple of scrapes on his left arm that would be impossible for him to reach very well while the right was still in the damn sling.

It was Anna or the clinic in town and after all the time he'd spent being poked and prodded by medical types over the last six months, Anna was definitely the lesser of two evils.

"Sit down," she ordered in a drill-sergeant sort of voice.

He gave her a mocking salute but was grateful enough to take the weight off his ankle and the throbbing pain. He tried his level best not to wince as he eased onto her couch, feeling a hundred years old, like some kind of damn invalid in a nursing home.

She watched him out of those careful, miss-nothing eyes and he saw her mouth firm into a tight line. He suspected he wasn't fooling her for a moment.

"I just have to gather up a few first-aid supplies and I'll be right back," she said.

"I'm not going anywhere," he answered, which was the absolute truth.

Conan had disappeared into the kitchen—probably to find his Dog Chow, Max figured. If he'd been thinking straight, he should have stopped off and picked up the juiciest, meatiest steak he could find for the hero of the hour.

He leaned back against the sofa cushions and closed his eyes, ready for a little of the calm and peace he had always found in these rooms.

An elusive effort, he discovered, especially since the scent of Anna seemed to surround him here, sweet and sultry at the same time.

He allowed himself the tiny indulgence of savoring that delectable combination for only a moment before she bustled back with her arms loaded down by bandages and antiseptic.

"I don't need all that. Do I really look that terrible?"

She gave him a sidelong look and for just a moment, he sensed something in her gaze that stunned him to the core, a thin thread of attraction that seemed to tug and curl between them.

She was the first one to look away, busying herself with the first-aid supplies. "You want the truth, you look like you just tangled with a mountain lion."

He ordered his pulse to settle down and reminded himself of all the dozens of reasons there could be nothing between them. "Nope," he answered, trying for a light tone. "Just the mountain."

She smiled a little, then reached for the iodine. "Let's take care of the cut on your face first and then I'll check out your arm."

"I can do the face. I just need a mirror for that. I, uh, would appreciate a little help with the arm, though."

For a moment, she looked as if she wanted to argue and he wasn't sure if he was relieved or disappointed when she finally reached for his arm.

Her fingers were deliciously warm on his skin. Sensation rippled from his fingertips to his shoulder and to his vast chagrin, his heartbeat accelerated with the same thick jolt of adrenaline that hit him just as his bird lifted into the air.

Anna was some seriously potent medicine. One touch and he completely forgot about all his other aches and pains.

She gripped his arm firmly with one hand while she used her other hand to dab antiseptic on the scrapes along his forearm. He welcomed the cold, bracing sting of the medicine to counterbalance her heat.

His sudden hunger was a normal response to a lovely woman, he knew. It had been just too long and she was just too pretty for him to sit here without any reaction to her soft curves and silky skin.

"Tell me if I'm hurting you," she said after a moment.

Oh, you have no idea. Max choked down the words.

"Don't worry about it," he muttered instead.

"I mean it. You don't have to be some kind of tough-guy, stoic soldier. If this stings or I'm not careful enough, just tell me to stop."

"I'll be fine," he said gruffly, though it was a bald-faced lie. He couldn't tell her just how badly he wanted to close his eyes and lean into the gentleness of her touch.

What the hell was wrong with him? He had been fussed and fretted over by soft, pretty nurses for the last six months and none of them had ever sparked this kind of reaction in him.

He tried to tell himself it was just a delayed reaction to the adrenaline buzz of his fall—a sort of spit-in-the-face-of-death response. But he wasn't quite buying it.

Her sweep of hair brushed his skin as she bent over his arm and he wondered if she could see the goose bumps rising there.

She didn't appear to notice as she reached for a tube of antibiotic cream and slathered it on with the same slow, careful movements she seemed to do everything.

"You have a choice," she said after a moment.

"Do I?" he murmured.

"I can leave it like this or I can put bandages on the scrapes to protect them for a few days. It's up to you. I would recommend the bandage to keep things clean but it's your decision."

He wanted to tell her to stop but after he had spent several extra weeks in the hospital from a bad infection, he knew he couldn't afford to take any chances.

"Go ahead and wrap it. I might as well look like something out of a horror movie."

She smiled. "Wise choice, Lieutenant."

She pulled out gauze from her kit and wound it carefully around his arm. "If you need me to rewrap this anytime," she said as she worked, "I've got plenty."

"Right."

He figured he'd rather gnaw off his arm than endure this again.

He caught a flicker of movement in the room. Grateful for any distraction, he shifted his gaze and found Conan watching him with what looked like a definite smirk in his eyes, as if he knew exactly how tough this was for Max.

He gave the dog a stern look. *Thanks for the backup.*

When she finished his arm, she stepped back. "Are you sure you don't want me to take care of your face while you're here and all the stuff is out?"

"No. Thanks anyway."

Just the thought of her touching his face with those soft, competent fingers sent shivers rippling through him.

"Anywhere else on you I need to take care of?"

Though his mind instantly flashed a number of inappropriate thoughts, he clamped down on all of them.

"Nope. I'm good. Thanks for the patch job. I appreciate it."

He rose and took only one step toward the door when her voice stopped him.

"You were limping when you came in and you still seem hesitant to put weight on your left foot. What's that all about?"

He turned back warily. "Nothing. I twisted my ankle a little when I fell but it's really fine. Just a little tender."

"You twisted your ankle and then you hiked back

down to the trailhead and drove all the way here? Why
didn't you say something? We need to put some ice on it."

He had to be the world's clumsiest idiot and right now
he just needed to put a little space between himself and
the enticing Anna Galvez before he did something he
couldn't take back.

"It's really not a big deal. I can take care of it upstairs.
You've done enough already."

*More than enough. Or at least more than I can han-
dle!*

"Oh, stop it! How can you possibly take care of it
when you can't use your shoulder?" she pointed out with
implacable logic. "I'm willing to bet your foot is swollen enough that you won't be able to even take off your
boot by yourself, even if you didn't have your shoulder
to contend with as well."

He knew she was right but he wasn't willing to concede defeat, damn it. He'd figure out a way, even if he
had to slice the boot off with a hacksaw.

With his eye firmly on his objective—escape—he
took another few steps for the door. "You can stop worrying about me anytime now. I can take care of myself."

"I'm sure you can. But you don't always have to,"
she answered.

He had no response to that so he took a few more
steps, thinking if he could only make it to the door, he
was home free. She couldn't physically restrain him, not
even in his current pitiful condition.

But Abigail's blasted dog had other plans. Before he
could take another step, Conan magically appeared in
front of him and planted his haunches between Max and
the doorway, looking as if he had absolutely no intention
of letting him leave the apartment.

He faced the dog down. "Move," he ordered.

Conan simply made a sound low in his throat, not quite a growl but a definite challenge.

"You might as well come back," Anna said, and he heard a thread of barely suppressed laughter in her voice. "Between the two of us, we're here to make sure you take care of that ankle."

He gave Anna a dark look. "Are you really prepared for the consequences of kidnapping an officer in the United States Army, ma'am?"

She laughed out loud at that. "You don't scare me, Lieutenant."

I should, he thought. *I damn well should.*

Once again, he felt foolish for being so churlish when she was only trying to help. He could spend an hour trying to wrestle the boot one-handed or he could let her help him and be done in five minutes.

He sighed. "I would appreciate it if you would help me take off the boot. I can handle the rest from there. I've got ice upstairs."

"Of course. Come back and sit down."

He ignored Conan's look of triumph as he slowly returned to his spot on the sofa. Instead, he cursed his stupid arm and shoulder all over again.

If not for the crash and his subsequent injury, none of this would be happening. He would still be carrying out his duty, he would be flying, he would be in control of his world instead of here in Oregon wondering what the hell he was going to do with the rest of his life.

She knelt on the floor and worked the laces of his hiking boot. Her delicious scent swirled around him again and he told himself the fact that his mouth was watering had more to do with missing dinner than anything else.

Conan seemed inordinately interested in the proceedings. The dog plopped down beside Anna, watching the whole thing out of curious eyes.

The dog was spooky. Max couldn't think of another word for it. Though he felt slightly crazy for even contemplating the idea, he was quite certain Conan understood him perfectly well.

Throughout the day he had carried on a running commentary with him and Conan barked at all the proper places.

He was trying to distract himself, thinking about the dog. It wasn't quite working. He still couldn't seem to avoid noticing the curve of Anna's jawline or the little frown of concentration on her forehead as she tried to ease his tight hiking boot over his swollen ankle.

He jerked his gaze away and his attention was suddenly caught by an open doorway and the contents lined up on shelves inside.

"You kept…" His voice trailed off and he realized he couldn't just blurt out his surprise that she had kept his aunt's extensive doll collection without revealing that he knew about the collection in the first place.

"Yes?"

He couldn't seem to hang on to any thought at all when she gazed at him out of those big dark eyes.

"Sorry. I, um, was just thinking that it, uh, looks like you've kept the original woodwork in the house."

"Actually, not in this room. There was some old water damage and rot issues in here and the trim was beyond saving. I was able to find a decent oak pattern that was a close imitation, though not exact."

"You wouldn't know it's not original to the house."

"I have an excellent carpenter."

"You must have to keep him on retainer with a house of this size."

She made a face, tugging a little harder on the stubborn boot. "Just about. It helps that he only lives a few houses down. And he's marrying Julia Blair, the woman who lives on the second floor."

As she spoke, she finally managed to tug the boot off his ankle.

Before he could jerk his foot away, she rolled the sock down and then gasped. "Oh, Max. That looks horrible! Are you sure it's not broken?"

His entire ankle was swollen to the size of a small cantaloupe and it was already turning a lovely array of colors. He felt like a graceless idiot all over again.

"It's only a little sprain. I just need to wrap it and everything will be fine. Thanks again for your help."

He was determined this time he would make it out of the apartment as he picked up his boot and leaned forward to rise to his feet.

"Max—" she started to argue, and he decided he just couldn't take another word.

Driven by the slow, steady hunger of the last half hour and his own frustration at himself, he bent his head and captured her mouth with his, knowing just a moment's satisfaction that at least he had discovered an effective way of shutting her up.

Okay, it was just about the craziest thing he had ever done in a lifetime of crazy stunts but he couldn't regret it. Not when her mouth was soft and slightly open with surprise and when she tasted like cinnamon and sugar.

Before this moment, he would have thought a kiss where only two sets of lips connected would lack the fire and excitement of a deep, full-body embrace, when he could feel a woman's soft curves against him, the silky smoothness of her skin, each pulse of her heart.

But standing in Anna Galvez's living room with every muscle in his body aching like a son of a bitch, simply touching her mouth with his was the most intense kiss he had ever experienced.

He felt the electrifying heat of it singe through him like a lightning strike, as if he stood atop Neah-Kah-Nie Mountain with his arms outstretched in the middle of a thunderstorm, daring the elements.

Hunger surged through him, a vast, aching need, and he couldn't seem to think straight around it.

This wild heat made no sense to him and contradicted every ounce of common sense he possessed.

If she wasn't a con artist, she was at least an opportunist. She struck him as tight and contained. Buttoned-down, even. Very much not the sort of woman to engage in a wild, fiery romance with a wounded soldier who would be leaving in a few weeks' time.

Despite what logic was telling him, he couldn't ignore her reaction to his kiss. Instead of jerking away—or even slapping his face—she made a breathy kind of sound and leaned in closer.

That tiny gesture was all it took to send his control out the window and he pulled her closer, suddenly desperate for more.

CHAPTER SEVEN

SOME TINY, LOGICAL corner of her brain that could still function knew this was completely insane.

What was she thinking to be here kissing Harry Maxwell—she barely knew him, he was her tenant, and right now the man couldn't even stand upright, for heaven's sake!

Usually she tried to listen to that common-sense corner of her mind but right now she found it impossible to focus on anything but the heat of him and his strong, commanding mouth on hers.

As he pulled her closer, she wrapped her arms around his waist. This was a little like she imagined it would feel to stand in the midst of the battering force of a hurricane, holding tight to the hard, immovable strength of a centuries-old lighthouse. His body was all heat and hard muscles and she wanted to lean into him and not let go.

She closed her eyes and savored the taste of him, heady and male, and the thrum of her blood as his mouth explored hers.

The house faded around her and she was lost to everything but the moment. Right now she wasn't a struggling businesswoman or an out-of-her-league homeowner. She wasn't a failure or the victim of fraud or an unwilling dupe.

She was only Anna and at this frozen moment in time she felt beautiful and feminine and *wanted*.

She didn't know how long they kissed, wrapped together in her living room with the sounds of their mingled breathing and the creaks and sighs of the old house settling around them.

She would have been quite willing to stand there forever. But that still-functioning corner of her mind was aware of him shifting his weight slightly and then of his sudden discordant intake of breath.

Awareness washed over her like the bitter cold of a January sneaker wave and she froze, blinking out of what felt like a particularly delicious dream into harsh reality.

What was wrong with her? He was a stranger, for heaven's sake! She'd known him for all of twenty-four hours and here she was entangled in his arms.

She knew nothing about this man other than that he could be kind to her dog and he disliked being fussed over.

This absolutely was not like her. She always tried to be so careful with men, taking her time to get to know them, to give careful thought to a man's positive and negative attributes before even considering a date with him.

And wasn't that course of action working out just great for her? a snide little voice sneered in her mind.

She pushed it away. She barely knew the man. Not only that, but he was injured! He could barely stand up and here she was throwing herself at him. She couldn't even bring herself to meet his gaze, mortified at her instant, feverishly inexplicable reaction to a simple kiss.

Why had he kissed her, though? That was the real question. One moment she had been urging him to take it easy with his sprained ankle—okay, nagging him—and the next moment his mouth had been stealing her breath, and whatever good sense she possessed along with it.

This sort of thing did *not* happen to her.

Still, she found some consolation that he looked as baffled and thunderstruck as she was.

In fact, the only one in the room who didn't look like the house had just imploded around them all was Conan, who sat watching the two of them with an expression that bordered on smug delight, oddly enough.

Max was the first one to break the awkward silence.

"Well, your nursing methods might be a little unorthodox, but I suddenly feel a hell of a lot better."

Her flush deepened. "I'm so sorry. I don't know what... I shouldn't have..."

He held up a hand. "Stop. I was trying to make a stupid joke. I completely started it, Anna. I kissed you. You have nothing to apologize about."

She tried to remember the steps in the circle breathing Sage was always trying to make her practice but her mind was too scrambled to focus on the calming method. She also still couldn't quite force herself to meet his gaze.

"I was way out of line," he added. "I don't know quite what to say, other than you can be sure it won't happen again."

"It won't?" Now why did that make her feel so blasted depressed?

"I don't make it a habit of accosting people who are only trying to help me."

"You didn't accost me," she mumbled. "It was just a kiss."

Just a kiss that still seemed to sing through her body, moments later. A kiss she could still taste on her lips and feel in her racing pulse.

"Right," he said after a moment. "Uh, I'd better get

out of your way and let you get back to…whatever you were doing before we showed up."

She fiercely wanted him gone so she could try to regain a little badly needed equilibrium. At the same time, she couldn't help worrying about his injuries.

"Are you sure you'll be able to make it up the stairs?"

"Unless Conan stands in my way again."

"He won't," she promised. If she had to, she would lock the dog in her bedroom to keep him from causing any more trouble.

He paused at her door. "Good night, then. And thank you again for all your help."

A shadow of something hot and intense still lingered in the hazel depths of his eyes.

She told herself she shouldn't be flattered by it. But her ego had taken a beating the last few months with the trial and Gray Fletcher's perfidy. She felt stupid and incompetent and ugly in the knowledge that Gray had only pursued her so arduously to distract her from his shady dealings at her company—and that she had been idiot enough to fall for it.

Harry Maxwell didn't work for her, he didn't want anything from her. He seemed as discomfited by the heat they generated as she was.

At the same time, the fact that this gorgeous man was at least interested enough in her to kiss her out of the blue with such heat and passion was a soothing balm to her scraped psyche.

He grabbed his boot and headed into the foyer. Though she knew his ankle had to be killing him, he barely limped as he headed up the stairs.

Abigail would have followed him right upstairs with

cold compresses and ibuprofen for his ankle, no matter what the stubborn man might have to say about it.

But Anna wasn't Abigail. She never could be. Yes, she might invite the man over to breakfast to make him feel more welcome in Cannon Beach and she might fill his room with guidebooks and put a little first-aid ointment on his scrapes.

But Abigail had possessed unfailing instincts about people. She didn't make the kinds of mistakes Anna did, putting her trust in the completely wrong people who invariably ended up hurting her....

Though she knew he wouldn't appreciate her concern, she waited until she heard the door close up on the third floor before returning to her living room.

She closed the door and sagged into Abigail's favorite chair, ignoring Conan's interested look as she pressed a hand to her mouth.

What just happened here? She had no idea a simple kiss could be so devastatingly intense.

She had certainly kissed men before. She'd been engaged, for heaven's sake. She had enjoyed those kisses and even the few times she and her fiancé had gone further than kisses.

But she had always thought something was a little wrong with her in that department. While she enjoyed the closeness, she had never experienced the raw, heart-pounding desire, the wild churn in her stomach, that other women talked about.

Until tonight.

Just another reason why her reaction to a wounded soldier was both unreasonable and dangerous. She wanted to throw every caution to the wind and just enjoy the moment with him.

How on earth was she going to make it through the next few months with him living just upstairs?

Julia and the twins would be back in a week. Their presence would at least provide a buffer between her and Max.

Whether she wanted it or not.

SHE DIDN'T SEE Max Saturday morning before she left for the store. His SUV was gone and the lights were off on the third floor, she saw with some relief as she backed her van out through a misting rain that clung to her windshield and shimmered on the boughs of the Sitka spruce around Brambleberry House.

He must have left while she was in the shower, since his vehicle had been parked in the driveway next to hers when she returned with Conan from their morning walk on the beach earlier.

She spent a moment as she drove to By-the-Wind wondering where he might have gone for the day. Maybe the Portland Saturday Market? That was one of her favorite outings when she had the time and she was almost certain this was the opening weekend of the season. But would Lieutenant Maxwell really enjoy wandering through stalls of produce and flowers and local handicrafts? She couldn't quite imagine it.

Whatever he had chosen to do with his Saturday was none of her business, she reminded herself. She only hoped he didn't overdo.

She had fretted half the night that he wouldn't be able to get up and down the stairs with his ankle, that he would be trapped up on the third floor with no way of calling for help.

It was ridiculous, she knew. The man was a trained

army helicopter pilot who had survived a crash, for heaven's sake, and she had no idea what else during his service in the Middle East. A twisted ankle was probably nothing to someone who had spent several months in the hospital recovering from his injuries.

Her worry was obviously all for nothing. With no help whatsoever from her or Conan, he had managed to get down the stairs, obviously, and even behind the wheel of his vehicle.

Since he was apparently mobile, she needed to stop worrying about the man, especially since she had a million other things within her control she could be stressing over.

She barely had time to even think about Max throughout the morning. Helen Lansing, her wonderful assistant manager who led the weekly preschool story hour on Saturday mornings—complete with elaborate puppets and endless energy—called in tears, with a terrible migraine.

"Don't worry about it," Anna told her as she mentally reshuffled her day. "Just go lie down in a quiet, dark room until you feel better. Michael and I can handle story hour."

The rain—or probably their parents' cabin fever—brought a larger than average crowd to the story hour. It might have been not quite as slick and polished as Helen's shows usually were but the children still seemed to enjoy it—and as a business owner, she certainly enjoyed the sales generated by their parents as they waited for their little ones.

By the time the last child left just before lunch, she was ready for a little quiet.

"I'll be in the office for a few moments working on

invoices," she told Michael and Kae, her two clerks. "Yell if you need help."

She had just settled into her desk chair when her office phone rang. She didn't recognize the number and she answered rather impatiently.

"Sorry. Is this a bad time?"

Her mood instantly lifted at the voice on the other end of the line. "Sage! No, of course it's not a bad time. It's never a bad time when you call. How are you? How are Eben and Chloe?"

There was an odd delay on the line, as if the signal had to travel a long distance, though the reception was clear enough.

"Wonderful. Guess where I'm calling from?"

Eben owned a chain of hotels around the world and he and Sage frequently traveled between them, taking his daughter, Chloe.

Last month Sage had called her from Denmark and the month before had been Japan.

"Um, New York City?" she guessed.

"A little farther south. We're in Patagonia!"

"Really? I didn't know Spencer Hotels had a location down there."

"We don't. But Eben's considering it. He wants to capitalize on the high-end ecotourism trend so we're scouting locations. Chloe is having a blast. Just yesterday we went horseback riding through scenery so incredible, you can't imagine. You should have seen her up on that horse, just like she's been riding her whole life."

Sage's love for her stepdaughter warmed Anna's heart. When she and Sage inherited Brambleberry House, she used to be so envious of Sage for her vivid, outgoing personality.

Sage was much like Abigail in that every time she walked into a room, she walked out of it again with several new friends.

Anna never realized until they had become close friends how Sage's exuberance masked a deep loneliness.

That was gone now. Sage and Eben—and Chloe—were genuinely happy together.

"Sounds like you're having a wonderful time."

"We are. And how are things there? What's going on with the trial? I tried to call a few times last week to check in and got your voice mail."

"I know. I got your message. I'm sorry I haven't called you back. I've just been busy..."

Her voice trailed off and she sighed, unable to lie to her friend. "Okay, truth. I purposely didn't call you back."

"Ouch. Screening my calls now?"

"Of course not. You know I love you. I just... I didn't really want to talk about the trial," she finally admitted.

"That bad?"

The sympathy in Sage's voice traveled all the way across the phone line from Patagonia and tears stung behind her eyes.

"Not at all, if you enjoy public humiliation."

"Oh, honey. I'm so sorry. I should have been there. I've been thinking all week that I should have just ignored you when you said you didn't want either Julia or me to come with you. You're always so blasted independent but sometimes you need to have a friend in your corner. I should have been there."

"Completely not necessary. We're on the homestretch now. The defense should wrap up Monday, with closing arguments Tuesday, and a verdict sometime after that."

"I'm coming home," she said after that short delay. "I should be there with you, at least for the verdict."

"You absolutely are not!"

"You're my friend. I can't let you go through this on your own, Anna."

"I can handle it."

She would rather have her tongue chopped into little pieces than admit to Sage how very much she longed for her friends to lean on right now.

"You handle everything. I know. And usually you do a marvelous job at it. But you shouldn't have to bear this burden by yourself."

"If you cut short your dream trip to Patagonia with your family on my account, I will never forgive you, Sage Benedetto-Spencer. I mean it. You and Eben have already done more than enough."

"I should be there."

"You should be exactly where you are, horseback riding through incredible scenery with your husband and daughter."

Sage was silent for a moment and Anna thought perhaps the tenuous connection had been severed. "And you have to deal with a new tenant in the middle of all this, too. He's arriving any day now, isn't he?"

She rolled a pencil between her fingers. "Actually, he showed up a few days ago."

"And…?" Sage prompted.

"And what?" she said, stalling.

"What's he like?"

She had a wild, visceral image of his mouth on hers, of those strong muscles surrounding her, of his skin, warm and hard beneath her exploring fingertips.

How should she answer that? He was gorgeous and stubborn and infuriating and his kiss was magic.

"I don't really know. He's only been there a few days. So far everything has been…fine."

It was a vast understatement and she could only be grateful Sage was thousands of miles away and not watching her out of those knowing eyes of hers that missed nothing.

"Any sign of Abigail since your wounded soldier showed up or is she giving him a wide berth?"

"No ghostly manifestations, no. Everything has been quiet on the paranormal front."

"What about Conan? Does he like him?"

"Well, he did try to attack him last night in my apartment, but other than that, they get along fine."

"Excuse me? He attacked him? Our fierce and mighty watchdog Conan, who would probably lick an intruder to death?"

She sighed, wishing she'd kept her big mouth shut. Sage was far too perceptive and Anna had a sudden suspicion she would read far more into the situation.

"He and Conan went hiking yesterday on Neah-Kah-Nie Mountain and Lieutenant Maxwell fell and was scraped up a bit. He's already got an injury from a helicopter crash so it was hard for him to tend his wounds by himself but he's the, uh, prickly, independent type. He wasn't thrilled about me having to bandage his cuts. But Conan and I can both be persuasive."

"Okay, now things are getting interesting. Forget some stupid old trial. Now I want to know everything about the new tenant. Tell me more."

"There's nothing to tell, Sage. I promise."

Other than that she had kissed him and made of fool

of herself over him and then spent the night wrapped in feverish dreams that left her achy and restless.

"What does he look like?"

Anna closed her eyes and was chagrined when his image appeared, hazel eyes and dark hair and too-serious mouth.

"He looks like he's been in a hospital too long and is hungry for fresh air and sunlight. Conan adores him and is already extremely protective of him. That's what last night was about. Conan didn't want him to go up the stairs until I'd taken a look at his swollen ankle."

"And did you? Get a good look, I mean?"

Better than she should have. "Sage, drop it. There's nothing between me and Lieutenant Maxwell. I'm not interested in a relationship right now. I can't afford to be. When would I have the time, for heaven's sake, even if I had the energy? Besides, I obviously can't be trusted to pick out a decent man for myself since my judgment is so abysmal."

"That's why you need to let Abigail and Conan do it for you. Look how well things turned out for Julia and for me?"

Anna laughed, feeling immeasurably better about life, as she always did after talking to Sage. "So what you're saying is that a fictitious octogenarian spirit and a mixed-breed mutt have better taste in men than I do. Okay. Good to know. If I ever decide to date again—highly doubtful at this point in my life—I'll bring every man home to Brambleberry House before the second date."

They talked a few moments longer, then she heard Chloe calling Sage's name. "You'd better go. Thanks for calling, Sage. I promise, I'll call you as soon as I know anything about the verdict."

"Are you sure you don't want me there?"

"Absolutely positive. When you and Eben and Chloe come back to Cannon Beach at Easter, we'll have an all-nighter and we can read the court transcripts together."

"Ooh, can we do parts? I've got the perfect voice for that weasel Grayson Fletcher."

She pitched her voice high and nasal, not at all like Gray's smooth baritone, but it still made Anna laugh. "Deal. I'll see you then."

She hung up the phone a few moments later, her heart much lighter as she focused on all the wonderful ways her life had changed in the last year.

Yes, she'd had a rough few months and the trial was excruciatingly humiliating.

But she had many more blessings than hardships. She considered Sage the very best gift Abigail had be-queathed to her after her death. Better than the house or the garden or all the antique furniture in the world.

The two of them had always had a cool relationship while Abigail was alive, perhaps afflicted by a little sub-tle rivalry. Both of them had loved Abigail and perhaps had wanted her affection for themselves.

Being forced to live together in Brambleberry House had brought them closer and they had found much com-mon ground in their shared grief for their friend. She now considered Sage and Julia Blair her richest blessings, the two best friends she'd ever known.

She had a beautiful home on the coast, she had close friends who loved and supported her, she had two busi-nesses she was working to rebuild.

The last thing she needed was a wounded soldier to complicate things and leave her aching for all she didn't have.

CHAPTER EIGHT

FEW THINGS COULD send his blood pumping like a heavy storm roiling in off the ocean.

Max walked along the wide sandy beach with Conan on his leash, watching the churn of black-edged clouds way out on the far horizon. Even from here, he could see the froth of the sea, a writhing mass of deep, angry green.

It wouldn't be here for some time yet but the air had that expectant quality to it, as if everything along the coast was just waiting. Already the wind had picked up and the gulls seemed frantic as they soared and dived through the sky, driven by an urgency to fill their stomachs and head for shelter somewhere.

At moments like this, Max sometimes wondered if he should have picked a career in the coast guard.

He could have flown helicopters there, swift, agile little Sikorsky Jayhawks, flying daredevil rescues on the ocean while waves buffeted the belly of his bird.

He had always loved the ocean, especially *this* ocean—its moods and its piques and the sheer magnificence of it.

Conan sniffed at a clump of seaweed and Max paused to let him take his time at it. Though he didn't want to admit it, he was grateful for the chance to rest for a moment.

Considering his body felt as if it had been smashed

against the rocks at the headland, he figured he was doing pretty well. A run had been out of the question, with his ankle still on the swollen side, but a walk had helped loosen everything up and he felt much better.

The ocean always seemed to calm him. He used to love to race down from the house the moment Abigail returned to Brambleberry House from picking him up at the airport in Portland. She would follow after him, laughing as he would shuck off his shoes and socks for that first frigid dip of his toes in the water.

Max couldn't explain it, but some part of him was connected to this part of the planet, by some invisible tie binding him to this particular meshing of land and sea and sky.

He had traveled extensively around the world during his youth as his mother moved from social scene to social scene—in the days before Meredith sent him to military school. He had served tours of duty in far-flung spots from Latin America to Germany to the gulf and had seen many gorgeous places in every corner of the planet.

But no place else ever filled him with this deep sense of homecoming as he found here on the Oregon coast.

He didn't quite understand it, especially since he had spent much longer stretches of time in other locations. When people in social or professional situations asked him where he was from, as Anna had done at breakfast the other day, he always gave some vague answer about moving around a lot when he was kid.

But in his heart, when he thought about home, he thought of Brambleberry House and Cannon Beach.

He sighed. Ridiculous. It wasn't his. Abigail had decided two strangers deserved the place more and at this point he didn't think he could do a damn thing about it.

If his military career was indeed over, he was going to have to consider his options. Maybe he would just buy a fishing boat and a little house near Yachats or Newport and spend his days out on the water.

It wasn't a bad scenario. So why couldn't he drum up a little more enthusiasm for it, or for any of the other possibilities he'd been trying to come up with since doctors first dared suggest he might not ever regain full use of his arm?

He flexed his shoulder as he watched the gulls struggle against the increasing wind. They ought to just give up now, he thought, before the wind made it impossible for them to fly. But they kept at it. Indeed, they seemed to revel in the challenge.

He sighed as his ankle throbbed from being in one place too long. He felt weaker than a damn seagull in that headwind right now.

"Come on, Conan. We'd better head back."

The dog made a definite face at him but gave one last sniff in the sand and followed as Max led the way back up the beach toward Brambleberry House.

The storm clouds were edging closer and he figured they had maybe an hour before the real fun started.

Good. Maybe a hard thunder-bumper would drive this restlessness out of him.

He was grateful for his fleece jacket now as the temperature already seemed to have dropped a dozen degrees or more, just in the time since they set off.

The moment he opened the beach access gate at Brambleberry House, Conan bounded inside, barking like crazy as if he had been gone for months.

Max managed to control him enough to get the leash off and the dog jumped around with excitement.

"You like storms, too, don't you? I bet they remind you of Aunt Abigail, right?"

The dog barked in that spooky way he had of acting as if he understood every word, then he took off around a corner of the house.

As Max followed more slowly, branches twisted and danced in the swell of wind, a few scraping the windows on the upper stories of the house.

He planned to start a fire in the fireplace, grab the thriller he had been trying to focus on and settle in for the evening with a good book and the storm.

Yeah, it probably would sound tame to the guys in his unit but right now he could imagine few things more enjoyable.

A quick image of kissing Anna Galvez while the storm raged around them flashed through his mind but he quickly suppressed it. Their kiss had been a one-time-only event and he needed to remember that.

"Conan? Where'd you go, bud?" he called.

He rounded the corner of the house after the dog, then stopped dead. His heart seemed to stutter in his chest at the sight of Anna atop a precarious-looking wooden ladder, a hammer in her hand as she stretched to fix something he couldn't see from this angle.

The first thought to register in his distinctly male brain was how sexy she looked with a leather tool belt low on her hips and her shirt riding up a little as she raised her arms.

The movement bared just the tiniest inch of skin above her waistband, a smooth brown expanse that just begged for his touch.

The second, more powerful emotion was sheer terror as he noted just how far she was reaching above the ladder—and how precarious she looked up there fifteen feet in the air.

"Have you lost your ever-loving mind?"

She jerked around at his words and to his dismay, the ladder moved with her, coming away at least an inch or more from the porch where it was propped.

At the last moment, she grabbed hold of the soffit to stabilize herself and the ladder, and Max cursed his sudden temper. If she fell because he had impulsively yelled at her, he would never forgive himself.

"I don't believe I have," she answered coolly. "My ever-loving mind seems fairly intact to me just now."

"You might want to double-check that, ma'am. That wind is picking up velocity with each passing second. It won't take much for one good gust to knock that ladder straight out from under you, then where will you be?"

"No doubt lying bleeding and unconscious at your feet," she answered.

He was not going about this in the correct way, he realized. He had no right to come in here and start issuing orders like she was the greenest of recruits.

He had no right to do anything here. He ought to just let her break her fool neck—but the thought of her, as she had so glibly put it, lying bleeding and unconscious at his feet filled him with an odd, hollow feeling in his gut that he might have called panic under other circumstances.

"Come on down, Anna," he cajoled. "It's really too windy for you to be safe up there."

"I will. But not quite yet."

He wasn't getting her down from there short of toppling the ladder himself, he realized. And with a bad ankle and only one usable arm right now—and that one

questionable after the scrapes and bruises of the day before—he couldn't even offer to take her place.

"Can I at least hold the ladder for you?"

"Would you?" she asked, peering down at him with
delight. "I'm afraid I'm not really fond of heights."

She was afraid of heights? He stared at her and finally
noticed the slight sheen of sweat on her upper lip and the
very slightest of trembles in her knees.

A weird softness twisted through his chest as he
thought of the courage it must be taking her to stand
there on that ladder, fighting down her fears.

"And so to cure your phobia, you decided to stand fifteen feet above the ground atop a rickety wooden ladder
in the face of a spring storm. Makes perfect sense to me."

She made a face, though she continued hammering
away. "Ha ha. Not quite."

"Well, what's so important it can't wait until after
the storm?"

"Shingles. Loose ones." She didn't pause a moment
in her hammering. "We need a new roof. The last time
we had a big storm, the wind curled underneath some
loose singles on the other side of the house and ended
up lifting off about twenty square feet of roof. The other
day I noticed some loose shingles on this side so I just
want to make sure we don't see the same thing happen."

"Couldn't you find somebody else to do that for you?"

She raised an eyebrow. "Any suggestions, Lieutenant
Maxwell?"

"You could have asked me."

She finally stopped hammering long enough to look
down at him, her gaze one of astonishment as she looked
first at his arm in the blasted sling, then at his ankle.

He waited for some caustic comment about his current

physical limitations. Instead, her lovely features softened as if he'd handed her an armload of wildflowers.

"I...thank you," she said, her voice slightly breathless. "That's very kind but I'm sort of in the groove now. I think I can handle it. I would appreciate your help holding the ladder while I check a couple of shingles on the porch on the east side of the house."

He wanted to order her off the ladder and back inside the house before she broke her blasted neck but he knew he had no right to do anything of the sort.

The best he could do was make sure she stayed as safe as possible.

He hated his shoulder all over again. Was he going to have to spend the rest of his life watching others do things he ought to be able to handle?

"I'll help you on one condition. When the wind hits twenty knots, you'll have to stop, whether you finish or not."

She didn't balk at the restriction as she climbed down from the ladder. "I suppose you're going to tell me now you have some kind of built-in anemometer to know what the wind speed is at all times."

He shrugged. "I've been a helicopter pilot for fifteen years and in that time I've learned a thing or two about gauging the weather. I've also learned not to mess around with Mother Nature."

"That's a lesson you learn early when you live on the coast," she answered.

She lowered the ladder and he grabbed the front end with his left hand and followed her around the corner of the house. The house's sturdy bulk sheltered them a little from the wind here but it was still cold, the air heavy and wet.

"I thought you said you kept a handyman on retainer," he said as together they propped the ladder against one corner of the porch.

She smiled. "No, you're the one who said I should. I do have a regular carpenter and he would fix all this in a second if he were around but he's been doing some work for my friend Sage's husband on one of Eben's hotels in Montana."

"Your friend's married to a hotel owner?"

He pretended ignorance while his stomach jumped as she ascended the ladder again.

"Yes. Eben Spencer owns Spencer Hotels. His company recently purchased a property here in town and that's how he met Sage."

"She's the other one who inherited Brambleberry House along with you, right?"

She nodded. "She's wonderful. You should meet her in a few weeks. She and Eben bought a house down the coast a mile or so and they come back as often as they can but they travel around quite a bit. She called me this afternoon from Patagonia, of all places!"

She started hammering again and from his vantage point, he had an entirely too clear view of that enticing expanse of skin bared at her waist when she lifted her arms. He forced himself to look away, focusing instead on the Sitka spruce dancing wildly in the wind along the road.

"Does she help you with the maintenance on the house?"

"As much as she can when she's here. And Julia helps, too. The two of us painted my living room right after Christmas."

"She's the one who lives on the second floor, right? The one with the twins."

"Right. You're going to love them. Simon will probably talk your leg off about what it's like to fly a helicopter and how you hurt your shoulder and if you carry a gun. Maddie won't have to even say a word to steal your heart in an instant. She's a doll."

His heart was a little harder to steal than that. Sometimes he wondered if he had one. And if he did, he wasn't sure a little girl would be the one to steal it.

He'd never had much to do with kids. He couldn't say he disliked them, they just always seemed like they inhabited this baffling alien world he knew little about.

"How old are the twins?" he asked.

"They turned eight a month ago. And Sage's stepdaughter, Chloe, is nine. When the three of them are together, there's never a dull moment. It's so wonderful."

She loved children, he realized. Before he'd gotten to know her a little these last few days, that probably would have surprised him. At first glance, she had seemed brusque and cool, not at all the sort to be patient with endless questions or sticky fingers.

But then, Anna Galvez was proving to be full of contradictions.

Just now, for instance, the crisp, buttoned-down businesswoman he had taken her for that first night looked earthy and sexy, her cheeks flushed by the cold and the exertion and her hair blown into tangles by the wind.

He wasn't interested, he reminded himself. Hadn't he spent all day reminding himself why kissing her had been a huge mistake he couldn't afford to repeat?

"There. That should do it," she said a moment later.

"Good. Now come down. That wind has picked up again."

"Gladly," she answered.

He held the ladder steady while she descended.

"Thank you," she said, her voice a little shaky until her feet were on solid ground again. "I'll admit, it helped to know you were down there giving me stability."

"No problem," he answered.

She smiled at him, her features bright and lovely and he suddenly could think of nothing but the softness of her mouth beneath his and of her seductive heat surrounding him.

They stood only a few feet apart and even though the wind lashed wildly around them and the first few drops of rain began to sting his skin, Max couldn't seem to move. He saw awareness leap into the depths of her eyes and knew instinctively she was remembering their kiss as well.

He could kiss her again. Just lean forward a little and all that heat and softness would be in his arms again...

She was the first one to break the spell between them. She drew in a deep breath and gripped the ladder and started to lower it from the porch roof while he stood gazing at her like an idiot.

"Thanks again for your help," she said, and he wondered if he imagined the tiniest hint of a quaver in her voice. "I should have done this last week. I knew a storm was on the way but I'm afraid the time slipped away from me. With an old place like Brambleberry House, there are a hundred must-do items for every one I check off."

She was talking much more than she usually did and seemed determined to avoid his gaze. She obviously didn't want a repeat of their kiss any more than he did.

Or at least any more than he *should*.

"Where does the ladder go?"

"In the garage. But I can return it."

He ignored her, just hefted it with his good arm and carried it around the house to the detached garage where Abigail had always parked her big old Oldsmobile. Conan and Anna both followed behind him.

Walking inside was like entering a time capsule of his aunt's life. It looked the same as he remembered from four years ago, with all the things Abigail had loved. Her potting table and tools, an open box of unpainted china doll faces, the tandem bicycle she had purchased several years ago.

He paused for a moment, looking around the cluttered garage and he was vaguely aware of Conan coming to stand beside him and nudging his head under Max's hand.

"It's a mess, I know. I need to clean this out as soon as I find the time. It's on my to-do list, I swear."

He said nothing, just fought down the renewed sense of loss.

"Listen," she said after a moment, "I was planning to make some pasta for dinner. I always make way too much and then feel like I have to eat it all week long, even after I'm completely sick of it. Would you like some?"

He was being sucked into Anna's life, inexorably drawn into her web. Seeing Abigail's things here only reminded him of his mission here and how he wasn't any closer to the truth than he'd been when he arrived.

"No," he said. "I'd better not."

His words sounded harsh and abrupt hanging out there alone but he didn't know how else to answer.

Her warm smile slipped away. "Another time, then."

They headed out of the garage and he was aware of Conan glaring at him.

The sky had darkened just in the few moments they had been inside the garage and it now hung heavy and gray. The scattered drops had become a light drizzle and he could see distant lightning out over the ocean.

"I should warn you we sometimes lose power in the middle of a big storm. You can find emergency candles and matches in the top drawer in the kitchen to the left of the oven."

"Thanks." They walked together up the front steps and he held the door for her to walk into the entryway.

He headed up the stairs, trying not to favor his stiff ankle, but his efforts were in vain.

"Your ankle! I completely forgot about it! I'm an idiot to make you stand out there for hours just to hold my ladder. I'm so sorry!"

"It wasn't hours and you're not an idiot. I'm fine. The ankle doesn't even hurt anymore."

It wasn't quite the truth but he wasn't about to tell her that.

He didn't want her sympathy.

He wanted something else entirely from Anna Galvez, something he damn well knew he had no business craving.

UPSTAIRS IN HIS apartment, Max started a fire in the grate while his TV dinner heated up in the microwave.

The wind rattled the windowpanes and sent the branches of the oak tree scraping against the glass and he tried to ignore the delicious scents wafting up from downstairs.

He could have used Conan's company. After spending the entire day with the dog, he felt oddly bereft without him.

But he supposed right now Conan was nestled on his rug in Anna's warm kitchen, having scraps of pasta and maybe a little of that yeasty bread he could smell baking.

When the microwave dinged to signal his own paltry dinner was ready, he grabbed a beer and settled into the easy chair in the living room with the remote and his dinner.

Outside, lightning flashed across the darkening sky and he told himself he should feel warm and cozy in here. But the apartment seemed silent, empty.

Just as he was about to turn on the evening news, the rocking guitar riff of "Barracuda" suddenly echoed through his apartment.

Not tonight, Mom, he thought, reaching for his cell phone and turning it off. He wasn't at all in the mood to listen to her vitriol. She would probably call all night but that didn't mean he had to listen.

Instead, he turned on the TV and divided his attention between the March Madness basketball games and the rising storm outside, doing his best to shake thoughts of the woman downstairs from his head.

He dozed off sometime in the fourth quarter of what had become a blowout.

He dreamed of dark hair and tawny skin, of deep brown eyes and a soft, delicious mouth. Of a woman in a stern blue business suit unbuttoning her jacket with agonizing slowness to reveal lush, voluptuous curves…

Max woke up with a crick in his neck to find the fire had guttered down to only a few glowing red embers. Just as she predicted, the storm must have knocked out power. The television screen was dark and the light he'd left on in the kitchen was out.

He hurried to the window and saw darkness up and down the coast. The outage was widespread, then.

From his vantage point, he suddenly saw a flashlight beam cutting across the yard below.

His instincts hummed and he peered through the sleeting rain and the wildly thrashing tree limbs to see two shapes—one human, one canine—heading across the lawn from the house to the detached garage.

What the hell was she doing out there? She'd be lucky if a tree limb didn't blow over on her.

He peered through the darkness and in her flashlight beam he saw the garage door flapping in the wind. They must not have latched it quite properly when they had returned the ladder to the garage.

Lightning lit up the yard again and he watched her wrestle the door closed then head for the house again.

He made his way carefully to his door and opened it, waiting to make sure she returned inside safely. Only silence met him from downstairs and he frowned.

What was taking her so long to come back inside?

After another moment or two, he sighed. Like it or not, he was going to have to find out.

CHAPTER NINE

SHE LOVED THESE wild coastal storms.

Anna scrambled madly back for the shelter of the porch, laughing with delight as the rain stung her cheeks and the churning wind tossed her hair around.

She wanted to lift her hands high into the air and spin around wildly in a circle in some primitive pagan dance.

She supposed most people would find that an odd reaction in a woman as careful and restrained as she tried to be in most other areas of her life. But something about the passion and intensity of a good storm sent the blood surging through her veins, made her hum with energy and excitement.

Abigail had been the same way, she remembered. Her friend used to love to sit out on the wraparound porch facing the sea, a blanket wrapped around her as she watched the storm ride across the Pacific.

Since moving to Brambleberry House nearly a year ago, Anna tried to follow the tradition as often as she could. Sort of her own way of paying tribute to Abigail and the contributions she had made to the world.

Conan shook the rain from his coat after their little foray to the garage and she laughed, grateful she hadn't removed her Gore-Tex parka yet. "Cut it out," she exclaimed. "You can do that on that side of the porch."

The dog made that snickering sound of his, then settled into the driest corner of the deep porch, closest to the house where the rain couldn't reach him.

Conan was used to these storm vigils. She would have thought the lightning and thunder would bother him but he seemed to relish them as much as she did.

Her heart still pumped from the wild run to the garage as she grabbed one of the extra blankets she had brought outside and used a corner of it to dry her face and hair from the rain.

Lightning flashed outside their protected haven and she shivered a little as she grabbed another quilt and wrapped it around her shoulders, then headed for the porch swing that had been purposely angled into a corner to shelter its occupants as much as possible from the elements.

She had barely settled in with a sigh and rattle of the swing's chains when thunder rumbled through the night.

Before it had finished, Conan was on his feet, barking with excitement.

"Settle down, bud. It's only the storm," she assured him.

"And me."

She gasped at the male voice cutting through the night and quickly aimed her flashlight in the direction of it. The long roll of thunder must have muffled Max's approach. He stood several feet away, looking darkly handsome in the distant flashes of lightning.

Her heart, already racing, began to pump even faster. This had nothing to do with the storm and everything to do with Lieutenant Maxwell.

"Is everything okay out here?" he asked, coming closer. "I saw from my window when you went out to the garage to close the door. When I didn't hear you come back inside, I was worried you might have fallen out here or something."

He was worried about her? A tiny little bubble of warmth formed in her chest but she fought down the reaction. He didn't mean anything by it. It was just simple concern of one person to another. He would have been just as conscientious if Conan had been out here in the storm.

More so, maybe. He loved her dog, while she was just the annoying landlady who wouldn't leave him alone, always inviting him to dinner and making him help her nail down loose shingles.

"I'm fine," she finally answered, unable to keep the lingering coolness from her voice after his abrupt refusal to share pasta with her earlier. "Sorry I worried you. I was just settling in to watch the storm. It's kind of a Brambleberry House tradition."

"I remember," he answered.

She gave him a quizzical look, wondering what he meant by that, though of course he couldn't see her expression in the dark.

"You remember what?" she asked.

An odd silence met her question, then he spoke quickly. "I meant, I remember doing the same thing when I visited the coast several years ago. A coastal storm is a compelling thing, isn't it?"

He felt the same tug and pull with the elements as she did? She wouldn't have expected it from the distant, contained soldier.

"It is. You're welcome to join us."

In a quick flash of lightning, she saw hesitation flicker over those lean features—the same hesitation she had seen earlier when he had refused her invitation to dinner.

Never mind, she almost said, feeling stupid and presumptuous for even thinking he might want to sit out on a cold porch swing in the middle of a rainstorm.

But after a moment, he nodded. "Thanks. I was watching the storm from upstairs but it's not quite the same as being out here in the thick of things, is it?"

"I imagine that's a good metaphor for the life of an army helicopter pilot."

"It could very well be."

"There's room here on the swing. Or you could bring one of the rockers over from the other side of the porch, but I'm afraid they're a little damp. This is the safest corner if you want to stay out of the rain."

"Says the voice of experience, obviously."

After another odd, tense little moment of hesitation, he sat down on the swing, which swayed slightly with his weight.

The air temperature instantly increased a dozen degrees and she could smell him, spicy and male.

Lightning ripped through the night again and her blood seemed to sing with it—or maybe it was the intimacy of sitting out here with Max, broken only by the two of them wrapped in a warm cocoon of darkness while the storm raged around them.

They settled into a not uncomfortable silence, just the rain and the thunder and the occasional creak and rattle of the swing's chains.

"Are you warm enough?" she asked. "I only brought two blankets out and one is wet but I've got plenty more inside."

"I should be okay."

"Here. This one should be big enough for both of us." She pulled the blanket from around her shoulders and with a flick of her wrists, sent it billowing over both of them.

Stupid move, she realized instantly. Stupid and naive. It was one thing to sit out here with him, enjoying the storm. It was something else indeed to share a blanket while they did it. Though they weren't even touching underneath it except the occasional brush of their shoulders as they moved, it all still seemed far too intimate.

He made no move to push the blanket off, though, and she couldn't think of a way to yank it away without looking even more foolish than she already must.

"I imagine you've seen some crazy weather from the front seat of a helicopter," she said in an effort to wrench her mind from that blasted kiss the day before.

"A bit," he answered. "Sandstorms in the gulf can come up out of nowhere and you have to either play it through or set down in the middle of zero visibility."

"Scary."

"It can be. But nothing gets your heart thumping more than trying to extract a wounded soldier in poor weather conditions in the midst of possible enemy machine-gun fire."

"You love it, don't you?"

He shifted on the swing, accompanied by the rattle of creaky chains. "What?"

"Flying. What you do."

"Why do you say that?"

She shrugged. "I don't know. Your voice just sounds… different when you talk about it. More alive."

"I do love it." He paused for a long moment as the storm howled around them. "I did, anyway."

"What do you mean?"

This time, he paused so long she wasn't sure he would answer her. She had a feeling he wouldn't have if not for this illusive sense of intimacy between them, together in the darkness.

When he spoke, his voice was taut, as hard as Haystack Rock. "The damage to my shoulder is...extensive. Between the burns and the broken bones, I've lost about seventy percent range of motion and doctors can't tell me whether I'll ever get it back. Worse than that, the infection damaged some of the nerves leading to my hand. At this point, I don't have the fine or gross motor control I need to pass the fitness test to remain a helicopter pilot in the army."

"I'm so sorry." The words sounded ridiculously lame and she wished for some other way she could comfort him.

"I'm damn lucky. I know that."

He spoke quietly, so softly she almost didn't hear him over the next rumble of thunder. "The flight medic and my copilot didn't walk away from the crash."

"Oh, Max," she murmured.

He drew in a ragged breath and then another and she couldn't help it. She reached a hand out and squeezed his fingers. He didn't seem in a hurry to release her hand and they sat together in the darkness, their fingers linked.

"What were their names?" she asked, somehow sensing the words were trapped inside him and only needed the right prompting to break free.

"Chief Warrant Officer Anthony Riani and Specialist Marybeth Shroeder. Both just kids. Marybeth had only been in country for a couple of months and Tony's wife was pregnant with their second kid. They both took the brunt of the missile hit on that side of the Black Hawk and probably died before we even went into the free fall."

She couldn't imagine what he must have seen, what he had survived. She only knew she wanted to hold him close, touched beyond measure that he would share this with her, something she instinctively sensed he didn't divulge easily.

"The crew chief and I were able to get the wounded soldier we were transporting out before the thing exploded. We kept him stable until another Black Hawk was able to evacuate us."

"Was he okay? The soldier?"

"Oh. Yeah. He was a Humvee gunner hit by an improvised explosive device. He lost a leg but he's doing fine, home with his family in Arkansas now."

"That's good."

"Yeah. We were both at Walter Reed together for a while. He's a good man."

He finally let go of her fingers and though she knew it was silly, she suddenly felt several degrees cooler.

"I can't complain, can I?" he said. "I've still got all my pieces and even with partial function, I should eventually be able to do almost anything I want. Except fly a helicopter in the United States Army, I guess. It's looking like I'll probably have to ride a desk from now on or leave the military."

"A tough choice. What will you do?"

He sighed. "Beats me. You have any ideas? Flying helicopters is the only thing I've ever wanted to do. I never wanted to be some hotshot fighter jet pilot or anything fancy like that. Just birds. I'm not sure I can be content to sit things out on the sidelines."

"What about being a civilian pilot?"

He made a derogatory sound. "Doing traffic reports from the air or flying executives into the city who think they're too busy and important for a limousine? I don't think so."

"You could do civilian medevacs."

"I've thought about it. But to tell you the truth, I don't know that I'm capable of flying anything at this point, civilian or military. Or if I ever will be. We're in wait-and-see mode, according to the docs, which genuinely stinks when you're not a very patient person."

The storm seemed to be passing over, she thought. The lightning flashes were slowing in frequency and even the rain seemed to be easing. She didn't want this moment to end, though. She was intensely curious about this man who had survived things she couldn't even imagine.

"I'm sure you'll figure it out, Max. My friend Abigail used to say a bend in the road is not the end, unless you fail to make the turn. You just need to figure out which direction to turn. But you will."

"I'm glad one of us has a little faith."

She smiled. "You can borrow mine when you need it. Or Abigail's. She carried enough faith and goodness for all of us and I'm sure some still lingers here at Bramble-berry House."

He was again silent for a long time. Then, to her shock, he reached for her hand again and held on to it as the storm continued to simmer around them. They sat for a long time like that in the darkness, while Conan snored in the corner and the storm gradually slowed its fury.

Anna's thoughts were scattered but she was aware of overriding things. She was more attracted to him than any man in her entire life. To his strength and his courage and even to his sadness.

He had been through hell and though he hadn't directly said it, she sensed he suffered great guilt over the deaths of his crew members and she wanted to ease his pain.

She was also, oddly, aware of the scent of freesia drifting over the earthy smell of wet leaves and the salty tang of the sea.

If she were Sage or Julia, she might think Abigail was making her opinion known that Harry Maxwell was a good man and she approved.

She couldn't believe Abigail was here in spirit. Abigail had been such a wonderful person that Anna couldn't believe she was anywhere but in heaven, probably doing her best to liven up things there.

But at times, even she had to admit Abigail seemed closer than at others. The smell of freesia, for instance, at just the moment she needed it. She tried to convince herself Abigail had loved the scent so much it had merely soaked into the walls of the house. But that didn't explain why it would be out here in the middle of a March rainstorm—or why she thought she caught the glitter of colorful jewels out of the corner of her gaze.

She shivered a little, refusing to give in to the urge to turn her head. Max, sitting too close beside her to miss the movement, misinterpreted it. "You're freezing. We should probably head in."

"I'm not. It's just…" She paused, feeling silly for even bringing this up but suddenly compelled to share some of Sage and Julia's theory with him. "I should probably confess something here. Something I should have told you before you rented the apartment."

He released her hand abruptly. "You're married."

She laughed, though it sounded breathless even to her. "No. Heavens, no. Not even close. Why would you even think that?"

"Not even close? Didn't you say you were engaged once?"

"Yes, years ago. I'm not close to being married right now."

"What happened to the engagement?"

She opened her mouth to tell him it was none of his business, then she closed it again. He had shared far more with her than just the painful end to an engagement that should never have happened in the first place.

"He decided he wanted a different kind of woman. Someone softer. Not so calculating. His words. At least that's what he wrote in the note he sent with his sister on the morning of what was supposed to be our wedding day."

She knew it was ridiculous but the memory still stung, even though it seemed another lifetime ago.

"Ouch."

His single, abrupt word shocked a laugh out of her. "It's been years. I rarely even think about it anymore."

"Did you love him?"

"I wouldn't have been a few hours away from marrying him if I didn't, would I?"

"Seems to me a hard, calculating woman like you wouldn't need to love a man in order to marry him. My mother never did and she's been married five times since my father died."

Now that revealed a wealth of information about his life, she thought. All of it heartbreaking.

"I'm not hard or calculating! I loved Craig. With every ounce of my twenty-four-year-old heart, I loved him. That first year afterward, I was quite certain I would literally die from the pain of the rejection. I couldn't wait to move away from my friends and family in Utah and flee to a place where no one knew me or my humiliating past."

"What's humiliating about it? Seems to me you had a

lucky escape. The guy sounds like a jackass. Tell me the truth. Can you imagine now what your life would have been like if you had married him?"

She stared, stunned that he could hit right to the heart of things with the precision of a sharpshooter. "You are so right," she exclaimed. "I would have been completely miserable. I was just too young and stupid to realize it at the time."

It was a marvelously liberating discovery. She supposed she had known it, somewhere deep inside, but for so long she had held on to her mortification and the shame of being jilted on her wedding day. Somehow in the process, she had lost all perspective.

That day had seemed such a defining moment in her life, only because she had allowed it be, she realized.

She had become fearful about trusting anyone and had learned to erect careful defenses to keep people safely on the perimeter of her life. She had focused on her career, on first making By-the-Wind successful as Abigail's manager, then on building the company after she purchased it from her and then adding the second store to further cement her business plan.

Though she didn't think she had completely become what Craig called her—hard, calculating, driven—she had certainly convinced herself her strengths lay in business, not in personal relationships.

Maybe she was wrong about that.

"So if you're not married, what's your big secret?"

She blinked at Max, too busy with her epiphany to follow the trail of conversation. "Sorry. What?"

"You said you had some dark confession to make that you should have told me before I rented the apartment."

"I never said dark. Did I say dark?"

"I don't remember. I'm sure it was."

"No. It's not. It's just...well, rather silly."

"I could use more silly in my life right now."

She smiled and nudged his shoulder with hers. "All right. What's your opinion on the paranormal?"

"I'm not sure I know how to answer that. Are we talking alien visitations or bloodsucking vampires?"

"Neither. I'm talking about ghosts. Or I guess ghost, singular. As in the ghost that some residents of Brambleberry House believe shares the house with us. My friend Abigail."

"You're saying you think Abigail still walks the halls of Brambleberry House."

"I didn't say *I* believed it. But Sage and Julia do. They won't listen to reason. They're absolutely convinced she's still here and that Conan is her familiar, I guess you could say. She works through him to weave her Machiavellian plans. Though I don't really know if one should use that word when all her plans seem to be more on the benevolent side."

The rain had slowed and a corner of the moon peeked out from behind some of the clouds, lending enough light to the scene that she could clearly see his astonished expression.

He stared at her for an endless moment, until she was quite certain he must believe her barking mad, then his head rocked back on his neck and he began to laugh, his shoulders shaking so much the swing rocked crazily on its chains and Conan padded over to investigate.

She had never seen Max so lighthearted. He looked years younger, his features relaxed and almost happy. She could only gaze at him, entranced by this side of him.

The entire evening, she had been trying to ignore how

attracted she was to him. But right now, while laughter rippled out of him and his eyes were bright with humor, the attraction blossomed to a hot, urgent hunger.

She had to touch him. Just for a moment, she told herself, then she would go back inside the house and do her best to rebuild her defenses against this man who had survived horrors she couldn't imagine but who could still find humor at the idea of a ghost and her dog.

Her heart clicked just like the rain on the shingles she had just fixed as she drew in a sharp breath, then leaned forward and brushed her mouth against his.

CHAPTER TEN

HER MOUTH WAS warm and soft and tasted like cinnamon candy.

For all of maybe three seconds, he couldn't seem to move past the shock of it, completely frozen by the unexpectedness of the kiss and by the instant heat that crashed against him like those waves against the headland.

He forgot all about his amusement at the idea of his aunt Abigail using a big, gangly dog to work her schemes from the afterlife. He forgot the rain and the wind and the vow he had made to himself not to kiss her again.

He forgot everything but the sheer wonder of Anna in his arms again, of those soft curves beside him, of her scent, sweet and feminine, that had been slowly driving him insane all evening long as she sat beside him, tugging at him until his senses were filled with nothing but her.

Her arms twisted around his neck and he deepened the kiss, breathing deeply of that enticing, womanly scent and pulling her closer until she was nearly on his lap.

For the first time since he had sat down on the porch swing next to her, he was grateful for the blanket around them. Now it was no longer a curse, lending an intimacy he didn't want. Instead, the blanket had become a warm, close shelter from the cold air outside, drawing them closer.

Nothing else existed here but the two of them and the wild need glittering between them.

Kissing her again had a sense of inevitability to it, as if all day he had been waiting for only this. Suspended in a state of hungry anticipation to once again feel her hands in his hair, her soft curves pressed against him, the rapid beat of his heart.

Since the first time he kissed her, his body had been aching to have her in his arms again. That's why he had punished his ankle with a long walk on the shore, why he had spent the morning at the gym he'd found in Seaside working on his physical therapy exercises, why he had done his best to stay away from Brambleberry House all day.

Now that he had rediscovered the wonder of a woman's touch—*this* woman's touch—he couldn't manage to think about anything else. And even when he wasn't consciously thinking about it, his subconscious had been busy remembering.

This was better than anything he might have dreamed. She was warm and responsive, her mouth eager against his.

It was an intense and erotic kiss, just the two of them alone in the night in this warm shelter while the storm battered the coast around them, and he wanted it to go on forever.

Still, he had a vague awareness even as their bodies heated that the storm was calming—or at least moving farther inland, leaving them behind. The lightning strikes became more infrequent, the rolling thunder more distant.

He didn't care. Nothing else mattered but having her in his arms, slaking this raging thirst for her.

She moved a little, her soft curves brushing against his sling, but she quickly drew back.

"Sorry," she exclaimed.

"You don't have to be careful. I'm sorry my arm is in the way."

"It's not. I'm just afraid of hurting you."

"Let me worry about that."

"Are you? Worried about it, I mean?"

"What red-blooded male in his right mind would worry about a stupid thing like a cast on his arm right now?" he murmured against her mouth.

Her low laugh sent chills rippling down his spine.

"Do that again," he said.

In the darkness, she blinked at him. "Do…what?"

"Laugh like that. I would have to say, Ms. Galvez, that was just about the sexiest sound I've ever heard."

"You're crazy," she said, though she gave a self-conscious laugh when she said it and he thought he just might be content to sit there all night letting his imagination travel all sorts of wicked roads inspired by the sound.

"I must be. That's what six months in an army hospital will get you."

"I'm so sorry you had to go through that," she whispered. "I wish I could make everything okay."

To his shock, she planted a barely there kiss on the corner of his mouth then one on the other side. It was a stunningly sweet gesture and he felt something hard and tight that had been inside him for a long time suddenly break loose.

Had anyone ever shown such gentle compassion to him? He sure as hell couldn't remember it. To his dismay, tears burned behind his eyelids and he wanted to lean into her and just lose himself in her touch.

A fragile tenderness wrapped around them like Aunt Abigail's morning glory vines. He pulled her more firmly on his lap, solving the quandary of his cast by lifting the whole thing out of the way and resting his arm against her back as she nestled against his chest.

They kissed and touched for a long time, until he was aching with need, until she was shivering.

"Are you cold?"

Her laugh was rough. "Not even close."

Still, even as she said the words, she let out a long breath and he sensed her withdrawal, though she didn't physically pull out of his arms.

"This is crazy, Max. What are we doing here? This isn't… I don't do this kind of thing. I…we barely know each other."

He was having a hard time making his addled brain think at all but the still-functioning corner of his mind knew she was absolutely right. He had only been here a few days and in that time, he had been anything but honest with her.

But he didn't agree when she said she barely knew him. Right now, he felt as if she knew him better than anyone else alive. He had told her things he hadn't been able to share with the shrinks at Walter Reed.

"I don't know what this thing is between us but I'm fiercely attracted to you."

She let out a shaky breath and pulled out of his arms with a breathless little laugh. "Okay. Good to know."

"But then, you probably figured that out already."

"I believe I did, Lieutenant. And, uh, right back at you. So what do we do about it?"

He had a number of suggestions, none of which he was willing to share with her.

Before he could answer at all, the porch was suddenly flooded with lights as the electricity flashed back on.

Her eyes looked wide and shocked and she slid away from him on the porch swing as Conan gave a resigned-sounding sigh.

"Is that some kind of message?" Max asked with a rueful laugh. "Maybe the ghost of Brambleberry House is subtly telling us it's time to go inside."

"Ha. Doubtful. If I bought in to Sage and Julia's theory, Abigail's ghost would more likely be the one who cut the power in the first place," she muttered.

"You didn't tell me they had a theory about the ghost. I just figured she maybe wanted to hang around and make sure you treated her house the way she wanted."

He couldn't quite imagine Abigail as a malicious poltergeist. Not that she didn't love a little mischief and mayhem, but she wouldn't have caused it at any inconvenience or expense to someone else.

Though he might have expected things to be awkward with the heat and passion that still sparkled between them, he felt surprisingly comfortable with Anna.

He enjoyed her company, he realized. Whether they were talking or kissing or sitting quietly, he found being with her soothing, as if she settled some restless spirit inside him in a way nothing else ever had.

"Abigail was always a bit of a romantic," Anna answered. "She would have enjoyed setting the scene like this. The rain, the storm. All of it."

While he was trying to picture his aunt working behind the scenes as some great manipulator, Conan ambled off the porch steps and out in the misting rain.

"You don't really think some…ghost had anything to do with what just happened, do you?"

"I'm afraid my feet are planted too firmly on the ground for me to buy in to the whole thing like Sage and Julia do. And besides, while I firmly believe Abigail could have done anything she set her mind to, cutting off power along the entire coast so the two of us could…" Her voice trailed off and he was intrigued to see color soak those high, elegant cheekbones. "Could make out is probably a little beyond her capabilities."

Just as she finished speaking, the porch lights flickered off for maybe two seconds before they flashed back on again.

When they did, her eyes were bright with laughter.

"I wish you could see your face right now," she exclaimed.

He scanned the porch warily. "I'm just trying to figure out if some octogenarian ghost is going to come walking through the walls of the house any minute now with a bottle of wine and a dozen roses."

She laughed. "I don't believe you have anything to worry about. I've never seen her and I don't expect to."

Her smile faded and her dark eyes looked suddenly wistful, edged with sadness. "I wish Abigail *would* walk through that wall, though. I wish you could have known her. I think you would have loved her. She was…amazing. That's the only word for it. Amazing. She drew everyone to her in that way that very few people in the world have. The kind of person who just makes people around her feel happy and important, whether they're billionaire hotel owners or struggling college students."

"She must have been a good friend."

"More than that. I can't explain it, really. I just think you would have loved her. And I *know* she would have adored you."

"Me? Why do you say that?"

"She was always a sucker for a man in uniform. She was engaged to marry a man who died in Korea. He was her one true love and she never really got over him."

He stared. "I never…" Knew that, he almost said, but caught himself just in time. "How do you know that?"

"She told me about him once and then she never wanted to talk about him again," Anna answered. "She said he was the other half of her heart and the best person she'd ever known and she had mourned his loss every single day of her life."

Why had Abigail never told him anything about a lost love? He supposed it might not be the thing one confided in a young boy. What bothered him more was that he had never once thought to ask. He had always assumed she loved her independent life, loved being able to come and go as she pleased without having to answer to anyone else.

He found it terribly sad to think about her living in this big house all these years, mourning a love taken from her too soon.

"I would think a heartbreak like that would have given her an aversion to military men."

Anna shook her head, her eyes soft. "It didn't. I know she had a nephew in the military. I don't even know what branch but she was always so proud of him."

"Oh?"

"Her Jamie. I never met him. He didn't visit her much but she was still crazy about him. Abigail was like that. She loved wholeheartedly, no matter what."

Her words were a harsh condemnation, and the hell of it was, he couldn't even defend himself. He might not have visited Abigail as often as he would have liked, but it wasn't as if he had abandoned her.

They had stayed in touch over the years, he just hadn't been as conscientious about it while he was deployed.

"She sounds like a real character," he said, his voice gruff.

She flashed him a searching look and opened her mouth but before she could speak, Conan bounded back up the porch steps and shook out his wet coat on both of them.

Max managed to pull the blanket up barely in time to protect their faces.

"Conan!" she exclaimed. "Cut that out!"

The dog made that snickering sound he seemed to have perfected, then sauntered back to the corner.

"If you're looking for a signal to go inside, I believe that's a little more concrete than some ghostly manifestation."

"You're probably right," he said, reluctance in his voice.

"You're welcome to stay out here longer. I can leave the lantern and the blankets."

"I'd rather have you."

The words slipped out and hovered between them. "Sorry. I shouldn't have said that. Forget it."

She blinked. "No, I—I..."

She looked so adorably befuddled in the glow from the porch light—and just so damn beautiful with that thick, glossy dark hair and that luscious mouth—that he couldn't help himself.

One more kiss. That's all, he promised himself as he pulled her closer.

She sighed his name and leaned into him. She was

small and curvy and delicious and he couldn't seem to get enough.

He touched the warm, enticing skin above the waistband of her jeans. She gave a little shuddering breath and he felt her stomach muscles contract sharply. Her mouth tangled with his and she made a tiny sound of arousal that shot straight to his gut.

He feathered his fingers along her skin, then danced across it until he met an enticing scrap of lace. He curved his thumb over her and felt her nipple harden. She arched into him and a white haze of hunger gnawed at him, until all he could think about was touching her, tasting her.

She gasped his name.

"I need to stop or I'm afraid I won't be able to."

"To what?"

He gave a raw laugh and kissed her mouth one last time then leaned his forehead against hers, feeling as breathless as if he were a new recruit forced to do a hundred push-ups in front of the entire unit.

He wanted to take things further. God knew, he wanted to. But he knew it would be a huge mistake.

"To stop. I don't want to but I'm afraid what seems like a brilliant idea right now out here will take on an entirely different perspective in the cold light of morning."

After a long moment, she sighed. "You're probably right."

She rose from the porch swing first and though it was one of the toughest things he had ever asked of himself, he helped her gather the blankets and carry them inside the foyer.

"Good night, Anna," he said at her apartment door. "I enjoyed the storm."

"Which one?" she asked with a surprisingly impish smile.

He shook his head but decided he would be wise not to answer.

His last sight as he headed up the stairs to his apartment was of Conan sitting by Anna's doorway looking up at him, and he could swear the dog was shaking his head in disgust.

His TV had switched back on when the power returned and some Portland TV weatherman was rambling on about the storm that was just beginning to sweep through town.

He turned off the noise then went to the windows, watching the moonlight as it peeked between clouds to dance across the water.

What the hell was he going to do now?

Anna Galvez was no more a scam artist than his aunt Abigail.

He didn't know about Sage Benedetto but since he had come to trust Abigail's judgment about Anna, he figured he should probably trust it with Sage as well.

Anna had loved his aunt. He had heard the vast, unfeigned affection in her voice when she had talked about her, when she had told him how she wished he could have known Abigail.

She loved Abigail and missed her deeply, he realized. Maybe even as much as he did.

He would have to tell her the truth—that he was Abigail's nephew and had concealed his identity so he could basically spy on her.

After the heated embrace they had just shared, how was he supposed to come clean and tell her he had been lying to her for days?

It sounded so ugly and sordid just hanging out there like that, but he knew he was going to have to figure out a way.

AS WAS OFTEN the case after a wild coastal storm, the morning dawned bright and cloudless and gorgeous.

Anna awoke in her bed in an odd, expectant mood. She rarely slept with the curtains pulled, so that she could look out at the sea first thing in the morning. Today, the waves were pale pink frothed with white.

Conan must have slept in. He was usually in here first thing in the morning, begging for his run, but she supposed the late-night stormwatching had tired him out.

She wished she could say the same. She had tossed and turned half the night, her body restless and aching.

She sighed and rolled over onto her back. She was *still* restless and achy and she was very much afraid Harry Maxwell had ruined stormwatching for her for the rest of her days. How could she ever sit out on the porch watching the waves whip across the sky without remembering the heat and magic of his arms?

Blast him, anyway.

She sighed. No. It wasn't his fault. She had known she was tempting fate when she kissed him but she hadn't been able to control herself.

She wanted a wild, passionate fling with Harry Maxwell.

She drew in a shaky breath. How was that for a little blunt truth first thing in the morning?

She was fiercely attracted to the man. More attracted than she had ever been in her life. She wanted him, even though she knew he would be leaving soon. Maybe *because* she knew he would be leaving soon.

For once in her life, she didn't want to fret or rehash the past. She wanted to live in the heady urgency of the moment.

She blew out a breath. Even if she ever dared tell them—which she wouldn't—Sage and Julia would never believe she was lying here in her bed contemplating such a thing with a man she had only known for a matter of days.

How, exactly, did one go about embarking on a fling? She had absolutely no idea.

She supposed she could take the direct route and go upstairs dressed in a flimsy negligee. But first she would have to actually go out and *buy* a flimsy negligee. And then, of course, she would have to somehow find the courage to put it on, forget about actually having the guts to walk upstairs in it.

She sighed. Okay, she didn't know exactly how she could work the logistics of the thing.

"But I *will* figure it out," she said aloud.

Conan suddenly barked from the doorway and she felt foolish for talking to herself, even if her only witness was her dog, who didn't seem to mind at all when she held long conversations with herself through him.

"Thanks for the extra half hour," she said to the dog.

He grinned as if to say *you're welcome,* then headed to the door to stand as an impatient sentinel, as was his morning ritual. She knew from long experience that he would stay there until she surrendered to the inevitable and got dressed to walk him down the beach.

This morning she didn't make him wait long. She hurried into jeans and a sweatshirt then pulled her hair back into a ponytail and grabbed her parka against the still-cold March mornings.

Conan danced on the end of his leash as she opened the door to Brambleberry House, then even he seemed to stop in consternation.

The yard was a mess. The storm must have wreaked more havoc than she'd realized from her spot on the seaward side of the house. The lawn was covered with storm debris—loose shingles and twigs and several larger branches that must have fallen in the night since she was certain she would have heard them crack even from the other side of the house.

Okay, she was going to have to put her tentative seduction plans for Harry Maxwell on the back burner. First thing after walking Conan, she was going to have to deal with this mess.

CHAPTER ELEVEN

She cut Conan's walk short, taking him north only as far as Haystack Rock before turning back to head down toward home and all the work waiting for her there.

At least it was an off-season Sunday, when her schedule was more flexible. As a small-business owner, she always felt as if she had one more thing she should be doing. But one of the most important things Abigail had taught her was to be protective of her time off.

You've got to allow yourself to be more than just the store, Abigail had warned her in the early days after she purchased By-the-Wind. *Don't put all the eggs of yourself into the basket of work or you're only going to end up a scrambled mess.*

It wasn't always possible to take time off during the busier summer season, but during the slower spring and winter months she tried to keep Sundays to herself to recharge for the week ahead.

Of course, cleaning up storm debris wasn't exactly relaxing and invigorating, but it was better than sitting in her office with a day full of paperwork.

Her mind was busy with all that she had to do as she walked up the sand dunes toward the house. She let Conan off his leash as soon as she closed the gate behind her and he immediately raced around the corner of the house. She followed him, curious at his urgency, and was stunned to find Max wearing a work glove on his uninjured hand and pushing a wheelbarrow already piled high with fallen limbs.

Her heart picked up a pace at the sight of him greeting Conan with an affectionate pat and she thought how gorgeous he looked in the warm glow of morning, lean and lithe and masculine.

"Hey, you don't have to do that," she called. "You're a renter, not the hired help."

He looked up from Conan. "Do you have a chain saw?" he asked, ignoring her admonition. "Some of these limbs are a little too big to cart off very easily."

"Abigail had a chain saw. It's in the garage. I'm not sure when it was used last, though, so it's probably pretty dull."

She hesitated, trying to couch her words in a way to cause the least assault to his pride. "Um, I hate to bring this up but don't you think your shoulder might make running a chain saw a little tough?"

He looked down at the sling with frustration flickering in his eyes, as if he had forgotten his injury.

"Actually, she also had a wood chipper," she added quickly. "I was planning to just chip most of this to use as mulch in the garden in a few weeks' time. The machine is pretty complicated, though, and it's a two-person job. To tell you the truth, I could use some help."

"Of course," he answered promptly.

She smiled, lost for just a moment in the memory of all they had shared on the porch swing the night before.

She might have stood staring at him all morning if Conan hadn't nudged her, as if to remind her she had work to do.

"Let me just find my gloves and then we can get to work."

"No problem. There's plenty out here to keep me busy."

She hurried inside the house and headed for the hall tree, where she kept her extra gardening gloves and the muck boots she wore when she worked out in the garden.

The man had no right to look so gorgeous first thing in the morning when she could see in the hall mirror that she looked bedraggled and windblown from walking along the seashore.

The idea of a casual fling had seemed so enticing this morning when she had been lying in bed. When she was confronted with six feet of sexy male in a denim workshirt and leather gloves, she wondered what on earth she had been thinking.

She had a very strong feeling that a casual fling with a man like Lieutenant Maxwell would turn out to be anything but casual.

Not that a fling with him seemed likely anytime in the near future. He had seemed like a polite stranger this morning, in vivid contrast to the heat between them the night before.

She sighed. It was a nice fantasy while it lasted and certainly helped take her mind off Grayson Fletcher and the misery of the trial, which would be resuming all too soon.

When she returned to the yard, she couldn't see Max anywhere. But since Conan was sprawled out at the entrance to the garage, she had a fairly solid idea where to find him.

Inside, she found him trying to extricate the chipper, which was wedged tightly behind an old mattress frame and a pile of two-by-fours Will had brought over to use on various repairs around the house.

The chipper had wheels for rolling across the lawn but it was still bulky and unwieldy. She stepped forward to give him a hand clearing a path. "I know, this garage is a mess. With every project we do on the house, we seem to be collecting more and more stuff and now we're running out of places to put it all."

"You'll have to build a garage annex for it all."

She smiled. "Right. A garage for the garage. Sage would love the idea. To tell you the truth, I don't know what else to do. I hate to throw anything away. I'm so afraid we'll toss an old lamp or something and then find out it was Abigail's favorite or some priceless antique that had been in her family for generations."

"You can't keep the house like a museum for her."

"I know. She wouldn't want that and what little family she had doesn't seem to care much about maintaining their heritage. But I still worry. My parents brought very little with them from Mexico when they came across the border. Their families were both poor and didn't have much for them to bring but sometimes I wish I had more old things that told the story of my ancestors and what their lives might have been like."

An odd expression crossed his features and he opened his mouth to answer but before he could, she pulled the last obstacle out of the way so they could pull out the chipper.

"Here we go. That should give us a clear path."

They pulled the chipper out of the chaotic garage and into the sunshine while Conan watched them curiously.

"Any idea how to work this thing?" Max asked.

She smiled. "A year ago, my answer to that question

would have been a resounding no, but I've had to learn a few things since I've been at Brambleberry House. This home ownership thing is not for the weak or timid, I'll tell you that much. I've become an expert at removing wallpaper, puttying walls, even wielding a toilet snake. This chipper business is easy compared to that."

For the next two hours, they worked together cleaning up the yard while Conan lazed in whatever dappled bit of sunbeam he could find. It was a gorgeous, sunny early spring day, the kind she always considered a gift from above here in Oregon.

When the fallen branches were cleared and the beautiful wood chips from them stored at the side of the garage for a few more weeks until she had time to prepare the flower beds, Max helped her gather up the loose shingles and replace the gutter that had blown down.

"Anything else we can do?" he asked when they finished and were sitting together on the porch steps taking a breather.

"I don't think so. Not right now, anyway. It's an endless job, this home maintenance thing."

"But not a bad way to spend a beautiful morning."

She smiled, enjoying his company immensely. Even with only one good hand, he worked far harder than most men she knew. He carried heavy limbs under one arm and though he quickly figured out he couldn't push the wheelbarrow with one hand without toppling it over, he ended up dragging out Abigail's old garden wagon and pulling the limbs and wood chips in that.

"I used to hate gardening when I was a kid," she told him. "My parents always had a huge vegetable garden. We would grow peppers and green beans and sweet corn and of course we kids always had to do the weeding. I vowed I was going to live in a condominium the rest of my life where I wouldn't have to get out at the crack of dawn to pick beans."

"But here you are." He gestured to the house.

"Here I am. And you know something weird? Taking care of the garden and yard has become my favorite part of living here. I can't wait until the flowers start coming out in a few weeks. You will be astonished at Abigail's garden. It's a magic place."

He made a noncommittal sound, as if he wasn't quite convinced, and she smiled. "I guess you don't have much opportunity for gardening, living in base housing as you said you've done."

"Not in the army, no," he said in what she had come to think of as his cautious voice. "Various places I've stayed, I've had the chance to do a little but not much."

"You can do all you want at Brambleberry House while you're here. All hands are welcome in Abigail's garden, experienced or not."

"I'll keep that in mind."

Conan brought over a sturdy twig they must have missed and dropped it at his feet. Max obliged him by picking it up and tossing left-handed for the dog to scamper after.

It was a lovely moment and Anna found she didn't want it to end. "Do you feel like a drive?" she asked suddenly.

"With a specific destination involved or just for the ride?"

"A little of both. I need to head down to Lincoln City to drop off some items that were delivered by mistake to the store up here. I'd love some company. I'll even take you to lunch at my favorite restaurant at Neskowin

Beach on the way down. My way of paying you back for your help today."

"You don't owe me anything for that. I didn't do much."

She could have argued with him but she decided she wasn't in the mood to debate. "The offer's still open."

He shifted on the step and looked up at the blue sky for a long moment and then turned back at her with a rather wary smile. "It *is* a gorgeous day for a drive."

She returned his smile, then laughed when Conan gave two sharp barks, whether from anticipation or just plain excitement, she couldn't guess. "Wonderful. Can you give me about half an hour to clean up?"

"Only half an hour?"

She grinned at him as she climbed to her feet. "Lieutenant, I grew up with three brothers in a little house with only one bathroom. A girl learns to work her magic fast under those circumstances."

She was rewarded with a genuine smile, one that warmed her clear to her toes. She hurried through her shower and dressed quickly. And though she would have liked to spend some time blow-drying her hair and fixing it into something long and luxurious and irresistible, she had to be satisfied with pulling it into a simple style, held away from her face with a yellow bandeau that matched her light sweater.

She did take time to apply a light coat of makeup, though even that was more than she usually bothered with.

"It's not a date," she assured Conan, who sat watching her with curious eyes as she applied eyeliner and mascara.

This is not a date and I am not breathless, she told herself when the doorbell rang a few moments later.

She answered the door and knew that last one was a blatant lie. She felt as if she were standing on the bluffs above Heceta Head with the wind hitting her from every side.

He wore Levi's and a brushed-cotton shirt in a color that matched the dark spruce outside. Hunger and anticipation curled through her insides.

"Do you need more time?" he asked.

"Not at all. I only have to grab my purse. Oh, and Conan's leash. Are you okay with him coming along? He pouts if I leave him alone too long."

"I expected it."

That was one of the things she appreciated most about him—his wholehearted acceptance of her dog.

Conan raced ahead as they headed out to her minivan and waited until she opened the door. His customary spot was in the passenger seat but he seemed content to sprawl out in the cargo area this trip, along with the boxes she had carefully strapped down the day before.

She backed with caution out of the driveway and waited until they were on the road heading south before she spoke. "I know you've been at least as far south as Neah-Kah-Nie Mountain. Have you gone farther down the coast?"

"Not this trip," he answered. "It's been several years."

"I've been driving to Lincoln City two or three times a week for nine months and I still never get tired of it."

"Is that how long you've had the store there?"

She nodded, then fell silent, remembering her starry dreams of last summer, when she had first opened the second store. She had wanted so desperately for the store to succeed and had imagined opening a third and maybe even a fourth store someday, until everywhere on the coast, people would think of By-the-Wind when they thought of books and unique gift items.

Now her dreams were in tatters and most days when she drove this road, she arrived with tight shoulder muscles and her stomach in knots.

"Did I say something wrong?" Max asked, and she realized she had been silent for a good mile or more.

"No. It's not you. It's just..."

She hesitated to tell him, though the trial was certainly common knowledge.

No doubt he would hear about it sooner or later and it was probably better that she give him the information herself.

Her hands tightened on the steering wheel. "My professional life is a mess," she admitted. "Once in a while I'm able to forget about it for an hour or so at a time but then it all comes creeping back."

She was almost afraid to look at him to gauge his reaction but she finally dared a quick look and found his expression unreadable. "Want to talk about it?"

"I don't want to ruin your enjoyment of the spectacular coastal scenery with such a long, boring, sordid story."

"Can a story be boring and sordid at the same time?"

The tongue-in-cheek question surprised a laugh from her when she least expected to find much of anything amusing. "Good point."

And a good reminder that she shouldn't take herself so seriously. She hadn't lost any team members to enemy fire. She hadn't been shot down over hostile territory or suffered severe burns or spent months in the hospital.

This was a tough hurdle and professionally and personally humiliating for her but it wasn't the end of the world.

She didn't know where to start and she didn't want to look like an idiot to him. But he had been brutally honest with her the night before and she suddenly found she wanted to share this with Max.

"I trusted the wrong person," she finally said. "I guess the story all starts with that."

COULD THE WOMAN make him feel any more guilty, however unwittingly?

As Max listened to Anna's story of fraud and betrayal by the former store manager of her Lincoln City store, shame coalesced in his gut.

She talked about how she had been lied to for months, how she had ignored warning signs and hadn't trusted her gut.

How was Max going to tell her he had lied about his identity?

He had a strong suspicion her past experience with this charlatan wasn't going to make her the forgiving sort when he came clean.

"So here we are six months later," she finally said. "Everything is such a disaster. My business is in shambles, I've got suppliers coming out of the woodwork with invoices I thought had been paid months ago and worse, at least two dozen of my customers had their credit and debit cards used fraudulently. It's been a months-long nightmare and I have no idea when I'll ever be able to wake up."

Max remembered his speculation when he read the sketchy information online about the trial that maybe she had been involved in the fraud, a partner who was letting her manager take the fall while she reaped the benefits.

The thought of that now was laughable and he was sorry he had even entertained the idea. She sounded sick about the trial, about the fraud, especially about her customers who had suffered.

"You said this Fletcher jerk has been charged?"

"Oh, yes. That's part of the joy of this whole thing, out there in the public eye for everyone to see what an idiot I've been."

"It's not your fault the guy was a scumbag thief."

"No. But it is my fault I hired the scumbag thief to mind my store and gave him access to the personal information of all my customers and vendors who trusted me to protect that. It's my fault I didn't supervise things as closely as I should have, which allowed him more room and freedom to stick his fingers in as many pies as he could find."

"That's a lot of weight for you to bear."

"My name is the one on the business license. It's my responsibility."

"When will the trial wrap up?"

"This week, I think. Closing arguments start tomorrow and I'm hoping for a quick verdict soon after that. I'll just be so glad when it's over."

"That bad?"

She shrugged and tried to downplay it but he saw the truth in her eyes. "Every day when I walk in the courtroom, I feel like they ought to hand me a dunce cap and a sign to hang around my neck—World's Biggest Idiot."

"You've sat through the entire trial?"

"Every minute of it. Grayson Fletcher stole from me,

he stole from customers, he stole from my vendors. He took my reputation and I want to make sure he pays for it."

He had seen seasoned war veterans who didn't have the kind of grit she possessed in order to walk into that courtroom each day. He was astonished at the soft tenderness seeping through him, at his fierce desire to take her hand and assure her everything would be okay.

He couldn't do it. Not with his own deception lying between them.

"Anna, I need to tell you something," he said.

"What?" For just an instant, she shifted her gaze from the road, her eyes wary and watchful.

"I haven't been..." Honest, he started to say, but before the words were out, Conan suddenly interrupted him with a terrible retching sound like he had a tennis ball lodged in his throat.

Until this moment, the dog had been lying peacefully in the cargo area of the minivan but now he poked his head between the driver and passenger seats, retching and gagging dramatically.

"Conan!" she exclaimed. "What's going on, bud? You okay?"

The dog continued making those horrible noises and Anna swerved off the road to the wide shoulder, turned off the van and hurried to the side to open the sliding door.

Conan clambered out and walked back and forth a few times on his leash. He gagged once or twice more, then seemed to take care of whatever had been bothering him.

A moment later, with what seemed like remarkable nonchalance, he headed to a clump of grass and lifted his leg, then wandered back to the two of them, planted his haunches in the grass and looked at them expectantly.

Anna watched him, a frown on her lovely features. "Weird. What was that all about?"

"Carsick, maybe?" Max suggested.

"Conan's never carsick," she answered. "I swear, he has the constitution of a horse."

"Maybe he just needed a little fresh air and a convenient fern."

"So why the theatrics? Maybe he just needed attention. Behave yourself," she ordered the dog as she let him back into the back of the vehicle.

Conan grinned at both of them and Max could have sworn the dog winked at him, though of course he knew that was crazy.

"We're almost to Neskowin and my favorite place," Anna said as she returned to the driver's seat. "Are you ready for lunch?"

He still needed to tell her he was Abigail's nephew. But somehow the time didn't seem right now.

"Sure," he answered. "I'm starving."

"Trust me, you're going to love this place. Wait until you try the chili shrimp."

HE COULDN'T REMEMBER the last time he had permitted himself to genuinely relax and have fun.

In the military, he had been completely focused on his career, on becoming the best Black Hawk pilot in his entire division. And then the last six months had been devoted to healing—first the burns and the fractures, then the infection, then the nerve damage.

All that seemed a world away from this gorgeous stretch of coastline and Anna.

While they savored fresh clam chowder and crab legs at a charming restaurant with a spectacular view, they watched the waves roll in and gulls wheel overhead as they laughed and talked.

She told him about growing up with three older brothers in Utah and the trouble they would get in. She told him about her father dying in an industrial accident and her mother's death a few years later from cancer.

She talked about her brother the biologist who lived in Costa Rica with his wife and their twin toddler girls, who knew more Spanish than they did English and could swim like little guppies. About her brother Daniel, a sheriff back home in Utah and his wife, Lauren, who was the only physician for miles around their small town and about her brother Marc, whose wife had just left him to raise their two little boys on his own.

He would have been content just to listen to her talk about her family with her hands gesturing wildly and her face more animated than he had seen it. But she seemed to expect some conversation in return.

Since he didn't think she'd be interested in the stepsiblings he had barely known even when his mother had been married to their respective fathers, he told her instead about his real family. About his army unit and learning to fly his bird, about night sorties when it was pitch-black beneath him as they flew over villages with no electricity and he felt like he was flying over some lunar landscape, about the strength and courage of the people he had met there.

After lunch, they took a short walk with Conan along the quiet, cold beach before continuing the short trip to Lincoln City.

Though he had been careful not to touch her all day, he was aware of the heat simmering between them. He would have to be dead to miss it—the kick of his heartbeat when she smiled, the tightening of his insides when she laughed and ran after Conan on the beach, the burning ache he fought down all day to kiss her once again.

She was the most beautiful woman he had ever known but he couldn't find any words to tell her so that didn't sound corny and artificial. As they reached the busy outskirts of Lincoln City, he watched, fascinated, as his lighthearted companion seemed to become more focused and reserved with each passing mile.

By the time they drove into a small district of charming storefronts and upscale restaurants and pulled up in front of the cedar-and-brick facade that said By-the-Wind Two, she seemed a different person.

"You can wait here if you'd like," she said after she had turned off the engine.

"I'd like to see your store, if that's okay with you," he said. There was a much smaller likelihood of anyone recognizing him as Abigail's nephew in Lincoln City than if he'd gone into the original By-the-Wind, he figured. Beyond that, he really did want to see where she worked.

"Can I carry something for you?" he asked.

"I've got six boxes here. They're extremely fragile so we would probably be better off making a few trips rather than trying to haul everything in at once," she said.

He picked up a box with his good arm and followed her to a side entrance to the store, which she unlocked and propped open for them. They carried the boxes into what looked like a back storage room then they made two more trips each, the last one accompanied by Conan.

After they set down the last boxes, Anna led the way into the main section of the store.

He looked around with curiosity and found the shop comfortable and welcoming, very much in the same vein as Aunt Abigail's Cannon Beach store. Something jazzy and light played on a hidden stereo system and the wall sconce lighting in the bookstore area made all the books seem mysterious and enticing. Plump chairs invited patrons to stay and relax and apparently they did. Several were occupied and he had the feeling these were regular customers.

A long-haired gray cat was curled up atop a low coffee table in one corner. Conan hurried immediately over to the cat and Max braced himself for a confrontation but the two of them seemed to have an understanding.

The cat sniffed, gave him a bored look, then sauntered away just as a woman with a name badge that indicated she worked at the store caught sight of them and hurried over to greet Anna.

She looked thin and athletic, with long, salt-and-pepper hair pulled back in a ponytail and round wire-rim glasses that didn't conceal her glare.

"Excuse me, what are you doing here? Get out."

Anna tilted her head, much as the long-haired cat had done. "Last I checked, I still own the place."

The older woman all but shook her finger at her. "This is supposed to be your day off, missy. What do I have to do, hide your van keys so you take some time off?"

Anna laughed and hugged the other woman. "Don't nag. I know. I just brought the shipment of blown glass floats that was delivered to the other store. They're all in the back waiting to be stocked. You should see them, they're every bit as gorgeous as the few samples we received. I was afraid I wouldn't have time to drop them off before court tomorrow and I know they're already a week overdue."

"We would have gotten by without them for another day or two."

"I know, but it was a lovely day for a drive. Sue Poppleton, this is my new tenant, Lieutenant Harry Maxwell."

The woman gave him a friendly, curious smile, then turned back to Anna. "Since you're here, do you have five minutes to help me figure out what I'm doing wrong when I try to cancel a preorder in the system?"

"Of course. Max, do you mind just hanging out for a moment?"

"Not at all," he answered.

He headed for a nearby display of local travel books and was leafing through one on local history when he heard the front door chime. He didn't think much about it, until he realized the entire section of the store had gone deadly quiet.

CHAPTER TWELVE

"GET OUT," HE heard Anna say with a coldness in her voice Max had never heard before.

Conan growled suddenly—whether at her tone or at something else, Max had no idea but he now burned with curiosity.

Not knowing quite what to expect, he stepped away from the display so he could get a clear view of the door.

The man standing just inside the store didn't look threatening at all. He was one of those academic-looking types with smooth skin, artfully tumbled hair, intense eyes behind scholarly looking glasses. Exactly the sort one might expect to find sitting in a bookstore on a Sunday afternoon with a double espresso and the *New York Times* crossword puzzle.

So why the dramatic reaction? Conan was standing in front of Anna like he was all set to rip the man apart and even her employee looked ready to start chucking remaindered books at his head.

The guy seemed completely oblivious to their animosity, his gaze focused only on Anna.

"Come on, Anna. Cut me a break here. I was across the street at the coffee shop and saw your van pull up. I left an excellent croissant half-eaten in hopes you might finally give me a chance to explain."

"I don't need to hear any explanations from you. I need you out of my store right now."

Her voice wobbled, just a little, but in that instant Max figured it out. This must be the bastard who had screwed her over.

He took a step forward, thinking he could probably knock the guy out cold with one solid left hook, but he paused. Maybe it would be better to see how things played out.

Besides, she looked as if she had plenty of help.

"Call off your mutt, will you?"

The dog Max had never seen do anything but enthusiastically lick anyone who so much as looked at him still stood in a protective stance in front of Anna, low growls rumbling out of him.

"I ought to let him rip your throat out after what you've done."

"Come on, baby. Don't be like this."

He raked a hand through his hair and gave Anna what Max figured he probably thought was some kind of melting look.

Anna appeared very much frozen solid. "Like what?" she asked quietly. "Like a woman who finally found her brain about six months too late and figured out what a *cabrón* you are."

Max didn't know much Spanish but he'd heard that particular term in the army enough to know it was not a particularly affectionate or flattering one.

Sue chortled, which seemed to infuriate the man even more. His face turned ruddy beneath his slick tan and he took a step forward, only to pause when Conan growled again.

His mouth hardened but he stopped. "How long did

you have to practice that injured victim act you played so well in court when you testified?"

"Act?" Anna's voice rose in disbelief.

"Come on. You knew what was up the whole time. You just preferred to look the other way."

Anna drew in a shaky breath and even from here, Max could see the fury in her eyes. "Get out. That is your last warning before I call the police. I'm sure the judge will just love to find out you've been in here harassing me."

"Careful, babe. *Harassment* is an ugly word. You don't want to be throwing it around casually. Of course, sometimes it's a perfectly appropriate word. The exact one, really. Like when a business owner coerces an employee to sleep with her."

Her features paled and she looked vaguely queasy. "I never slept with you, thank the Lord."

"She didn't coerce you into anything and you know it, you disgusting piece of vermin," Sue snapped, and Fletcher blinked at her as if he'd forgotten she was there.

"Every single employee of By-the-Wind could testify about how you were the one constantly putting out the vibe, hitting on her every time she turned around," she went on. "Sending her flowers, writing poems on the employee bulletin board, taking credit for everybody else's ideas just so you could convince her you were Mr. Wonderful."

Anna drew in a deep breath, not looking at all thrilled by the other woman's defense of her. Instead, her color flared even higher. "Uh, Sue, maybe you should start unpacking those floats I brought so you can make sure none of them shattered in transit."

The other woman looked reluctant to leave but something in Anna's gaze must have convinced her to go.

With one last glare at Grayson Fletcher, she headed for the stockroom.

As soon as she was out of earshot, Anna turned back to the man. "You are way out of line."

He shrugged. "Maybe. But if, say, I spoke to the local newspaper reporter covering the case, I could probably spin things exactly my way. You wouldn't look like the sainted victim then, would you?"

Anna opened her mouth to retort, but he cut her off before she could. "Of course, I could always keep my mouth shut, under the right circumstances."

"What circumstances?"

He shrugged. "If I *am* convicted on these bogus charges, maybe, just maybe, you could see your way clear to testifying on my behalf in the sentencing hearing."

She narrowed her gaze. "That sounds suspiciously like blackmail."

"Another ugly word. That's not it at all. I would just think in the interest of making things right, you would want to tell the judge you've had second thoughts and have had time to look at things a little differently," he said calmly.

She gazed at him for a long time. Just before Max was ready to step forward and kick the guy out of the store, she spoke in a quiet, determined voice.

"Go to hell, Grayson. Of course, I can comfort myself with the thought that by this time next week that's exactly where you're going to find yourself—the hell that passes for the Oregon State Penitentiary in Salem."

The other man's face turned a mottled red, until any trace of anything that might have been handsome turned ugly and mean. He took another step forward, not even stopping when Conan barked sharply.

"You should have left things alone." His low, intense voice dripped with rancor. "I would have paid everything back eventually. I was working on a plan. I tried to tell you that, but you were too damn uppity to listen. Well, you'll listen to me now. I have enough dirt on you that I can ruin you. You harassed me, you assaulted me, you threatened to fire me if I didn't sleep with you. That's the story I'm going to be feeding the pretty little local reporter. And then you framed me to hide your own crimes. When my civil suit is done, you're going to be lucky if I leave you with so much as a comic book. I'll take this store and your other one and that damn house you love so much. Then where will you be? A stone-cold bitch left with nothing."

She seemed to freeze, to shrink inside herself. Max, however, did not. He stepped away from the shelves and faced the other man down.

"Okay, time's up, bastard."

Anna lifted shocked eyes to his, as if she'd forgotten his presence. Max had dealt with enough of Fletcher's type in the military that he wasn't at all surprised to see his bullying bluster fade when confronted with direct challenge.

"Says who?" he asked warily.

"Between me and the dog, I think it's safe to say we can both make it clear you've outstayed your welcome."

Fletcher looked between Conan and Max, as if trying to figure out which of them posed the bigger threat, then he gave a hard laugh, regaining a little of his aplomb. "What are you going to do? Club me with your cast?"

Max gave the same grim, dangerous smile he used on recalcitrant trainees. "Try me."

The four of them stood in that tableau for several long

seconds until Conan barked sharply, as if to add his two cents to the conversation. Fletcher stared at them again then gave Anna one last look of sheer loathing before he turned and stalked out of the store.

SHE WANTED TO DIE.

To walk down to the beach and dig the biggest, deepest hole she could manage and just bury herself inside it like a geoduck clam.

Bad enough that she had been caught unawares by Grayson and had stood there like an idiot letting him rant on and on with his damning—but completely ridiculous—allegations.

How much worse was it that Max had been a party to her disgrace?

Not exactly the best way to seduce a man, to show him unmistakable evidence what an idiot she was. When she remembered how she had actually thought she was coming to care for that piece of dirt, she just about thought she would be sick.

"Well, that was the single most humiliating ten minutes of my life."

Max moved closer and she alternated between wanting to bury her face in her hands so she didn't have to look at him and wanting to curl against that hard chest of his.

"You have no reason to feel humiliated. I'm the one who should feel humiliated. I didn't even get one good swing with my cast."

His disgruntled tone surprised a shaky laugh out of her. "I'm sure you can still chase him down at the bakery with his half-eaten croissant," she said. "Or send Conan over to bring him back."

"That kind of instant problem solving must be why you're the boss."

She laughed again, then realized her knees were wobbling. "Excuse me, I need to sit down."

She plopped down on the nearest couch, still fighting the greasy nausea in her belly, the sheer mortification that she had once been stupid and gullible enough to be attracted to a slimy worm like Grayson Fletcher.

"I told you my life was a mess."

"You've still got By-the-Wind."

"For now."

"Any chance he can make good on those threats?"

She sighed and pressed a hand to her stomach. Sexual harassment. How low could the man stoop?

"He can try, but there's absolutely no evidence backing him up. I refused to even date him for months. I didn't want any appearance of impropriety. The other employees can all confirm that. But he was so damn persistent and I was…flattered. That's what it comes down to. I only dated him for a month, but I swear I never slept with him."

Oh, why couldn't she keep her mouth shut? Did she really need to share that particular detail with Max?

"Then don't worry about it. I know his type. He's all bluff and bluster up front but the minute you confront him, he runs away like the rat he is."

"I'm just sorry you were tangled up in the middle."

"Funny, I was just thinking how glad I am that I was here to back you up."

She stared at him for a long moment, at the solid strength of his features, the integrity that seemed so much a part of him. The contrast between a sleazy, dishonest slimebag like Grayson Fletcher and this honorable soldier who had sacrificed so much for his country and still bore the scars for it was overwhelming.

"Thank you," she whispered.

With a full heart, she leaned across the space between them to kiss him softly. Compared to their heat and passion of the night before, this was just a tiny kiss of gratitude, just a slight brush of her lips against his, but it rocked her clear to her toes.

She was crazy about this man. She was aware she had only known him a few days but she was in serious danger of falling head over heels.

She eased away from him, feeling shaky and off balance.

"You're welcome," he murmured, and she wondered if she imagined that raspy note in his voice.

"What did I miss?"

At the sound of her employee's voice, Anna tried to collect her scattered wits. She took a deep breath and found Sue had come out of the stockroom carrying two of the colorful glass floats.

"Not much. He's gone."

"Good riddance. I don't care what you say, I'm calling the cops the next time he has the nerve to come in here."

"Sounds like a plan," Anna said. "Did I answer what you needed to know on canceling an order?"

"Yes. And now you need to get out of here and enjoy the rest of your day off." Sue had on that bossy mother-hen voice that Anna was helpless to fight. "Go have some fun. You deserve it."

She rubbed her hands on her slacks and turned back to Max as a customer came up to Sue and asked her for help locating an item.

"You're welcome to look around more if you'd like."

"I think I'm done here," he answered.

"Are you ready to go home, then?"

A strange light flickered in his eyes and she wondered at it, until she remembered his transitory life. The concept of home probably wasn't one he was used to considering.

"Good idea," he said after a moment, and his words were punctuated by Conan barking his approval.

Dusk was washing across the shore as they reached the outskirts of Cannon Beach and the setting sun cast long shadows across the road and saturated everything with color.

Brambleberry House on its hill looked graceful, welcoming, with its gables and gingerbread trim and the wide porch on all sides.

"I love coming home this time of day," she said as she pulled into the driveway. "I know it's silly but I always feel like the house has been waiting here all day just for me."

"It's not silly."

"Abigail used to say a house only comes alive when it's filled with people who love it." She smiled, remembering. "She used to have this quote on the wall. 'Every house where love abides and friendship is a guest, is surely home, and home, sweet home, for there the heart can rest.'"

He was quiet for a long time, gazing as she was at the house gleaming in the fading sunlight. "You do love it, don't you?" he asked, finally breaking the silence.

"With my whole heart. Rusty pipes, loose shingles, flaking paint and all."

"She knew what she was doing when she left it to you, didn't she?"

It seemed an odd question but she nodded. "I hope so. Sometimes I'm overwhelmed with the endless responsibility of it, especially when the rest of my life seems so chaotic right now. I have no idea why she left things as she did and bequeathed Brambleberry House to Sage and to me out of the blue, but I love it here. I can't imagine ever leaving."

He let out a breath, his eyes looking suddenly serious in the twilight. "Anna—"

Whatever he intended to say was lost when Conan began barking urgently from the cargo area of the van, as if he had expended every last ounce of patience.

She laughed. "Sorry. That sounds dire. I'd better take him down the beach a little to work out the kinks from the car ride. You interested?"

She thought she saw frustration flicker across his features but it was quickly gone.

"Sure. I've got kinks of my own to work out."

Conan leaped out of the van as soon as she hooked on his leash and practically dragged her behind him in his eagerness to mark every single clump of sea grass on the beach trail.

Just before they reached the wide stretch of beach, Max reached for her hand to help her around a rock and he didn't let go. They walked hand in hand with Conan ahead of them and warmth fluttered through her despite the cool spring wind.

She didn't want to the day to end. Even with the humiliation of the encounter with Gray Fletcher, it had been wonderful, the most enjoyable day she'd spent in longer than she could remember.

Conan obviously didn't share her sentiments, however. The dog could usually run for miles along the beach at any time of the day or night. But though he had been so insistent earlier, as soon as he had taken care of his pressing need, now he didn't seem nearly as enthusiastic to be walking. One moment he planted his haunches stubbornly in the sand, the next he tried to tug her back the direction they had come.

The third time he tried the trick, she gave a tug on the leash. "You don't know what you want, do you?"

"As a matter of fact, I do."

She looked over at Max and found him watching her in the fading sunlight, a glittery look in his hazel eyes that made her catch her breath.

"I was talking to Conan," she murmured. "He's being stubborn about the walk. I think he's ready to go back."

"Not yet," Max said quietly.

Before she could ask him why not, he pulled her against him as the sun slid farther down the horizon.

All the heat and wonder they had shared the night before during the storm came rushing back like the tide and she couldn't seem to get enough of him.

She tried to be careful of his sling and his arm but he lifted the sling out of the way so he could pull her against his chest.

He kissed her for long moments, until they were both breathing hard and the sun was only a pale rim on the horizon.

"If we keep this up, we're going to be stuck down here in the dark and won't be able to find our way back."

"Conan will lead the way," she murmured against his mouth. "He hasn't had dinner yet."

He laughed roughly and kissed her again. She wrapped her arms around his waist, a slow heat churning through her. She couldn't seem to get close enough to him, to absorb his hard strength and the safe harbor she felt here.

She didn't know how long they stood there accompanied by the murmur of the sea, a salty breeze eddying around them. She would have been quite content to stay all night if Conan hadn't finally barked with thinly veiled impatience.

The moon had started to rise above the coastal range, a thin sliver of light, but all was dark and mysterious around them.

"I guess we should probably head back."

She couldn't see his features but she was quite sure she sensed the same reluctance that was coursing through her.

Somehow she wasn't surprised when he pulled a flashlight from his keychain in the pocket of his leather bomber. He was a soldier, no doubt prepared for anything.

"I don't have night-vision goggles with me so this will have to do," Max said. He reached for her hand and they walked back up the beach toward Brambleberry House, whose lights gleamed a welcome in the darkness.

Her insides jumped wildly with nerves and anticipation. She didn't want this to end but how could she possibly scramble for the courage to tell him she wanted more?

They said little as they made their way back home. Even in his silence, though, she sensed he was withdrawing from her, trying to put distance between them again.

Her instinct was confirmed when they reached the house. She unlocked her apartment and opened the door for Conan to bound inside to find his food. She and Max stood in the foyer and she didn't miss the tight set of his features.

Desperate to regain the fleeting closeness, she drew in a shaky breath and lifted her mouth to his again.

After a moment's hesitation, he returned the kiss with an almost fierce hunger, until her thoughts whirled and her body strained against him.

After a long moment, he wrenched his mouth away. "Anna, I need to tell you something."

Whatever it was, she didn't want to hear it. Somehow she knew instinctively it was something she wouldn't like and right now she couldn't bear for anything to ruin the magic of this moment.

"Just kiss me, Max. Please."

He groaned softly but after a moment's hesitation he obliged, tangling his mouth with hers again and again until nothing else mattered but the two of them and the fragile emotions fluttering in her chest.

"I have been trying to figure out all day how to seduce you," she admitted softly.

His laugh was rough and strummed down her nerve endings. "I think it's safe to say you don't have to do anything but exist. That's more seduction than I can handle right now."

She smiled with the heady joy rushing through her. He made her feel delicate and beautiful, powerful in a way she had never known before.

"Come inside," she said, her voice soft.

He froze and she knew she didn't mistake the indecision on his features. "Anna, are you sure?"

"Please," she murmured.

With a ragged sigh, he yanked her against him and an exultant joy surged through her.

This was right. She was crazy about him, she thought. Head-over-heels crazy about this man.

She knew he wasn't going to be here forever, that he wanted to return to active duty as soon as possible and she would be alone again.

But for now, this moment, he was hers and she wasn't going to waste this precious chance fate had handed her.

A soft, silken spell wove around them as they kissed their way inside her bedroom.

The rest of her house was tasteful and subdued, all whites on wood tones. Her bedroom was different. It was soft and feminine, with lavenders and greens and yellows.

How was it possible that Max could seem so over-whelmingly masculine amid all the girly stuff, the flounces and frills? she wondered. He had never seemed so dangerously, enticingly male.

She led the way to her bed, with its filmy white hangings and mounds of pillows. Max looked at the bed for a moment then back at her and his expression was raw with desire.

"I should probably warn you I haven't done this in a while. I've been redshirted for a while with my injury and before that I was in a country where there wasn't a hell of a lot of opportunity for extracurricular activities."

She couldn't seem to think with these nerves skating through her. "Good to know. I haven't, either. My engagement ended five years ago and I haven't been with anyone else."

His eyes darkened, until the pupils nearly obscured the green-gray of the irises.

"I don't know if I can take things slowly. At least not the first time."

She smiled. "Good."

He gave a rough laugh and kissed her again, then lowered her to the bed. "As much as I want nothing more than to take hours undressing you and exploring every inch of that glorious skin, I'm a little clumsy with buttons right now. With this damn cast, I can barely work my own."

"I've got two hands," she answered. Her fingers trembled a little as she slowly worked the buttons of her shirt and pulled her arms free. At least she had worn one of her favorite bra-and-panty sets, a lacy creation in the palest peach.

He swallowed hard. "I definitely don't think I can take things slowly."

He pressed his mouth to her bared shoulder, then trailed kisses along the skin just above the scalloped edge of her bra. She shivered, arching against him as he slid a hand along the bared skin at her waist then up until he touched her intimately through the lace.

She wanted more. She wanted to feel his skin on hers. He must have shared her hunger because he pulled the sling off, revealing the cast underneath that ran from his wrist to just above his elbow and began working the buttons of his shirt.

"Let me help," she said.

He leaned back to give her more access and she helped him out of his shirt and then went to work on the snaps on his Levi's.

"I can take it from here," he told her.

In moments, they were both naked and he was everything she might have dreamed, all hard muscles and lean strength.

Then she caught her first view of the full extent of his injuries and her heart turned over in her chest.

For some reason, she had thought the damage was

contained to his arm and shoulder. But rough, red-looking burns spread out from his collarbone to his pectoral muscles on the right side, crisscrossed by scars that were still blinding white against his skin.

"Oh, Max," she breathed.

Regret slid across his features. "I should have kept my shirt on. I'm so used to it by now I forget how ugly it is."

"No. No, you shouldn't have. I am so sorry you had to go through that."

She pressed her mouth just above the raw-looking skin at the spot where his shoulder met his neck, then again in the hollow above his collarbone.

"Does it hurt?"

He looked as if he wanted to deny it but he finally shrugged. "Sometimes. Right now, no. Right now, all I can think about is the incredibly sexy woman in my arms. Come up here and kiss me."

"Absolutely, Lieutenant," she said with a smile and settled in his arms.

They kissed and touched for a long time, exploring all the planes and hollows and secret places while those tensile emotions twisted through her, wrapping her closer to him.

He said he couldn't take things slowly but it seemed to her their teasing and touching lasted for hours. At last, when she wasn't sure she could endure another moment, he braced above her on his left forearm and he entered her.

She gasped his name and tightened her arms around him, hunger soaring inside her like bright, colorful kites on the wild air currents of the beach.

Had she ever known this sense of wonder, the feeling of completion, that scattered pieces of herself had only right this moment fallen into place?

She was floating higher and higher, her heart as light

as air as he moved inside her, slowly at first and then faster, his mouth hard and urgent on hers with a possessive stamp that thrilled her to the core.

She held tight to him, her body rising to meet his, and then he pushed slightly harder and she gasped suddenly as she broke free of gravity and went soaring into the air.

He groaned her name, then with one last powerful surge he joined her.

Oh, heaven. This was heaven. She held him tightly as a delicious lassitude slid over her.

CHAPTER THIRTEEN

ABIGAIL WOULD HAVE APPROVED.

Anna lay next to Max, her arm across him, feeling his chest rise and fall with each slow, steady breath as he slept. Pale moonlight filtered in through her open window and played across his features, and she thought how vulnerable he looked in sleep, years younger than the hard-eyed soldier he appeared at times.

Abigail would have loved him. She didn't quite know why she was so certain but somehow she knew her friend would have been quick to include him in the loose circle of friends that Sage had called her lost sheep—people who were lonely or tired or grieving or who just needed to know someone else believed in them.

Max would have been drawn into that circle, whether he wanted it or not. Abigail would have taken him in, would have filled him with good food to ease all the hollows from those months in the hospital. If he ended up leaving the army, Abigail would have been right there helping him figure out his place in the world.

He made a soft sound in his sleep and her arm tightened around him. She rested her cheek against his smooth, hard chest, astonished at the sense of peace she found here in his arms, the tenderness that seemed to wind through her with silken ties.

She was in love with him.

The truth shimmered through her, bright and stunning, and she drew in a sharp breath, astonished and suddenly terrified.

Love. That wasn't in the plan. She was supposed to be having a casual fling, nothing more. The man had made no secret of his plans to leave as soon as he could. This whole situation seemed destined for disaster.

He wasn't the stick-around type. He couldn't have made that more plain. He had told her himself that he considered his base in Iraq more of a home than anywhere else he had lived. She remembered how sad that had seemed when he told her. It was even more tragic now that she had come to know him better, since she had seen a certain yearning in his eyes when he looked at Brambleberry House.

He needs a home. A place to belong. That's what he's always needed.

The words whispered into her mind and she frowned. Why on earth would such a thought even enter her mind, let alone with such firm assurance? It made absolutely no sense, but she couldn't shake the unswerving conviction that Harry Maxwell needed Brambleberry House, maybe more even than she did.

She couldn't make him stay. She knew that with the same conviction. She might want him to, with sudden, fierce desperation, but she couldn't hold him here.

When his shoulder healed, he would return to his unit, to his helicopter, and would go wherever he was needed, no matter how dangerous.

Even if his arm didn't heal as well as he hoped, she couldn't see him sticking around. Brambleberry House was a temporary stop on his life's journey and there was nothing she could do to change that.

She sighed, just a tiny breath of air, but it was enough to awaken him. Watching him come back to consciousness was a fascinating experience. No doubt it was the soldier in him but he didn't ease into wakefulness, he just instantly blinked his eyes open.

Her brothers always told her she did the same thing—one minute, she could be in deep REM sleep, the next she was wide-awake and ready to rock and roll.

They used to tease her that she slept with the proverbial one eye open, as if she was afraid one of them would sneak into her room during the night and steal her dolls. Not that she ever had many, but could she help it if she liked to protect what little she had from pesky older brothers?

"Hi," Max murmured, a sexy rasp to his voice, and Anna forgot all about brothers and dolls and sleeping.

"Hi yourself." She smiled, determined to savor every single moment she had with him. Why waste time wishing he could be a different sort of man, the kind who might be happy rattling around an old house like this for the rest of his life?

"Have I been asleep long?"

She shook her head. "A half hour, maybe."

"Sorry. I didn't mean to doze off on you."

"I didn't mind. It was…nice." A major understatement, but she wasn't about to risk scaring him off by revealing just how much she had treasured a quiet moment to savor being in his arms.

He gazed down at her, an oddly tender expression in his hazel eyes that stole her breath and left her stomach doing cartwheels again.

"It has been. Everything. I never expected this, Anna. You have to know that."

She smiled, her heart full and light. "I didn't, either. But a gift can be all the more rare and precious when it's unexpected."

"Is that more of Abigail's wisdom?"

"No. Just mine."

With surprising dexterity, he tugged her with his left arm so she was lying across his chest, then he twisted his hand in her hair so he could angle her mouth to meet his kiss. "You are a wise woman, Anna Galvez."

She smiled. "I don't know about that. But I'm learning."

They kissed and touched and explored for a long time there in the dark, quiet intimacy of her room. At last he pulled her atop him, letting her set the pace.

Their first union had been all heat and fire. This was slower, sweet and sexy and tender all at the same time.

I love you.

She almost blurted the words just before she found release again, but she caught them in her throat before she could do something so foolish.

He wasn't ready to hear them yet—and she wasn't sure she was ready to say them.

It took a long time for his heartbeat to slow back to anything resembling a normal pace. He lay in the dark watching the moonlight dance across the room and listening to Anna breathe beside him.

The soft tenderness seeping through his insides scared the hell out of him.

This wasn't supposed to happen. He wasn't supposed to care so much. But somehow this woman, with her tough shell that he had discovered hid a fragile, vulnerable core, had become fiercely important to him.

She soothed him. He didn't know how she did it but these last few days with her had been filled with a quiet peace he only now realized had been missing since his helicopter crashed.

He had been so damn restless since he was injured. But with Anna, the future didn't seem like a scary place anymore. She made him think he could handle whatever came along.

Except telling her the truth.

He let out a long, slow breath, guilt pinching away at the tranquility of the moment. He had to tell her Abigail was his aunt. The very fact that he was lying in her bed having this conversation with himself while she was naked and warm in his arms was evidence that he had allowed the deception to go on far too long.

But how, exactly, was he supposed to tell her that now? She would be furious and hurt, especially after they had shared this.

He stared up at the ceiling, trying to figure out his options. He ached at the idea of hurting her but he couldn't see any way out of it. Maybe it would be best all the way around if he just left town before this could go on any further.

She would be hurt and baffled if he suddenly disappeared. But what would hurt her more—wondering why he left or discovering he had deceived her, that he had slept with her under false pretenses?

What he had done was unconscionable. He could fool himself that his intentions had been honorable, that he had only wanted to make sure Abigail had been competent in her last wishes when she left the house to Anna and Sage Benedetto. He had been compelled to do something, if only to assuage his own guilt over his negligence these last few years.

Then he had come to Brambleberry House and Anna had made Abigail's French toast for him and bandaged his wounds and kissed him senseless and everything had become so damn tangled.

He hated the idea of leaving her. It seemed the height of cowardice, especially after what they had shared tonight. But what would cause the least harm to her?

"Will you come with me next week when the verdict is read?"

Her voice in the darkness startled him and he shifted his gaze from the ceiling to see her watching him out of those huge dark eyes.

"I thought you were asleep," he said.

"No. I was just thinking."

"About the trial?"

"Sorry. Everything comes back to that right now. I'll be so glad when it's over."

He kissed her forehead, pulling her into a more comfortable position. "It's been rougher on you than you let on, hasn't it?"

She didn't answer but he thought her arms tightened around him. "I've been okay. I have. I just... I think I could use someone else in my corner during the verdict. Would you come?"

Like his aunt, Anna was a strong, independent woman. He had a feeling asking for anything was difficult for her. The fact she had asked him to stand by her touched him deeply.

He could stay a few more days. He owed her that, and perhaps giving her the support she needed at this critical time would be a small way to atone for his deception.

"Yeah. Sure. I'll come with you," he answered. "And if he's found not guilty, we've always got clubbing him senseless with my cast to fall back on as Plan B."

She laughed and kissed him. He pulled her close, pushing away the chiding voice of his conscience for now.

A few more days of this sweet, seductive peace. That's all he wanted. Surely that wasn't too much to ask.

"ARE YOU READY for this?" Max asked her three days later as they sat on a park bench outside her store in Lincoln City enjoying the afternoon sunshine, the first since Sunday.

She made a face, her stomach fluttering with nerves. "Do I have a choice?"

"You always have a choice. You could just forget the whole thing and catch the next fishing boat out of town. Or I could make a phone call, get us a helicopter in here to fly us down the coast to an excellent crab shack I've heard about in Bandon."

"You're not helping."

He gave her an unrepentant grin and she couldn't help thinking how much lighter he had seemed these last few days. The occasional shadow still showed up in his gaze but he laughed more and seemed far more comfortable with the world.

The time they'd spent together since Sunday night had seemed magical. She never would have expected it, but the last two days of the trial passed with amazing swiftness. Even listening to the defense's closing arguments, where she had been painted as everything from an incompetent manager to a corrupt manipulator, hadn't stung as much as it might have a few days earlier.

Now she saw it for what it was—Grayson's desperate ploy to escape justice.

Between the trial and trying to stay on top of administrative duties at both stores, her days had been as packed and chaotic as always.

But the nights.

They had been sheer heaven.

When she returned to Brambleberry House Monday night, Max and Conan had been waiting for her with what he called his specialty—take-out Chinese. After dinner, Max started a fire in her fireplace and read a thriller with Conan at his feet while Anna did payroll and caught up on paperwork.

Eventually she gave up trying to concentrate with all this heat jumping through her insides. She had joined him on the couch and Max had tossed her reading glasses aside and kissed her while rain clicked against the window and Conan snored softly beside them. Later—much later—she had fallen asleep holding his hand.

Tuesday had been largely a repeat, except he had grilled steaks for her out in the rain while she held an umbrella over his head and laughed at the picture he made in one of Abigail's frilly flowered aprons.

That was the moment she knew with certainty that what she felt for him wasn't some passing infatuation, that she was hopelessly in love with him—with this wounded soldier with the slow smile and the secrets in his eyes.

She had no idea what she was going to do about it— except for now, she was going to live in the moment and enjoy every second she had with him.

Her cell phone rang suddenly and she jumped and stared at it.

"Are you going to get that?" Max asked.

"I'm working up to it."

She knew it must be the prosecutor, calling to tell her the verdict was in and about to be read.

The jury had been deliberating for four hours and Max had been with her for two of those hours. She had called him as soon as the jury had started deliberations and he had rushed down to Lincoln City immediately, even after she told him it might be hours—or possibly days—before the jurors reached a verdict.

She was immeasurably touched that he had kept his promise to come with her when the verdict was read—and she was grateful now as she answered her phone with fingers that trembled.

"Hello?" she said.

"They're back," the prosecutor said. "Can you be here in fifteen minutes?"

"Yes. I'll be right there."

She hung up the phone and sat, feeling numb and shaky at the same time.

Max reached for her hand. "Come on. I'll drive your car. We can come back for mine."

He kept his hand linked with hers as they walked into the courthouse. "What will you do if he's exonerated?" he asked, the question she had been dreading.

A few days ago, she was quite certain that possibility would have devastated her. But she had learned she had a great deal in common with Abigail's favorite sea creatures. Like the by-the-wind sailors her store was named for, she would float where fate took her and manage to adapt. Even on that fishing boat Max joked about.

"I'll survive," she said. "What else can I do?"

He squeezed her fingers and didn't let go as they walked into the courtroom and sat down.

So much of her life the last several months had been tied up with this trial but in the end, the verdict was almost anticlimactic. When the jury foreman read that jurors had found Grayson Fletcher guilty on all counts of fraud, Anna let out a tiny sob of relief and Max immediately wrapped her in his arms and kissed her.

Max stayed by her side as she hugged the prosecutor, who had worked so tirelessly for conviction, and as she received encouraging words from several others in the community who had come to hear the verdict.

She finally allowed herself to glance at Grayson and found him looking pale and stunned, as if he couldn't quite believe it was real. A tiny measure of pity flickered through her, even though she knew he deserved the consequences for what he had done.

Still, she wasn't going to hold a grudge the rest of her life, she decided. Life was just too short for her to be bitter and angry at being duped.

"We need to celebrate," Max said after they left the courtroom. "I'm taking you to dinner tonight. Where would you like to go?"

"The Sea Urchin," she said promptly, without taking even a moment to think about her answer. "Sage's husband owns it and since it's a Spencer Hotels property, of course it's fabulous. The food there is unbelievable. The best on the coast."

"I love a woman who knows what she wants."

If only he truly meant his words, she thought, then pushed the thought away. She was deliriously happy right now and she wasn't going to spoil it by worrying about the future.

SHE HAD A hard-and-fast rule never to use her cell phone while she was driving except in an absolute emergency, especially on the sometimes curvy coastal road, but she was severely tempted as she drove her van home from Lincoln City to phone everyone in her address book to give them the happy news.

She restrained herself, focusing instead on following Max's SUV, since they had both driven down separately, and trying to contain the happiness bubbling through her.

Still, even before she had a chance to greet Conan, her cell phone rang the moment she walked in the door at Brambleberry House. She grinned when she saw Sage's name and number on the caller ID.

"All right, that's just spooky. How did you know the verdict was in?" she asked, without even saying hello.

Sage shrieked. "It is? I had no idea! Sue called me from the store hours ago when the jury went out for deliberation. I was just checking the status of things since I haven't heard from you. Tell me!"

Anna took a deep breath, thinking again how her life had changed since she inherited this house. A year ago, she would have had no one to share this excitement with except her employees. Now she had dear friends who loved her. She was truly a lucky woman.

"Guilty. Guilty, guilty, guilty!"

"Yes!" She heard Sage shouting the news to Eben and even over the phone, Anna could hear her husband's delighted exclamation.

"Oh, that's wonderful news. I hope they throw the book at the little pissant."

"This, from the world's biggest bleeding heart?" she teased.

"I care about things that deserve my time and energy," Sage said primly. "Grayson Fletcher does not."

"True enough," Anna replied.

"Oh, I'm so happy. I'm only sorry I wasn't there. With Julia gone, too, you're not going to have anyone to celebrate with!"

"Am, too," she answered. "For your information, I'm going to the Sea Urchin for dinner with Max."

There was a long, pregnant silence on the other end of the phone. "Max? Upstairs Max?"

Anna smiled, wondering how he would react to that particular nickname. "That's right."

"All right. What other secrets have you been keeping from me, you sly thing?"

Anna grimaced. She probably shouldn't have let that slip. But now that she had, she knew she wouldn't be able to fool Sage for long. "Nothing. Well, not much, anyway. It's just that Upstairs Max has been spending most of his time downstairs the last few days," she finally confessed.

That long pause greeted her again. "So does Conan like him?"

"Adores him. He treats him like his long-lost best friend."

"And have you smelled any freesia lately?'

Anna made a face. "Cut it out. Abigail's not matchmaking in this situation. She must be taking a break."

"Or maybe he's not the one for you."

Her heart gave a sharp little tug. "Of course he's not," she answered promptly. "He's only here a short time and then he's leaving again. I know that perfectly well."

"Are you sure?"

She wasn't certain of anything, other than that she

was fiercely in love with Harry Maxwell. But she wasn't about to reveal that little tidbit of information to Sage.

"You know I'm going to insist on a full report from Julia as soon as she gets back. And the minute we get back to the States, I'm coming up there, even if I have to use up all my carbon offsets for the year."

"Sage, honey, stop worrying about me, okay? You don't have to come up here to babysit me. Max is a wonderful man and I know you'll love him. But I also know this is only temporary. I'm fine with that."

After she hung up the phone some time later, those words continued to echo through her mind. Had she ever lied to Sage before? She couldn't remember. This one was a doozy, though. She wasn't fine. No matter how cool and sophisticated she tried to be about things, she knew she would be devastated when he left.

And he would leave. She knew that, somewhere deep inside of her, with a certainty she couldn't explain. Her time with him was limited. Even now, he could be preparing to leave.

Fight for him. He needs you.

The words whispered through her mind, so strong and compelling that she looked around the room to find a source.

He needs you.

The smell of freesia floated across the room and Conan looked up from his rug, thumped his tail on the floor, then went back to sleep.

Anna shivered, her heart pounding, then she quickly caught herself before her imagination went crazy. That's what happened when she talked to Sage. She lost every ounce of common sense and started believing in ghosts.

Not that it was bad advice. If she loved Max, shouldn't she be willing to fight for the man?

Starting tonight, she decided, and went to her closet for her favorite dress, a shimmery sheath in pale green that made her dark skin and hair look exotic and sultry.

She might not have a matchmaking ghost on her side, but she could take control of her own fate.

Max wouldn't know what hit him.

CHAPTER FOURTEEN

MAX RANG THE doorbell to Anna's apartment, aware of the sense of foreboding in his gut.

He was going to tell her tonight after dinner. No more excuses. He had put things off far too long and the time had come to confess everything. Maybe she would be so happy at the guilty verdict that she would be in a forgiving sort of mood.

Or maybe she would evict him and throw all his belongings out of her house.

He hoped not. He hoped she would find it in her to understand his motives. But either way, he owed her the truth.

Conan barked behind the door and a moment later, it swung open, revealing a vision in pale green.

From the first time he saw her, Max had considered Anna Galvez beautiful, with those huge brown eyes and her glossy dark hair and classically lovely features.

But right now she was truly breathtaking.

She had piled her hair up in a loose, feminine style, with curls dripping everywhere. She wore a sexy dream of a dress with a low back that showed off fine-boned shoulders and all that luscious skin of hers. She also wore more jewelry than he'd seen on her—a diamond choker and matching bracelet and slim, dangly earrings that glittered in the foyer light.

She looked lush and sensual and he wanted to stand in the foyer of Brambleberry House all night just looking at her.

"Wow," he murmured. "You look incredible. I know that sounds completely lame but I can't think of another word for it."

"Incredible is good." She smiled. "Come in. I'm just about ready."

He wanted to devour her but he was afraid of messing up perfection so he stood inside the doorway while she picked up a filmy scarf from a side table and wrapped it around her shoulders, then grabbed one of those tiny little evening bags women managed to cram huge amounts of paraphernalia into.

Conan padded over to her wearing one of his pathetic take-me-with-you looks. The dog brushed against her and Max held his breath. Meredith—hell, most women he knew—would have gone ballistic to have dog hairs on one of her fancy party dresses but Anna simply laughed and scratched the dog's chin.

"I'm sorry, bud, but you know you can't go with us to the Sea Urchin. You wouldn't want to. You'd be bored senseless, I promise. But we'll be back later and we'll play then."

The dog heaved a massive sigh and headed for his favorite rug, but in that instant, that tiny interaction, Max felt as if the entire house had just collapsed on top of him.

Emotions washed through him, thick and raw and terrifying, and for an instant of panic, he wanted to turn on his heels and walk out of Brambleberry House and just keep on going.

He was in love with Anna Galvez. Not because she

was achingly beautiful or because she made his heart race and the blood pool in his gut.

But because she was strong and courageous and smart and she made him believe in himself again.

He was in love with her. How the hell had that happened?

One minute, his life had been going along just fine. Okay, maybe not perfect. His shoulder problems were proving to be a major pain and he had no idea if he would still be in the army in a few weeks. But he had been dealing with the setbacks in his own way.

And then this woman, with her stubborn independence and her brilliant smile and her ambitious dreams, had knocked him on his butt. She talked to her dog and she knew her way around a wood chipper and she filled his soul with a peace he never realized had been missing.

"Max? Is everything okay?"

How long had he been staring at her? Too long, obviously. He drew in a ragged breath and realized she was watching him with concern while Conan seemed to be grinning at him.

"Yeah. Yeah. Fine. You just dazzle me."

He could tell she thought he was talking about her appearance and he decided not to correct the misconception.

"Thank you." She smiled. "The jewelry is Abigail's. She never went anywhere, even to the grocery store, without glittery stuff dripping from every available surface. She used to tell me, 'My dear girl, a woman my age has to use every available means at her disposal to distract the eye from all these wrinkles.'"

He could hear Abigail saying exactly that and he suddenly missed his aunt desperately.

"You don't need any jewels," he said. "You're stunning enough without them. The most beautiful woman I've ever known."

Her mouth parted slightly as her eyes softened. "Oh, Max," she whispered. "I do believe that's the sweetest thing anyone has ever said to me."

"It's the truth," he said gruffly.

She smiled with stunning sweetness and stepped forward to press her mouth against his.

His heart seemed to flop around in his chest like a rockfish on the line and he could barely breathe around the tenderness inside him. He kissed her, almost desperate with the need to touch her, taste her, burn every moment of this in his mind.

The magic he always found with her began to coil and twine around them and he closed his eyes as she wrapped her arms around his neck, holding him as if she couldn't bear to let go.

He was wondering just how long it might take for her to fix herself up again if he messed up all this perfection when Conan suddenly barked urgently and raced to the door.

A moment later, he heard the front door to the house open and children's laughter echo through the house.

Anna pulled away from him with a startled gasp, then her face lit up with joy. If she was breathtaking before, right now with her eyes bright and a wide smile lighting her features, she was simply staggering.

"They're back!" she exclaimed.

He couldn't seem to make his brain work. "Who?"

"Julia and the twins! Oh, this just makes this entire day perfect. Come on, you've got to meet them."

She looked a little windblown from the passion of their

kiss but she linked her hand with his and opened the door. Conan rushed out first, just about tripping over his feet in his rush to greet two dark-haired children who were starting up the stairs, their arms loaded with backpacks.

"Conan!" both children shouted, dropping their bundles and hurrying back down the stairs.

The dog barked and jumped around them, licking first one and then the other while the boy and girl giggled and hugged him.

"Hey, I need a little of that love."

"Anna Banana!"

The little boy jumped up from hugging the dog and launched himself at Anna. She gave him a tight hug then turned to gather the less rambunctious girl to her as well.

"How are you, my darlings? I know you've only been gone a week, but I swear you've grown a foot in that time! What have you been eating, Maddie? Ice cream for breakfast, lunch and dinner?"

The girl giggled and shook her head. "Nope. Only for breakfast and lunch. We had pizza and cheeseburgers the rest of the time."

"You've been living large in Montana, haven't you?"

"We had tons of fun, Anna! You should have come with us! We went on a horseback ride and we went sledding and skiing and then we went to Boise and visited Grandma and Grandpa for three whole days," the boy exclaimed.

The girl—Maddie—dimpled at her. "You look superpretty, Anna. Are you going to a ball?"

Anna smiled and hugged her again. "No, sweetheart. Just to dinner at Chloe's dad's hotel."

"Ooh, will you bring me a fortune cookie?" the boy asked. "I love their fortune cookies."

"I'll see what I can do," Anna promised, just as a slim blonde woman tromped through the door carrying a suitcase in each arm. She dropped them as soon as she walked into the foyer and saw Anna greeting the children, and Max watched while the two women embraced.

"I just heard. Sage just called me. Oh, Anna, I'm so happy about the guilty verdict. Will is, too."

"Yeah," Maddie said with a grin. "You should have heard him yelling in the car. My ears still hurt!"

Anna laughed and looked behind them. "Where is Will?"

"He's getting the rest of our luggage off the roof rack. He should be here in a moment."

The woman glanced over Anna's shoulder at Max and though she gave him a friendly smile, he thought he saw a kind of protective wariness there. It made him wonder what Anna might have told her friends about him.

"Hi," she said. "You must be Harry Maxwell."

The false name scraped against his conscience like metal on metal. He didn't know what to say, loath to perpetuate the lie any more than he already had.

Anna saved him from having to come up with a response. "I'm sorry," she exclaimed with a distracted laugh. "I was so happy to see you all again, I forgot my manners. Max, this is Julia Blair and her children Maddie and Simon. Julia, this is Lieutenant Harry Maxwell."

He nodded hello, then reached forward to shake Julia's outstretched hand.

"We're interrupting something, aren't we?" she said. "You both look wonderful and you're obviously on your way out."

"We're heading to the Sea Urchin to celebrate the verdict," Anna said.

"We can do it another time," Max offered. "I'm sure you two probably want to catch up."

"No, go on. Keep your plans," Julia said. "We can catch up later tonight over tea when the kids are in bed."

Max said nothing, though he thought with fleeting regret of the last two nights when he had slept with her in his arms.

"I was going to shut Conan in my apartment while we're at dinner but you're certainly welcome to take him upstairs with you. I'm sure he'll be so much help while you're trying to unpack."

"Thanks," the other woman said dryly.

"Let me help you with your luggage," Max said.

Julia gave a surprised glance at his omni-present sling. "You don't have to do that."

"You'd better let him," Anna said with a laugh. "The man doesn't take no for an answer."

"Doesn't he?" Julia murmured.

Max felt his face heat and decided he would be wise to beat a hasty retreat. He picked up one of the suitcases and carried it up and set it on the landing outside the second-floor apartment. He was just heading back down for the second suitcase, when he heard a male voice from the foyer below.

"We were only gone eight days. Why, again, did we need all these suitcases?"

Max froze on the stairway, his heart stuttering. He knew the owner of that voice.

And worse, the man knew him.

"Wow, Anna. You look fabulous!"

Anna beamed at Will Garrett, who lived three houses down. Will was not only a gifted carpenter who had done most of the renovation work on Brambleberry House but, more importantly, he was a dear friend.

"I would say the same for you if I could see you behind all the suitcases," she said with a laugh.

"Here. How's that?" He set down the luggage and pulled her into a close hug. She hugged him back, her heart lifting at the smile he gave her. Every time she saw Will, she marveled at the changes in him these last six months since he and Julia had fallen in love again.

Before Julia and her twins came to Brambleberry House, Will had been a far different man. He had been lost in grief for his wife and daughter who had been killed in a car accident three years ago.

Anna had grieved with him for Robin and Cara. She and Sage—and Abigail, before her death—had worried for him as he pulled away from their close circle of friends, drawing inside himself in the midst of his terrible pain.

They had all rejoiced when Julia moved in upstairs and they learned she had been his first love, when they were just teenagers.

The two of them had rediscovered that love and together, Julia and her twins had helped Will begin to heal.

"I heard the good news about that idiot Fletcher," Will said, too low for the children to overhear. "I couldn't be happier that he's finally getting what's coming to him. Maybe now you can put the whole thing behind you and move forward."

She thought of the progress she had made, how she had brooded far too long about everything. Her perspective had changed these last few days, she realized, thanks in large part to Max.

She *was* ready to move forward, to refocus her efforts

on saving both stores. Through hard work, she had built something good and worthwhile. She couldn't just give up all that because of a setback like Gray Fletcher.

She looked up and saw Max standing motionless on the stairs. She smiled up at him, awash in gratitude for these last few days and the confidence he had helped her find again.

"I need to introduce you to our new tenant. Will, this is—"

He followed her gaze and suddenly his eyes lit up. "Max! What are you doing here?"

Max walked slowly down the stairs and Anna frowned when Will gave him that shoulder tap thing men did that seemed the equivalent to the hug of greeting she and Julia had shared.

"Why didn't anybody tell me you were living upstairs? This is wonderful news. Abigail would have been thrilled that you've finally come home."

Anna stared between the two men. Will looked delighted, while Max's expression had reverted to that stony, stoic look he had worn so often when he first arrived at the house.

Her pulse seemed unnaturally loud in her ears as she tried to make sense of this new turn of events. "I don't understand," she finally said. "You two know each other?"

"Know each other? Of course!" Will exclaimed. "We hung out all the time, whenever he would visit his aunt. A couple weeks every summer."

"His...aunt?"

Will gave her an odd look. "Abigail! This is her nephew. The long-lost soldier, Max Harrison."

Anna drew in a sharp breath, her solar plexus contracting as if someone had socked her in the gut. She stared at Max, who swallowed hard but didn't say anything.

"That's impossible," she exclaimed. "Abigail's nephew's name was Jamie. Not Harry or Max. *Her Jamie*. That's what she always called him."

"My full name is Maxwell James Harrison. Abigail was the only one who called me Jamie."

She was going to hyperventilate for the first time in her life. She could feel the breath being slowly squeezed from her lungs. "Max Harrison—Harry Maxwell. I'm such an idiot. Why didn't I figure it out?"

"I can explain if you'll let me."

Lies. Everything they shared was lies. She had kissed him, held him, slept with him, for heaven's sake. And it had all been a lie.

She pressed a hand to her stomach, to the nausea curling there. First Grayson and now Max. Did she wear some invisible sign on her forehead that said Gullible Fool Here?

All her joy in the day, the triumph of the guilty verdict, the fledgling hope that she could now regain her life seemed to crumble away like leaves underfoot.

Julia, with her usual perception, must have sensed some of what was racing through Anna's head. She quickly stepped in to take control of the situation.

"Will, kids, let's get these suitcases out of the entryway and upstairs to the apartment. Come on."

The children grumbled but they grabbed their backpacks and trudged up the stairs, Conan racing ahead of them in his excitement at having them all back.

In moments, the chaos and bustle of their homecoming was reduced to a tense and ugly silence as she gazed at the man she thought she had fallen in love with.

Most people call me Max. She remembered his words, which very well might have been the only honest thing he had said to her since he moved in.

She moved numbly back into her apartment, only vaguely aware that he had followed her inside.

A hundred thoughts raced through her head but she could only focus on one.

"You lied to me."

"Yes," he answered. Just that, nothing else.

"What am I missing here?" she asked. "Why would you possibly feel like you had to lie about your relationship with Abigail and use a false name?"

He rubbed a hand at the base of his neck. "It was a stupid idea. Monumentally stupid. All I can say is that it seemed like a good idea at the time."

"That tells me nothing! Who wakes up in the morning and says, 'gosh, I think I'll create a false identity today, just for kicks'?"

"It wasn't like that."

"Then explain it to me!"

Her hands were shaking, she realized. This felt worse than the slick, greasy feeling in her stomach when her accountant had discovered the first hint of wrongdoing at the store. She was very much afraid she was going to be sick and she did her best to fight down the nausea.

"I was stationed in Fallujah when Abigail died. I didn't even know she died until several months later."

"Wrong!" she exclaimed. "Sage notified Abigail's family. I know she did! Not that it did any good. Not a single family member bothered to come to her funeral."

"Sage notified my mother. Not the same thing at all.

I told you my relationship with my mother is difficult at best and she never liked Abigail. The only reason she let me come here all those summers was because she thought Abigail was loaded and would eventually leave everything to me. Meredith didn't think to mention to me that Abigail had even died until two months after the fact, and then only in passing."

"How can I believe anything you tell me?"

He closed his eyes. "It's true. I loved Abigail. I doubt I could have swung leave to attend a great-aunt's funeral but I would have moved heaven and earth to try."

"So how do we get from here to there?"

He sighed. "My mother is between husbands, which means that, as usual, she's short on cash. She suddenly remembered Abigail had this house that was supposed to be worth a fortune and she seemed to think it should have come to me, as Abigail's only living relative. And of course, to her by default if something happened to me in the Middle East. Imagine her dismay when she found out Abigail had left Brambleberry House to someone else. Two strangers."

The nausea roiled in her stomach, mostly that he could speak of his own mother regarding his possible demise with such callousness. "This was about money?"

"I don't give a damn about the money!" he said, with unmistakable vehemence. "My mother might but I don't. This was about making sure Abigail knew what she was doing when she left the house and its contents to two complete strangers."

"Strangers to you, maybe, but not to Abigail!" Anna's temper flared with fierce suddenness. "She was our friend. Sage and I both loved her dearly and she loved us. Obviously more than she loved some nephew who never even bothered to visit her."

He drew in a sharp breath. "It was a little tough to find time for social calls when I was in the middle of a damn war zone!"

She had hurt him, she realized. She wanted to take back her words but how could she, when her insides were being ripped apart by pain?

She loved him and he had lied to her, just like every other man she'd ever been stupid enough to trust.

She could feel hot tears burning behind her eyes and she was very much afraid she was going to break down in front of him, something she absolutely could not allow. She blinked them back, focusing on the anger.

"Let me get this straight. You came here because you thought I was some kind of scam artist? That Sage and I had schemed and manipulated our way into Abigail's life so she would leave us the legacy that should have been yours."

He compressed his mouth into a tight line. "Something like that."

"And where did sleeping with me fit into that?"

CHAPTER FIFTEEN

HER WORDS HOVERED between them, a harsh condemnation of his actions these last few days. In her eyes, he could see her withdrawal, the hurt and fury he fully deserved.

Why had he ever been stupid enough to think coming to Cannon Beach was a good idea? He thought of the events he had set into motion by that one crazy decision. He hated most of all knowing he had hurt her.

"Everything between us has been a lie," she said, her voice harsh.

"Not true." He stepped forward, knowing only that he needed some contact with her, but she took a swift step back and he fought hard to conceal the pain knifing through him.

"I never expected any of this to happen. I only intended to spend a few weeks running recon here, getting the lay of the land. I just wanted to check things out, make sure everything was aboveboard. I felt like I owed it to Abigail because…"

Because I loved her and I never had a chance to say goodbye.

"Well, my reasons don't really matter. I swear, I tried to keep my distance but you made it impossible."

"What did I do?"

"You invited me to breakfast," he said simply.

You fixed up my scrapes and bruises, you listened

with compassion when I rambled on about my scars, you kissed me and lifted me out of myself.

You made me fall in love with you.

The words clogged in his throat. He wanted desperately to say them but he knew she wouldn't welcome them. He had lost any right to offer her his love.

"I figured out a long time ago that you genuinely cared about Abigail and there was nothing underhanded in you and Sage Benedetto inheriting Brambleberry House."

"Well, that's certainly reassuring to know. Was that before or after you slept with me?"

"Anna—"

"So tell me, Max. As soon as you figured out I wasn't some con artist, why didn't you tell me who you were?"

He raked a hand through his hair. "I wanted to, a hundred times. I tried, but something always stopped me. The dog. The storm. I don't know. It just never seemed like the right time."

He sighed, wishing she would give him even the tiniest of signals that she believed any of this. "And then after we made love, I felt like we were so entangled, I didn't know how to tell you without hurting you."

Her laugh was bitter and scorched his heart. "Far easier to go on letting stupid, oblivious Anna believe the fantasy."

"You're not stupid. Or oblivious. I deceived you. Though I might have thought I had good intentions, that I owed something to Abigail's memory, it was completely wrong of me to let things go as far as they did."

She said nothing and he scanned her features, looking for any softening but he saw nothing there but pain and anger. "I never meant to hurt you," he said.

She stood in a protective stance with her shoulders

stiff, and her arms wrapped tightly around her stomach, and he didn't know how to reach her.

"Isn't it funny how people always say that after the fact?" she said, her voice a low condemnation. "If you truly never meant to hurt me, you should have told me you were Abigail's nephew after you kissed me for the first time."

He had no defense against the bitter truth of her words. She was absolutely right.

He had no defense at all. He was wrong and he had known it all along.

"I'm sorry," he murmured, hating the inadequacy of the words but unable to come up with anything better. He should leave, he thought. Just go before he made things worse for her.

He headed to the door but before he opened it, he turned back and was struck again by how beautiful she was. Beautiful and strong and forever out of his reach now.

"Aunt Abigail knew exactly what she was doing when she left Brambleberry House to you," he said, his voice low. "She would have hated to see me sell this house she loved so much and she must have known that with my career in the army, I wouldn't have been able to give it the love and care you have. You belong here, in a way I never could."

He closed the door softly behind him and headed slowly up the stairs, every bone in his body suddenly aching to match the pain in his heart.

That last he had said to her was a blatant lie, just one more to add to the hundreds he had told.

She belonged here, that much was truth. But he couldn't tell her that these last few days, he had begun to think perhaps he could also find a place here in this house that had always been his childhood refuge.

The words to the poem she had quoted echoed through his memory. *Every house where love abides and friendship is a guest, is surely home, and home, sweet home, for there the heart can rest.*

His heart had come to rest here, with Anna. She had soothed his restless soul in ways he still didn't quite understand. He had come here hurting and guilty over the helicopter crash and the deaths of his team members, wondering what he could have done differently to prevent the crash.

He had been frustrated about his shoulder, worried about the future, grieving for his team and for Abigail.

But when he was with Anna, he found peace and comfort. She had helped him find faith again, faith in himself and faith in the future.

The thought of walking away from her, from this place, filled him with a deep, aching sorrow. But what choice did he have?

He couldn't stay here. He had made that impossible. He had been stupid and selfish and he had ruined everything.

"How is it humanly possible for one woman to be such a colossal idiot when it comes to men?"

Two hours after Max walked out of her apartment, Anna sat in Julia's kitchen. The children were in bed, exhausted from their journey, and Will had returned to his own home down the beach, the house where he and Julia would live after their marriage in June.

"That is a question we may never answer in our lifetimes." Sage's voice sounded tinny and hollow over the speakerphone.

"Sage!" Julia exclaimed, a frown on her lovely features.

"Kidding. I'm kidding, sweetheart. You know I'm kidding, Anna. You're not an idiot. You're the smartest woman I've ever met."

"So why do I keep falling for complete jerks?"

Conan whined from his spot on the kitchen rug and gave her a reproving look similar to the one Julia had given the absent Sage.

"Are you sure he's a complete jerk?" Julia's voice was quiet. "He is Abigail's nephew, after all, so he can't be all bad. I've been wracking my memory and I think I might have met him a time or two when we stayed here during the summers when I was a girl. He always seemed very polite. Quiet, even."

"I'm afraid I never met him so I can't really offer an opinion either way," Sage said on the phone. "He came to stay several years ago before he shipped out to the gulf but I was on a field survey down the coast the whole time. I do know Abigail always spoke about him in glowing terms, but I figured she was a little biased."

Anna remembered the solid assurance she had experienced several times that Abigail would have approved of Max and her growing relationship with him. It hadn't been anything she could put her finger on, just a feeling in her heart.

Fight for him. He needs you.

She suddenly remembered those thoughts drifting through her mind earlier in the evening when she had been preparing for the celebration that hadn't happened.

She was almost certain that had been a figment of her

imagination. But was it possible Abigail had been trying to give her some kind of message?

She hated this. She couldn't trust him and she certainly couldn't seem to trust herself.

"He lied to me, just like Gray and just like my fiancé. With my history, how can I get past that?" she asked out loud as she set her spoon back in the bowl of uneaten ice cream.

She hadn't had much of an appetite for it in the first place but now the cherry chocolate chunk tasted terrible with this bitterness in her mouth.

"Maybe you can't," Sage said.

Julia said nothing, though an expression of doubt flickered over her features.

"You don't agree?" Anna asked.

The schoolteacher shrugged. "Do I think he should have told you he was Abigail's nephew? Of course. Deceiving you was wrong. But maybe he just found himself in a deep hole and he didn't know how to climb out without digging in deeper."

"And maybe he should have just buried himself in the hole when he got down far enough," Sage said.

Though Anna knew Sage was only trying to offer her support, she suddenly found she wanted to defend him, which was a completely ridiculous reaction, one she quickly squashed.

"I've been lied to so many times. I don't know if I forgive that."

"You're the only one who can decide that, honey," Julia said, squeezing her fingers. "But whatever you do, you know we're behind you, right?"

"Ditto from the Patagonia faction," Sage said over the phone.

Though she was quite certain it was watery and weak, Anna managed a smile. "Thank you. Thank you both. As tough as this is, I'm grateful I have you both."

"And Conan and Abigail," Sage declared. "Don't forget them."

The dog slapped his tail on the floor at the sound of his name but didn't bother getting up.

"How can I?" she said. She and Julia were saying goodbye and preparing to hang up when Sage suddenly gasped into the phone.

"The letter! We've got a letter for Abigail's nephew, remember?"

"That's right," Anna exclaimed. "I completely forgot it!"

"What letter?" Julia asked.

"From Abigail," Anna explained. "She left it as part of her estate papers for her great-nephew. Her Jamie."

"It was another of those weird conditions of her will," Sage added. "He could only receive it if and when he arrived in person to Brambleberry House. I was all in favor of mailing it to him in care of the army but Abigail's attorney stipulated her wishes were quite clear. We weren't even supposed to tell him about it until he showed up here."

"Why was she so certain he would come back to Brambleberry House after her death? Especially since she had gone to such pains to leave the house to you two, leaving him with no reason to return at all?" Julia asked with a puzzled frown.

"I don't know. I wondered that myself," Anna admitted.

She remembered how sad she had thought it that Abigail seemed so desperate for her nephew, who hadn't visited her much when she was alive, to come here, even after her death.

"She was right though," Sage said. "Just like she always was. He came back, just as she seemed to know he would."

Anna shivered at the undeniable truth of the words.

"You have to give it to him," Sage continued. "Do you know where it is?"

"In the safe in my office," she answered promptly. "I kept it there with all the other estate documents."

"I'd give anything to know what's in that letter. What do you think Abigail had to say to him?" Sage asked.

Anna wondered the same thing after she and Julia had said goodbye to Sage and she had returned downstairs to her own apartment and retrieved the letter from her safe.

She sat looking at the envelope for a long time, at Abigail's familiar elegant handwriting and those two words. *My Jamie.*

For the first time, she allowed herself to look at this from Max's perspective. He said he had loved his aunt and she knew she had hurt him tonight when she said Abigail must not have loved him enough to leave the house to him.

It had been a cruel thing to say, especially since she knew from the way Abigail talked about her nephew that she had adored him.

What would Anna have done if a beloved elderly relative had left a valuable legacy to two strangers? She probably would have been suspicious as well. Of course, she would have wanted to find out the circumstances. But would she have lied about her identity to investigate?

She couldn't answer that. She only knew that some of

her anger seemed to be subsiding, drawing away from her like low tide.

She gazed at the letter. *My Jamie.* She was going to have to give it to him, but she knew she couldn't go knocking on his apartment door. She wasn't ready to face him again. Not yet. Maybe in the morning, she would be more in control of her emotions.

Still, some instinct told her she needed to deliver this tonight, whether she faced him or not. Praying she wouldn't encounter him wandering around in the dark, she moved quietly up the stairs and slipped the letter through the narrow crack under the door.

There you go, Abigail, she thought, and was almost certain she felt a brush of air against her cheek.

The task done, she stood for a long moment on the landing outside his apartment, her emotions a tangled mess and her heart a heavy weight in her chest.

MAX BACKED HIS SUV out of the Brambleberry House driveway just as the sun crested the coast range. His duffel and single suitcase were in the backseat and the letter that had been slipped under his apartment door was on the seat beside him.

He knew the letter was from Abigail. Who else? Even if he hadn't recognized her distinctive curlicue handwriting, he would have known from only the name on the outside.

My Jamie.

He had stared at that envelope, his heart aching with loss and regret. It even smelled like her, some soft, flowery scent that made him think of tight hugs and kisses on the cheek and summer evening spent in the garden with her.

Finally he had stuck it in the pocket of his jacket and walked down the stairs of Brambleberry House for the last time.

He knew of only one place he wanted to be when he read her final words to him. It seemed fitting and right that he drive to the cemetery to pay his last respects before he left Cannon Beach. He had been putting it off, this final evidence that Abigail was really gone, but he knew he couldn't avoid the inevitable any longer.

He found the cemetery and drove through the massive iron gates under winter-bare branches. Only when he was inside looking at the rows of gravestones, surrounded by tendrils of misty morning fog, did he realize he had no idea where to find his aunt's plot amid the graves.

At random, he picked a lane and parked his SUV halfway down it then started walking. He had only gone twenty feet before he saw it, a tasteful headstone in pale amber marble under a small statue of an angel, with her name.

Abigail Elizabeth Dandridge

Someone had angled an intricate wrought-iron bench there to look over the grave and the ocean beyond it. Anna? he wondered. Somehow it wouldn't have surprised him. It seemed the sort of gesture she would make, practical and softhearted at the same time.

He sat at the bench for a long time, until the damp grass began to seep through his boots and the wrought-iron pressed into the back of his thighs. He wasn't quite sure why he was so apprehensive to read Abigail's final words to him.

Maybe because of that—because it seemed so very

final. Silly as it seemed, he hated that this was the last time anyone would call him the nickname only she had used.

Finally he opened the envelope. A tiny key fell out, along with several pieces of cream vellum. He frowned and pocketed the key then unfolded the letter, his insides twisting.

My dear Jamie,

I suppose since you're reading this, it means you have come home to Brambleberry House at last. I say home, my dear, because this is where you have always belonged. During the rough years of your childhood, while you were off at military school, even when you were off serving your country with honor and courage, this was your home. You have always had a home here and I hope with all my heart that you have known that.

By now you must be thinking I'm a crazy old bat. I'm not so sure you would be wrong. I want you to know I'm a crazy old bat who has loved you dearly. You have been my joy every day of your life.

So why didn't I leave you the house? I'm sure you're asking. If you're not, you should be. I nearly did, you know. Since the day you were born, I planned that you would inherit Brambleberry House when I left this earth. Then a few years ago, something happened to change my mind.

I began to want something more for you than just a house. You see, houses get dry rot or are bent and broken by the wind or can even crumble into the ocean.

Love, though. Love endures.

I knew love when I was a girl, a love that stayed with me my entire life. Even though the man I loved died young, I have carried the memory of him inside me all these years. It has sustained me and lifted me throughout my life's journey.

I wanted the same for you, my Jamie. For you to know the connection of two hearts linked as one. So I began to scheme and to plot. You needed a special woman, someone smart and courageous, with a strong, loving heart.

I knew from the moment I met Anna, she was perfect for you.

He stopped and stared at the gravestone as a chill rippled down his spine. Impossible. How could Abigail have known from beyond the grave that he would find Anna, that he would fall in love with her, that he would feel as if his heart were being ripped out of him at the idea of walking away from her? With numb disbelief, he turned his attention back to the letter.

I wanted you to meet her, Jamie. To see for yourself how wonderful she is. I thought if I left you the house outright, you would quickly sell it and return to the army, leaving all you could have found here behind without a backward glance.

Anna and Sage would watch over my house with loving care, I knew. And I also knew that if I left the house to them, eventually you would come home to find out why. I thought perhaps when you did, you would find something far more valuable here than bricks and drywall and a leaky roof.

It was a gamble—a huge one. I only wish I could be there to see if it paid out. Of course, there was always a chance you might fall for Sage, but I had other plans for her, plans that didn't include you.

I can't even contemplate the eventuality that you might not fall for Anna. You are too smart for that—or at least you'd better be!

Please know that my dearest wish is that you will find joy, my darling Jamie.

All my love, forever,

Abigail.

P.S. In case you're wondering, the key is to a safe-deposit box at First National Bank of Oregon where you will find record of my investment portfolio. The proceeds are all to go to you, as the legal documentation in the safe deposit will attest and my attorney can confirm. I've played the market well over the years and I believe you'll find the value of my portfolio far exceeds the worth of an old rambling house on the seashore. I pray you will put my money to good use somewhere, even if I'm wrong about you and Anna being perfect for each other.

He stared at the letter for a long, long time, there in the cemetery with only the wind sighing in the trees and a pair of robins singing and flitting from branch to branch as they prepared their spring nest.

All these years, he had no idea his great-aunt was a sly, manipulative rascal.

He ought to be angry at her for luring him here. She had set him up, had played him every step of the way.

Instead, he laughed out loud, then couldn't seem to

stop. He laughed so hard the robins fluttered into the sky, chattering angrily at him for disturbing their work.

"Oh, Abigail," he said out loud. "You are one in a million."

How could he be angry, when her actions had been motivated only by love for him? And when she was absolutely right?

Anna was a smart, courageous woman with a strong, loving heart. And she was perfect for him.

He couldn't just walk away from her, from the chance to see if he could find what Abigail wanted so much for them both.

He was gone.

Anna sat on the porch swing where Max had held her so tenderly the night of the storm and gazed out at the sleeping garden, at the rose bushes with their naked thorns and the dry husks of daylily leaves she hadn't cut down in the fall and the bare dirt that waited in a state of anticipation for what was to come.

He was gone and she was quite certain he wouldn't be back. His SUV was gone when she awoke and when she had let Conan out, she had found the key to his apartment hanging on her doorknob, along with a simple note.

I'm so sorry, he had written, without even signing his name.

The morning was cold, with wisps of fog coming off the sea to curl through the trees and around the garden. She shivered from it. She really should go inside and get ready for work but she couldn't seem to move from the porch swing.

Conan, his eyes deep with concern, padded to her and placed his head in her lap.

Just that tiny gesture of comfort sent the first tear trickling down her cheek, then another and another until she buried her face in her hands and wept.

She gave into the storm of emotions for only a few moments before she straightened and drew in a shaky breath, swiping at the tears on her cheeks. Of course he was gone. What did she expect? She had made it quite clear to him the night before that she couldn't forgive him for lying to her. Did she expect him to stick around hoping she would change her mind?

Would she have?

It was a question she didn't know the answer to. This morning, her anger had faded, leaving only an echo of hurt that he had maintained the deception even after they made love.

Julia's words kept running through her head.

Maybe he just found himself in a deep hole and he didn't know how to climb out without digging in deeper.

Yes, he had lied about his identity. But she couldn't quite believe everything else was a lie. He had stood up to Grayson for her that day in the store, he had come with her to the verdict, had held her hand when she was afraid, had kissed her with stunning tenderness. What was truth and what was a lie?

She loved him. That, at least, was undeniably true.

She let out one last sob, her hands buried in Conan's fur, then she straightened her spine. He was gone and she could do nothing about it. In the meantime, she had two businesses to run and a house to take care of. And now she needed to find a new tenant for her third-floor apartment so she could pay for a new roof.

Conan suddenly jerked away from her and went to the edge of the porch, barking wildly. She turned to see what had captured his attention and her heart stuttered in her chest.

Max walked toward her through the morning mist, looking lean and masculine and dangerous in his leather bomber jacket with his arm in the sling.

The breath caught in her throat as he walked toward her and stopped a half-dozen feet away.

"I made you cry."

"No, you didn't. I never cry."

He raised an eyebrow and she lifted her chin defiantly. "It's just cold out here and my allergies must be starting up. It's early spring and the grass pollen count is probably sky-high."

Now who was lying? she thought, clamping her teeth together before she could ramble on more and make things worse.

"Is that right?" he murmured, though he didn't look as if he believed her for an instant.

"I thought you left," she said after a moment.

He shrugged. "I came back."

"You left your key and vacated the apartment."

Where did this cool, composed voice of hers come from? she wondered. What she really wanted to do instead of standing out here having such a civil conversation was to leap into his arms and hold on tight.

He shrugged, leaning a hip against the carved porch support post. "I changed my mind. I don't want to leave."

"Too bad. You can't walk out on a lease agreement and then waltz back in just because you feel like it."

Amusement sparked in his hazel eyes. Amusement and something else, something that had her pulse racing. "Are you going to take me to court, Anna? Because I have to tell you, that would look pretty bad for you. I would hate to pull out the pity card but I just don't see how you could avoid the ugly headlines. 'Vindictive landlady kicks out injured war veteran.'"

She bristled. "Vindictive? *Vindictive?*"

"Okay, bad choice of words. How about, 'Justifiably angry landlady.'"

"Better."

"No, wait. I've got the perfect headline." He slid away from the post and stepped closer and her pulse kicked up a dozen notches at the intent look in his eyes.

"How about 'Idiotic injured soldier falls hard for lovely landlady.'"

"Because only an idiot would be stupid enough to fall for her, right?"

He laughed roughly. "You're not going to make this easy on me, are you?"

She shrugged instead of answering, mostly because she didn't quite trust her voice.

Just kiss me already.

"All right, this is my last attempt here. How about 'Ex-helicopter pilot loses heart to successful local business owner, declares he can't live without her.'"

Conan barked suddenly with delight and Anna could only stare at Max, her heart pounding so loudly she was quite certain he must be able to hear it. She didn't know quite how to adjust to the quicksilver shift from despair to this bright, vibrant joy bursting through her.

"I like it," she whispered. "No, I love it."

He grinned suddenly and she thought again how much he had changed in the short time he'd been at Brambleberry House.

"It's a keeper then," he said, then he finally stepped forward and kissed her with fierce tenderness.

Tears welled up in her eyes again, this time tears of joy, and she returned his kiss with all the emotion in her heart.

"Can you forgive me, Anna? I made a mistake. I should never have tried to deceive you and I certainly shouldn't have played it out so long. I never expected to fall in love with you. That wasn't in the plan—or at least not in *my* plan."

"Whose plan was it?"

"I've got something to show you. Something I'm quite sure you're not going to believe."

He eased onto the porch swing and pulled her onto his lap as if he couldn't bear to let her go. She was going to be late for work, Anna thought, but right now she didn't give a darn. She didn't want to be anywhere else in the world but right here, in the arms of the man she loved.

"I'm assuming you're the one who slipped the letter from Aunt Abigail under my door."

She nodded. "She was quite strict in her instructions that you not receive it until you returned to Brambleberry House in person. Sage and I didn't understand it but the attorney said that was nonnegotiable."

"That's because she was manipulating us all," he answered. "Here. See for yourself."

He handed her the letter and she scanned the words with growing astonishment. By the time she was done, a single tear dripped down the side of her nose.

"The wretch," she exclaimed, then she laughed out loud. "How could she possibly know?"

"What? That you're perfect for me?"

Her gaze flashed to his and she saw blazing emotion there that sent heat and that wild flutter of joy coursing through her. "Am I?" she whispered, afraid to believe it.

"You are everything I never knew I needed, Anna. I love you. With everything inside me, I love you. Abigail got that part exactly right."

She wanted to cry again. To laugh and cry and hold him close.

Thank you, Abigail. For this wonderful gift, thank you from the bottom of my heart.

"Oh, Max. I love you. I think I fell in love with you that first morning on the beach when you were so kind to Conan."

He kissed her, his mouth tender and his eyes filled with emotion. "I'm not the poetry type of guy, Anna. But I can tell you that my heart definitely found a home here, and not because of the house. Because of you."

This time her tears slipped through and she wrapped her arms around him, holding tight.

Just before he kissed her, Anna could swear she heard a sigh of satisfied delight. She opened her eyes and was quite certain that over his shoulder she caught the glitter of an ethereal kind of shadow drifting through the garden, past the edge of the yard and on toward the beach.

She blinked again and then it was gone.

She must have been mistaken, she thought, except Conan stood at the edge of the porch, looking in the same direction, his ears cocked.

The dog bounded down the steps and into the garden. He barked once, still looking out to sea.

After a long moment, he barked again, then gave that silly canine grin of his and returned to the porch to curl up at their feet.

EPILOGUE

It was easy to believe in happy endings at a moment like this.

Max sat in the gardens of Brambleberry House on a lovely June day. The wild riot of colorful flowers gleamed in the late-afternoon sunlight and the air was scented with their perfume—roses and daylilies and the sweet, seductive smell of lavender that melded with the brisk, salty undertone of the sea.

Julia Blair was a beautiful bride. Her eyes were bright with happiness as she stood beside Will Garrett under an arbor covered in Abigail's favorite yellow roses while they exchanged vows.

The two of them were deeply in love and everyone at the wedding could see it. Max was glad for Will. He had been given a small glimpse from Abigail's letters over the years of how dark and desolate his friend's life had been after the deaths of his wife and daughter. These last three months, Anna had shared a little more of Will's grieving process with Max and he couldn't imagine that kind of pain.

From what he could tell, Julia was the ideal woman to help Will move forward. Max had come to know her well after three months of living upstairs from her. She was sweet and compassionate, with a deep reservoir of love inside her that she showered on Will and her children.

"May I have the rings, please?" the pastor performing

the ceremony asked. Then he had to repeat his request since Simon, the ring bearer and best man, was busy making faces at Chloe Spencer.

"Simon, pay attention," his twin sister hissed loudly. To emphasize her point, she poked him hard with the basket full of the flower petals she had strewn along the garden path before the ceremony.

"Sorry," Simon muttered, then held the pillow holding the rings out to Will, who was doing his best to fight a smile.

"Thanks, bud," Will said, reaching for the rings with one hand while he squeezed the boy's shoulder with the other in a man-to-man kind of gesture.

As Will and Julia exchanged rings, Max heard a small sniffle beside him and turned his head to find Anna's brown eyes shimmering with tears she tried hard to contain.

He curled his fingers more tightly around hers, and as she leaned her cheek against his shoulder for just a moment, he was astounded all over again at how very much his world had changed in just a few short months.

She had become everything to him.

His love.

When the clergyman pronounced them man and wife and they kissed to seal their union, he watched as the tears Anna had been fighting broke free and started to trickle down her cheek.

He pulled a handkerchief from the pocket of his dress uniform, and she dabbed at her eyes. For a woman who claimed she never cried, she had become remarkably proficient at it.

She had cried a month earlier when Sage Benedetto-Spencer told them she and Eben were expecting a baby, due exactly on Abigail's birthday in November.

She'd cried the day the accountant at her Lincoln City store told her they were safely in the black after several record months of sales.

And she had cried buckets for him when, after his latest trip to Walter Reed a month ago, he had come to the inevitable conclusion that he couldn't keep trying to pretend everything would be all right with his shoulder; when he had finally accepted he would never be able to fly a helicopter again.

Max could have left the army completely at that point on a medical discharge, but he had opted instead only to leave active duty. Serving part-time in the army reserves based out of Portland would be a different challenge for him, but he knew he still had much to offer.

The ceremony ended and the newly married couple was immediately surrounded by well-wishers—Conan at the front of the pack. Though he had waited with amazing patience through the service, sitting next to Sage in the front row, the dog apparently had decided he needed to be in the middle of the action.

Conan looked only slightly disgruntled at the bow tie he had been forced to wear. Maybe he knew he'd gotten a lucky reprieve—Julia's twins had pleaded for a full tuxedo for him but Anna had talked them out of it, much to Conan's relief, Max was quite certain.

"What a gorgeous day for a party." Sage Benedetto-Spencer approached them with her husband. "The garden looks spectacular. I've never seen the colors so rich."

"Your husband's landscape crew from the Sea Urchin did most of the work," Anna said.

"Not true," Eben piped in, wrapping his arms around his wife. "I have it on good authority that you and Max had already done most of the hard work by the time they got here."

Max considered the long evenings and weekends they had spent preparing the yard for the ceremony as a gift— to himself, most of all. Here in Abigail's lush gardens as they'd pruned and planted, he and Anna had talked and laughed and kissed and enjoyed every moment of being together.

He loved watching her, elbow-deep in dirt, Abigail's floppy hat on as she lifted her face to the evening sunshine.

Okay, he loved watching her do anything. Whether it was flying kites with the twins on the beach or throwing a stick for Conan in the yard or sitting at her office desk, her brow wrinkled with concentration as she reconciled her accounts.

He was just plain crazy about her.

They spoke for a few more moments with Eben and Sage before Anna excused herself to make certain the caterers were ready to start bringing out the appetizers for the reception.

When she still hadn't returned a half hour later, Max went searching for her.

He found her alone in the kitchen of her apartment, which had been set up as food central, setting bacon-wrapped shrimp on etched silver platters. Typical Anna, he thought with a grin. Sure, the caterer Julia and Will had hired was probably more than capable of handling all these little details, but she must be busy somewhere else and Anna must have stepped in to help. She loved being involved in the action. If there was work to be done, his Anna didn't hesitate.

She was humming to herself, and he listened to her

for a moment, admiring the brisk efficiency of her movements, then he slid in behind her with as much stealth as
he could manage. She wore her hair up and he couldn't
resist leaning forward and brushing a kiss along the elegant arch of her bared neck, just on the spot he had
learned, these last few months, was most sensitive.

A delicate shiver shook her frame and her hands
paused in their work. "I don't know who you are, but
don't stop," she purred in a low, throaty voice.

He laughed and turned her to face him. She raised her
eyebrows in a look of mock surprise as she slid into his
arms. "Oh. Max. Hi."

He kissed her properly this time, astonished all over
again at the little bump in his pulse, at the love that
swelled inside him whenever he had her in his arms.

"It's been a beautiful day, hasn't it?" she said, soft joy
in her eyes for her friends' happiness.

"Beautiful," he agreed, without a trace of the cynicism he had expected.

His own mother had been married six times, the most
recent just a few weeks ago to some man she'd met on
a three-week Mediterranean cruise. With his childhood
and the examples he had seen, he had always considered
the idea of happy endings like Julia and Will's—and Sage
and Eben's, for that matter—just another fairy tale. But
this time with her had changed everything.

"Anna, I want this," he said suddenly.

"The shrimp? I know, they're divine, aren't they? I
think I could eat the whole platter myself."

"Not the shrimp. I want the whole thing. The wedding, the flowers. The crazy-spooky dog with the bow
tie. I want all of it."

She blinked rapidly, and he saw color soak her cheeks.
"Oh," she said slowly.

He wasn't going about this the right way at all. He had a feeling if Abigail happened to be watching she would be laughing her head off just about now at how inept he was.

"I'm sorry I don't have all the flowery words. I only know that I love you with everything inside me. I want forever, Anna." He paused, his heartbeat sounding unnaturally loud in his ears. "Will you marry me?"

She gazed at him for a long, drawn-out moment. Through the open window behind her, he was vaguely aware of the band starting up, playing something soft and slow and romantic.

"Oh, Max," she said. She sniffled once, then again, then she threw herself back into his arms.

"Yes. Yes, yes, yes," she laughed, punctuating each word with a kiss.

"A smart businesswoman like you had better think this through before you answer so definitively. I'm not much of a bargain, I'm afraid. Are you really sure you'll be happy married to a weekend warrior and high-school physics teacher who's greener at his new job than a kid on his first day of basic training?"

"I don't need to think anything through. I love you, Max. I want the whole thing, too." She kissed him again. "And besides, you're going to be a wonderful teacher."

Of all the careers out there, he never would have picked teaching for himself, but now it seemed absolutely right. He had always enjoyed giving training to new recruits and had been damn good at it. But high-school students? That was an entirely different matter.

Anna had been the one who'd pointed out to him how important the teachers at the military school Meredith sent him to had been in shaping his life and the man he had become. They'd been far more instrumental than his own mother.

Once the idea had been planted, it stuck. Since he already had a physics degree, now he only had to finish obtaining a teaching certificate. This time next year, he would be preparing lesson plans.

It wasn't the path he had expected, but that particular route had been blown apart by a rocket-fired grenade in Iraq. Somehow this one suddenly seemed exactly the right one for him.

He couldn't help remembering what Abigail used to say—*A bend in the road is only the end if you refuse to make the turn.* He was making the turn, and though he couldn't see it all clearly, he had a feeling the path ahead contained more joy than he could even imagine.

He rested his chin on Anna's hair. Already that joy seemed to seep through him, washing away all the pain. He couldn't wait to follow that road, to spend the rest of his life with efficient Anna—with her plans and her ambitions and her brilliant mind.

Suddenly, above the delectable smells of the wedding food, he was quite certain he smelled the sweet, summery scent of freesias.

"Do you think she's here today?" Anna asked him.

He tightened his arms around her, thinking of his aunt who had loved them all so much. "Absolutely," he murmured. "She wouldn't miss it. Just as I'm sure she'll be here for our wedding and for the birth of our children and for every step of our journey together."

Anna laughed softly. "We'd better hold on tight, then. If Abigail has her way, I think we're in for a wild ride. A wild, wonderful, perfect ride."

* * * * *

New York Times bestselling author

RaeAnne Thayne

brings you back to Haven Point—a place made for second chances...

Following in the footsteps of her critically acclaimed novel *If You Only Knew*, multi-bestselling author

KRISTAN HIGGINS

returns with a pitch-perfect look at the affection— and the acrimony—that binds sisters together.

Ainsley O'Leary is so ready to get married—she's even found the engagement ring her boyfriend has stashed away. What she doesn't anticipate is for Eric to blindside her with a tactless breakup he chronicles in a blog…which (of course) goes viral. Devastated and humiliated, Ainsley turns to her half sister, Kate, who's already struggling after the sudden loss of her new husband.

Kate has always been so poised, so self-assured, but Nathan's death shatters everything she thought she knew—including her husband—and sometimes the people who step up aren't the ones you expect. With seven years and a murky blended-family dynamic between them, Ainsley and Kate have never been overly close, but their shared sorrow dovetails their faltering worlds into one.

Despite the lifetime of history between them, the sisters must learn to put their differences aside and open their hearts to the inevitable imperfection of family—and the possibility of one day finding love again.

Available January 31!

Order your copy today.

www.HQNBooks.com

PHKH925

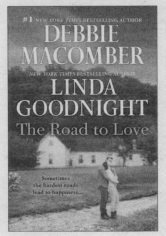

New York Times bestselling author

JODI THOMAS

In the heart of Ransom Canyon, sometimes the right match for a lonely soul is the one you least expect.

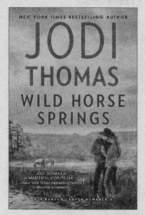

Dan Brigman may not lead the most exciting life, but he's proud of what he's achieved: he's a respected lawman, and he's raised a bright, talented daughter on his own. But finding a lone, sparkly blue boot in the middle of a deserted highway gets him thinking maybe the cowgirl who lost it is exactly the shake-up he needs.

After losing her baby girl to pneumonia, Brandi Malone felt like her soul died along with her daughter. Now singing in small-town bars to make ends meet, she's fine being a drifter—until a handsome sheriff makes her believe that parking her boots under his bed is a better option.

College grad Lauren Brigman has just struck out on her own in downtown Dallas when a troubling phone call leads her back home to Crossroads. Her hometown represents her family, friends and deepest hopes, but also her first love, Lucas Reyes. Will Lauren's homecoming be another heartbreak, or a second chance for her and Lucas?

Available January 24!

Order your copy today.

PHJT927

REQUEST YOUR FREE BOOKS!

2 FREE NOVELS
FROM THE ROMANCE COLLECTION, PLUS 2 FREE GIFTS!

YES! Please send me 2 FREE novels from the Romance Collection and my 2 FREE gifts (gifts are worth about $10). After receiving them, if I don't wish to receive any more books, I can return the shipping statement marked "cancel." If I don't cancel, I will receive 4 brand-new novels every month and be billed just $6.49 per book in the U.S. or $6.99 per book in Canada. That's a savings of at least 18% off the cover price. It's quite a bargain! Shipping and handling is just 50¢ per book in the U.S. and 75¢ per book in Canada.* I understand that accepting the 2 free books and gifts places me under no obligation to buy anything. I can always return a shipment and cancel at any time. Even if I never buy another book, the two free books and gifts are mine to keep forever.

194/394 MDN GH4D

Name   (PLEASE PRINT)

Address   Apt. #

City   State/Prov.   Zip/Postal Code

Signature (if under 18, a parent or guardian must sign)

Mail to the **Reader Service:**
IN U.S.A.: P.O. Box 1867, Buffalo, NY 14240-1867
IN CANADA: P.O. Box 609, Fort Erie, Ontario L2A 5X3

Want to try 2 free books from another line?
Call 1-800-873-8635 or visit www.ReaderService.com.

*Terms and prices subject to change without notice. Prices do not include applicable taxes. Sales tax applicable in N.Y. Canadian residents will be charged applicable taxes. Offer not valid in Quebec. This offer is limited to one order per household. Not valid for current subscribers to the Romance Collection or the Romance/Suspense Collection. All orders subject to credit approval. Credit or debit balances in a customer's account(s) may be offset by any other outstanding balance owed by or to the customer. Please allow 4 to 6 weeks for delivery. Offer available while quantities last.

Your Privacy—The Reader Service is committed to protecting your privacy. Our Privacy Policy is available online at www.ReaderService.com or upon request from the Reader Service.

We make a portion of our mailing list available to reputable third parties that offer products we believe may interest you. If you prefer that we not exchange your name with third parties, or if you wish to clarify or modify your communication preferences, please visit us at www.ReaderService.com/consumerschoice or write to us at Reader Service Preference Service, P.O. Box 9062, Buffalo, NY 14240-9062. Include your complete name and address.